CHASING THE SUN

The launch wire pulled taut and lifted off the grass –

The glider leaped away, tail rising, leaving its attendants behind. Icarus went up in a single smooth sweep. You could hear the wind whispering over its wings . . .

The glider's canopy snapped open on its rear hinge.

The glider started to stand on its tail. Two people inside it, lying with their feet up to heaven.

"It's an airbrake! Tipping them backwards! Cut the winch!"

The canopy burst in a spray of spinning pearls.

When he came back from the landing field, when they were hauling his damaged glider towards the sheds, when his girlfriend, sitting on the grass, had surrendered to someone's cup of tea, Michael Tranter walked towards Munro. He looked a little shaken, but otherwise unmoved. Was it an act, or a real assumption of immortality?

"Don't worry, Bob. I'm not going to let a mishap like that kill me. I found out what life's all about at seventeen, and I certainly haven't had enough yet."

"What," Munro asked, "is it about?"

Michael looked towards Ruth Clifford, and towards his top-of-the-range glider, his executive toy, beyond. Seen from the side, his grin was carnivorous. "Sex," he said. "And money."

Also by the same author,
and available from Hodder
and Stoughton Paperbacks:

The Highest Ground
Frankenstein's Children
Shadow Hunters

About the author

David Mace was born in Sheffield. He is the author of six internationally published novels: DEMON-4, NIGHTRIDER, FIRE LANCE, and the highly-acclaimed THE HIGHEST GROUND, FRANKENSTEIN'S CHILDREN and SHADOW HUNTERS. He and his wife and son live in North Lancashire.

DAVID MACE

CHASING THE SUN

CORONET BOOKS
Hodder and Stoughton

All persons, products, organisations and events figuring in this story are entirely imaginary and bear no relation to any real persons, products, organisations or events.

British Library C.I.P.
Mace, David
  Chasing the Sun.
  I. Title
  823.914[F]

ISBN 0 340 58782 2

Printed and bound in Great Britain for Hodder and Stoughton Paperbacks, a division of Hodder and Stoughton Ltd, Mill Road, Dunton Green, Sevenoaks, Kent TN13 2YA (Editorial Office: 47 Bedford Square, London WC1B 3DP) by Clays Ltd, St Ives plc. Typeset by Hewer Text Composition Services, Edinburgh.

For Alexander, my son

I wish to thank Pelham Gore for his contribution towards the writing of this book. Departures from fact, either error or invention, are entirely my own responsibility.

CONTENTS

Prologue

Icarus, 1989

ONE

The sun burned through Wedgwood blue. Not a cloud, not a contrail, not a flaw or fault in a perfect vault. It was a summer sky straight from childhood.

Michael Tranter was playing childish games. If he's dragged me up here on a Sunday, Munro thought, just to watch ...

The glider club occupied a field bounded by trees on two sides, by the lip of a descending slope at the far end, and by a fenced and embankmented road marking the long southern boundary. There were cars half-hidden like glistening tanks behind that embankment, and sightseers in sentry groups along the fence. They were watching a busy, low-budget production.

The club owned a trio of wide-doored sheds at the end of its access lane, but most of the gliders came in streamlined road trailers that looked like wingless airliner embryos. The canteen was an open-sided van selling hot dogs, sandwiches, soft drinks and tea. The control tower was conjured out of two Transits connected by a cable. One had half its top cut away to make an open platform, where a man and a woman with headsets sat in front of microphones. The other was full of radio equipment and everyone's discarded jackets or sweaters: it had a mast topped by dipoles bolted to its back, and its out-of-tune engine chugged constantly. The dipoles, wobbling with the breeze, glinted in the afternoon sun, while a steady brown exhaust perfumed the grass. Gliding can be a more or less quiet, more or less clean sport.

Michael Tranter came back from the rabble of sun-planished cars parked on the grass beside the sheds. His vehicle was the white Land Cruiser. His girlfriend was the redhead walking by his side – Ruth Clifford, recently a fieldworker with the World Assist charity, now an employee in Tranter's public relations department. Padding beside him in trainers and faded jeans, she was as tall as Michael Tranter. He wasn't a tall man at all.

"How do you like – " Tranter gave in to the sudden noise. The towing aircraft revved up beyond the sheds to take a two-seater into the air, and the winch tractor at the far end of the field started its own roar. The winch launch was the faster affair. The glider waiting on the end of the cable, beside the two Transits, was suddenly wrenched along the grass. It bounced once on its single wheel – then it swooped up into the air, dragged by the cable under its nose, pushed by the wind under its wings. It aimed towards the afternoon sun, it kicked the cable loose, it arced up into the empty west. From the distant winch to the towing hook over the mid-point of the field, the cable dropped to the grass like an envious snake, sighing. The glider was already high over the westward slope, over the valley, and turning south.

The towing aircraft went out with its glider to chase it.

"How do you like," Michael Tranter said again, as the aircraft and its gliding caravan receded over the valley, "our little club, Robert?" He pointed to the bald Pennine hills where the day's launches were aimed. "That's limestone country. And somewhere round there, past the trees, down in the haze – that's Buxton. My old university's gliding club used to fly up here. That's how I got the taste for it."

"It's a beautiful view," Munro said. He narrowed his eyes at it. His glasses had a light-sensitive coating, but they only darkened so far. They weren't exactly sunglasses. He scanned the summer dazzle sitting on the hills. It was all he'd had to do since they'd left the damned pub where they met at lunchtime.

"Not a patch on bonnie Scotland, I suppose?"

"I grew up in Glasgow. The part where we lived wasn't bonnie."

"Are you from Glasgow?" Ruth Clifford asked. "You don't sound Scottish to me."

"No," he said. "I don't, do I?" He'd worked hard on it, levelling out the accent. The English business élite disliked anyone exotic doing well in their world.

"Ruth's from Sheffield," Michael said. "But you wouldn't really know."

"London School of Economics," she explained. "And then the big wide world." She smiled.

She had a nice smile. She had a nice face – and long red hair waving down over her shoulders. Completely fashion free.

"The view," Michael said, "is even better from up there." He pointed straight up, hand raised to shoulder height. "Doesn't it tempt you? No nasty engine noise. Just the swish of the wind."

"No," Munro said.

"Well – Ruth's a little bit braver. I'm taking her up for her first flight."

"Michael wants everyone to fly," Ruth Clifford said. "He's hooked on it. I've been trying to tell him he should do something really ambitious. A non-stop round the world flight would be just the thing to suit his ego."

"It's been done," Michael said. "Two Americans."

"It hasn't been done solo. That would be something."

"I'll think about it." Michael looked round, past the canteen van. "Here comes Icarus now."

Half a dozen people, stooping, were wheeling a glider over the grass from the sheds. It was one of those sport models – an elongated teardrop nose with integral canopy, endless tapering wings, a dragonfly's rear fuselage no fatter than a telegraph pole, and a high T-bar tail. Under the long canopy, one behind the other in tandem, were two reclining things that passed for seats.

"Icarus?" Ruth Clifford was saying. "Your glider's called Icarus?"

5

"Don't worry." Michael glanced up at the sky, then down at her face. "I'll grant you it's warm – but Icarus has no wax that could melt in the sun." He looked at Munro. "You needn't worry about my tendency to do wild and dangerous things. There's no family to inherit my shares, you know, so there'd be no new outsider owning a big slice of the outfit. If we make you chief executive officer, you'd be the most powerful man in the shop. Once I was out of the way."

Munro shrugged. It was the first he'd heard of the title in connection with himself. Perhaps the Sunday drive up half the length of England wasn't going to be a waste of time. On the other hand, when you're being head-hunted, which at the age of fifty is a flattering thing . . . "Chief executive officer. I've been under the impression I'd be taking over finance."

"Oh yes, you'll be finance director. I was thinking CEO would make a nice title for someone combining finance director and deputy managing director. Don't you?"

"It makes a nice title," he said. And a very nice role, he thought, if the power is also there.

"I want you to shape the company for me, Robert. I'll be the king and you can be the general. I read your restructuring proposal last night."

Saturday night. A financial wizz-kid, in his mid-thirties and head of a burgeoning and heavily diversified empire, could only have done it by working all the time. It would try his new girlfriend's patience, eventually. It wrecked even mature marriages. Munro knew all about that. "It doesn't have the details. I can't give you new details until you let me see the existing ones."

"Not until you're on the payroll, Bob. May I call you Bob?"

Munro shrugged. He hated it, he only let people he needed get away with it – such as bosses. Barbara used to call him Robbie, but that was different again. She'd reverted to Robert the day the divorce came through.

"Well – let's look at Icarus," Michael said, and led the way past the chugging Transits of the control tower. "Tell Ruth about your plan. I didn't have time."

Munro fell into step beside Ruth Clifford. He didn't expect her to ask.

"Well," she said. "What's the plan? In a nutshell. I'm interested, but my mind's on this bloody glider flight."

In a nutshell, he thought, in the middle of the Derbyshire Pennines on a sunny Sunday afternoon. Is this an offbeat interview technique – or a different kind of test? Charm Michael's girlfriend and it proves you're an all-right guy. Munro wasn't interested in the business deception of being an all-right guy.

"Well?" she said again. "Would you keep MT Holdings?"

"Yes. I'd expand its downward control. I'd give it three main subsidiaries – Siltech, with the whole computer business underneath it, Orbis Air with its own subsidiaries, and a newly created company. The new company would be another holding company with no outside investors. Is this boring you yet?"

"No." But she was looking at the glider and the people round it. Michael Tranter was talking with the black bloke who seemed to be overseer of the ad hoc ground crew.

"The new company would be there to administer a pyramid of further subsidiary companies – all the green-image ones."

"Natural medicines," she recited. "Rainforest management, agricultural products, food wholesaling, paper recycling, fair-wage Third World farming, chlorine-free bleach. Michael has a clever phrase for it. Thematic diversification."

"It needs tidying into a single subsidiary structure," Munro said. "At the moment the coherence only comes from pandering to anyone who wants to look at the world through green-tinted spectacles." He was looking at the world through glasses with a maximum fifty per cent absorption. The grass-green colour was real, and blinding. "That's what the marketing strategy amounts to."

But she was transfixed by the glider in front of her. He wasn't going to find out whether she actually believed in Michael Tranter's marketing strategy. Probably she did.

"Bob?" Michael was beckoning him. "Come and meet Chester."

Chester must be Chester Alby, the man he'd heard about over the pub lunch – the man from Toxteth who left school at fifteen, but later did A levels in evening class and then took an aeronautics degree. The man who couldn't find recognition in the aero-industry, who was kicking around as a maintenance engineer at the British end of the ailing Air Global's transatlantic route. The man Michael spotted when he took over the airline and transformed it from a broken American outfit into the British independent, Orbis Air. The man who coached Michael for his pilot's licence on powered aircraft, and who was now a director of Orbis Air and of a tiny subsidiary which built light aircraft at a place somewhere north of Nottingham. No one had thought to say Chester Alby was black.

Chester Alby shook hands. "Nice to meet you." He was more or less forty. "I design Michael's aircraft. What do you do?"

"Bob's going to be joining us, all being well," Michael said. "Did you notice the towing aircraft, Bob – the one that took off a few minutes ago? Chester designed that. A Trantair Solomaster. It's my donation to the club." Michael turned his attention back to the glider. The canopy had been swung up on its rear hinge and was pointing into the sky. The cockpit rim was barely more than knee high. It was as narrow as a coffin. "Controls all working, Chester?"

"Everything's checked, Michael." Alby glanced round for something that didn't seem to be there yet. "I'll get them to bring up the winch cable."

Chester Alby walked across to the open-topped Transit. A woman club member was explaining something to Ruth Clifford. Munro was already wondering again if he was here on nothing more than a Michael Tranter whim after all.

Michael leaned over the cockpit and rested his hands on the rim each side of the rear seat. Then he stepped into the well from which the joystick rose, and started to find his way down. He ended up almost as much lying as sitting, his knees raised on each side of the stick, his head propped against the upturned headrest. The fit was as tight as a racing car.

Michael looked up, unaffected by his low-line position. He was unshakably the boss, one hundred percent of a slim, compact, self-made man. "The new holding company you propose, Bob. We'll call it Orbis. I'll take a four percent stake. Forty-eight will be held by MT Holdings, and twenty-four each by Siltech and Orbis Air. I'll reduce my stakes in each of those to four percent. The rest of their shares will be held equally as mutual cross-shares, and by Orbis, by MT and by outside investors. Will that tie everything together?"

"Yes," Munro said. "None of the three could be prised loose, so they'd be pretty much immune to takeover."

"Exactly what's wanted. I'll be MD of each of the three, plus MT Holdings, plus some of the lower-tier subsidiaries." Michael put his hand on the stick and started to waggle it methodically. He twisted his head to look over his shoulder. Ailerons moved near the tips of the long wings.

He was standing in Michael Tranter's sky. He felt very exposed indeed. "You're not thinking of pinching my ideas without hiring me, by any chance?"

Michael twisted himself onto his shoulder so that he could watch the tail surfaces move. "I need you to do all those details – and to run the result. My present company secretary certainly couldn't. You can." He settled in his seat again. He turned a knob which moved a pointer on one of the tiny group of dials backing against the headrest of the front seat. The dial called itself *altimeter*. "You'll be CEO, that is finance director and deputy MD, of – and only of – MT Holdings. To be blunt, if I involved you in the next tier as well, you'd be too powerful. I'll be stocking the Orbis board with people like George Connor from Siltech and Andrew Carlyle from Orbis Air. They'll keep their seats on the other boards. You've met them, haven't you? What do you think?"

Munro shrugged. Was it safe to tell Michael Tranter that his chosen men were mediocre? "They're competent."

"They're moderately competent, Bob. But they're *intensely* loyal, which is what I want. However, I need you to be a man who won't agree with me just because I want you to. Everyone else always does, and sometimes it isn't much help." He leaned forward to look past Munro's legs. "Ah, here's my passenger at last."

Ruth Clifford arrived, wearing the remnants of a brave smile. Carefully, she started to step into the cockpit and wriggle her way into the front seat. There was no joystick to intrude between her knees. The mounting was there on the floor, but the stick had been removed. No untutored interference wanted.

Chester Alby had appeared on the other side of the glider. He reached up, ready to close the canopy.

"Well," Michael said, "that's settled. Salary and so on to be sorted tomorrow. There'll be no company car, by the way. That's rigid policy. I object to the tax dodge, so I add the value of a car to the salary instead. Also, it's very good for our PR image." He smiled up at Chester Alby. "Right, let's close the lid."

Munro moved out of the way. I'm *in*, he thought. I'll be getting my terms, and I'll be getting an entire company to shape into my version of what suits the boss. Michael Tranter's expanding empire is a rising star company. He's hot stuff in the City, it's a good place to be. I've been blocked by senior time-servers at the Bryce McFadden Group, so when the head-hunter came, I got ready to jump. Now I've landed somewhere big enough, and new. So let's get out from under the gloom that settled after the divorce.

Under the glider's canopy, down among the thighs of the assorted ground crew, Michael had put on a headset and seemed to be conversing with the woman up in the control tower Transit. His girlfriend, tucked in the front seat, would be able to hear what he said but wouldn't be interfering with communications. Contact with the co-ordinating ground mattered – there were eight gliders somewhere in the sky, on the drive up they'd seen a pair of hang gliders, and it was

10

probably the kind of weather that brought out the microlights. Not to mention RAF low-flyers playing at jet-powered Biggles. Someone had to know what was going on.

Ruth Clifford was getting agitated. She was pointing at the catches which locked the front of the canopy. People outside were nodding and giving her thumbs-up signs.

Two men hauled up the launching wire and grovelled on hands and knees to hook it to the belly under the cockpit, right in front of the single wheel. Chester Alby started waving people back. A woman took hold of the left wingtip, a man took hold of the right. They balanced the glider on its fuselage wheel and its tail skid.

Ruth Clifford was still unhappy about something. Backing off, Chester Alby gave her another thumbs-up. At the far end of the field, the winch tractor revved, belching brown exhaust smoke at the sky. Michael Tranter, ever rising star, was about to follow the smoke towards the sun – with the conceit of a man whose glider is called Icarus . . .

Chester Alby had come over to stand beside him. "Well, here they go. Michael's settled your appointment, I gathered."

Munro nodded. He was watching Ruth Clifford twisting to say something to Michael Tranter, and Tranter just smiling in reply. I'm the boss – trust me, don't bother me.

"You'll like it in Michael's outfit. He's the best."

The tractor revved again. The launch wire pulled taut and lifted off the grass –

The glider leaped away, tail rising, leaving its attendants behind. Its little wheel rumbled over the ground.

Icarus went up in a single smooth sweep, like something coming out of the bottom of a roller coaster ride. You could hear the wind whispering over its wings.

"Nice lift," Alby was saying . . .

The glider's canopy snapped open on its rear hinge.

The glider started to stand on its tail. Two people inside it, lying with their feet up to heaven.

"Jesus!" Alby yelled. "It's an airbrake! Tipping them backwards!"

Red blossomed from the front passenger's head. For a moment he thought it was blood. Slashed in the face by something. Such a nice face, he noticed himself thinking . . . Then he realised it was hair.

The glider was standing vertical on its tail. The winch would haul it down. The winch would haul it tail first into the ground.

"Cut the winch!" Alby was waving his arms and starting to jump. "If they cast the wire like that they'll come straight down! Cut the winch!"

He could see the elevators at the tail pitched right over. They wouldn't do any good –

The canopy burst in a spray of spinning pearls. The sound arrived like a handclap. The empty canopy frame shook. Icarus shook with it.

The tail came up slightly. The glider was beginning to arc again on the end of a wire still vibrating into the winch. Without airspeed it couldn't fly. Any fool could see that.

The canopy frame was snapping like an inverted, tooth-less jaw.

The arc went up to forty-five degrees.

The cable cast loose from the glider. The man on the winch tractor started running away.

The glider's nose came down.

The cable was going back like an aborted slingshot, the hook overtaking the wire.

The glider's nose came down in a dive. The canopy frame still gaped amazement.

The cable hook went over the tractor and disappeared. The wire sliced off the exhaust stack.

The glider dived out of its little piece of sky. And disappeared below the end of the field –

A noise like shredding –

The noise shot clean overhead. The towing aircraft was coming in to land. The man on top of the Transit was flailing

12

his arms at it. The woman was yelling at the microphone. The man from the tractor at the far end of the field was waving *go away, go away*.

"Jesus God Almighty," Alby was whispering.

The towing aircraft touched down once, then bounced back up into the air and roared towards the sky.

"Jesus God Almighty. Michael's only got airspeed. No thermals down in the valley. Nothing but airspeed to climb out with."

"Can they land?" He'd forgotten what it was like. The kids were grown up and away at university, Barbara had divorced him. He'd forgotten what it was like, even for a moment, to be frightened for someone else. "In a field?"

"It's all outcrops and stone walls." Alby started shaking his head. "Michael won't – "

The glider, silent, came up on the left, beyond the road. The sentry groups of people at the fence started to turn, like a sparse but choreographed chorus line.

The glider, silent, with its chattering upper jaw, started to turn in a shallow curve. It came across towards the road, and the gate to the glider field.

The only sound left was the engine of the second Transit. It crossed over the road. Jump and you'd catch it.

It went overhead with a sweet whoosh, and a snap.

The dipole from the very top of the Transit's radio mast spun free.

The glider turned across the front of the sheds, one wingtip down near the grass, the other up in front of the wall of trees.

The dipole landed in front of Munro's feet. It stuck in the ground like a toy javelin.

The glider was flying in front of the trees at tree-trunk height. Down went the flaps, up went the real airbrakes.

It hit hard and went at a diagonal across the far end of the field. Alby started running. Everyone else was running. The canopy frame was still gasping its disbelief.

He looked at the dipole in front of his feet. What did

13

that mean? Why did the disaster try to take a little shot at me?

When he looked up, the glider had stopped next to the winch tractor. Icarus was back on the ground.

No wax to melt, and it didn't get anywhere near the sun . . .

Ruth Clifford got out so fast she fell over the rim. She pushed people away who tried to help her. She started a zigzag run back along the field.

Michael Tranter stood up in the cockpit and lifted the loose frame back to the vertical, a mockery of hinging it open. Then he stepped out onto the grass.

He knows how to make a myth of himself, Munro thought. He might be a brilliant glider pilot who's just saved himself and his passenger from death. But first and foremost, he's a showman.

Ruth Clifford, hair awry, face pure white, was stumbling past the Transit tower. A woman was trying to coax her round towards the canteen van, but she was searching for a better place to hide. She looked at him. Anyone she recognised would do. "I won't go up again," she said. "I won't ever go up again!"

When he came back from the landing field, when they were hauling his damaged glider towards the sheds, when his girl-friend, sitting on the grass, had surrendered to someone's cup of tea, Michael Tranter walked towards Munro. He looked a little shaken, but otherwise unmoved. Was it an act, or a real assumption of immortality?

"Don't worry, Bob. I'm not going to let a mishap like that kill me. I'm thirty-seven." He shook his head. "I found out what life's all about at seventeen, and in twenty years I certainly haven't had enough yet."

"What," Munro asked, "is it about?"

Michael looked towards Ruth Clifford, and towards his top-of-the-range glider, his executive toy, beyond. Seen from the side, his grin was carnivorous. "Sex," he said. "And money."

14

Part 1

Cold Dreams, 1991

TWO

There was snow frozen on the windows as high as the twelfth floor. Not even the east wind could scour it away from the glass. February was turning as ferocious as the recession – and like a blizzard in London, the economic blitz wasn't supposed to happen at all.

"Right," Michael said. He switched off his desktop and gazed for a second at the departed screen. In there, written on the hard disk, was the virtual world that he most of all liked, where things could be moved and mutated to suit him. The stuff of cold dreams. In there, even on his office machine, were some of his secrets, protected by a castle of program layers from company network snoopers. It was time, though, that he took those secrets home. He looked across at Ruth. She was sitting in one of the conference chairs. "Nine o'clock. Time to go."

"Where," she asked, "are we going? I mean, you're not thinking of trying to get to Oxford in this weather, are you?"

He shook his head. She was sitting with one foot drawn up on the edge of the seat, knee angled outwards over the arm of the chair. Her jeans had folds focussing at the top of her thighs. It had been her idea to do it in a conference chair, after-hours sex, illicitly, at the very focus of executive power. He'd never done it in the office before. It had to be a conference chair – the carpet, after all, got walked on, the tables were glass and would be adorned with imprints, and his desk chair had tipped over. It used to be great fun, the affair with Ruth. But now he was

17

beginning to get bored. "The new hairstyle," he said. "It suits you."

"Think so?" She turned and tipped her head, demure. She'd had her long hair shorn and shaped in an extremely short bob, tapered and layered. It made her jawline firmer – less indecisive.

"Also, it's just the thing for the modern PR woman. And it's perfect with the Orbis jeans-and-sweater look."

"I know," she said, unfolding her leg and then standing up. "We are going to my place, aren't we?"

"After we give Bob Munro a lift. He isn't even trying to get home in this. He's staying the night at his club."

"Can't he get a taxi? They're still running."

"I want to talk to him, Ruth."

Robert Munro came out of his office into the corridor, briefcase in hand, exactly on time. He had his mohair coat over his arm. Every single thing about the man was dark – black winter coat, dark-grey suit, russet and slate-green tie. His hair, despite the grey and the retreating hairline, was dark. The rims of his glasses were black, his Mercedes in the basement was black. His mood was sombre. So, too, would be his depths. I wonder, Michael thought, I often wonder – how dangerous might those be?

They walked along the corridor of the executive floor. Munro had his coat, Ruth was wearing her green-toned parka with the weightless lining. Michael just had his jacket, sweater and open-necked shirt. Munro pressed for the lift. It was waiting, and opened its doors.

"You're not chancing it to Guildford, Robert?" Ruth said as she pushed the button for ground.

Munro shook his head. "Not without four-wheel drive. Michael, I'm beginning to worry about Orbis Air."

The lift was dropping silently, a little box of intimate voices. When Munro said he was worried, it sounded like a problem that wasn't going to go away. It surrounded them in the lower third of the MT building. The lower third was rented to Orbis Air.

"The Gulf war isn't helping," Michael said, refusing the real subject until he'd mustered his thoughts.

"It isn't the war."

"I know, Bob." He looked up, past Munro, at the floor indicator over the door. Three, two, one – "Let's have a little chat." Mezzanine – "About flying."

Ground.

They stepped out into the lobby. The security woman at the desk started checking them out of the building on her screen.

"Goodnight, Selena." He had half a head full of faces and names. It did a world of good. They love the boss who knows them well. Munro couldn't compete with that.

"Night, Mr Tranter. Mr Munro. Miss Clifford."

They took the stairs down to the garage. At the second flight the wall turned to white-painted blocks. Both of the doors at the bottom were still two-way unlocked, but they'd buzz in sequence at the desk upstairs. The whole of MT-Orbis cultivated a friendly image, but that didn't make it a friendly world.

The garage was cold, very cold, and empty. Fluorescent fans echoed off concrete ceiling, columns and floor. Around behind the services core, in the executive bay, was Munro's black Mercedes, and his own Volvo and the white Land Cruiser. The BMW was snowbound at the cottage in the Chilterns.

Randall Wild was waiting in the driver's seat of the Land Cruiser. An Afro-Caribbean from Birmingham, he was chauffeur and bodyguard. Randall started the engine, then twisted round to start opening the doors.

Randall drove them up the ramp. It had been shovelled free and gritted. So had a narrow strip down the centre of the entry MT Holdings shared with the merchant bank next door. The road itself was a disaster, ruts of ice and furrows

19

of slush wriggling along between irregular spoil-heaps of snow. Pedestrians must have spent the day struggling through freezing deeps.

He put Ruth in the front with Randall. As the Land Cruiser ground its way over the temporary ice age of English civilisation, he watched Munro in the sliding streetlights of the back seat.

Robert Munro waited until they'd reached the long emptiness of Queen Victoria Street. "An airline is very recession sensitive," he said. "Business spends less on travel. People have less disposable income, so the private passengers go, too. Inflation makes it worse. Fuel price panics make it worse still. And besides all that, Orbis Air is very exposed." He turned his head, eyes almost hidden in the half-dark behind tinted glasses. "Too America focussed. You never cracked the European cartel, Michael."

"Not for want of trying, Bob." You didn't take on the collective might of the European national flag carriers, plus their hand-in-glove governments, without a fund of patience. You waited, year after year. But the Commissioners in Brussels stayed too scared to deregulate their airspace. The national paymasters wouldn't like it.

Munro shrugged, heavy shoulders inside heavier coat. "Orbis Air's biggest single revenue is the transatlantic route, which unfortunately is business oriented and exceptionally recession sensitive. On top of that, it's been hit by the war scare. A *ninety* percent drop in trade. All those bloody Americans, fighting abroad and shit-scared of any consequences."

"I know, Bob. A jumbo's already flown west to east with a total of four passengers on board."

"Then you have the drought on the US domestic market – less people flying, and American parochiality making them avoid a foreign-owned carrier in times of trouble. I've seen the figures on what the company's losing on its US network, Michael. Losses on that scale can't be sustained for much more than six months."

"I know, Bob. And I know it's worse because the bottom's

20

gone out of the package tour business, so Orbis Travel isn't feeding profits up to Orbis Air."

"And it all comes on top of the write-offs for the Orbis Pacific Tours fiasco."

"I wouldn't quite call it a fiasco, Bob. The American carriers ganged up to keep me out of the Pacific market."

"I told you they would, Michael." Munro was looking at him again, through shadows. "On a smaller scale, Trantair has been operating at a profit until this quarter, but it hasn't earned back more than a fraction of the start-up cash you put into it six years ago. That hurts Orbis Air. And now Trantair's showing a loss."

"Well – a recession stops people buying little aeroplanes."

"It stops them buying everything. The whole of MT-Orbis is hurting. Nobody believes the upturn's going to be here by the summer. Without major changes, I don't think the corporation can carry Orbis Air beyond the end of the year."

They went past Blackfriars station and came round onto the Embankment. It was a cold snap, really, not an ice age – the river was still dark water, reflecting lights. But it felt like an ice age, a vast intervention of economic fate. We're fat enough to survive, he thought, but at a cost. For me, it might turn into a hidden cost as well. "What do you suggest, Bob?"

"Don't wait until Orbis Air is no longer a going proposition, with debts big enough to negate its assets. That includes its subsidiaries, of course."

It included the glamour. He started out in computers, and got rich. But something you can do so easily, reputedly as a computer genius, soon ceases to be fun. So he bought the airline. Then came the marketing masterstroke, the expansion into anything and everything tinged with fashionable green, and finally the consolidation and restructuring Munro had organised. But it was aviation that was the playground, it was Orbis Air which was the headquartered tenant in the brand new MT building. And besides, it was tiny little Trantair which had a special mission to perform. "I don't want to sell Orbis Air, Bob."

"I didn't think you would. Let me start putting figures on some options. There's no hurry. It isn't an emergency yet."

Silence in the front seats, Randall driving and Ruth watching the white night, two privileged eavesdroppers on the machinations of the mighty. We're ordinary chaps, you know. Really we are. Our professional problems are just that bit bigger. That's all.

So he nodded, watching the snow-blanketed gardens going by. "All right, Bob. Small options as well as big ones."

"Right." Munro didn't shift his position, or relax. He was very good at hiding his pleasure at achieving a compromise. It made him a poker player. Once again, how dangerous might those dark depths be? "What did you want to talk to me about, Michael?"

"The project, of course." Munro's going to have to trade now, a bit of quid pro quo. He's going to have to give a much less grudging agreement. "We're ready to build."

"I was afraid you might be." Munro watched the lights of Hungerford Bridge swing by. He didn't like the project at all, of course, but he would have known from the start that he couldn't block it on anything but cost grounds. And those costs eventually turned into investment risk against future return. Everything in business – and life – is the same.

Randall took them on a four-wheeled icy turn towards Trafalgar Square. Ruth looked round, briefly, and smiled. She didn't smile at Munro. She seemed to have difficulty with older men. Munro was fifty-two to her thirty-one.

"You're going to tell me," Munro said, "that the spare capacity at Trantair is just right for building the aircraft. No customer orders being lost because those orders aren't coming in. You're going to appeal to my socialist heart by pointing out that it keeps the workforce busy and dodges the issue of lay-offs. You're also going to remind me that Trantair specialises in GRP construction, so you won't have to buy in any expertise for this one-off aeroplane. You won't be parting with money to anyone outside the company, which is what I disliked about the design stage."

"I had to buy the program to design the aircraft, Bob, as well as time on a big number-cruncher to run it. We don't write or build anything of the sort at Siltech – that's out of our league altogether. And you've seen the figures on what it's saved us in wind tunnel testing."

"The building costs will still be a pure loss for Trantair. And once the thing's built, you'll tell me it would be foolish to throw away the investment without doing your flight tests first. That's more money. How are you going to recover it?"

"Invoice Orbis, in effect. Keep it all in the family."

"And Orbis will pay the costs out of the sponsorship money you'll raise, with the net going to charity – if there is any net."

"I think there'll be a net." He decided to start with a small smile. "You're weakening, aren't you, Bob?"

"You haven't got a single penny pledged. You haven't even got a sponsor, Michael – or any charity lined up."

Time, he thought, to bring in the infantry. "The charities will be easy. What about your old friends, Ruth – World Assist?"

"They'd take the money," she said. "They wouldn't have any ideological problems taking money from a capitalist just because he was advertising himself in the process."

"They're pragmatists," Michael said. "Once a beneficiary is on the bandwagon, with a piece of good work in the Third World lined up as a final destination for the money, the big charities will want to come in on it. They know the punters wouldn't like to part with their own donations, and then see the charities turning down some big money sponsored by the fat cats of industry. Very bad politics, that. Don't worry about the charity side."

"Think of the advertising," Ruth said. "Masses of free advertising for MT-Orbis. That's where your profit will be. Your return on the investment."

Munro shook his head. "Not without sponsors."

They were cruising sedately through Trafalgar Square. Snow and freezing slush everywhere, and not another vehicle

23

in sight except a couple of cabs. London was empty in its unnatural night.

"If I had a sponsor," Michael said, "what would be your response? We can build the aircraft in three months."

Munro looked less than happy. He watched the opening of Pall Mall approach, the way to his club. "If you build it, you'll want me to let you fly it. And once you've flown it, you'll want to fly the bloody thing round the world. Won't you?"

Michael gave him a broad smile. "That's the idea, Bob. That's what they'd be sponsoring, in return for all the publicity."

"So?"

Michael shrugged. Got you on this one, Bob Munro. You're not going to stop me having my fun. "I've got a sponsor."

They dropped Munro at his club, then came out on St James's Street and turned into Piccadilly. A snow trench along the pavements, snow half-burying the barricades, a disgusting deep dirtiness of defiled white covering the road – there was no one walking and no one driving anywhere.

But London wasn't empty in its wiped out winter night. There were heaps and bundles in shop doorways, in the arch of the Royal Academy, along under the Air Street arcade. They huddled under blankets, involuntary igloos and cardboard collapses. They were inhabitants of the economic other-world, phantoms from the occupying army that haunted the free market age. I'll do anything, Michael thought, I'll play the rules, bend the rules, break the rules. It's worked so far. These ice-bound ghosts are intimations of the death of money. I'll do *anything* to stay away from the bottom of the pile. Be a lion, not a lamb, at the constant slaughter.

Ruth had said something about the people littering the streets. He hadn't even heard it. Take refuge in the cynical. "Misery is the only part of the free market they got to work properly."

In the front seat, she sniffed. "My, don't you sound like the poor little rich boy."

"Do I? What do you think, Randall?"

Randall Wild had his black-wire hair levelled in a top so flat you'd wonder if he could think at all. He came from a family as broken as it could get, he had a criminal record, he'd been bumping along the bottom of the world. Now he had his own house, sharp clothes, and access to some very expensive cars. Randall shook his head. "I don't think, Mike. I drive."

He drove them halfway up Shaftesbury Avenue, into Wardour Street and round to the Orbis building. Michael let him take the Land Cruiser home.

Ruth's Golf was the last car still waiting inside the street-level car park. He settled in the passenger seat and began some serious planning. Ruth drove them towards her own little home, battling upwards into the winter-wasted streets of Muswell Hill.

THREE

On the Sunday, after heavy snow and four days of unbroken sub-zero, the police were still telling people not to attempt the M1 through the Midlands without four-wheel drive. The Land Cruiser, of course, could cope. So Michael told Ruth to pack enough underwear, and they set off. The drive up to Wragby had never been so empty or so easy.

Wragby Aerodrome was north of Nottingham, out past the far end of Sherwood Forest. It had been a wartime bomber field, had fallen into disuse, and one day the Ministry of Defence had decided to sell it. Now it belonged to Orbis Air.

The main aircraft maintenance was done at Wragby, and went on seven days a week during the peak season. The air taxi and executive charter fleets were based there, and were on twenty-four-hour call for transatlantic and all-Europe.

The tiny Trantair company leased a quarter of the workshop and staff provisions, and coped with over-capacity orders, when they came, by round-the-clock working. Michael got maximum use out of the capital tied up in the airfield, and did it with a minimum workforce. All it cost was productivity bonuses, dormitory facilities for the staff – and a little time, a lot of interest, and some attention to remembering names.

With all air operations suspended since mid-week, Wragby should for once have been deserted. The only people who actually had to be there were the security guards, and their activities were limited to checking the gate and patrolling the buildings, since the perimeter was protected by drifts half as high as the fence. However, seven Orbis Air and four Trantair staff had been marooned there since Wednesday evening. Chester Alby, as well. He lived in Reigate, on-call for the sharp end of the airline work at Gatwick. But he also ran the engineering side of Trantair.

And he'd designed Michael's special aircraft.

They drove the snow-ploughed road from the gate, dumped their bags in the staff building, then crunched across the parking area to the Trantair offices. Moving outside, with black-boned trees along the perimeter, snow-capped workshops and hump-roofed hangars retreating in a silent line, and a vast frozen-lake flatness beside them, it was like creeping near the edge of some Christmas cake made on a heavenly scale and forgotten in the back of God's freezer.

The offices, by comparison, were warm.

"John's here," Chester said, grinning middle-aged colour. He didn't grin at Ruth. He never did. "Came in when he heard you were on your way." Chester pointed down the corridor to the design office, and let Ruth go first. His problem with Ruth was jealousy. Michael had picked him out of his career dead-end and put him on the board, so in return Chester put his whole life into his work, and taught Michael to fly powered aircraft as a personal thankyou. Michael repaid with friendship – but after living the high life with Sylvia Symes until it was time to dump her, Michael put Ruth in her place and in turn

26

coached her, even against her initial resistance, to her own pilot's licence. In Chester's view, Ruth was just a low-profile gold digger. "So – Munro gave in? We're building!"

"We're building." Michael touched Chester on the arm, just enough of a touch to slow him. Ahead, Ruth was turning through the office door. Take the time to check, he thought. With Chester it always pays to check. "You okay at the moment?" he asked quietly. "Not under a cloud?"

"I'm fine, Michael." Chester looked ashamed, and sincere. You could trust him, because Chester himself didn't trust anyone else. A secret, allowed for and never exploited, is another way of tying someone happily to your coat tails.

Chester brightened up. "The slippery shell bit's going to be easy. We can make the moulds for the monocoque skin in two to three weeks. It's the structural frame that's going to take the time. Unless you want to forget composites and go back to metal?"

"Be too heavy," Michael said. "Wouldn't it?"

"We'd lose fuel capacity and get into trouble with the range. We'd have to increase the wing, which increases drag, which requires more engine power, which increases weight. The spiral goes on forever." They'd reached the door, and Chester was letting him go first. "Stick with the answer we've got, I'd say."

"Right." Michael went into the design office. At the far end, past the tilted drawing tables and the computer screens, Ruth was talking to John Coates. Michael smiled at the man with the beard, and the man with the beard smiled back. He didn't like an aircraft engineer to wear a beard – all the science teachers at school had worn beards, and all the lab technicians at university. For some reason it seemed an inadequate professional cliché. "Glad to see you here, John. Haven't you got *anything* better to do on a Sunday?"

"My wife thought I might dig the snow off the drive." John shrugged. "An expedition out here seemed a good excuse."

"Me, too." He scanned the walls of the room, a wrap-around pinboard for structural drawings. "My PA was trying to tie me in the office all week. And Munro's getting heavy about the recession." The original sketch for the Trantair Solomaster was still there, signed by Chester. The Solomaster had been the man's first complete design, it was Trantair's bread-and-butter success and Chester had gone on a long binge to celebrate after the first batch of orders came in. His nerves had been stretched at breaking point for too long, he'd been proving himself much too personally. It was something he suffered from. Since then he'd developed aerobatic and crop-spraying variants, and then a twin-engined successor. The rest of the wall space was taken up with work in progress, detailed drawings for the proposed executive jet. That, in the economic present, was strictly pie in the sky.

The miracle of the moment was spread in colour printed sheets along the table beside Ruth and John Coates.

The single-seat machine was unique, a radical solution to a one-off problem. On black grounds, it rotated and pitched frame by frame in CAD presentations, a spectrum of colours showing the air flows and the structural loads. It had come into existence in rented time on a parallel processor, using a computer-aided design program derived from work at Nasa's Ames Laboratory – leagues of hardware and software that Michael's original company, Siltech, couldn't possibly provide. It was a beautiful ghost from an information machine, waiting for a body to be born in.

It was a rear-engined craft with a tall fin but no tailplane. It had an elongated nose graced with slender foreplanes. The wings were high-mounted and were nearer the tail than the nose, a concept like a delta-wing combat aircraft. But this was no supersonic delta. It was a broad-shouldered, propeller-driven aircraft with long, tapering, straight-edged wings. It would be efficient at take-off, it would be smooth in the air, it could carry a huge load of fuel. And it would fly a very long way indeed . . .

"Who is this first sponsor?" Chester asked. He was looking at the pictures of his creation the way a father might behave in the ultrasound room at a maternity clinic. Transfixed, dubious, amazed.

"Geo-Petro," Michael said. "A mines and minerals outfit."

"They have an image problem," Ruth said – to John, though, more than to Chester. "Open-cast mines, ore-processing plants spewing filth into lakes and rivers all over the Third World. They have a lot to gain by sponsoring a charity benefit flight."

"Once the charity and the sponsorship stuff starts to come together," John said, and looked at Michael, "who's going to look after it all? You won't have time."

"Ruth will." Michael smiled. "Who else? Her background is in Third World aid, and she's done two years with Orbis PR."

Chester nodded, meaning: if you say so, Michael. Ruth nodded, more probably meaning, if you really think I can. I'm surrounded, he thought, by inadequates. I always am. They try to make up for it with loyalty, which is exactly what I want from them. It renders them safe. Let as few of the self-contained people as possible into the power positions in the company, or into the intimate areas of your life. The self-contained people are the dangerous ones. Like Sylvia Symes, who I got rid of. Like Munro, who I need. Keep them to a minimum, and keep them under control.

"We'll need a name." John waved a hand over the drawings.

"We do," Ruth said. "We need a name."

"Angel," Michael said.

They thought about it.

"Angel," Chester repeated. "That's a good name."

"Which Angel?" Ruth asked.

Michael shrugged. "I don't know many angels. There's Raphael, but everyone thinks he's a painter. Then there's Gabriel, but if I remember my Bible, Gabriel goes round making women pregnant and blaming it on God. And I can't name it after the archangel Michael, because everyone would think me terribly conceited. Which leaves Lucifer. Now

29

Lucifer's a fallen angel, isn't he? Bit of an all-round devil. That would be nearer the mark."

Ruth nodded. "So we're naming it after you?"

Chester cut in. "When are we going to start work, Michael? Trantair's got spare capacity at the moment."

"I know," he said. "So we'll start tomorrow."

Part 2

Angel

FOUR

Angel flew at five thousand feet. The taxiing checks and airstrip hops were things of the past, the five-hundred-foot circuits had gone like a dream – now it was time for emptier air. They had nothing but blue, with spring green and ploughed fields below, and a raft of cloud sliding in from the east. The weather front wouldn't be here until long after the test flight was ended.

Ruth watched the VSI and nudged the handlebar controls. Two years ago she'd refused ever to think of flying again. Now she had her pilot's licence and forty hours in the log. Michael could be very persuasive – you never, in the end, said no. He provided the tuition and the aircraft free, and in the end you had the fun of it and the satisfaction from the accomplishment. If she'd been able to fly in the Ethiopia days, working at the airfield base camp for World Assist, then the skill would even have been useful. Now she flew her part in a rich man's role-playing game . . .

She watched the block of vertical situation instruments on the panel, and nudged the controls to keep the heading, altitude and the attitude smooth. For a very small aircraft, the Trantair Solomaster was beautifully steady. It had been Chester Alby's masterpiece, his all-round graduation design. Next to them in the air was his personal apotheosis.

Chester was watching it fixedly, as if his head had locked looking out to his right. She had to lean forwards or back to see past his skull and the plastic wings of his headphones. She wanted to see. Angel was a fascinating thing.

The aircraft had a long and tapering nose, a smooth belly, and a very short and high-line tail. On top of the tail stood the fin with its integral rudder. Behind the base of the fin was the boss for the four-blade pushing propeller. Without the fin, for a moment you could have thought it was going backwards through the air.

Angel was green, brilliant green, the Orbis credo colour – all of it green except the AGS registration letters and the windows of the cockpit canopy. Sitting inside it, head and shoulders in sight, Michael was even wearing an Orbis-green overall. The colour of the fabric wasn't quite so bright, because the cockpit roof was opaque and shaded him from the sun. On endless days chasing the sun round the equator, he'd need the protection from its light.

Angel's wings were high-mounted on the fuselage behind the cockpit, giving an unbroken top surface from wingtip to wingtip. The leading edges were straight, the trailing edges swept forward to taper the wings from the deep chord of the huge shoulders to the slender section of the tips. The wings were wider than the aircraft was long. Angel, at the start of its flight, would be carrying a massive load of fuel.

There was no tailplane at all. Instead, a pair of knife-thin foreplanes adorned the forward fuselage halfway between the cockpit and the tip of the nose. The foreplanes were the secret of the radical design. Their control surfaces could tip the nose up or down to climb or dive, they provided pitch stability as well as any tailplane – and they generated lift, adding to the carrying capacity of the wings. The tailplane of a traditional aircraft exerts a downward pressure to balance the machine in the air, because the centre of gravity is forward of the wings' centre of lift, and left to itself the aircraft will nod nose down and stick in a dive. The wings have to hold the aircraft up against its own weight, plus the downthrust at the tail. Foreplanes keep an aircraft in balance by exerting an upward pressure. So foreplanes and wings pull together to beat the weight.

Angel was a very efficient machine. It had to be, if it was going to circle the world.

"You're drifting out," Chester said. She had his voice in her earphones although his face was turned away. There was a snap in his voice. "Close up. Come on, close up."

Ruth nudged the rudder a fraction right. Station keeping would be easier if his head wasn't constantly in the way of her view, but saying so was a waste of time. Her opinion never meant very much to Chester. Her microphone was off. Chester's was on, and he could choose whether he spoke to her, to Michael across the air, or to John Coates on the ground at Wragby. The way they'd set up the channels, no one else could hear what he said to her, so that their own cockpit communication didn't interfere with Michael's link with Wragby. That meant it didn't hurt so much when Chester treated her like a novice. Nothing to get excited about. When women complain of mistreatment they're only being hysterical – everyone knows that.

"You're drifting. Close up again."

"I'm not bloody drifting," she said past the dead microphone and into the engine noise. The heading scale on the VSI confirmed that she wasn't. If he'd turn his head for a moment he'd see. "If anyone's bloody drifting, it's Michael."

Chester didn't hear, of course, and didn't answer. Instead he started talking to Wragby. "How are we on radar, John?"

"You look fine from here. Your immediate airspace is clear at the moment. The nearest aircraft is a private at four thousand feet and seven miles to your northeast, heading north. There's also what looks like a microlight at eight hundred feet and nine miles to your south, heading west. The RAF aren't supposed to be flying through here today."

"They'll get a surprise if they do," said Michael's voice. "Bet they'll think I'm a Russian spy plane. Or a UFO."

"Then you'd better hope they don't shoot you down."

"Nobody would shoot my Angel down, John."

Chester was shaking his head. He had a still camera in his

lap, and his fist had clenched on it. "Now you're coming too close. Move out, woman. Move out."

She hadn't left the heading. The VSI scale said so. She tipped her head back to see past Chester's plastic ear. Angel was definitely too close. Michael had the luminous green wingtip slightly high, as if he was letting the aircraft lean to its right in the air. But he wasn't banking in order to make any gentle turn out to the side. Angel was simply driving forwards.

"I said move out. You're coming too close."

Slowly, Angel's wingtip came down again. Michael was still settling in on the new machine. Ruth switched on her microphone. "I'm staying on the heading, Chester. It's Michael who's drifting. Look, he's rolling, too. You can see that."

"Move out. Will you just move out before we get any closer?" Chester actually turned his head and looked round at her.

It wasn't a nice look at all. His eyes never went anywhere near the VSI scale. It must be something to do with women, she thought, and probably whites as well. He might be a director of three companies, and he might be Michael's champion aircraft designer, but he still carried an ethnic chip on his shoulder. You can't fight that.

So she nudged the rudder left, and watched past Chester's head as the separation opened up again. To hell with holding the correct heading. Instead she'd just keep pace with Michael's wobbles.

"Michael," Chester was saying, "how's stability?"

"No problem, Chester."

"Ruth here thinks you're drifting and getting a bit of roll."

"I'm not drifting, Chester. The drag on Angel is balanced perfectly. Yaw stability's very sensitive, but it isn't giving me any trouble. It's just the long-nose, short-tail effect. We're on minimum ballast, aren't we? With more weight on board, the pendulum will be heavier and the tendency to swing will disappear. Angel's fine."

36

He's drifting out, Ruth thought. Admit it or not, he's falling off to the right. Don't say anything. Just follow him.

"And more weight will add to the roll stability, won't it, Chester?"

"That's right, Michael. Is roll being a bit tricky?"

"No," said Michael's voice. "No problem at all."

Ruth peered past Chester's ear. Michael had his left wing down and his right wing up, and she could see clear across the entire top surface from tip to tip. No bloody problem at all. Michael denied it and Chester couldn't see it, so the conspiracy was complete. The club closed ranks and did its routine doublethink: Michael was the perfect pilot and Angel was Chester's flawless creation. It was true because the men knew so. Men, one after the other, had been the problem all her life. No bloody problem at all.

When the drizzle was beginning in the afternoon, Michael slid into the driving seat of his BMW and closed the door. He turned the key and then put the wipers on intermittent. Through the cleared arc, a dust of little droplets, reflecting cloud grey, sat on the white bonnet. The start of a dreary ending to a not entirely happy day.

"Well," he said, "what's bothering you?"

She shrugged. She fastened her seatbelt instead. "Are we going back to London?"

"No." He switched on the CD in the console, and intercepted its autoplay to *stop*. "My place. I want to do some work on the computer." His place was an exclusive cottage in the Chilterns, a few miles off the M40. "And tomorrow morning I want a chat with George Connor."

Ruth nodded. George Connor was Michael's number two at Siltech, the man who minded the computer company for him most of the time. So Michael was going to leave her to amuse herself in Oxford, while he busied himself with men's affairs at the Siltech offices. There were worse towns to waste a morning in. Sheffield, for instance. That's where all the man trouble had begun. With her father.

37

Michael programmed a disk from the magazine. It loaded with a little whirr into the playing head. "London after lunch." He turned the key and started the car. The 735's engine purred.

"I wanted some time at my own desk, Michael."

"Why?" He treated her to a smile. "Don't you think you're earning your salary? We need a pilot for the pacer aircraft, no one else is available, you're ideal. It's all work on the project. It isn't what I'd call taking time off." He started the BMW rolling and pulled around across the concrete space in front of the staff building. "Don't worry."

"I am worried. It's this logjam with the sponsors. We've got an entire list of sponsors, but I can't get any one of them to move towards a firm commitment. They're all very interested, all very keen to come in at a future date. They're all saying profits are too tight at the moment, or they haven't finished costing the returns they'd expect from the promotion they'd get from the sponsorship. Not one of them will even talk about signing. It's been going on for weeks, and I don't know how to crack it."

Michael swung the BMW onto the roadway to the gate and started to accelerate. They purred past airfield grass on the left and a line of trees which was coming closer on the right. He – or rather one of his companies – owned Wragby Aerodrome, so he allowed himself the privilege of ignoring its speed limit. "Don't worry, Ruth. Wait until we're back in London. I know what to do about it."

They reached the trees, and followed the bend of the road into an avenue arched with drizzle-wet green. Straight ahead was the perimeter, gate open, barrier down, with the red stop light shining on top of the security booth.

On the CD Michael pressed *play*. Something with a piano started up slowly – something by Schubert. She didn't know what.

"Relax," Michael said.

Ahead, the barrier went up and red turned to green. Michael remembered to wave at the security booth as they cruised through the gate. They left Michael's part of the world, and went out into the rest of it.

FIVE

She called herself Terri Sabuli. Her mother came from Gloucester, her father from Ghana. Her skin was a perfect chocolate brown. Her hair was black, and straight, and she wore it pinned tight by combs to the back of her oval skull, from where it arched in a single plait to the nape of her very long neck. She was slender, she was tall. She was beautiful.

She wore a ruby suit – a tight skirt wrapping itself round half her thighs, a waisted jacket, a white blouse with red chalk stripes. Her tights were black, but her patent leather shoes were red. Her shoulder bag was black with a ruby-red clasp. Her lipstick and her fingernails were matching red, like rich blood. She wore a ruby stud in each ear, and a ruby on the ring finger of her right hand. She was a piece of sheer perfection that a man or woman would see once, and never forget.

She wasn't possible. Such a woman can't really exist.

She sat in the conference chair, legs crossed, hands resting relaxed on the chair arms. She didn't fidget, didn't pose, didn't do anything at all. She didn't tie Michael's eyes to her. She didn't need to. He could look away, move round his office, behave with outward self-control. But inside his head he wouldn't be seeing anything but her.

She wasn't fair. She just really wasn't fair.

I did it with Michael once in that chair, Ruth thought, in that very same chair. He might, with reasonable luck, still remember. But I can't compete with this. With this – presence. She isn't a vision. She's much more than that. Touch her, a man must think – if she'd ever let you – and your nerves would burn. It really, *really* isn't fair.

39

Terri Sabuli had turned her head. It emphasised the length of her neck, from ear to collar bone. It silhouetted the arc of the single plait, from head to neck like the handle on a vase – but soft and pliable, yielding, like the body might be . . . If I can hear this single symphony of sexual dreams she's playing, Ruth thought, what on earth must it do to a man?

Michael was by the window, thumbs hooked in his belt and the wings of his jacket pushed aside. He turned back from his view of the NatWest Tower, modern London's money symbol, and faced this other icon of enviable success. "Well," he said, "what do you think of the idea?"

Terri Sabuli had turned her head, but not far enough round to see Michael while he stood behind her. The impression was a regal one: I've been waiting. "Flying round the world?" she said. "Or taking on the PR?"

"Either."

She turned her head forward, slowly. "I wouldn't fly round the world, except in an airliner." She was looking at Ruth when she said that.

She knows, Ruth thought. Somehow she's seen it. Michael did bother to mention, in passing, that the idea originally was mine. This woman knows that he'll fly Angel, and I won't, and a place for me in the pilot's seat will never ever be free.

"The PR sounds interesting. Would I be running it?"

"Answerable directly to me." Michael started to stroll back from the window. "How do you feel about your work at Orbis Travel?"

"I assume you don't mean how I feel about the boss?" There was a darkness in her tone which said that the publicity boss, in her opinion, wasn't worth his salary. "To be candid, I've been wasting my time since I joined the department. I suspect Orbis Travel might be starting to go to the wall. The phones, as they say, have stopped ringing, and the money isn't coming in." Now she was watching Michael again, head turned and face slightly lifted. The pose offered neither condescension nor womanly admiration. Fall in, it seemed to suggest, to these eyes, these lips, these arms . . . She wasn't a woman

40

at all. She was an android which had built itself to feed on men's hijacked dreams.

"We'll be taking care of things at Orbis Travel." Michael sat down, smiling. The smile would be a mask. He didn't like anyone on his staff to comment on the health of his companies – except Munro, who was there to do specifically that job. But if anyone else could get away with it, this creature would.

"Tell me about the project," the creature said. "Don't tell me about the aeroplane – it's green, and you're probably going to paint sponsors' logos all over it. Tell me *how* you're going to do it solo. How long will the flight take?"

"Four days." Michael crossed his legs and folded his hands affably in his lap. But he was on the defensive, Ruth could see. He really wasn't sure of himself, as the interview situation was turned around.

"Two Americans did it a few years ago in seven or eight days, I think. They took it in turns to fly and sleep. How are you going to do it solo – shoot the pilot up with amphetamines?"

Michael grinned. "After three or four days you'd have a totally disoriented zombie. In fact, you'd have a pilot guaranteed to kill himself. Drugs are completely out. We'll be relying on the autopilot."

"And other aircraft? Weather? Mountains?"

"Angel will have an anti-collision radar, with an alarm to wake the pilot. The sleep periods will be over ocean, not over land. The autopilot will be connected to a central computer which is programmed with an exact plan of the entire course. The pilot, really, is for the landing and the take-off. Otherwise, he's just the human interest without which the publicity circus doesn't roll. Angel's computer will control a satellite communication dish so that we have direct and constant contact between the pilot and our mission control. We'll be able to steer round any weather. Navigation will be absolutely precise because Angel will have a satellite navigation receiver as good as the military people use, and it will be backed up by a state of the art inertial navigation system. These avionics packages are being provided free by a non-paying sponsor. The route program is going to be my job."

"And who is the non-paying sponsor?"

"Haysburg Instruments. An American outfit."

"And all the others are pledged to pay?"

"Ah – now that's where a certain problem lies." Michael's spotlight smile turned. "Isn't it, Ruth?"

He was bringing her back into the conversation on the issue of her own failure. It didn't help at all. She tried to be relaxed. She stretched out her legs, crossed at the ankles, the heel of her trainer bedding itself into the carpet. Faded denim shirt with the sleeves rolled up, stonewashed jeans, clean white trainers – she fitted perfectly within the casually cultivated Orbis public image. It wasn't on the mud hut level, but it was at best corner shop or back-street hairdresser compared to Terri Sabuli's public relations architecture of glittering glass and steel. That was why Michael was adding this creature to the team. The problem wasn't one of separating money from the high street punters. It was about squeezing big finance out of the wrought-iron hearts of the business world. Those people went for things like the NatWest Tower. All glittering, and glass, and steel.

The creature's eyes were on her again. Brown, not unfriendly, but blank.

"We've got a hundred companies interested," Ruth said. "Of those, twelve have already agreed that they'd come in at a sponsorship rate of ten pounds per mile. It doesn't sound much, but for the completed circumnavigation that would mean a quarter of a million per company. Twelve of them would just about cover the basic costs, wouldn't they, Michael?"

He nodded. "The absolute basic costs. But there'd be nothing left over for charity."

"And," Ruth said, "so far no one's signed."

Terri Sabuli just pressed her lips together. A minimum

effort which said: oh dear, you've got a problem, your project's still flat on its back.

Michael was content to wait. Now he's enjoying this, Ruth thought. He likes women who are prepared to move in and take charge. Where does that leave me? Still in command of his bed. I hope.

The lips parted, rich blood separating slowly. "Tell me," said Terri Sabuli, "about the route."

"A great circle," Michael answered. "What else? Try flying round at the latitude of England, and you're only doing about half the maximum distance. It has to be a great circle. One extreme would be the equator, the other would be over the poles. The polar route would be easy, with no real worries at all, but it's boring – all empty ice and endless ocean, down the Atlantic and up the Pacific. Whatever. No photo opportunities, not much green-awareness stuff besides penguins, whales and ozone holes. It wouldn't attract sponsors."

"And the equator?"

"Not much better. Pacific Ocean and Indian Ocean with one or two islands passing by. African jungle, Atlantic Ocean, and then Amazon jungle. The jungle's very green, of course, with all that destruction going on, but it amounts to just two helpings of exactly the same thing. Also, the Andes are a bit in the way. And I really can't see the American media taking much interest if there's no contact to the United States along the route. They are so very parochial, the Americans. And if we can't deliver the American media, the sponsorship issue is dead."

"So what are you going to do? Start from England, cross the equator somewhere in the Indian Ocean, go down as far as New Zealand, come back up across the Pacific, cross Panama and wave at the US Army, then back up the Atlantic to good old Blighty?"

Michael shook his head. "The winds aren't favourable. On a venture like this, the difference between head winds or tail winds is worth thousands of miles. Besides which, there'd be no way of avoiding either the Middle East or

43

the Horn of Africa. We don't want to fly over anybody's war."

"Well, then." The woman's smile was slight, with levelled eyes. "Why don't you let me stop guessing?"

That was something which certainly didn't please Michael. He decided, though, to let it ride. "We start in Florida, cross to southern California, swing past the Hawaiian Islands, then go to Australia. Then we come up the Indian Ocean to East Africa, cross some rainforest in Zaire, fly over some other countries – including Ghana, by the way – then cross the Atlantic back to Florida."

"That's east to west. Is that the best way to go?"

"It gives us tail winds for three-quarters of the distance. No other route is better. We might be having a little difficulty with our sponsors, I'll grant you – but I do know about flying."

Terri Sabuli did no more than blink at the rebuke. After all, she was still measuring the company boss she'd never met before. But she didn't feel the need to pace out the man's ground on tiptoes. "MT-Orbis is a British outfit. Your sponsorship base is the UK. If your route neither starts nor finishes in the UK, you'll never get your sponsors to sign."

Silence.

Ruth quite liked it. She hoped it didn't show.

Michael didn't like it. He was wearing his masking smile again, this time the mildly questioning version. But, if she knew him well enough, it was the conclusion he didn't like, and not the fact that the woman had dared to say it. We've got a superbly sexy version of a Robert Munro here, Ruth thought – someone who isn't afraid to tell him what he doesn't want to hear. I wish, oh how I wish, I'd recognised such an obvious problem.

Michael still had nothing to say.

"How," asked Terri Sabuli, "are you getting your aeroplane to Florida? Taking it over in pieces and putting it together there?"

"No." Michael's tone was guarded, as if he was afraid of walking straight into another hole. "The idea is to fly it

44

out under its own power. The stage to Florida would take about twenty hours, which gives us a proving rehearsal for the real thing."

"And where would you start?"

"From Wragby, where we've built it."

"Then make sure you leave the UK – actually fly out over the coast, where you can expect the TV people to take some romantic pictures – at Plymouth."

"Why?" Michael looked at Ruth. "Why Plymouth?"

"Sir Francis Chichester," Terri Sabuli said.

Ruth just shrugged for Michael's benefit.

Terri Sabuli lifted her hand, palm upwards. It was the first major gesture she'd made – an offering, in friendship, from an oracle. She had the smooth, minimising control of an actress. On television she'd take them all by storm. "For a stunt like this, you need to plug into everything that's available. National consciousness is available. This is a nation of lost little souls, still stunned by the end of the empire. At the moment you've got the recession, rising unemployment, the inflation rate problem, the feeling that there's a primary school government in charge which doesn't know what to do about anything. People are depressed. And on top of that, the tabloids are terrifying them about bloodsucking Euros who want to take away their pounds, their biscuits, their undemocratic electoral system and their right to be kicked by the boss. People are not at all happy. So – plug into national consciousness. Give them something they'll love you for."

Michael frowned. "Sir Francis Chichester?"

"He was the last one who did it – in the sixties, when you had devaluation, and west of Suez, and UDIs everywhere. He did something completely useless, but it made everybody feel wonderful again. He won the first single-handed transatlantic yacht race – solo, in other words. And he did the first solo voyage right round the world. He's real school history book sort of stuff. He's in there with Alfred's cakes and Nelson's blind eye and all that. And he always started from Plymouth. I'll have to check, but he might even be buried there."

"Ah," Michael said. "Right. I see. That's good. We could time the UK-to-Florida stage so that we just have a stopover in Florida, enough for the pilot to get a final night's rest before setting off on the real thing. It's good. I like it."

"It isn't good enough, though." The offering hand had disappeared again, had withdrawn to its repose on the arm of the chair. "It's a *token* UK start. It helps, but you need more. So how about this? Your circumnavigation thing is from Florida all the way round to Florida again. That's the history book stuff – first non-stop solo and so on. If the Florida route is the best route, there's no changing that – and it has the advantage that it includes some of the United States. Fine. But let's suppose the flight goes well, the pilot's still up to it by the end, and the aeroplane hasn't got any bits falling off it or anything. Why land again at Florida? Why not turn there and fly on all the way back to England, still solo, still non-stop? Could your aeroplane do it? Could it carry enough fuel?"

Michael took a deep breath. Then he let the air out slowly through his open mouth. "I don't know. I don't think so. It would mean some modifications. I'll talk to my design team about it."

"And what about the extra strain for the pilot? You are definitely going to be the pilot, aren't you?"

"Yes." He didn't even look at Ruth. "I could handle it."

Terri Sabuli nodded. "What you do then, is you offer the Florida-to-UK bit as a bonus stage. The basic sponsorship agreements are for the circumnavigation only. But you make the rate per mile you're already pushing look a little bit – grudging – on the part of the sponsors. As if they could really do better. And you do that by inviting sponsors to *double* their payout if you also complete the bonus stage. Some will feel obliged to agree, the rest will feel they're getting off lightly by sticking with the basic sponsorship. You get the same money you've been aiming at, plus a lot more if you do manage to fly the bonus stage. And the trick is, you don't actually have to fly it to put a UK landing in the plan for the whole thing. It will work just the same – you intend to land in good old England if you and your aeroplane can get that far. Of course, ideally you do in fact do it, because of the money and the great big show you'll get out of it."

Silence. A different silence from the previous one.

Slowly, Michael began to nod. He'd been a lot smarter than he realised when he asked Orbis Travel to send their crack new publicity specialist upstairs for a chat. Ruth knew Michael was thinking exactly that. She *knew* he was. Clever, clever me.

And I'm outclassed, she thought. Eclipsed completely.

"I'll talk to my design team." Michael stood up, began a first stride towards his desk – then stopped. "Oh – we still didn't get an answer to my original question, Terri. How do you feel about running the publicity on this? It means co-ordinating the sponsors and charity stuff as well, not just doing the media. So?"

Terri Sabuli allowed herself another slight smile. "I'll have a go at it, Michael." She stood up, a rising presence of ruby and black. She was taller than Michael. He didn't seem to mind. "I'll need someone to bring me up to date on things."

"Ruth can do that." He put on his charmer's face. "Can't you, Ruth?"

"Yes," she said. "Obviously."

They didn't leave late. Michael wanted to head home to his cottage in the Chilterns. They travelled down to the garage in the company of a trickle of departing staff. Michael did his royalty bit, waving and smiling and saying something friendly to everyone they met along the way. There wasn't any privacy until they'd walked round the services core into the executive parking bay.

"Land Cruiser today," Michael said. "I've let Randall take the BMW, and the Volvo's in for its service. I've had this Land Cruiser more than two years." He pulled the key from his pocket and flipped it out of its little Aigner wallet. "Time I replaced it."

Ruth stopped dead, trainers scuffing slightly on the concrete. She was hugging her briefcase anyway. She hugged it tighter. "You've had me more than two years."

Michael stopped, key in the lock of the passenger door. He turned his head and looked at her. "What does that mean?"

"Work it out."

He turned the key and the buttons popped up inside all the doors. "I see." He opened the passenger door wide, backing along the Land Cruiser's wing. Then he started to squeeze through between the front bumper and the concrete wall. He opened his mouth again, talking –

A starter motor reverberated from round the corner in the garage. Then the engine was treated to three macho-driver revvings, foot flat and a noise like avalanches. Then the gears were stripped and the car went roaring and resonating away towards the ramp.

Michael shook his head. "A green-image company, and people like that work for us. Ruth, I was saying – if we're going to have a fight, at least let's do it in the car." He half-opened the driver's door, walked round it, then opened it wide. He looked at her again across the seats.

Ruth shrugged. Might as well get in. She could always get out again, go to her own little Golf and drive home to Muswell Hill. But it's tricky when you bed the boss. Walk out on him, and you might be quitting your job as well. Sylvia Symes, his previous girlfriend, had departed from both positions at once.

"Right," Michael said as she was climbing into the seat. He hauled himself up behind the wheel, and heaved his door closed. "So what's the matter? Terri Sabuli? Come on, close the door. Look, I haven't *demoted* you. You're still in charge of the charities and the sponsorship tie-in from their side. You've got all the right connections for the job, for God's sake. Come on, will you close the door?"

Ruth put her briefcase down between her feet under the parcel shelf. She wasn't going to close the door. It was her own self-imposed control. It would stop her shouting at him.

"You've brought her in over my head. Now I'm her assistant. *She's* your assistant. *She's* the one close to you."

"And what's that supposed to mean? You saw the way she picked up immediately on the big flaw in the project – the reason we're having trouble with the sponsors – *and* came up with the solution."

"You're giving her an office here at MT, even though the main operation is based over at Orbis. You're putting her in this building. I'll be over at the other building."

"She's moving up a few floors, from Orbis Air to MT Holdings. She already was in this building."

"Yes, Michael. But in what other ways is she moving up?"

Michael put on his oh-dear-Ruth's-got-a-problem face.

It was the face you could hit.

Michael turned the face away and stared through the windscreen at the concrete wall for a while. "Do you think," he said at last, "that just because she presents herself like a fuck-me fantasy, fuck her is what I'm going to do?"

Ruth folded her arms. Let him explain himself. Let Michael reveal the cracks in his own perfection. "You tell me."

Michael put his hands on the wheel. He pushed his arms out straight, forcing his shoulders into the back of the seat. "Look – the weather's too cold for May, isn't it?"

"What the bloody hell – ?"

"The weather's too cold. But the economic weather's worse – much worse. The recession's getting deeper. MT-Orbis is dependent on exposed markets – computers, air travel, package tours, and loads and loads of green products. We're getting in a *mess*. We're going to land flat on our back. Munro's starting to push for a major restructuring. And I *don't* want him going over the finances with a bloody magnifying glass. Believe me, I don't. Not under any circumstances."

"So?" So what did that mean? Poor Michael needed the use of a super-sexed android for some rest and recuperation?

"So I need a big idea. I want a huge image boost that will put the company back on its feet. Put us back in profit. Put us out of reach of restructuring. I want a *big idea*. And flying

Angel round the world for charity is exactly that. It's *different*. It stands out. I *need* to do it. So I need the best – the most outstanding – publicity manager I can find for the project. *That's* what Terri Sabuli is for. And for *nothing* else. Okay?"

Ruth thought about it. Michael didn't act as though he was desperately worried about his empire. But then he hid everything inside. Access to Michael's head didn't exist, really. Once she believed she enjoyed it uniquely – that she alone understood the sensitive man concealed behind the brash business persona. But gradually, imperceptibly, she'd learned that the off-duty Michael was just another front, a pose, a personality that he wore. It seemed you were never going to see the real Michael Tranter.

He'd turned his head and was looking at her, waiting. Now he'd manoeuvred her into a sulk. He'd defeated her. "Okay?" he said again. "So let's close the door, and then we can go home."

SIX

Chester Alby's response was worse than Michael expected. Chester stayed out of sight for a few days. Michael finally intercepted him at Gatwick, on the Orbis Air sector of the staff car park. He could have cornered Chester at his home in Reigate, of course, but that wouldn't have been a very good move. Part of their understanding was that Chester kept the recurrence of his bad days under control, and Michael didn't rub the man's nose in the mess.

Michael left Randall with the Volvo, and walked over to Chester's Saab 9000. Chester was still getting out, moving slowly as if he hadn't seen the big, blue 960. Chester was arriving for work mid-morning. He wore a suit and a tie and looked tidy and shaven. His eyes, though, were

50

tightened up against the light. His brown face, today, looked old.

He slowed his movements to a stop for a moment, then he proceeded to close the car door. Click, it went, in the car park breeze.

"Morning, Chester." Michael stuffed his hands into the pockets of his jacket, slouching like a philosophical loser during a day at the races. Be relaxed, put the man at ease. "They told me you were expected in today."

Chester just looked at the key dangling from his hand. "It's a lot to ask, Michael."

"I know."

Chester flipped the key into his fist.

"So," Michael said. "What's the answer going to be?"

Chester turned and walked to the boot of his car. Michael stayed put. Don't crowd him.

"On the Florida-Florida course," Chester said. "With ideal weather all the way, needing no detours." He opened the hatchback and helped the door wheeze sweetly up into its wide open rest. "You'd have a margin of unused fuel of only four percent."

"I know, Chester."

"And with the likely weather, it would be just two percent. And for the worst we can cope with, it would be no percent at all." Chester studied the interior of the boot, like a man whose treasure chest is empty. "To fly from Florida back to England means flying nearly five thousand miles. Even with the tail wind, it's still well over four thousand air miles. You'd need eighteen percent more fuel. Twenty percent, if you want a safety margin."

"We wouldn't fly the bonus stage unless we came out of the main course with that maximum fuel margin in the first place." He tried a wry smile for Chester. "Nobody's actually asking for miracles."

Chester just reached into the boot, and hauled out his leather flight bag. In it he kept the hard hat, overalls and ear protectors he carried around in case the maintenance teams asked him to look at something for them. He hitched the strap of the bag over his shoulder. "You still need fifteen or sixteen percent, Michael. Angel couldn't fly with that much fuel on board. She'd never get off the ground."

"We can't save weight anywhere else, I suppose?"

"You're talking about more weight than the pilot and the engine combined. You can't do without either of those." Chester reached into the boot again, and brought out his briefcase. "You're human, Michael. You can't make Angel float through the air."

It was a tired jibe from a washed-out man. Michael fenced it with a little shake of the head. Wait – and let Chester make the start along the positive road.

Chester slammed the hatchback. He came back to the driver's door and locked the car. The door buttons closed like soft finger raps on metal.

Chester took his first step across the empty tarmac, aiming past the front of the big blue Volvo. "If we add that much weight to Angel, we have to add lift as well. Not as much lift as we're adding weight, because Angel can cope with some of it as she's built now. But not all of it. So we'd have to add lift."

Michael nodded. Slowly, he started to follow at Chester's shoulder. Slowly, Chester pulled himself onwards, eyes down to the ground.

"If we redesign the wing for more lift, we get two problems. First, we throw away half of the aircraft we've already got, and take months to get it back in the air. You don't want that, Michael. Do you?"

"No, Chester. I've set my heart on going this summer."

"Second, you get more structural weight and more drag when you add more wing. So then you need more power. So then you need a bigger engine, which means more weight. Which means you need more wing, and so on."

"I do know about aircraft design, Chester."

"So you won't ever get the compromise you need like that. Angel already *is* the compromise. We'd have to try a different trick."

52

They got to the front of the Volvo. Inside, Randall was reading some sort of paperback propped on the wheel.

"Fuel tanks mean structural weight, besides the weight of the fuel they contain. That's a problem. It's wasted weight, once the fuel tank's empty." Chester stopped walking. He finally looked up again, a narrow eye squinting through the daylight. "Isn't it?"

Michael nodded. Chester, going his private and crisis-loaded way, had come up with the only solution that seemed at all likely to succeed. If Chester had found it independently, then it was probably the right answer. Prompting him might have saved Chester some of the agony, but it wouldn't have provided a valid support for the solution. "An external tank," Michael said. "A drop tank."

Chester sort of shrugged. "It isn't a magic solution. It still adds the fuel weight, it still adds the weight of the tank, it still adds drag. It still lumbers us with all the penalties. But at least, once the fuel's used up and the tank is empty and the fuel weight penalty is gone, you can throw the tank weight and the extra drag away. It's a start, I suppose."

Michael frowned, acting the part of a man thoughtfully surprised by an idea. "Do you think the tank could be made big enough – could carry enough extra fuel – to compensate for the inefficiency in Angel's flight until the tank can be thrown away?"

"I don't know. I'll have to put some figures on it."

"But you do think it's worth working on?"

Chester tried for a weak little smile.

Michael beamed. He let Chester bathe in gratitude. He clapped Chester on the shoulder, his hand slapping the leather pad on the flight-bag strap. "That's great, Chester. I knew you'd come up with something. I knew you'd get me out of the woods."

Chester adjusted the strap on his shoulder. Michael's hand had already gone. Chester's thumb stayed hitched under the leather. He let the tiredness close his eyes. "I'll get to work on it, Michael. I'll have something by next week."

"Fine. And, well – stay dry for me, Chester. Okay?"

"I said I'll get to work on it." Chester opened his eyes. Now he wasn't pleased – their coded agreement had been bruised by the remark. It was a little kick in the pants. It was waking him up. "I'll have something by next week."

"Thanks, Chester. I know you will."

Michael watched Chester walk as far as the staff gate, then turned back to his Volvo. Talented cripples are worth the attention, the effort pays off in the end. Ruth Clifford was still worth the attention – at least until after the flight in Angel, probably for the rest of the year. But he wasn't going to carry her inferiority complex for ever. As every boss knows, a change is always due. Somewhere, sometime.

He got into the back, where his laptop was waiting on the seat. "London," he said to Randall. "Orbis."

Randall stuffed the paperback into the glove box, and started the engine.

Michael fastened his belt, then pulled the computer across his knees. He hinged up the screen, checked the file that was waiting was the right one, and pressed *enter*. "Put a disk in the CD, Randall. Anything you like."

Randall decided to play something muscular by Madonna. Thank God the man didn't like rap.

SEVEN

Munro buzzed Michael's office. He got the beep of the transfer, meaning Michael wasn't there. Pattie Lee answered instead, smooth and bland. "Michael isn't in the office, Mr Munro. I believe he's at the Orbis building. Can I take a message?"

Munro looked at the pin-printed sheets on his desk – a digest of the data going through the accounting machine.

It made a fuzzy snapshot of the present state of health of MT-Orbis. It was nothing more than a provisional projection, but it mattered just the same. "Is he intending to come back today?"

"No, I don't think so."

He fingered one of the sheets, the one with the bottom-line warning of disaster. Should he pick up the phone and try chasing Michael at Orbis, or have Michael's PA do the chasing, or let it ride until tomorrow? If Michael was indeed going to be in the office tomorrow, and not playing pilots up at Wragby. Pattie Lee wasn't any help. She never volunteered anything. Her voice was as blank and inscrutable as her face – when talking to her, you were confounded by Chinese clichés. She was the keeper of the seal on Michael's private book.

The figures, though, were dire.

"I've got the estimates for the current quarter in front of me. I think Michael should see them right away."

"Very well. I'll ask him to come back as soon as he's finished at Orbis. May I tell him precisely why?"

What she meant was, would Munro be so good as to justify the urgency of the situation to her? Munro, in fact, would not. He didn't get angry: there was no point in pretending he wasn't outside Pattie Lee's personal fortress line, drawn up to protect her boss from all and any avoidable intrusions. But he could still get mildly emphatic. "Just tell him I think he should see these figures right away."

Michael was there for the good news, then he got some sort of message and left. Bad news, it seemed, was piling up.

Ruth followed Terri Sabuli to the third floor, and along the corridor towards the back of the building. The all-conquering android had started this week by wearing white – white shoes, short white jacket, white slacks which were loose in the leg and gathered in a forest of tucks at the top, which said: look at these gorgeous hips, chaps, think of this slender waist. As a woman trying to hold your ground in the big male world, you could really hate her.

They arrived at the door and went into the empty room.

It had three unmodernised sliding sash windows. It had a blank end wall with the faded imprints of vanished charts stretching like ghosts between old drawing-pin holes. On the long wall opposite the windows, the daylight did its duty and picked out every single pit in the plaster left behind by the recently removed shelves. There was the wall with the door, next to which hung a clock reading seven twenty-three, the time on some long gone day or night when the battery had died. Pale carpet tiles covered the floor. The stacks of fast forwards and lever arch files had been taken away, the boxes of junk had gone. One single Orbis Airship sticker had escaped and lingered next to the skirting under the windows. The airship had been the key plaything in Michael's publicity drive in eighty-eight. He brought the airship to Ethiopia, part of his brief blitz of good works. That's where Ruth met him. As people might say, it had changed her life. On the surface.

Terri folded her arms, scanning the circuit of the floor. "No telephone point. We'll need a dozen. One mains socket there, and one here. We'll need at least eight. If we're going to run this like a proper Mission Control, they'll have to put in computers with all the stuff on the aeroplane, on the route, with info on the arrangements with local air traffic controls, and I don't know what else. We'll need a screen full-time just to handle the press contacts and camera teams we'll have waiting all round the world. Come to think of it, this will add up to quite a big oppo."

Ruth just nodded. Oppo. The android sounded like a military groupie.

Terri walked over to the Orbis Airship sticker, and squatted neatly on her heels to give it a better look. She didn't touch it. "Did I hear right, Ruth? You met Michael in Ethiopia?"

"I was there with World Assist. Second time, in fact."

"Mm." Terri stood up. "Bet you're glad you're not there now – rebels taking the capital, relief convoys being bombed, aid workers shot at. Did you just do fieldwork?"

Just do fieldwork. As if the sweat, the dirt, the constant battle to control the chaos, the bringing in of food, the organising of it up-country to feed people as thin as the skin-covered bones of their own dead cattle, the ceaseless war of negotiations with the increasingly brutal and belligerent government and rebel forces – as if all of that, the real and debilitating work at the sharp end, was just so much decoration on the charity industry's cake. On the other hand, the android was asking about administrative experience, which was a fair enough concern. "As well as fieldwork, I did a couple of years at the Africa desk here in London."

"Good," Terri said. "Good. So you're happy about running the charity liaison?"

"Yes," Ruth said. "I am."

Terri nodded. She glanced out of the window at the bald brickwork of the building's back alley. "Well, there'll be nothing to tempt us to stare at the lovely view when we ought to be working. I'll need someone to keep up with the media contacts once they start to come in – someone to run them for me while I'm juggling the whole show. Know of anybody? It doesn't matter if they're tied up with something else at the moment."

Meaning the android had been given the power to pull in anyone it wanted. "Mandy Rees," Ruth said. "She works here at Orbis. She's used to the press, and she knows about the project."

"Good. And I'm also going to need some tasty girls."

"Girls?"

"You know – pretty young women with friendly voices to run the phones and meet the gentlemen from the press. All of them dressed in the Orbis look, more or less like you are, but sexier. I'll talk to Michael about a T-shirt or something. We don't want to take it too far. Fresh, modern, youthful but responsible – that's the Orbis image, isn't it? Clean, not mean. And not a bit exploitative, which also means no overt sexual sell. Right?"

The android was looking straight at her for the first time since Michael got the message calling him back to the MT building. It was a look of mild interest, where the measuring up had already been done. It wasn't unfriendly, but if the walking publicity machine had done its measuring job, then where did any remaining interest come from? Time to confront the difference in professional skill – acknowledge that you can't do this kind of thing alone, any more than the android could fly an aircraft out of a hangar. Time to stop the working relationship, threatened by your own resentment, from sliding beyond retrieval. "How did you do it?"

"Do what, Ruth?"

"How did you get Geo-Petro to sign?"

"Oh – I played on their weakness. Their image problem. You didn't do your research properly."

"Why not?"

Terri smiled. "It isn't just the Third World where their name stinks, and it isn't the Third World where they're vulnerable. There's a court case proceeding against them in Australia at the moment, and there are three lawsuits pending against them in the United States. They need to do a highly visible nice turn. So – I thought I might try leaning on them."

"How?"

"I told them that *we* have an image problem – we can't take on too many so-called Third World exploiters without being rubbished as just a PR stunt for neo-colonialists, and all that. So at the moment, I told them, we're rationing ourselves to one company from each branch of industry. I was playing on my credibility there. I look like a piece of Third World glamour, don't I?"

Ruth just nodded. She wasn't going to start praising the android for its makeup, its wardrobe and its long, slinky walk.

"I didn't *mention* anybody, but I did suggest we had another interested party talking about offering more per mile – which the charities would like, of course. And I gave them a crude, but realistic, costing for an orthodox advertising campaign able to do their image as much good as the sponsorship will achieve.

They'd be spending a hundred million world-wide to get the same coverage. So they signed. At thirty per mile."

"*Thirty* pounds per mile?" Ruth walked headlong into the little surprise. "That comes to – three-quarters of a million for the complete circuit of the world. And a million and a half, if they double it with the bonus stage. Are they going for the bonus stage?"

Terri nodded. "We're starting to talk real money on this."

"Does Michael know?"

"Oh yes. He seemed quite pleased. It should help him with Munro, don't you think?"

Ruth nodded. Michael knew, but he didn't tell her. Terri Sabuli didn't tell her straight away. The closeness between Michael and his android had already begun.

"Richmond Alchem are coming in at twenty pounds per mile," the android added, smooth and self-satisfied. "Also with the bonus stage. Another half million doubling to one million. However, there's a condition attached to that, which we have to discuss with Michael. Any idea why he was called back to MT?"

Ruth shrugged. "Something about the figures for the current quarter."

"Oh." The android pouted its lips into a red, glistening circle. "Bet that's bad."

Ruth just shrugged again.

Then the android decided to turn on its heel. "Right." It started its sinuous strides towards the door. "Let's have a chat with Mandy Rees. Then we have to hurry over to MT Holdings." At the door it stopped and turned. "This does actually involve you, Ruth."

Terri Sabuli's car was a VW Corrado – red, of course. It was all part of the personal presentation. But it didn't let her move through town any faster than the rest of the choked-up traffic. One day, London is going to stop, thought Ruth. Every road is going to come to a complete standstill, and a decade later the veins of the city will still be one solid mass of painted rust. It's bound to happen, even if the marketing message gets out and many more firms take on Michael's strategy of green awareness.

Because the strategy is just a face. And wearing the face is a great big business trying to make – and not to lose – as much money as it possibly can.

Michael looked grim. They found him in Munro's office, where Ripley, the PA, showed them through. For a moment it was Ruth who was providing the walk-in access. And then she was back in the shade, eclipsed by the android.

"Mr Munro," the android said, sucking light into the middle of the room, "has Michael told you we've got one sponsor signed up, and another ready?"

"He has." Munro glanced at Michael. "And I've just handed him a conclusive argument for going ahead with the project."

Michael brightened slightly. "Now the sponsorship is coming in and we can recover costs, we'll be losing if we don't fly the mission. And Bob has just had to agree that we really could use a major publicity stunt." He looked straight at Ruth. "It's the profits, you see. They're a lot further in the red than we were expecting. I really don't like recessions." Then he looked at the android, and pointed his finger. For a moment, every hint of good humour disappeared. "And that's privileged information, and I do not joke about the fact."

Terri Sabuli nodded. She could cope with concealing privileged information. Being a publicist made her a professional liar.

"Anyway." Michael pressed his palms together for a second, a snatch of placatory prayer. "Perhaps God's just being even-handed. Last year the communists were wiped out, this year the capitalists are getting a squeeze on profits. Now then, back to the sponsors. What's the catch on the Richmond Alchem deal?"

"They want a backup pilot," the android said.

Michael looked at Munro, who raised an eyebrow behind

his glasses. Michael studied the android for a while, then he looked at Ruth.

Ruth just shook her head. Don't ask me, she thought. Neither you, nor anybody else, tells me much these days. Ask your android.

Terri Sabuli didn't bother to wait. "You were bound to run into it at some stage. These people are cautious. If they're pledging significant cash, they want reliability and a guarantee of payback built into the arrangement."

"By reliability," Michael said, "you mean accidents. But if I put myself in hospital, Angel doesn't fly, and no one donates a penny."

"But suppose you look at the sponsor's worst scenario. You, the only pilot. The publicity circus up and running. The very eve of take-off. Shocking news – you wrap your car round a tree. The sponsor sees himself losing out in two ways. First, everyone's been jumping up and down about the oodles of money due to flow to good works in the Third World. The pressure will probably be high enough to oblige the sponsor to make a token donation, even though the whole thing is off. Second, MT-Orbis has already harvested plenty of publicity – which wouldn't have been possible without a credible charity promotion, which requires the pledging of the sponsor's money – *and* you'll get a run-on for a while with the sympathy effect. MT-Orbis gets a lift lasting for months, while the sponsor scores a great big publicity zero. So the sponsor has put in, but got nothing back."

"Ah," Michael said. "I see."

"So they want a better guarantee that the aeroplane is going to fly. Which means that they want a backup pilot, just in case."

Michael folded his arms. He turned to Munro, and Munro merely nodded. It was obvious. They were businessmen. They understood.

Another point to the android. Ruth wasn't supposed to get these little kicks when Michael was caught out in the middle of his own plans. But she did just the same.

61

"Well," Michael said. "Any suggestions? It would have to be someone who fits the PR profile for the flight, plus the image for the company. Also, an insider would be ideal."

"The Orbis image is ecological responsibility and economic fairness," said Terri Sabuli. "The code at the centre of that is *balance*. You're a rich white male, so you'd get the most mileage out of a poor black female. But finding one on the payroll who can fly is a bit of a tall order. So, basically I'd go for a black. Failing that, a woman."

"Chester Alby," Munro said.

Michael didn't react.

"He's black," Munro added. "He isn't too old. He's a pilot. And he must understand the aircraft even better than you do."

Michael shook his head. "Not Chester Alby. I know what you mean, but it wouldn't work. He wouldn't be right. Believe me, Bob. I do know."

Munro just shrugged. He turned to the android. "Any other suggestions? As Michael said, an insider would be best."

The android, the beautiful android, turned its head and rested its deep brown eyes – on Ruth.

EIGHT

The sun shone sharp as glass through Wedgwood blue, a perfect sky straight from childhood's picture book. It made a flawless vault over the City's tangle of towers and trading temples. Even in the heart of London, the air smelled less than filthy in a chill north wind. It was the coldest start to June that anyone could remember. When they set out from the Chilterns at the brilliant beginning of the day, there'd been a frost.

Andrew Carlyle was in the lobby, at the reception desk.

The receptionist pointed at them as they came up the stairs. Carlyle looked round, said something like a thankyou to the receptionist, and came across to meet them at the lifts.

"Morning, Michael. Morning, Ruth." Carlyle went first into the lift. He turned dramatically to press the door hold button.

"Morning, Andrew," Michael said as he walked into the lift and took up position against the back wall. Michael showed signs of being very happy this week. Chester had solved the problem of extending Angel's range. "Lovely morning."

Ruth stood beside Michael. Andrew Carlyle was all slick suit and solarium smile hovering high up under a sweep of white hair that reached, neatly, to his collar. In the compact space of the lift, his fifties fitness was unbearably confined, and his indoor tennis aura was compressed to an almost visible brightness. It seemed possible that the deputy MD of Orbis Air, this marvellously mediocre man, would puff himself out, push aside the air, stretch the seams of the lift cage and jam it in the shaft.

"Damned chilly for June," Carlyle said, as the floors began to count themselves. Then he leaned down towards Michael, cutting off Ruth's view of the indicator over the door. From the side, she could see a well of concern surfacing in the man's evenings-and-weekend tanned face. "You do know, don't you, what Munro's up to?"

Michael used a small smile. Carlyle was his chosen top-rank dogsbody, and he knew how to play him. "What's that, Andrew?"

"Looking over our books. Same at Siltech, and Orbis. I know he's supposed to look over our shoulders, but this is a bit much."

"These are hard times, Andrew."

"I know full well, Michael. And I know you asked him a couple of months ago to take a look at the whole of MT-Orbis and start working out some recommendations. But I think he's going the whole hog – on his own say-so – and looking for chunks he can sell off." The lift stopped and the doors opened.

Carlyle took time to check the corridor at his floor was empty, then rammed the door hold button with his thumb again. "I did think you ought to know. You see, I'm beginning to think he's got his sights set on Orbis Air."

Michael continued with the small smile. Everything under control, it said. No surprises in the little big man's world. "I did actually okay Munro's activities, Andrew. And like you, I am aware that Orbis Air is our biggest loss-maker at the moment, as well as being the biggest single chunk we could put up for sale – if we were in a crisis that deep. But it's my judgement that we're not in that crisis. Also, Munro did ask me in February whether the sale of Orbis Air might be an option he should consider."

"Did he?" Carlyle said it quietly – but he looked as though his racket had been snatched away by a cross-court volley. "I didn't know, Michael."

Michael shook his head. He was keeping Carlyle in his grateful sit-up-and-beg posture. Ruth had given up wondering why the victim never saw the trick. First assert power by pointing out there's a higher level where things are done without the involvement of mere mortals – then show how magnanimous that power always proves to be.

"I told him no, Andrew."

Andrew Carlyle smiled, a sunrise of relief. A ball boy had brought the racket back, the umpire had disallowed the stroke. "I just thought, you know – I ought to make sure. I've been getting a little bit worried since Munro set up this special audit."

"Special audit?"

"Our accounts." Carlyle released the door hold and stepped out of the lift. "He's got someone going through the computer to get profiles on the loss areas. Anyway, as long as it's all right after all. Cheerio, Michael. Ruth." He gave a little drop-volley wave as the doors closed.

The lift continued to count floors.

Michael didn't say what he thought of Andrew Carlyle. He didn't say anything at all.

64

Ruth looked at his face. Michael's lips were pressed together, his eyes were staring a long way past the metal wall.

"What's the matter?" she said. "Michael?"

"My plans. I'm going to have to change my bloody plans."

"What plans?"

He turned his head. He stared at her for a second – then the mask came down. "That's my business." He turned back to the invisible metal wall. "Munro's fucking up my bloody plans."

The lift arrived at the executive floor. The doors opened, but for a moment Michael didn't react. Then he marched out, wheeled round, and stamped down the carpeted corridor.

Ruth followed, half-running. She'd almost caught him when he disappeared through the door to Munro's outer office. She paused in the doorway. Ripley, Munro's PA, was starting to stand up. Michael was already opening the inner door.

Ripley looked at Ruth while reaching for the intercom. Ruth shrugged and started across the room. Michael was already inside Munro's office –

"What the hell do you mean starting a special audit behind my back! Whose bloody company is this?"

As she followed Michael through, Ruth could see Munro sitting at his desk. He looked very surprised.

"You work for me, Bob." Michael had his back to Ruth, but there was something unmistakable in his posture, like a gunslinger about to draw. "That means you work *with* me. You *don't* work without me!"

Munro stayed seated. He put his hands on the top surface of his desk, one each side of the blotter. He wasn't going to spring to his feet the minute his superior barged in.

There was a click behind Ruth. Ripley had closed the outer door and sealed the confrontation off from the rest of MT Holdings.

"Come on. Tell me! Why have you started the special audit? And why in *hell* didn't you tell me first?"

"I've been telling you," Munro said, "since February."

"Have you? Have you indeed been bloody telling me? And

when did I say go ahead? Tell me when I said go ahead!"
Michael made fists at his sides. "*This is my company!*"

Munro nodded.

Ripley was right behind Ruth. She was closing the second
door. She was looking at Ruth: staying in or coming out?

Ruth reached backwards to help close the door. To shoo
Ripley away. She wasn't going to miss this . . .

"I said – this is *my* company!"

Munro nodded again. "I know it's your company, Michael."

"Well?" Michael's fists had started to quiver. "*So?*"

"So I'm looking after it for you." Munro's voice was very
quiet – far too quiet. Like a man prepared to quit before
he'd accept a dressing-down from a younger boss. "You hired
me to run MT-Orbis. You hired me to show an extremely
well-developed sense of responsibility to MT-Orbis. You did
not hire me to parrot yes Michael, no Michael, anything you
say Michael. Did you?"

"You're pushing it, Bob. You're *pushing* it."

"I'm pushing responsibility. At you, Michael. I'm pushing
it at you. You've seen the figures. You know what's happening.
MT Holdings is about to tip into massive losses. It's losing its
income because the whole of MT-Orbis is flat on its back, and
because Orbis Air is starting to sink. Before the end of the
year, Orbis Air is going to pull everything down. The recession
isn't my fault, it isn't yours. If you believe the politicians who
manage the economy, it isn't even theirs. But it's real. And
it's starting to do massive damage to this company. We have
to get ready to take action now – before we let a catastrophe
happen."

Michael didn't say anything. His fists were still clenched
tight.

Munro folded his arms – a quieter, colder, darker man.
"Every time I've asked you to let me start putting a rescue
plan together, you've stalled, you've said not yet, or you haven't
even answered. That's a mistake you've been making. It's my
job to make up for your mistakes, otherwise I'm a waste of
every penny you pay me. So if you won't accept what has to

be done – to stop your own company going under – I'll do it without waiting any longer. Am I making myself clear?"

"When?" Michael said. "When did you start the audits?"

"Last week. After we got the estimated figures."

"Last week. Without asking my permission."

"Without asking your permission for the fifth or sixth time."

Michael's fists were unfolding, a finger at a time. "You started last week. You could have had the courtesy to tell me."

Munro nodded. "I'll grant you that, Michael."

Michael lifted his hands. He pushed open the sides of his jacket and planted his hands on his hips. "You'll grant me that, will you? I just found out from that nonentity Andrew Carlyle. I think he was too bloody stupid to realise he knew something I didn't know. You shouldn't be doing that to me, Bob."

Munro shrugged, a dismissive gesture. It had already happened, and he'd already apologised – more or less. "What's so upsetting about the audit, Michael? I'm supposed to be in charge of MT's finances. Is there anything I'm not supposed to know?"

"It's – " Michael shook his head. "The damned principle. Oh, to *hell* with it." He turned half away from Munro, ending the confrontation.

Then his head turned all the way round, and he glared at Ruth.

"What," he said, "has this got to do with you?"

Ruth had an answer ready. The answer surprised her while she was saying it. "I was curious to see how big boys solve problems."

It surprised Michael. And Munro.

She was supposed to be discussing charity priorities with Terri Sabuli – how they should resolve conflicting claims on sponsored money when payout day arrived. But there was a note stuck to Terri Sabuli's door – sorry, gone to Wapping to keep some contacts warm.

Bloody considerate.

So Ruth took a taxi to the Orbis building in Soho, and charged the fare to MT Holdings. Then she decided to indulge herself in a telephone call at company expense, too. Recession or no recession, Michael's precious empire could afford it.

Her mother answered. Her father never did that now. He wouldn't even come to the phone when she asked for him. Nowadays, her mother didn't even bother to pass on the ritual request . . .

"You know how he is, love, sometimes. Busy with things, always at something. And you know it isn't easy for him with – "

"Yes, Mum. Never mind, Mum. Have you read anything about this Orbis charity flight? The thing Michael's doing."

"That would be your Michael, wouldn't it? Yes, I saw something on the box, love. Your dad doesn't think much of that sort of thing. Nobody's had any charity for him all his life."

"Did you hear we were modifying the aircraft so that we can make the flight even longer?"

"I might have, love. Oh, I'm sure I must have done."

"Anyway, that's nearly finished now. The thing is, in a week or two we're giving Angel – that's the aircraft – we're giving Angel a new test flight at Wragby. You know – Wragby Aerodrome, out Sherwood Forest way?"

A pause for thought in Mellors Road, Sheffield. "It's a long time since we went to Sherwood Forest, Ruth. Not since you were a little girl."

"Well the point is, when we test fly it, some press will be there to take a look – "

"Well yes, obviously. Your Michael Tranter's a very rich man, isn't he, and keeps doing these sorts of things. Like that other bloke with the balloons. Whatsisname. You'd *expect* the newspapers to be there. Will it be in the local rag?"

"Um – I don't know if the Sheffield paper will be there, Mum."

68

"Oh. Well, then. I mean, we don't get any other paper. Is there going to be any television?"

"Um – I don't know. We'll have to wait and see. I could ask our publicity co-ordinator and let you know what channel to watch. If there is any TV coverage, that is."

"I don't know, dear. There's so many horrid things on the news these days."

"Mum? Please? Can I get to the point. Look, I don't often phone, do I?"

"No, dear. Not as often as you should. Your dad never says anything, but I know he notices. It hurts him a lot. I suppose you want to tell me you're phoning because it's important."

"If it – if it hurts him a lot, why doesn't he talk to me when I'm on the phone? Why won't he?"

"Ruth, we don't want to go through that all over again, do we? You know perfectly well what it's all about, I'm sure. Your dad's as stubborn as you're contrary. There's no need to go raking things over all the time. Now what is it you're wanting to tell me? Have you got some news or something?"

"Yes, Mum. Exactly. I've got some news. Or at least, something that's going to be news. When we do the test flight for Angel – the aircraft – we're going to have a little press conference about progress on the project and so on. And that's when they're going to announce something. They're going to announce that I, Ruth Clifford – that I'm the backup pilot."

A long pause in Mellors Road.

"Backup pilot. Backup pilot. Is that like a copilot?"

"No, Mum. It means that I will be flying the aircraft – solo, all the way round the world – if Michael has an accident or falls ill. *I'm* the one who'll do it if anything happens to Michael."

Another long pause.

"You mean an understudy sort of thing."

"Um – yes, I suppose so. What do you think?"

"Oh – I'm sure that's very nice for you, love. I'm sure you'll manage, if you have to – though we'd better hope it doesn't come to that, if it means Michael Tranter having an accident. I'm sure your dad will be very pleased to hear it."

Ruth, when she was putting down the phone, was sure her father wouldn't.

NINE

Outside the open doors of the hangar, the rain had stopped and the wind had disappeared, but the apron was still wet and the distance was grey. Inside, Angel waited like some exotic creature of the air in a vast collecting box, too timorous to escape into the cold of an English June.

Ruth wanted Angel to escape. She sat in the cockpit and wished the bird would roll. Then she'd have to take command of Angel – of ungainly, wide-winged, short-tailed, long-nosed, foreplane-trimmed Angel – and fly the machine. She'd show that she could. She would put herself on the unique list of Angel's pilots. Because the pilot who flew Angel round the world, non-stop and solo, could be another Amy Johnson – could be a heroine in history's hall of aviation fame . . .

But they weren't going to let her fly.

So she sat in the cockpit, under its opaque roof, with both side windows slid fully open. She looked through the sleek slope of the windscreen, over the long nose and the wide blades of the foreplanes, at the wet world outside. Its sky was overcast, choked with waiting rain clouds. But up above the clouds, out of sight of this tangling drabness, was empty freedom and a summer sun to chase . . .

But they weren't going to let her fly.

Michael would sit here, in this seat, for four days – five, with the bonus stage. Just his autopilot, his central computer, his navigation system and the satellite voice from Mission Control for company. And afterwards, when he landed, the world would hand him more money and more fame. Those who already have shall have much, much more. And those who have not shall get nothing.

Michael would sit in this narrow space, instruments in front of him, throttle beside his left thigh, joystick beside his right, food and drink stowed in lockers behind him. For the short sleep periods he would crank the seat down like a dentist's chair until it was almost flat. That would be the beginning and the end of his freedom of movement. Five days sitting down was a very long time. Her father would know. Her father, of all people, would know . . .

They weren't going to let her fly.

Michael was going to do the test circuit with the external tank. Michael was going to fly every other test. Michael was going to fly round the world. Michael was going to steal from her. It always came out the same. First her father, who never forgave her for not being a son. Then Ashley, who told her to forget her university degree and her selfish fulfilment, and help him instead to bathe his own ego in saving the world. Now Michael, taking a childhood dream from under her nose – the Amy Johnson fantasy of escape, achievement and glory. Ruth, chasing the sun once more, had landed in another man's shadow. Sit on the sidelines, out of the light, and applaud the cartwheels of the conquering male.

It would never occur to Michael or to Chester that she should take Angel on one of the tests. Angel was Michael's personal ticket to another helping of fame. Angel was Chester's surrogate mate for the unattainable man in his life, destined to unite with Michael in one long and glorious matrimonial flight. That Ruth, the wrong pilot and the real lover, merely sat in the cockpit to get the feel of the controls was enough of an upset for Chester, like seeing the wrong person's hand slip inside Angel's knickers . . .

Terri Sabuli appeared at the hangar door, pausing for a moment like a stranger peering through a proscenium into a dark stage. She was wearing a raincoat, designer white and all epaulets, lapels, rifle patches and half-caped back. When she started to walk again, those long legs under the high, tight hemline let in glimpses between folded curtains of light. The gentlemen of the press, the few that were here, didn't stand a chance.

Terri Sabuli walked round the waist-high foreplane and came in towards the shadow of the wing. Terri Sabuli was tall, but the straight-edged wing was another head and shoulders taller. In front of its shelter, she walked to the cockpit side. Standing outside the open window, her eyes were no lower than Ruth's chin.

"Michael and Chester want to do the flight," she said. "Before the weather closes in again."

Ruth nodded. She touched the throttle with her left hand, stroked the joystick with her right. Goodbye to all this, she thought. Then she grabbed the assist handle under the roof, rested her forearm on the frame of the open window, and started to haul herself out of the seat and out of the side of Angel's cockpit. Don't tread on any instruments. Chester wouldn't like it. She got her body and her first leg through the window, placed her foot on the top of the little crew ladder, lifted her other leg out and then started to climb down. "What about the press?"

"Baker's dozen," Terri said. "And I think one of those is illiterate."

"Television?" Ruth jumped on tiptoes from the ladder to the concrete floor. "Have they turned up?"

"No." Terri was studying Angel. The press exposure for this event was a minor failure, and she didn't like it. Otherwise she wouldn't have left Mandy Rees minding the shop while she delivered a message. She pointed down at the attachment under the aircraft's belly. "I still can't get used to the sight of this. What you've got here is a *biplane*. Is this what Chester Alby's genius always looks like?"

"It's a clever idea," Ruth said. "It works."

The attachment was a streamlined boat shape, a narrow canoe, a conformal drop tank bolted under Angel's belly. It sat precisely against the aircraft's skin to minimise turbulence and drag, it blended smoothly with the underside of the fuselage from beneath the cockpit to the point where the upslope of the abrupt tail began. Made of GRP and finished in the same brilliant green, it looked as if it was an integral part of the machine.

What looked unusual, though, was the underwing.

Terri Sabuli pointed up and down the length of the square-ended underwing. It had a much shorter chord back to front, but it was fully half the span of the main wing above. Extending from the side of the canoe tank, the underwing was only knee-high off the ground as Angel sat on its landing gear. "It doesn't even have any struts up to the main wing or anything. Is it stable? Is it safe?"

Ruth shrugged. "It's stable. We've flown it once before. You don't think we'd really do the first flight in front of the press?"

"Actually – I did. I thought Michael meant it." She looked sideways at Ruth. "It seemed to fit the man's cocksure ego."

Ruth almost smiled. This woman is fallible after all, and it's a great relief. "Michael's ego takes better care of itself than that. He wouldn't risk any failure in public."

"I see. I'll make a note of it." Terri pointed at the canoe and its underwing again. "Why is it like this? I know the tank is that shape to reduce air resistance, and I know it's that *big* because it carries so much extra fuel. But what are these extra wings for?"

"They help carry the load. By far the heaviest part of Angel is the fuel, and the canoe tank increases the total fuel load by more than two-fifths. Angel couldn't get into the air without either a bigger wing, or an additional wing." Ruth shrugged. "If you go for a *bigger* wing, you increase the total drag and structural weight, and that has fuel penalties and so on, and you're stuck with your bigger wing from beginning to end of the flight. If you choose an *additional* wing, you increase drag and weight and you still get those fuel penalties, but you can throw away the extra wing when you no longer need it – in other words, when the tank is empty. You just drop the canoe and the underwing, and you've got back your original streamlined and efficient aircraft, fully loaded with internal fuel – but just about seven thousand miles into the flight. So you can go the extra distance for the bonus stage."

Terri nodded. "Two-fifths extra fuel for an extra seven thousand miles. Shouldn't that be ten thousand miles? The original course without the bonus stage is twenty-five thousand miles." She pointed at her own head, at her temple from which black hair was drawn straight back towards the base of that vase-handle plait. "We can do our sums in here, you know. We're not just a brown bimbo with a good line in male manipulation."

Ruth blinked. You don't actually expect people to confront you with your estimations of them. "Um – it's the drag. From the underwing. You have to balance airspeed against lift against fuel consumption to get your most efficient cruising speed. Angel's designed cruising speed without the canoe is two hundred and fifty knots. With the canoe and underwing, it will be only two hundred. That's with the engine using fuel at the same rate, which is its most efficient throttle setting, which is also critical. The constant power will drive Angel more slowly, but still give enough lift with the underwing. It means using more fuel per mile flown, which is why we only get seven thousand miles out of the canoe tank before we throw it away. Aerodynamics is all variables. You juggle them around to get the best balance."

"So I'm beginning to realise." Terri turned her head and looked at Ruth. "Why didn't Michael want Chester as his backup pilot?"

You mean, Ruth thought, why did he settle – at *your* suggestion – for crummy little me? "Chester has some personal problems. Most of them to do with being a black kid from Toxteth who's come a long way. One or two make him rather vulnerable." And that's enough freedom exercised over another human being's privacy. "And he doesn't seem the type who could easily handle the press."

Terri nodded. "Talking of which, Michael wants the flight

over and then we can hold our little briefing. Can you handle the press, Ruth?"

"Well, Terri – we're going to see."

Angel's flight was short and exactly to plan, twice over Wragby Aerodrome in a figure-eight. It was raining again before Michael had taxied the aircraft back to its hangar. The press briefing, in a workshop which was out of use because of the shortfall in Trantair's orders for Solomasters, was less of a smooth success. Nine men and four women spread themselves out among the chairs that had been awaiting a larger press presence, and which now signalled irrelevance, low interest, inside page footnote news. The excitement about the crazy aircraft had been real enough, but the thing wasn't going anywhere yet. From a low-key beginning, the briefing went steadily downhill.

Ruth sat between Michael and Terri. She didn't mind that Michael was having such a hard time keeping the questions trickling in. Sometimes he should have to work for it – and besides, it did him good. It let his hard-bitten charisma shine in the eyes of his faithful disciples.

Ruth was suddenly realising that she wasn't his disciple any more.

So silently that she hadn't even noticed it happen, Michael had changed. He was no longer light and strength. He was the man who took her idea, turned it into Angel, and made it exclusively his own. He was a shadow. He was a weight holding her down. Slowly, but inexorably, he was on his way to join the ranks of the fathers and the Ashleys in Ruth's life.

The discovery was so mesmerising that she lost track . . .

Terri's foot tapped Ruth's foot under the table. She looked into Terri's brown eyes, and the brown eyes flicked immediately to the questioner, the woman in the sparse second row. The question was obviously over. The woman was waiting.

Michael wasn't going to help. He clearly didn't mind if Ruth did some of the work. He could use a break by now.

Terri rested her elbows on the table. She put her hands

together, fingers over fist, red nails against brown knuckles, and leaned her forehead against her hands. Tired and despairing of this limping farce. She lifted her head and stared wearily over her fingers. "Why," she whispered, "would *you* want to fly round the world?"

"Um – " Ruth said to the journalist. "That's a good one. I don't know – really. I suppose you mean apart from the fame and the glory and all that?"

The reporter didn't even nod her head.

"Um – I suppose it goes back to – dreams and things. Escaping from everyday life. Doing something out of the ordinary. I suppose we all want to be a hero or a heroine. When we're children, I mean. We all want to do brave and wonderful things. I remember when I was a little girl, I got this book about Amy Johnson. You know, the flier. In the days when aeroplanes were all open cockpits and canvas and stuff. She set new records with solo flights to Australia, Japan and South Africa. I thought, if she could do things like that, so could I. Wouldn't it be wonderful to be famous and brave like Amy Johnson? When I was a little girl I thought it would be just the thing for me. I suppose – well, it's all a bit silly, really."

It didn't even raise a smile.

The next morning, Terri Sabuli phoned while Ruth was still wondering about breakfast. Michael had something urgent to do concerning company finances, and wanted to do it in private on his computer at home. He was at his cottage in the country, Ruth was in Muswell Hill.

Something had started to change, all right.

Terri didn't sound displeased. "Ruth, I don't suppose you stoop to reading the tabloids, do you? You're a *Guardian* and *Independent* type."

"Yes. No. Why?"

"Because you struck gold, that's why! How about this for a front page, second lead headline? 'Plucky Ruth – Our New Amy Johnson'."

"What?"

"Note the *our*. This brave girl belongs to the great British public! They've used our standard pic and printed it up fairly well. You look absolutely human, and they didn't feel the need to airbrush better shadows under your tits."

"*What?*"

"On the fabric of your shirt, Ruth. Inside they've got a pic of the aeroplane, and – "

"Plucky? *Plucky?*"

"It's a tabloid. It's a headline. Give the poor hacks a break. Inside, they've got a pic of the aeroplane in the air, a little pic of you next to Michael at the briefing, and they've even pulled the stops out and added a couple of hundred words of text. And get this for a journalist's ability to use her word processor's thesaurus. At one point they call you an *aviatrix*. Latin literacy is a must in the popular press. What do you think?"

"Um – of the coverage? I'm a bit surprised."

"Well I'm a bit pleased. I told Michael the kind of image he needed to add, if he expected to capture the popular imagination on the national pride angle. And I was right. You're it. You're even kosher with the mass circulations, because you're white. But that, Ruth, is only half of it. That's only half."

"What's the other half?"

"How early can you get up tomorrow morning, be awake, and be out in the big wide world?"

"Pardon? Why?"

"I'll meet you at the Orbis building at six tomorrow. At six, and don't be a minute late. This one's too good to miss. They need you in really early for makeup, briefing and run-through. I'll hold your hand as long as possible – "

"Who want me? What for?"

"Breakfast TV. I'll hold your hand until the last possible moment, but you'll be by yourself in front of the camera. Live, of course. Try not to start worrying about it yet. You've got twenty-four hours – plenty of time to work up a decent panic. You'll only be on for sixty seconds between news and round-up slots, after all. But it's real PR, Ruth. It's publicity paydirt. You did it!"

Part 3

Blood Money

TEN

Robert Munro had furnished his office in dark oak. It made a contrast with the light-green carpet, it left the functional elements clearly defined – conference table, chairs, the desk, his executive chair with upholstered arms and tailored back. It talked to its occupant of precision and order. Ripley, Mrs Anne Ripley, with her tweed skirt and jacket, her white blouse and her perfect grey pageboy hair, had added potted plants which threw screens of living green along the window sills. They put life inside the glass and steel of the building's skin, they demonstrated real biology and shamed the symbolism of the image-conscious floor. They talked to Munro of human beings with untidy personal worlds who did all the work and created the entity called MT-Orbis.

It was far too easy to forget, to take the mathematics of profit and loss, of capital and credit, to be the truth, the whole truth and nothing but the truth about the company. Salaries, pension costs, work-station costs, production attainments and productivity profiles appeared deep down in the details of the balance sheets. The people never did.

But it was the people who were going to suffer when the mathematics veered out of line.

The problem was gearing, the ratio between borrowed money and capital invested by shareholders. The borrowed money was debt, with interest to be paid. When the trading profit sank below the level of interest due, and the losses began to come in . . .

MT-Orbis as a whole wasn't all that high-geared. Two

years ago, during the restructuring, he'd seen the problem coming and had blocked Michael's plans. Michael wanted immunity from takeover threats, and had intended to reduce the proportion of company funds raised as equity from investors: fewer outsiders holding fewer shares are fewer slices of your company which can be bought by someone who wants to swallow you up. It keeps you semi-private, and protects you. But a largely private company has to get its money somewhere, which means massive borrowing, which incurs heavy interest charges. You can cover the cost when the trading profit stays high. But when a downturn comes, and then plunges into recession . . .

Munro had a better way to build in takeover protection. He set up the subsidiaries at the bottom of the pyramid to be low-geared, with most of their funds raised through shares. Higher up the pyramid, a company had fewer outside investors and more of its funds supplied through shares held by its parent company. Siltech and Orbis Air were minority-owned by outsiders while the majority of each outfit, together with the entirety of Orbis, was held through mutual cross-shares, and by MT Holdings at the top of the tree. MT itself had high borrowing and was high-geared. MT was immune to a hostile takeover. So were Orbis, Siltech and Orbis Air. Any predator would have to take chunks of all the lower-tier subsidiaries and gradually strangle the upper levels into some kind of negotiated submission. The exercise would be costly and very lengthy. It would give MT-Orbis time to defend itself. It was a good solution.

But it still required that high borrowing and high gearing at the top. Fine when the money's coming in . . .

The way Michael had originally wanted to set up MT-Orbis, it would already have gone to the wall. Munro had saved them all from that. But the losses were coming in and hurting very hard. It was time to sell off the worst loss-maker and use the money raised to pay back some of the debt at the top, maintaining the takeover protection and reducing the gearing of MT Holdings – making it fitter and leaner for the future.

The biggest loss-maker was Orbis Air. Unfortunately, Michael didn't want it to go. Not yet. It was supplying the entire base for his crazy project. Perhaps he was right, perhaps the PR value of Angel's flight would be so great that the market share of MT-Orbis would rise and the problems would disappear. Certainly, there'd be some useful improvement.

But not enough.

In particular, it wouldn't make a damned bit of difference to the developing disaster at Orbis Air. And the wipe-out of the earnings from its Orbis Air stake was going to plunge MT Holdings into the red during the next quarter. MT would get no pick-up from Siltech or Orbis to help it through – the computer market was worse than static, and the green products bonanza had gone into reverse. Things would get critical long before the end of the year.

But for some reason, Michael didn't seem to care.

And Munro couldn't see any obvious way to do anything about it, since Michael Tranter was by far the biggest partner in MT-Orbis's ecology of power.

And the longer Michael ignored the advent of the inevitable, the more people were going to get hurt when the emergency surgery took place . . .

His office door opened and Ripley looked in. "There's a Mandy Rees on the line. She wants to speak to you urgently."

"Who," he said, "is Mandy Rees?"

"She's on the Angel project at Orbis. She's Terri Sabuli's deputy. Apparently she can't get Miss Sabuli, nor Mr Tranter."

Munro shook his head. "Michael's sulking at home. Put her through." It had better, he thought, be a genuine panic about something big.

Ripley closed the door. He picked up the internal phone, the red one. The black telephone on his desk was a private line that didn't go through the MT exchange and couldn't be overheard, except at Ripley's desk. He even paid for the line and the call charges himself. It was a provision he'd specified when they moved into the new building. A lot of Michael's time-serving loyalists didn't take security seriously enough unless it involved good old-fashioned locks on doors. Munro took it very seriously indeed.

"Mr Munro?" said a woman's voice. "I'm sorry to disturb you, but I've got a serious problem, and I can't find Michael, and Terri Sabuli's still on her way back from the TV studio with Ruth Clifford. So I thought – well, it is that serious."

It really had better be. "What is the problem, Miss Rees?"

"We've just had a call from one of the charities – World Assist. They've been contacted by Geo-Petro – that's our biggest sponsor. I believe you're familiar with the way the – "

"And what's the problem?"

"Sorry. Yes. The thing is, Geo-Petro have warned World Assist that they're going to break contract and pull out."

"Pull out?"

"Cancel their sponsorship. Pay the default penalty and walk away from the deal."

He waited. He listened to the slight hiss on the phone. If he remembered the figures correctly on a deal he hadn't run himself, walking out would cost Geo-Petro seventy-five thousand. It wouldn't be the cheapest change of mind, even though the penalty was peanuts. "Do we know why they want to pull out?"

"It seems they've picked up what World Assist describes as a firm rumour about us."

"And what is the firm rumour?"

"That – that MT-Orbis is in serious trouble. That Orbis Air is about to fold, or be offered for sale at a knock-down price, and that several smaller subsidiaries are on the point of collapse. So the project won't be going ahead, and Geo-Petro can't afford to be associated with the fiasco. World Assist say they'll have to consider pulling out, too, if the rumour is substantiated."

He could imagine they would. No one wants to be caught in the whirlpool of a collapse in confidence. It sucks everyone down. The first victim into the vortex would be MT-Orbis. If the rumour was substantiated . . .

And it would count as substantiated the minute any one single person acted on it.

Damn, he thought. Damn the whole business to hell – Michael and his mad project. He's made us all hostages of the crazy affair. If it folds, or if it's cancelled, people will point and say the rumour must be real – MT-Orbis couldn't afford to go ahead, not even when the project must have been a last and desperate attempt to raise the crippled company's profile and profits. MT-Orbis, they'll say, is sinking. Confidence will follow the project down the drain. And then the investors will start to sell, the creditors will call in their loans. The floor will fall out . . .

"Mr Munro? I phoned you because I didn't know what else to do. We've still got another dozen sponsors hovering on the brink of signing. Something like this will frighten them all off, and I can see the whole project collapsing overnight. I'm sure that something has to be done very fast, before that happens. Only I don't know what. So I thought you might be able to get through to Michael for me. I'm really sure it's urgent."

"I think it probably is, Miss Rees. At least as far as the project is concerned." And the whole damned company, too. Michael and his bloody bright ideas. The project tail was starting to wag the corporate dog. Save the project you don't need, or face the loss of it you can't afford . . .

"Can you get hold of Michael for me?"

"Yes. Eventually. Meanwhile, courier everything you've got on Geo-Petro to me *now*. The sponsorship contract, the company profile, its image and its market position – everything. Get Miss Sabuli to contact me the minute she comes in. Don't talk to anyone else about this, and make sure your staff do the same. We don't want to be the ones spreading the rumour ourselves. If, God help us, there's any press inquiry, don't comment, don't issue a denial. Say the project is going ahead as planned, and questions about MT-Orbis should be referred to MT's public relations office. Got that?"

"Yes."

"Good. Keep me informed. I'll be back to you in due course." Then he put down the receiver.

No, and no again, and a thousand times no. He did *not* need this – not now, and not at any other time. Michael just had to be missing when the bombs started falling. Typical bloody Michael.

Well, Robert Munro could deal with this as effectively as Michael might – probably more effectively, given his contacts and his years in the City. He'd bring Michael in and let the man sweat his share, but first he had to get the situation mapped out on the desk in front of him. From that beginning, he could start trying to put it right. He pressed the intercom.

"Ripley, get me everything we have on Geo-Petro. In particular, their bankers and their major business partners and shareholders. I'll take it on screen, but I'll want a printout as well." He glanced at his appointments diary, a double page filled out in Ripley's handwriting. Free until nine forty-five for his own office work that was now out of the window, and then meetings right through until mid-afternoon. "Cancel all my appointments. Is there anyone here you think I should reschedule?"

"Yes – your eleven o'clock with Mr Carlyle."

Andrew bloody Carlyle, Michael's righthand yes-man at Orbis Air, the source, one way or another, of half the troubles. "Put him in for Monday afternoon. If he doesn't have time, let it slide. Anyone else?"

"I think so. Actually, your nine forty-five. Miss Trayhorn."

"And who's Miss Trayhorn?"

"She's from our accounts department. She's the one doing the special audit of Orbis Air, and she's turned up something she thinks you ought to know about."

"Has she?" Hopefully some cretin desperate to buy the airline and remove the problem once and for all. "Don't reschedule Trayhorn. I haven't got the time."

ELEVEN

By a quarter to twelve, Munro had one corner of the crisis nailed down, and a second corner more or less tight in his hand. But the mess was still flapping around like a loose sail in a storm, and the rocks of the City's shallows wait for any company drifting out of control among the banks and brokers . . .

He sent a personal fax to the chairman of Geo-Petro: it is not true that we are about to sell Orbis Air; it is not true that the charity project is about to be dropped; it is not true that MT-Orbis is in any form of difficulty; it would interest me to know the source of any such mischievous rumour; yours sincerely, Robert Munro, CEO, MT Holdings. The fax was the nail through the first corner. No one at Geo-Petro was obliged to believe it, and it didn't matter whether they did or not. What mattered was the silent message they'd receive if he *didn't* make a prompt and specific denial. Pulling in his head and hiding would prove that the ammunition being fired at MT-Orbis was live.

In fact, of course, it was.

The source of the rumour was unknown, and for the moment was likely to stay that way. But the reason behind it was obvious. One of the big operators who lived like vampires, feeding themselves by sucking the life out of other companies, had spotted MT-Orbis as a possible prey. Grab it despite its defences, because at the moment it's weak. Strip out and sell its assets. Drain everything out of its corpse. Pocket the blood money and move on.

It was easier, of course, if you could weaken the victim still further before you struck. A very well-placed rumour would help.

So someone had got hold of internal information, had blown it up to alarming proportions, and then put it into circulation at exactly the right place to precipitate a crisis – a loss of confidence, a drop in share values, a much lower price to pay for all those stranglehold stakes in the lower-tier subsidiaries . . .

The business jungle, swept by an economic famine that made even its biggest predators hungry, was suddenly looking like a very dark and dangerous place.

The second corner, the one he held in his hand, was the project timetable. There was a way to short-circuit rumours that you couldn't even afford to go ahead with the solo flight round the world. To tie that corner down, he needed to get Michael to move. That was for the afternoon. By the end of the morning, he'd got Michael moving fast along the motorway towards London. At least this was also spoiling Michael's day. Not that the man had seemed especially perturbed. He had an unnerving ability to keep his cool when it suited him, when he thought he could impress with his self-control. Michael might make an exasperating and unreliable bridge partner, but he'd be a fiendish opponent.

There were still two corners of the crisis loose. One of those had to be nailed tight before the initial alarm could subside. So Munro took a cab to his club to buy Geoffrey Simmington lunch.

Simmington tucked into his turbot. A man of traditional Catholic taste, he always ate fish on a Friday. He appreciated Chablis, as well – dry, clean and distinctly pale in the glass. He sipped his Vaudesir with positive pleasure. It seemed so unfair that a man who sat through a life of offices and business eating, who so favoured his food and his French wines, should be ageing so very tall and skinny. As he hunched slightly forward, steadily demolishing his turbot and sauce and potatoes, the waistcoat of his pin-stripe suit stood slightly proud from his chest. Geoffrey Simmington would never be overweight. You wondered why he threw such a natural advantage away by smoking his damned cigars.

"Now tell me, Robert – what makes you so confident it's been done with hostile intent?"

"The timing and the targeting," Munro said. "It's no secret that we have some problems at MT-Orbis. We've had to wind up one or two of the more adventurous subsidiaries – "

"Desert Life. Orbis Pacific Tours."

"And our mainstreams are computers and computer systems, and the airline and travel business. Siltech, like everyone else in the area apart from IBM and the big Japanese, is very much marking time at the moment. Orbis Air is one of the hardest hit airlines. But – we haven't got a crisis."

"I wouldn't have thought so, old chap, with you involved. You should be in charge, you know, instead of having a fancy title but no control over that boss of yours. How old is Tranter, anyway?"

"Thirty-nine. I'm fifty-two, and you, Geoffrey, are sixty. And Michael Tranter is richer than an army of the likes of you and me."

"But he hasn't got any damned style." Simmington eyed his glass of Chablis as if it was an icon and agreed with him. "And you, Robert, haven't got a crisis."

"However, the rumour claims that we have. It specifically singles out Orbis Air as the rotten part of our organisation, which means it delivers a double blow. If we were in trouble, Orbis Air would be the obvious parcel to unload, so the rumour is plausible, so it can talk us into trouble. But by making Orbis Air out to be such a serious liability, it also attempts to erode its selling price – meaning that we'd expect to get less, and are therefore pitched into even more of a mess. Someone, Geoffrey, wants our shares to take a tumble so they can pick them up cheap."

Simmington nodded. "And why pick on this project thingy?"

"Because if sponsors pull out, it will look like a judgement that MT-Orbis won't be around long enough to see the project through and honour the charity commitments. That would send us well on our way down the tubes. The share price would drop."

"Like a stone, Robert. Tranter's given you all a bit of an Achilles' heel there. And who do you think's behind it?"

Munro shook his head. He'd already handed out enough coded information about the actual state of affairs within MT-Orbis, and it was time for Simmington to volunteer something from his side, to prove that they were doing business together. "You're the merchant banker, Geoffrey. You tell me."

Geoffrey Simmington sat upright for a moment, communing at arm's length with his glass of Chablis on the table. "I'll preface by saying I have absolutely no information, neither fact nor rumour. But there is rather a feeling that Bryce McFadden are in the market again. I can't stress too strongly that it's only a feeling – a sort of match between the potential victims on the counter, and the length of time Bryce McFadden have been quiet." He transported his glass slowly towards his lips. "MT-Orbis isn't in a strong position at the moment, and has some assets which would be well worth stripping. You know them from the inside, Robert." He sipped his wine, then smiled past it. "Would old Lionel McFadden go so far as to hunt your company, just to get his own back on you?"

"No. There isn't any bad blood. I didn't take anything with me, I just changed jobs. If the Bryce McFadden Group were after us, it would be purely for business reasons." He sipped his own wine, slowly, letting its dry freshness linger in his mouth. "I left the Group because they'd stopped buying companies to do business, and had started doing business buying companies."

"Quite. In a nutshell. Must say, I'm no longer much of a takeover chappy myself. The Japs and the Jerries don't do it, and their economies aren't exactly in decline, are they?" Geoffrey Simmington returned his attention to his turbot. He placed a sliver of fish above a slice of potato on his fork, dabbed on sauce with the knife – and stopped with the morsel impaled in midair. "What is it you'd like me to do?"

Munro smiled, just enough to let Simmington see he appreciated the direct opening. It was all part of the contact dance. "Longman Short's security house is agent for at least one large shareholding in Geo-Petro. Longman Short holds a stake itself. Also, the bank administers a major slice of Geo-Petro's UK borrowing. And finally, you've offered a short-term loan to guarantee Geo-Petro's contingency fund, should it lose the pollution case in Australia and be slapped with huge fines. So I'd like you to lean on them."

Simmington nodded. "Along the lines, let's say – if they were to pull their sponsorship, it might prove detrimental to their outfit, which is already labouring under a cloud because of its pollution record. Is that what you have in mind?"

"Exactly that. It could produce what I believe is called an image-negative perception that they'd triggered the collapse – if collapse it should – of a very widely known and very definitely green project. It wouldn't be good for their business. More importantly, Longman Short are of the opinion that it wouldn't be good for their business."

"Hm. I thought that would be it. You know, it would mean we'd be tying together bits of information from different sides of quite a few Chinese Walls, old chap. Strictly not what one is, in fact, supposed to do."

Chinese Walls, Munro thought. An exquisite fiction built inside the imaginary world of finance. There is no such thing as money, it's just a scale for measuring debt and credit. And those totals of debt and of credit are mere phantom commodities that people swap back and forth. The Chinese Walls stop people working under the same roof from seeing or exchanging confidential information about clients. What they inevitably see and hear they must not know, and having pretended not to know it they must then avoid acting on it. A fantastic nonsense. "You'll just have to take a little Chinese stroll round those Chinese Walls, and send Geo-Petro a Chinese message, Geoffrey."

"Oh very jolly, Robert. There's no Chinese Wall without a chink, eh? I think I'll just stick to the good old quiet word in ear approach. It should do the trick, I'm sure. But it isn't *quite* ethical, and I'm afraid it won't be cheap."

"I'd hardly expect it to be, Geoffrey. What would you like in return?"

Simmington put down his knife and fork, little clicks on his porcelain plate. He sat upright, he tugged his waistcoat smooth against his chest. "A chance to grab the biggest slice of the cake when you sell Orbis Air."

On the button. Simmington had come to the lunch with his ideas already mapped out, and he'd decoded the information Munro had been feeding him. Orbis Air it would have to be from MT's side, and Orbis Air would be just the thing for which Longman Short could organise a buyers' consortium. "You'd like a little advance warning so that you could get things ready. Then when we announce the sale, you'd be in ahead of the field and we'd get a rapid conclusion."

"Exactly, old chap. And once again, not *quite* ethical."

"Not quite, Geoffrey. And I rather feel that the price is steeper than the service you're supplying with Geo-Petro. Unless you feel you've got me over a barrel, of course."

Geoffrey Simmington looked distinctly hurt. "Robert, I really *wouldn't* dream of doing any such thing to a friend. Might I suggest that we leave it part unpaid, as it were? You come back to me with something to make up the difference at a later stage. I'm sure there'll be something else I can do for you."

Oh there will be, Munro thought – something to help with manoeuvring Michael into letting Orbis Air go. Geoffrey Simmington was responding exactly according to plan. So he smiled again, and reached for his glass of wine. "That sounds fine, Geoffrey."

With his own fax, and with Geoffrey Simmington to wield the influence of Longman Short, he had two corners of the crisis firmly tied down. In the afternoon, Munro set about fixing the third corner, the one that depended on Michael.

The meeting was in Michael's office, at the conference table

– just Michael and Munro, and Pattie Lee. Michael's PA sat with her pad resting on the table, listening. She wore a blue cotton suit, blue shoes, a white blouse with a little blue bow tie. Her black hair was cut to a fringe on her forehead, and fell in a plain pageboy to her shoulders. High cheekbones, impassive face, almond eyes – the only cliché missing was the pair of glasses. Pattie Lee wore contact lenses instead.

"Right, now I'm up to date." Michael was putting finger-prints on the glass table with his index finger, building a slow grid. "I like the way you've handled it, Bob. This Simmington bloke – will he deliver?"

"Yes," Munro said.

"Did he want something in return?"

Munro shook his head. Lying comes easy when it's in a good cause. "He's the one in debt to me. I don't know whether he can do anything on the weekend, but he'll have brought Geo-Petro back into line by the end of Monday."

"Good." Michael smeared two diagonals through his grid of fingerprints, as if he was crossing out something only he could see. Something that mattered. "That should put things back under temporary control. You think it's only temporary, don't you, Bob?"

Munro nodded. "Someone's trying to talk us down. Some-one is after us – if they can get us cheap enough. All they have to do is keep planting the same rumour with your sponsors – and probably our creditors, too. We can deal with each individual instance, but eventually it's going to stick. It will become a widespread perception about us. It will work in the end."

Michael put his hand over the secret plan coded in fingertip smears on the table top. "I'm not – entirely – convinced that someone's after us with hostile intent."

Michael wouldn't be, of course. "I am, Michael."

"Yes." Michael glanced at Pattie Lee, but she was scrutinising her blank pad. He looked at the windows instead, out towards the NatWest Tower, a symbol of money as a mechanism of power. "It's certainly advisable to assume you're right, and that someone is after us. If that isn't the case, at least we'll be erring on the safe side. So, Bob – how would we stop the rumours coming back over and over again until they'd talked us down?"

"The target was the project. Make that out to be a wild promotional gamble by us – on the claim that we're already in a crisis – and then make it collapse. Then everyone's going to believe our last throw has failed, and we're going under." Munro folded his arms. You'll love this, Michael, he thought. The irony won't be wasted on you. I, of all people – the least enthusiastic man watching from the sidelines – turn out to be the one who makes this suggestion. "The way to block that tactic is to go ahead with the project. Fly your aircraft round the world – and do it *before* any damage is done."

"I see." Michael hid his amusement well. He kept his eyes on the NatWest Tower. "We're scheduled, more or less, to go in three months. In your scenario, with the hostile who's out to get us, that time is dangerously long. Isn't it?"

"In three months, someone who really wants us can ruin us."

Michael turned and looked at him. "You mean bring it forward."

"Bring it forward."

The amusement was starting to show. "How soon?"

"As soon as possible. Three weeks, if you can do it. The best way to stall rumours that we can't afford the project is to announce a take-off in three weeks, in mid-July. And the best way to sink the rumours is to do it."

"Three weeks." Michael grinned. "Three weeks, Bob?"

Munro shrugged, taking refuge in the matter-of-fact. It was best for the company, he'd said so, Michael had won the long wrangle about his crazy project hands down. No need to cry about the defeat. "Can you do it in three weeks?"

"It means a lot of work," Michael said. "It means finalising the charities, the sponsorship deals, the media hype, the flight permissions along the route. It means getting Angel ready. It means getting the navigation program ready. It means, in fact, doing in three weeks what we were going to do in three months." He turned to his PA. "Pattie, line up calls with Chester Alby and Terri Sabuli for me. They're going to get a surprise. Then start going through everything in my diary for the next three weeks and start cutting. Cut *anything* that can go."

Pattie Lee stood up. She lifted her pad off the table and walked towards the door. She had a smooth walk. With less of an ice-cold presentation, she could have been a woman your eyes would follow. She paused at the door. "Do the cuts include Ruth Clifford?"

Michael nodded. "I'm going to be busy."

When Pattie Lee had gone, Michael stood up and walked over to the windows. "Mid-July," he said. "Well, what a surprise. What a surprise indeed."

Munro watched from his seat at the conference table.

Michael strolled along the windows, in front of the mullion-bars of his high lair. "Quite a rush," he said. "It's going to be quite a rush. It's going to take all my time to do it. The navigation program still has to be written." He stopped as he came to his desk. He looked at Munro. "I'm sure I can leave the company safe in your hands, Bob."

Munro nodded.

Michael walked past the back of his desk. He patted the chair. He trailed his fingers across the top of the computer's monitor. "I can't tell you what it would mean to me if the project didn't go ahead. It would ruin all my plans." He giggled at a private joke. "Believe me, I *can't* tell you what it would mean, Bob."

Munro nodded. He shifted on his seat, turning as Michael paced around the corner behind his desk.

Michael strolled along his wall of Ligne Roset shelves. Books on ecology and the environment, on flying, on computers and on information technology – books grouped in squads and companies to reinforce his pose as the world's truly green-aware, fun-loving, up-to-the-minute businessman. Between the books – executive ivies, hand-thrown African

95

pots, a silver glider on a stick that was an aerobatics trophy, a model of the Orbis airship, pictures framing stations along a public image life. He walked in front of the shelves, but his eyes were on the margin of the floor.

He was walking like a compact human tiger in a cage, pacing the edge of his confinement. He'd never done this before. It was a loss of control, a surrender to freedom's frustration. It seemed triggered by the imminence of adventure. Of escape.

It had nothing to do with concern for his company.

Michael turned at the end of the shelves. He passed behind the filing carousel. He stopped in front of the huge poster blow-up of a slender glider in a perfect blue sky. The glider was Icarus, the one which had nearly killed him. "Just as long as you always come down in one piece. That's the trick when you fly with a lot of ambition. The flying and the ambition are pretty much a piece of cake. But getting away with it isn't quite as easy."

Munro just waited.

Michael took a deep breath. Slowly, he breathed goodbye for the moment to his aerial dreams. "Was that everything, Bob?"

"The hostile problem. It means we have a leak."

"Yes, I suppose it does." A faint smile, that ghost of mocking amusement again. "Do you think we've got a spy?"

"It might be just a blabbermouth, someone who talks too much when the wrong people are listening. A blabbermouth would be easy enough to find. You just list all the people who should have known the information that was leaked, and one of them is the culprit."

"And a spy, Bob?"

"Someone indulging in espionage will take steps to cover their tracks. They might also be dealing in information they're not supposed to have, which increases the list of suspects. They're also dangerous, because they do targeted damage."

Michael was nodding. "Talk to John Stallybrass about it on Monday, Bob. I know he's an old-fashioned type who thinks security begins with locks and ends with guard patrols, but he must have some up-to-date people somewhere in his department. Talk to John about it. Take any steps you think necessary."

"It means snooping on people, Michael."

"Yes. Unfortunately, yes." Michael shrugged his shoulders. "I'll leave it all to you, Bob."

TWELVE

John Stallybrass was ex-Army. Michael had made him security director of MT, as well as Orbis Air and Orbis, on the basis of his ability to set up patrols that covered every part of a place and ran to time. Apart from that, all he brought to his post was a serious sense of duty, square-shouldered loyalty, and more of that competent mediocrity which populated the boardroom courts in Michael's empire. To Stallybrass, computer security was trumped-up nonsense, and the notion of human espionage impossible. He lived within regimentally nurtured concepts of *us* and *them*: a traitor on the payroll was a near unthinkable thought.

Stallybrass assured Munro he'd start an investigation. He'd put people on it. He'd see what he could do.

Geoffrey Simmington called him early on Monday afternoon on the black telephone, his private line. Mission accomplished and all that. Our mutual friends in the mines and minerals business back on the good old straight and narrow.

Michael, girlfriend, publicist and project team were working away at sudden treble speed, and were finally out from under his feet. Munro could get on with the duties of the everyday, the background problem of a leak and an unknown agency of hostile intent, and the crucial task of finalising a rescue plan for MT-Orbis. The plan should be finished in time to present

97

to Michael when he dropped in again after flying round the world. The trouble with what amounted to a one-month timetable for the task, was that Munro was working alone. The people he would have called on to build a planning team were all Michael Men: sensing their master's dislike of the direction logic was driving MT-Orbis, they would tend to stall the work and skew the interpretations against selling off the beloved airline.

The problem was the absolute control Michael exercised through the club of courtiers he'd been building up since he founded Siltech seventeen years ago. The disloyal had all disappeared – the most recent being Sylvia Symes, who was ejected a few months before Munro joined the payroll. Michael had brought in Munro for the expertise he embodied, and specifically to balance up the gang of yes-men. But Michael never made anything easy. In two years, Munro had introduced a few minor pieces into the corporate chess game. He still didn't have a senior manager to call his own. Old Lionel McFadden would have been disappointed in the extreme . . .

He hadn't had a restful weekend. There'd been Friday's lost work to catch up on. There was the very nasty worry which Friday's upset had introduced. Life isn't easy for the administrator of an empire, when that empire has too many wars.

A steep drop in income flowing from the subsidiary provinces to the MT centre was bad enough. Barbarians stirring on the frontiers didn't help. Those barbarians were the small investors of the new age, panicking in a bear market or digging themselves into little foxholes during a recession. You could see them in any bank, standing in eager line for the thrill of instant share-dealing on the expert-guided screen. They were strictly down among the pin money when they thought out their share manipulations worth hundreds and even thousands of pounds. They were the kiddies in the capitalist toddler group. They did their cumulative pinpricks of damage, but that was all.

The frightening thing wasn't any number of barbarians at the gate. It was the forces of a bigger empire, unknown, drawn up beyond the horizon and waiting to attack . . .

It hadn't been a good weekend. Robert Munro decided to end his day early and head home to Guildford to eat – alone, and in peace. Early meant six thirty. He should be home by seven thirty.

The expectation started to slide when he stepped out of the lift into the lobby.

She stepped right in front of him before he had time to turn for the car park stairs. She was young, blonde, with hair in a long bob reaching almost to her collar and swept back to reveal her ears. She wore a grey checked jacket, black skirt above the knee, black shoes. She carried a leather briefcase, and she looked unhappy.

"Mr Munro?"

"Yes?" He stopped, letting his own case swing his arm with a little momentum, a pendulum clocking up the wait.

"I'm Geraldine Trayhorn – from accounts." She looked very unhappy. She seemed to regret wedging herself this close in front of a tall man. "I was due to see you on Friday morning." She took a step backwards to a more comfortable distance. "But something came up. And I'm told you're only taking priority meetings for the next few days."

"That's correct." He kept his case swinging, pressing the impatient point.

"But I think – I'm sure I have to inform you of something I've found. While I've been working on the audit of Orbis Air."

"And what's that?"

"I've run into – " She didn't step closer again, but she did glance round to make sure there was no one in sight but the woman at the reception desk. And she did lower her voice. "Fraud."

That stopped his case swinging.

Trayhorn's office was in the finance department, three floors below the executive plane. You got to it from the lift by weaving through the screens of an open plan area, bright with strip lights and distant windows. There were a few people still about, working silently or talking quietly, and none of them noticed the second most powerful man in the company go by.

The office was tiny, with a view to the south which would soak up the sun at the hottest time of the day. The blinds were down, but tilted open, and showed a clutter of modernist eruptions and post-modernist excrescences which choked out the older buildings squeezed below them. Somewhere through a gap was what might have been a bit of the Bank of England. Sliced by lateral lines, the window looked like a vast enlargement from a TV film on cultural self-destruction, showing a forest of profit-today monuments in the cold glow of an evening from a faltering summer. So many short-term promises failing to turn out true.

Trayhorn asked him to sit down, so he took the only spare chair. Trayhorn sat in the rotating chair in the angle made by her desk and the machine table. On the table was a printer, a screen, a keyboard and some printout sheets. The desk was like any desk. She sat with her back to it, and to the freeze-framed window on the world, her face partly protected by shadow. It wouldn't be an easy thing to ambush the senior executive on his way home and then drag him into a cubby hole of an office in order to upset him.

Munro put his briefcase flat on the floor. "Why did you wait for me downstairs, instead of coming up to my office?"

"I didn't know – if you were alone – or in a meeting. I needed to tell you this in private."

"Why?"

"Because it's sensitive. I mean, to stop rumours getting out before it's referred up. So as few people as possible know."

"Why did you come to me, instead of the accounts manager?"

"Well – the same reason. As I just said." She bit her lip.

In shadow against the window, she was busy looking at her screen, the wall, anything but her penultimate boss.

I'm starting to make a nervous young woman actually scared, Munro thought. If she looks at me, all she gets is a big man in a dark suit whose time costs a very great deal, who wanted to go home – and whose glasses reflect the bright window back at her. She can't find out what my eyes are doing. Give her a bit of a break from the Olympian act. "Actually, caution is a good idea. Fraud is a crime of secrecy. It might be perpetrated by the person sitting next to you at work, or anyone else in the entire organisation. If its discovery isn't kept equally secret, the perpetrator quietly closes down ahead of the investigation and is never found."

"I know. Exactly, I mean. Yes."

"So." He folded his hands in his lap. "Tell me what you've found." Tell me, he thought, for pity's sake, that it's something trivial, so I can hand it down to someone in your department, and someone in security, to deal with. MT-Orbis doesn't need to lose even more money at the moment, and it doesn't need the scandal of a major fraud. And I do not, I absolutely do not have the time.

Trayhorn hovered on the threshold for a moment. Then she grabbed the printout sheets from her table, and held them so that he could see the reams of figures. "If I take you through the – "

"I don't want to see the figures. *Tell* me about it so I have the initial picture, then we'll begin with the details."

"Oh." She put the sheets back on the table. "Yes."

"You've started the audit I asked for on Orbis Air. In what area have you found the fraud?" He waited, like a parent trying to start a tongue-tied child talking. "When did you find it?"

"Last week. I was looking at the net losses on Orbis Pacific Tours. The wind-up statements and the closing balances aren't good enough to show the how and why of it, so I was pulling out the actual accounting figures for the company."

"That's what I was expecting." The audit – once expanded to include every detail of Orbis Air and its subsidiaries, Orbis

101

Travel, Trantair and the defunct Orbis Pacific Tours – was intended to show exactly what was wrong with the set-up in clinical detail. He could then use it to tell Michael why surgery had to be drastic and immediate.

"Yes. Well – early last year, Orbis Air started paying emergency support to Orbis Pacific Tours. The payments were three hundred thousand a month, and were paid into the Pacific Tours account in Los Angeles. Everything on the account looks exactly right, but it seemed to me as though the interest was a little low for the quarter in which the first payment was made. I don't mean it was dramatic, but for the average level of the account over the period, it seemed a little low." Trayhorn turned her head away, looking longingly at the sheets of figures she wasn't allowed to use. "So I got the details and did the calculations, and found out it *was* too low. The missing interest could be a mistake by the bank, or something." She looked at Munro again – a glance at his reflecting glasses, then down at his hands in his lap. "But it would fit exactly with three hundred thousand missing from the account for ten days."

"I see," he said. Someone inside Orbis Pacific Tours had borrowed three hundred thousand from the account for ten days, done a share deal or made some interest with it, pocketed the profit and returned the money, and then fiddled the computer record to hide the fact. In the electronic banking age, it was just a hand dipping into the till. Small beer. Investigate and prosecute. No problem at all. "How serious do you think the fraud might be?"

"Well – if it was a one-off, I suppose you'd call it small. But it turns out to be the same every month. That's clever, really, because if you want to do a rapid check on whether the interest for any period is correct, you compare like with like – in other words, you compare quarters when the rescue payments were coming in. By doing the same thing with every payment, it has the same effect on the interest every time, and it doesn't show up in a like-with-like comparison. Only a movement-by-movement calculation over the whole quarter will show the apparent error in the interest credited to the account. Which is what I did."

He nodded. "You mean that in every month from – when did the payments start?"

"February."

"That in every month from February to when the outfit was wound up in November, three hundred thousand was missing for ten days? That's a third of each month. That's equivalent to three full months. What's the total loss in interest?"

"Only about sixty thousand."

"I see. That isn't exactly a major fraud. It's sixty thousand stolen from the company, but it's peanuts to MT-Orbis."

"If I'd been investing the sidelined money, I'd have felt free to put it into higher risk things – *and* I'd be accumulating and reinvesting interest from each cycle as I went along. I'd expect to make at least two hundred thousand."

Munro nodded again. He was starting to feel comfortable. A single fraud on that scale wasn't anything he had to worry about.

"Anyway, I thought about what was involved in fixing the computer record so that it masked the sidelining of the money. The bank's own computer wasn't involved, which means the fraudster wasn't drawing money out of the account and then paying it back ten days later. The thing is, the money is booked as appearing exactly when it should, according to when it was sent out, and that's that. So what's really happening? The fraudster is intercepting it at source, diverting it into a private account, then sending it on to the Orbis Pacific Tours account in Los Angeles ten days late. The Los Angeles bank doesn't know anything's wrong. The money just arrives, presumably with all the correct despatcher details."

"Why would the fraudster do it that way, instead of lifting the money from the Los Angeles account?"

"It simplifies the protection of the fraud. He intercepts the money on despatch, and it arrives at the bank ten days late. But he has to insert some sort of program into the Orbis Pacific Tours computer which creates the *false* information that the bank has reported the money arriving on time. If the report didn't appear, the people at Pacific Tours would get upset and start looking for the money. At the same time, the hidden program has to suppress the real report that comes in from the bank ten days later, or again it would give the game away. In other words, there has to be some manipulation on the computer at Pacific Tours to make it look as though everything's normal. Also, all instructions from Pacific Tours to the bank have to be checked by his program to ensure they're not going to move so much money that the temporary absence of three hundred thousand actually shows in a notably low balance. If an instruction like that comes along, the sidelined money has to be brought back early to cover it." Trayhorn shrugged. "That's getting fearfully complicated. If he was taking the money out of the account in the first place and having to hide that as well, it would be even worse."

Munro wasn't comfortable about this any more. The woman was telling him about a sophisticated fraud. "So he intercepts it."

"He intercepts it."

"Which means he's also manipulating the computer here, at the Orbis Air end."

"Exactly. Orbis Air sets up the instruction in its computer to despatch the money on a regular basis. He inserts a hidden program which changes the address to the account he's using, but makes the computer report it's used the correct Pacific Tours account address. The bank does what the fiddled computer has told it, and reports the fact to the computer, and the hidden program edits the report so that it also shows the Pacific Tours account address. So nobody here, or there, ever knows. I've checked – and there's no trace."

She'd lost her nervousness now. She hadn't been wrong in going straight to the top man, and was aware the top man knew it. Munro could feel the mess engulfing what was left of his time and his personal life. "You're talking about a very clever criminal."

"There's more. I've tried to see what was happening at the Orbis Air end, in case I could find out how it was done. I couldn't. But I did find that the rescue payments are still going out. There's no report of them, the system appears to have been shut down. But the money's going out at the same rate. Even though Orbis Pacific Tours hasn't existed since November."

That made his mouth open and close.

"I think it's being siphoned off from the same funds as before, which are fat enough to carry the drain without anyone noticing unless they look at all the pennies. Like I did. The computer says it isn't happening and there's no address for any recipient account at any bank. But the money's going just the same."

"This is June," he said. "That makes seven months. That makes two point one *million*."

"Yes," she said.

Munro took off his glasses. He put his hand over his eyes. Sixty thousand in stolen interest was one thing. More than two million in stolen cash was very different. And a crook penetrating the computers – the whole MT-Orbis *network*, damn it – and setting up something that clever and that well hidden was even worse. What he could do in one place, he could do anywhere else. Computer fraud is a security nightmare. Once inside the system, the evil-doer can slither anywhere and alter anything. The only limit is his skill in hiding what he does.

Munro uncovered his eyes and looked at Trayhorn. She sat there against the lateral-lined light of the window, round face and blonde hair ghosting themselves in an astigmatic smear. "If the fraudster gets the faintest hint of the fact that we know, he'll cut the connections and we'll never find him."

She nodded. "That's why I came to you. It's very skilled. It could be someone quite high up."

It could, God help them, be anyone at all. "Coming straight to me is probably the most intelligent decision I've seen made in this company." She didn't say anything, and he wouldn't have expected her to. "You're already doing a special audit on my instructions. The only thing that will change from now on is that I'll tell your chief you're reporting direct to me. As of tomorrow. You have my authority to look into *anything*, and you answer no questions at all. You can start by looking for similar opportunities for the same type of fraud. Let's find out how widespread this is. Then we'll worry about tracing it to a common source." He glanced at his watch, an overlap of distorted ovals with hints of hands that might be saying seven. "If you have time now, we can start putting together a strategy."

He put on his glasses again. Ten past seven. Later than you think.

THIRTEEN

After a week, Munro decided the internal hunt for the leak was going nowhere. He left Stallybrass to continue poking in all the wrong corners, and asked Geoffrey Simmington for a recommendation instead. Simmington suggested Smith and Brown Associates. So on Wednesday morning, Munro took a cab to a meeting in the coffee lounge of the Charing Cross Hotel. You could sit there and talk in quiet comfort, and you were surrounded by confidential space . . .

Darren Pierce was fearfully young for a private detective, and his yuppie-lookalike enthusiasm made him seem even more immature. His agency, though, specialised in business requirements and the intricacies of espionage – and their absolute respect for client confidentiality could be assumed from the fact that they'd ever attracted enough business to become specialists. One single leak of their own about a firm's internal affairs, and no one else would ever have engaged them.

"My advice." Pierce brought his coffee cup to hover over the saucer which balanced on the palm of his other hand. "My advice would be – keep the internal investigation running."

"Yes," Munro said. His own cup was empty, and was waiting on the occasional table in front of the two armchairs. "I fully intend to."

"Good." Pierce's cup finally landed on its saucer. "Your mole won't be in the least surprised by an internal investigation. But he or she *will* be surprised by its sudden cessation. Meanwhile, who do you actually suspect?"

"No one. I have no evidence at all, Mr Pierce."

"Darren, please." Darren Pierce let his smile swing away as he leaned forward and transferred his cup from his hand to the table. "Let's narrow the field, then. It could, in principle, be *anyone* inside MT-Orbis. Or their wives, husbands, girlfriends, boyfriends et cetera. Anyone on the inside can get inside information. But some would find it easier than others. Would you say it was likely to be someone higher up rather than lower down?"

"When the information concerns an overview of corporate finance – obviously."

"Then by the same token, this someone is more likely to be at MT Holdings than any of your subsidiaries. Now let's look at likely departments. Basically, there are four areas in any company where a spy should have access in order to be of value." Pierce prepared to count the areas off on his fingers. "Research, if it's about stealing products or processes and the like. Finance, if it's about deals and contracts and so on. The board is good, because all crucial information ultimately flits through the boardroom. And personnel can be very useful for showing up work dispositions, or for getting blackmail information on people. In this case, we'd be looking at the board, and at finance. It isn't cut and dried, but we're sorting out the most *likely* places to begin with."

"And what would you do?" Munro said. "To find a spy on the board or in our finance department? You can't put a tail on everybody."

"Gosh, no. Think of the cost." Pierce shook his head. "As a matter of fact, I suggest we don't even try to crack the problem from that end. You see, we know the spy is in MT-Orbis, and is most probably within a smaller group of people within MT Holdings. We know *where* the spy is, but not *who* it is among many candidates. But there's someone else involved."

"The company the spy is working for."

"Oh – yes, obviously. But I mean a specific individual. That is to say, the person who actually passed the information, in the form of a rumour, to someone at Geo-Petro. We don't know whether that was done during a visit to their offices, or by telephone or letter, or during an informal social interaction with one of their employees. This unknown individual represents the other end of the chain. If we could pinpoint this person, we could begin to work backwards towards the paymaster, and then the spy, you see? And if we were extremely lucky, it might even turn out that the spy's paymaster has also used the spy to pass the rumour to Geo-Petro." Pierce beamed. "And then you'd have learned everything you could wish to know."

Except the personal motive for betrayal, Munro thought. Which, come to think of it, would be nothing more esoteric than money. He nodded. "Very well, Mr Pierce, if that's – "

"Darren, please."

Darren, he thought. I'm to be hiring a bright young private eye called Darren, and no doubt he'll be wanting to call me Robert. Well I'm only fifty-two, but sometimes age can show. "If that's your advice – Mr Pierce – then we'll proceed along those lines. How will we be settling your bill? I don't exactly want to give the game away by having your firm invoice us directly."

"Oh, don't worry about that – Mr Munro. Our immediate fees can be deferred, and we can discuss setting up a holding account for us to draw against. No direct invoicing will ever be necessary. We work on a basis of trust, Mr Munro. You aren't going to run away without paying, any more than we are going to tell anyone what kind of service we're providing for you. On the subject of discretion, though." Pierce put his hands together, a little prayer of precaution. "I suggest that we continue for the present with out-of-house meetings. May I also suggest that you inform absolutely no one else at your offices that we are to be engaged on the case. If the spy is inadvertently warned, the spy evades us and all our efforts are wasted."

"What about co-ordination? Our internal investigation might produce something that would help you. Your results should be of use to us internally."

"Ah – that's where you come in. You will have access to everything we turn up, and to everything done in-house. You are the place where all information meets. Of course, that information must be sifted, evaluated and collated – but please be aware that you're engaging me as a consultant for that very purpose. The entire expertise of Smith and Brown Associates will be at your disposal."

Munro nodded. For their scale of fees, it had damned well better be. "Very well. What information will you need to begin with?"

"Oh, let me see. Not all that much, really. The date of the last meeting anyone had with Geo-Petro at which matters concerning the sponsorship were dealt with, plus the date when it first became clear they'd received a troublesome rumour. That narrows the time interval we're looking at in order to pin down their informant. It might be a help, though, if you could pass us some details from your personnel files."

"What kind of details?"

"Well, basically just names and photographs of all the top people from the prime areas of suspicion. That would be all the MT Holdings directors, all the managers and senior analysts in the finance department, and all their secretaries and PAs. We wouldn't need any other information at this stage, such as salary, position, address, family et cetera. You could withhold that – out of deference to the innocent people involved – without prejudicing our investigation. At this stage of the case I'm just being prepared, as it were. *If* we stumbled on a description that fitted one of the people from your suspects pool, that would speed things up enormously."

"Then I'll have names and photographs for you by the end of tomorrow." And I'll have more unscheduled after-hours work, Munro thought. He couldn't get anyone else to pull details on the relevant personnel and then photocopy file pictures – not unless he told them why.

"Good. Well – I suppose that's it for the moment." Pierce started to stand up.

Munro stood up with him. "How hopeful are you of obtaining a result, Mr Pierce?"

"Oh, entirely hopeful. Entirely. That isn't mere professional optimism on my part, you understand. It quite simply isn't possible to lose facts – only to *hide* them. However, finding those facts can take time. Often a great deal of time. Indeed to be quite frank, we can't achieve miracles if we intend to stay within the law. It can all turn out to be extremely pedestrian work. Very slow going, and all that." Pierce had suddenly started to look round the room, rather than at Munro. "I'm sure you see what I mean."

He's making a pitch, Munro thought. That's what it is. This yuppie gumshoe character is trying to tell me to ask a question, give a coded knock on a secret door so that he can show me what's inside. Speak, friend, and enter. Let's see what he's hinting at. "What if you don't stay within the law?"

"Oh – now." Pierce acted the young innocent. "That *would* open up possibilities of action – though one mustn't go too far, obviously. But of course, it gets *much* more expensive. Take telephone tapping. We'd risk having to pay a hefty fine. And we maintain a fund to compensate our operatives, should one of them – in an excess of zeal, as it were – exceed the law, get caught, and lose his or her licence. The costs soon add up."

"I see." It was the same in every line of business. Things could be done, but at a price. "Well then, let's stay within the law for the time being."

"My advice precisely, Mr Munro." Pierce offered his hand.

"So – I'll be managing the case for you, and we'll be in touch again tomorrow."

Munro shook the man's hand. The grip wasn't strong. It didn't inspire confidence. "By the way – Smith and Brown Associates. Is there really a Mr Smith and a Mr Brown?"

"Ah – Mrs Smith, actually. And Miss Brown. They added the *Associates* a year or two ago so we'd sound more kosher to you City types."

"Did they indeed? That was very considerate."

Geraldine Trayhorn was waiting in Ripley's outer office when he got back. He led her straight through into his own office, and looked at the sheaf of papers she put in his hand. More endless pin-printed figures, dates glossed with deposits, withdrawals and balances. Sheet after sheet of them, followed by pages of handwritten calculations linked in a chain of brought-forwards. Trayhorn had been working hard, and she'd been doing her sums with pen, paper and calculator. Set up on the computer, the sums might leave a retrievable trace.

"Another one?" he said.

"Desert Life. The actual fraud is the same. Desert Life started turning in a trading loss in nineteen eighty-nine. Orbis Foods began paying monthly funds to it from the end of that year. From the start, each monthly payment was intercepted and diverted for a period of five days before being delivered to the designated Desert Life account. It continued until Desert Life went into voluntary liquidation in March this year."

Munro scanned the account figures again. "The rescue payments were a quarter of a million per month. How much stolen interest are we talking about?"

"Only some ten thousand lost to the account. The Cairo bank wasn't offering particularly good rates."

"No." Nothing about Desert Life had made much sense. The subsidiary was already up and limping when Munro joined Michael's empire. It was one of Michael's image flagships – pesticide-free Sahel oranges and Yemeni grapefruits

111

for the green-aware and conscience-stricken middle classes of England.

"Might I ask," Trayhorn said, "why Orbis Foods waited so long before closing Desert Life down? It was never a going concern."

He looked at her, one finance specialist to another. "A slight difference of opinion at the top," he said. "It took some time before I won the argument."

She nodded. He could see her thinking: Munro and Tranter don't always see eye to eye. Is it in fact a good thing to be working all this closely with the man who's second from the top?

"I assume," he said, "that the rescue payments were terminated and are no longer registered as going out – but that money is still going from the funds at Orbis Foods?"

"Exactly," she said. "Four months, March to June. One million pounds."

"Right." Munro dropped the sheaf of data on his desk. "So far that's one fraud under Orbis Air, and another under Orbis. Start looking for the same kind of thing under Siltech. Our criminal does these things very cleverly. He's bound to have a sense of symmetry. Three branches to MT-Orbis, so three frauds."

FOURTEEN

Trayhorn took only five working days to find the fraud in the Siltech branch of MT-Orbis. The first discovery of the manipulation at Orbis Pacific Tours had been sheer chance. The Desert Life version of the same trick had proved the idea that the fraud would be found where a subsidiary had been in trouble. The difference was that everything in the Siltech branch was in a mess, but nothing had actually folded . . .

But there had been closures.

The subsidiary was Siltech Systems Service, which ran sales, aftersales and backup. Michael had tried to penetrate the South American market against the massive dominance of the US giants. The attempt had failed. The last Siltech Systems Service office in South America to go was in Buenos Aires. It was shut down a year ago, and its operating account at a local bank was closed.

But the money didn't come back.

According to the computer, the half million from the Buenos Aires account had been shunted in dozens of different parcels and diluted into other funds and holdings. But a precise examination of the actual balances at all those final destinations showed that no money had in fact arrived. Once again, it was the kind of thing that would never show up in a routine audit, since everything that the computer might tell an inquirer appeared to fit together perfectly. Only a very suspicious examination failed to find the money in question.

The half million was still in the account in the Buenos Aires bank, but the computer was unable to report the fact either on screen or in any printout. Its knowledge was blocked by some kind of program inserted by the fraudster. But it could still use its knowledge . . .

The Buenos Aires account had been maintained automatically at the half million reserve level. Excess money piling up from earnings by the local office would be siphoned back to London, excess drawings by the local office would be made good. The London computer would shunt money backwards and forwards as long as the account was in existence. During the year since the account was allegedly closed, there'd been no movement – even though the computer secretly knew the account was still there.

But the half million on the account was earning interest. If it hadn't topped the reserve level and been transferred to London, then that interest must be going sideways into some other account – to the benefit of the perpetrator of the fraud. Five hundred thousand pounds had been taken out of circulation, and a further fifty thousand pounds in interest had been stolen.

But that wasn't why Trayhorn, working alone, had been able to find the set-up in only five days.

Two weeks ago there'd been a movement through the Buenos Aires account – a phantom movement into non-existence, as far as the computer was able to report. A quarter of a million had vanished from the Siltech Systems Service account. Its disappearance had raised no single eyebrow at the company, since it was clearly marked as a routine movement triggered by an automatic instruction. The fact that there was supposed to be no account to transfer it to escaped routine inspection. Not even the withdrawal from the company account had been noticed, because the balance at that instant had remained constant.

The criminal had been very clever. He or she had withdrawn a quarter of a million from the hidden Buenos Aires account at the same moment as someone deposited an equal sum into the Siltech Systems Service company account. The Buenos Aires account went a quarter of a million below its reserve level, the computer immediately shunted a quarter of a million to Buenos Aires from London, and it happened at the same moment as a quarter of a million flowed into the London account from the other side. When you looked at the balances, nothing had happened. When you asked where the deposit into the London account had gone – well, there were whole queues of movements piling up on the printout, and only a full-scale audit would show up the loss. Trayhorn wouldn't have noticed, even though she was looking for a fraud, if it hadn't been for the single triggering of that automatic transfer into an account which was no longer supposed to exist.

Trayhorn had no explanation for that single movement at the end of June. Why do something that drew attention to such a well-hidden fraud, a nice little earner worth fifty thousand a year? There was no hope that the transfer could have escaped the next routine review of the company's finances. It would be seen, the fraud would be found, the alarm would be raised and the whole of MT-Orbis would be combed through in search of similar tricks.

The fraudster would then lose his entire illicit income, as well as risking the possibility that pooled information on all the frauds might be enough to trace him.

The coffee lounge of the Charing Cross Hotel, meanwhile, was having its mid-afternoon lull. Pierce was having pleasure in reporting a success.

"Two of our people posed as representatives of a certain clearing bank, you see, and went to ask Geo-Petro about the wisdom or otherwise of their sponsorship commitment. Word had leaked back that they'd heard something negative, et cetera. Geo-Petro were perfectly co-operative, because the bank is one of their major creditors. Our people were taken straight to see – "

"Wait a minute." Munro pulled himself upright again in the seductive armchair. "How did your people pass themselves off as bank representatives? When the masquerade is eventually found out, won't Geo-Petro realise something is going on?"

Pierce looked positively hurt. "Please, Mr Munro, do trust me in these matters. The bank in question is on good terms with us, because we are presently in a client relationship with them. Mutual co-operation is the order of the day, and they were happy to accredit our people without asking *any* questions. Accordingly, Geo-Petro was visited by accredited bank representatives, and nothing will ever arise to suggest that MT-Orbis might have been behind the inquiry. Discretion is our business, just as much as investigating breaches of discretion."

"Very well." Munro reached for his coffee cup. But he wasn't going to relax. This whole damned business was altogether unsettling. Especially the result it had produced. The result wasn't an answer: it was a fountain of new questions. "And your people got to see the employee of Geo-Petro who received the alleged information about MT-Orbis?"

"Exactly. It seems the meeting had taken place at midday

in a little bistro off Covent Garden, following an unsolicited telephone contact. Our suspect presented herself as a disaffected employee of MT Holdings. She claimed to be alarmed to see the company dragging others into an attempt to exploit charity, when the whole exercise was on the point of collapse. The upshot of the visit was that our people came away with a rather good description of the suspect. Chinese, plain hairstyle cut shoulder-length, contact lenses. It's very useful, you know, that the bloke at Geo-Petro noticed the contact lenses."

"Have you checked the dental appointment?" Munro pointed at the list on Pierce's knee. Pierce had asked for it two days ago – a tally of all the movements of all the shortlist suspects in and out of the MT building on the day in question, together with any available information on where they went. "Can you in fact check the dental appointment?"

Pierce smiled. "Oh, that was easy. One of our ladies phoned the practice posing as her secretary. Miss Lee is out of town, so is her appointments diary, and the secretary wants to check whether there was in fact an appointment recently, or whether she should discuss scheduling one with Miss Lee."

"And?"

"There was no dental appointment."

Munro nodded. Chinese, contact lenses, passing fake information to someone from Geo-Petro at the same time as she'd claimed to be out of the MT building at a dental appointment which had never in fact existed. It was circumstantial, but it was good enough. What capped it was that she had access to all the right information to construct plausible false facts about MT-Orbis – and to be able to give her other employer, her secret paymaster who had anything but friendly designs on the company, everything he could possibly need. She fitted the role of a spy, as well as being a dispenser of destructive rumours. And as a spy, she was sitting in the perfect place, the most damaging possible position.

She was Michael's personal assistant.

She was Pattie Lee.

* * *

116

Pierce advised a monitoring operation. A confrontation would get them nowhere. A spy as valuable as Pattie Lee would be commanding an enormous fee, and wouldn't throw it away by naming her paymaster. The only way to find the enemy was to unearth Lee's contact to her controller. All spies pass information. They have to do it along some kind of route.

Pierce could supply an intercept for Lee's telephone at MT Holdings. All he needed from Munro was protected access to her office out of hours in order to wire the little transmitter into her phone. Pierce could do the same for Pattie Lee's domestic phone, at the inevitably rising price. He seemed such a wholesome young man to be dabbling in activities on the other side of the law . . .

Munro wasn't going to worry about Pierce's moral health, any more than he was going to risk consulting his own conscience. Too many things were impinging at once. A trio of highly sophisticated frauds, one of which ended to date with an inexplicable move which guaranteed eventual detection and involved impossible timing. How had the perpetrator arranged to take exactly the right amount of money out of the lost Buenos Aires account at exactly the same moment as an equivalent sum was paid in, by someone else, to the Siltech Systems Service account in London? Unless it wasn't so much a theft of money from the company, as an exercise in sluicing money from somewhere else *through* the company and having it disappear in South America . . .

And now the spy turned out to be Pattie Lee.

Inscrutable Pattie Lee from Hong Kong, who managed Michael's personal finance, who handled his company appointments and all the information that converged on his office. No one but Munro, and Michael himself, would be better informed about the state of MT-Orbis. More than two years ago, Michael got rid of Sylvia Symes, his girlfriend and personal business assistant. He must have decided that combining business with pleasure had put too much power in one person's hands, so he terminated the possible threat. His business affairs were added to

Pattie Lee's workload. The move concentrated the potential for power.

Michael got rid of the wrong one.

Because it was Pattie Lee, fed a constant stream of secrets about the company and about its boss's affairs, who had been turned by an external enemy.

Munro wasn't going to tell anyone until he had enough evidence to prove it, and to unravel the plans of the hostile agency. He certainly wasn't going to tell Michael. If Michael's attitude to Pattie Lee changed in the slightest, she would know she'd been discovered. Tracing her paymaster would then be impossible.

Besides, having a spy as his PA might damage Michael in some people's eyes. And considering how careless and even obstructive Michael's attitude to the affairs of his own company had become, Munro was going to keep that card out of play for a while. Just in case.

In the evening, when the MT building began to go quiet, Munro called up finance data on his screen. From Trayhorn's figures he had the source code for that payment of a quarter of a million pounds. It was a privileged code, a translation by the computer from the actual originator information into a cryptic label. The labels were assigned to major investors and creditors in order to keep details of who owned and loaned what in the company restricted on a need to know basis. The less people aware of the financial dispositions of the moment, the fewer there were who might be tempted to exploit that information. Geraldine Trayhorn didn't belong to those who needed to know.

Munro did, of course.

He checked the code against the list, and read off the name of the originator of the quarter-million-pound payment into the Siltech Systems Service account. It wasn't a pension fund, a bank, an investment broker or a securities house.

It was starting to look as though the complex movement at the end of June, involving both the Buenos Aires and the

118

London accounts, was a money sluicing device – an operation designed to launder cash through MT-Orbis and ship it out of the country, and out of sight.

He thought about it for a very long time.

Then he went home.

He drove to Guildford across a splendid July sunset, arriving in the early dusk at ten. He'd started out so late, it would have made much more sense to go to his club, where he could have dined and then taken a room for the night. But he was in something approaching a state of shock, and didn't want to meet anyone at all until he had himself under control. He didn't like living alone, and expected he never would, but it was the first time since the divorce that he'd actually missed Barbara's presence. It would have been a relief to tell someone.

Because Munro knew who was running the frauds.

Part 4

Without Trace

FIFTEEN

The room on the third floor of the Orbis building – at the back, with a view of brickwork in an alley – got new white walls and new white paint on its old sash windows. It got a new and ideologically green carpet. It got tables and tubular frame chairs, and swivel chairs with armrests for the people who'd be minding the computers and running the communication with Angel during the flight. It got Terri Sabuli's power points and dozens of phone sockets on an exchange loop. It became Mission Control.

It got staff – good-looking young women with friendly voices. Michael had designed a project T-shirt: one of the friendly voices, suitably attired in complementary jeans and clean new trainers, showed it off, and then everyone was expected to wear one. The T-shirt was loose white cotton, with a bright-green print of Angel – minus the ungainly underwing – plastered across the front. No commemorative slogan yet, no *Angel Global Solo 1991*. That would be added for the merchandising phase, after the event had been a beautiful success.

Mandy Rees quite liked the T-shirt. Ruth didn't, but she wore it all the same. It turned her into a walking advert for Michael's coming glory, a placard for his ego.

Terri Sabuli didn't wear the T-shirt. She stayed true to her own carefully tuned image.

Terri Sabuli was no longer working with the sponsors. She'd landed the fish as required, and had moved on to different waters. She was bullying, tempting, teasing, manoeuvring the media into line, while at the same time nursing all those post-mission spin-offs and follow-through projects. There would be a series of videos on how the sponsored money did wonderful works in the grateful Third World. There would be the video of the mission to edit and market. Angel – the movie. Michael – the star.

Ruth – the also ran.

Ruth was still supervising the charity liaison, but there wasn't much left to do. The agencies were in the queue and were waiting for their money. All they needed was a little human contact now and then.

Ruth wasn't getting much of that.

Michael was so busy that he'd all but done a disappearing act. He tied up the sponsorship deals, he kept on top of the media production as it got ready to roll, he supervised the technical side of the mission – exclusive rentals on satellite channels to give constant contact between Angel and Mission Control, flight clearances for the overland stages, and so on. He looked over Chester's shoulder at Wragby as the avionics equipment was installed in Angel, and he flew Angel when it was tested. But above all, he wrote the navigation program.

Angel's central computer would contain a map of the entire route, a narrow virtual world representing a corridor of reality from Wragby to Florida, across oceans and continents and back to Florida, then up the Atlantic again to Britain. The map had to know everything, from topography to navigation beacons, that was relevant to an aircraft's flight. It had to know the political frontiers and the air traffic management boundaries.

The central computer read the map by listening to data coming in from the inertial navigation system, the INS, which told it how far it had moved in space from its starting point. It put the blind movements from the INS on its map, and found its position. It did that every ten seconds. Then it used the result to tell a slaved computer, which was steering the satellite dish in the nose, where to nudge the dish to keep it on line with the satellite. And every two hours it asked for a new satellite position fix from another slaved computer. The new satellite position would be accurate to thirty-three feet up, down or sideways. The central computer would promptly update the INS to eliminate its slight cumulative error, and then flash the precise position via the satellite link to Mission Control. At Mission Control they would have a second copy of the program running in parallel . . .

It was a massive piece of work. Nobody but Michael, the former computer genius, could have done it in the time.

Ruth saw him now and then in London, when he turned up to bathe everyone for a few moments in his smile, then disappeared for long consultations with Terri Sabuli. Apart from that, Michael didn't really exist in her world any more.

Nor, it seemed, did Ruth really exist in his.

The work went on for three weeks. And then Michael appeared on Tuesday afternoon at the Orbis building. He went to the third floor, to Mission Control.

He looked at the row of telephones waiting on tables backing on the windows. He inspected the array of communication equipment, he approved the trio of Siltech computers. He admired the map spread along the entire wall opposite the windows. All that was missing was the thin line marking the route.

"Well." He pushed the sides of his jacket open and hooked his thumbs in his belt. He looked at Mandy Rees, who'd followed him in from the project office, and at Ruth. "You can put the route on the map, now. It's finished."

"Great," Mandy said. "That means we're nearly ready to go!"

"It does." Michael nodded towards the computers. "I'll install the program while I'm here. I've got the disks in my car. Is Terri anywhere about?"

Mandy shook her head. "She's over at MT. Should I phone her?"

"In a minute. I want to check with her about which of the American TV channels will be on board. CNN were hinting at an exclusive on the Florida stuff. That would be a nice deal."

"It would." Mandy turned to Ruth. "Wouldn't it?"

Ruth nodded. Yet more coming in for the man who had it all. Michael exuded that sticky aura of success – so much sexy money. It glued ever more wealth to itself.

"What about the airfield in Florida?" Mandy asked. "Have you got exclusive use of it yet?"

"Yes. Tied the deal up yesterday evening." Michael was looking at the wall map, scanning the length of his glide to glory.

"Michaels Field?"

He smiled, still admiring the map. "Michaels Field. No airliners overshadowing us, no cocaine smugglers bothering us. And just about the ideal name. Not a bad little coup, that."

Mandy grinned. "Have you decided who'll be going out there?"

"Chester, with John Coates and most of their team, to do the servicing and engine change during the stopover. Terri and at least half of her team to do the media minding. Ruth, too." Michael looked at Ruth. "If I jump out of the cockpit too eagerly when I land, and break my ankle or something, Ruth has to be there to take over. Don't you, Ruth?"

Ruth nodded. Not a chance, she thought. No fall is ever going to break any part of Michael. Success protects him better than a posse of angels.

"You'll be staying in London, Mandy. You have to manage the British media while everyone's away." Michael shrugged. "And don't be too disappointed at missing Florida. They're all going to be flying out there in a cargo aircraft while I'm flying Angel, and they'll be flying back here the same way as soon as I've taken off again. They'll clock up two doses of jet-lag in about sixty hours. You won't be missing anything."

"I suppose I won't, really." Mandy shook her head. "Anyway, July isn't the best season for Florida. Shall I phone Terri?"

126

"Yes, please. Tell her I'll be over at MT in about two hours."

"Right." Mandy started towards the door. "I'll phone from the office." She pointed at the telephones on the row of tables. "These won't be connected until tomorrow."

Michael waited until Mandy had gone. Then he turned to Ruth again. He smiled. "Well?"

Ruth shrugged. "We don't see much of each other these days, do we, Michael?"

"No," he said slowly. "We haven't done these last few weeks."

"I know why, of course."

"Work," he said. "A bit of an emergency with the work."

She nodded. There was no point in pursuing a confrontation, no sense in provoking a fight. No mileage in asking why he'd never had time, not even late in the evening, and overnight, and at least as long as breakfast. At least once or twice. Michael did things his way, and you accepted it, and that was that. "Anyway, you've finished the navigation program."

"Yes," he said. "That's the biggest problem out of the way."

For you, she thought, perhaps. For me, the biggest problem is different. It's a mixture of the work overload on the project, the fact that I'm not flying Angel, jealousy that you are – and the way you've been excluding me from your life. I can try to deal with that last piece, at least, by making things nice again. "Well then, why not come to my place this evening? I'll cook dinner. We can have some peace and quiet, no one bothering us, a break from work. And we'll get very friendly. What do you think?"

"Ah," Michael said. "That's a bit of a pity. There's this last minute stuff I've got to check through with Terri. It's going to take all evening. But I tell you what – I'll interrupt the work long enough for us to meet for dinner. How about that?"

Ruth waited a moment, out of self-respect. She wanted to let the fury turn from pain to venom before she let it show. "Take your dinner, Michael," she said, "and shove it up your arse."

* * *

127

By the evening, Ruth was wrapped in guilt. Peace was still possible. It wasn't Michael's fault that the project had been brought forward from a September take-off to one in mid-July. It wasn't his fault that he had so much work to do. The blame lay with whoever it was who'd started the rumour against MT-Orbis. It wasn't even Michael's fault that she felt such resentment. As the one who planned the project, funded the work and provided the company workshops to do it in, Michael was obviously going to be the pilot who flew Angel round the world and put his name in the history books. Ruth's bitter envy was a torment of her own making. If only she didn't care . . .

But she cared so very much. She hated being a loser in the race to chase the sun, to keep up with the immortal *now* – to touch it, to make just one single mark on the receding hem of its garment of light. Before the dark night of ending rolls over you. And puts you out.

She didn't want to do it by phone. She drove to the MT building through the dull evening. One of Michael's cars was there, the big Volvo 960 – but Michael still had the BMW and the Land Cruiser to play with, not to mention taxis. Munro's Mercedes was there as well – but she didn't want to see Munro. There was no sign of Terri Sabuli's Corrado.

The huge building, sole home of MT Holdings and headquarters of Orbis Air, was quiet, was on its resting routine. But it wasn't deserted. There was the computer suite and there were the international offices, the security guards and the night canteen. It was a corporate head office, the heart and brain of a machine geared to making and managing money, and it never stopped. It had nothing to do with the green-alternative image of Orbis, the once beautiful creature which seemed to be decaying into a loss-making monster for the Frankensteinian genius who created it . . .

Michael wasn't there. Terri Sabuli wasn't in her office, either. Ruth went back to the lifts. She could hear the night lift running in its shaft as she pressed the down button.

When it arrived and the doors opened, Robert Munro was

inside. Ruth walked into the trapped conversation, and the lift continued down to the ground.

"I gather," he said, "that everything's ready to go, and you're just waiting for the weather to be right."

"Yes," she said.

Munro nodded, a tall and heavy man looming in possession of his half of the lift. "Were you looking for Michael?"

"Yes."

Munro nodded again. "I believe he went back to the Orbis building with Terri Sabuli. That's two or three hours ago."

"Oh." She watched the indicator over the door counting down. She couldn't decide straight away whether to go chasing after Michael any more. What if he wasn't at the Orbis building? Or what if he was, still going through page after lacquered fingernail page of some proposal in intimate closeness with Terri Sabuli? She wouldn't exactly want to interrupt . . .

Munro switched his briefcase from one hand to the other. "Have you eaten yet this evening?"

"No." The orange light was flicking behind the little number windows towards M for mezzanine.

"I'm on the way to my club. Why don't you dine with me?"

Mezzanine went by. The orange light moved to *ground*.

"Um – am I dressed right?" She was wearing black cotton trousers and a black linen jacket, with a green and white striped blouse underneath. The lift doors opened on the dim lobby and showed her in a softer light.

"When the club voted to allow women members and guests, the diehard chauvinists even gave in about trousers, but they drew the line at jeans. You aren't wearing jeans, and above all you're not wearing one of those bloody T-shirts with a green aircraft on the front. The club will let you in."

Outside the electronically locked doors, down in the pull-in bay at the foot of the steps, Munro's cab was already waiting.

SIXTEEN

Munro deposited his briefcase with the porter and then led Ruth to the bar. He ordered her a Campari and chose a brandy and soda for himself. Ruth eyed the oak panelling and the velvet upholstery. The place was smoke-free and smelled of rich men's drinks. It was filled with an atmosphere of well-mannered discretion – not so much suffocating tradition as self-confident élitism. They moved to the end of the bar to study the menu displayed under glass.

"Hello, Robert! Been working late again?"

Ruth turned, and looked up, to see a pin-striped streak of sixty-ish establishment holding two glasses of port. At his elbow, and Ruth's own height, was a blonde woman.

The pin-stripe nodded at the menu. "Try the salmon. Lovely, wasn't it, Sylvia?"

"Delicious," said his blonde companion. She was probably forty, she was City-suited in tones of grey. "We haven't met." She offered her hand – to Munro, not to Ruth.

"Sylvia Symes," said the pin-stripe. "This is Robert Munro, Michael Tranter's top man. Robert, you *must* know Sylvia."

"Only by name," Munro said. "You left a few months before I came in, didn't you?"

"End of eighty-eight, actually," said Sylvia Symes.

Ruth had started to smile. She felt the smile freeze in place. Stay polite, she thought, don't lose points by letting anyone see you're put out. This is Sylvia Symes – *the* Sylvia Symes – the woman who went before me through Michael's bed. She looks cool, and tough – one of the sharks who cull a living in the City.

Munro turned to Ruth. "This is Ruth Clifford. Ruth, this

130

is Geoffrey Simmington. Geoffrey's one of the senior people at Longman Short."

"Merchant bank," Simmington said. He shook her hand – carefully, the way old-fashioned men worry about weak women. "Ruth Clifford, eh? The intrepid lady pilot, bit of a jet-set Amy Johnson. Pleased to meet you."

Ruth managed to bring her smile back to life. Then she risked Sylvia Symes. "You were Michael's business assistant, weren't you?"

"For five years," the woman said. She didn't offer to shake hands. It was the only indication of discomfort. Apart from that, she exuded superiority.

"And now?"

"I'm with Rowe Spitta Pitts." She offered no explanation. If Sylvia Symes was forty, she would be nine years older than Ruth, and she wasn't going to shrink from wielding that seniority. Or, of course, she could be jealous of the new and younger model.

"Securities house," Simmington said. "Sylvia's one of their analysts."

"Rowe Spitta Pitts," Munro said, "has clients with shares in every level of MT-Orbis except MT Holdings itself. So does Geoffrey's bank."

"I see," Ruth said. Shareholders and share administrators, the paymasters of capitalism. Sharks, who cull a living in the City.

"We were just talking about you, Robert," Simmington said. "That is, about the company. Weren't we, Sylvia?"

"Yes, Geoffrey. Do you think I could have my drink, by the way?" Sylvia Symes pointed at the glasses of port.

"Of course. Sorry." Simmington handed over one of the glasses. "Sylvia's going to come in on this consortium thingy, Robert. Since you're here, we could firm up the expectations on this sale, don't you think?"

"I think so." Munro glanced briefly at Sylvia Symes, as if she was an eavesdropper of dubious credentials. "The bank seems to be sorting out its side, Geoffrey."

Simmington nodded. He glanced at Ruth. It was the same kind of caution, as if he wondered whether Ruth should hear what was going to be said. "If you can give me a week's warning before Orbis Air goes up for sale, I can move in with an offer on behalf of a solid consortium – say as soon as the Orbis Air shares have taken their initial fall. We'll put in an over-the-odds offer, of course, in order to tie it up before any rivals get in on the act. But there's a bit of a catch, Robert."

Orbis Air? They were talking about a *sale* of Orbis Air? Ruth looked at Sylvia Symes, and got a twitch of a smile in return. The woman certainly thought Ruth was Michael's tell-tale.

"What might the catch be, Geoffrey?"

"Well, Orbis Air won't look like a viable *entity* at that stage, so in fact the bank will want the profitable part, the tour group – Orbis Travel and the charter stuff."

"I see." Munro sipped his brandy. "You'd want it carved up at the time of sale, so that you don't have to unload losses later."

"Excuse me," Ruth said. "Excuse me, but I didn't realise Orbis Air was going to be sold. I mean, not yet, anyway."

Munro blinked at her through his glasses. "It isn't. Yet."

"I suppose," Simmington said, "we could sweeten it by buying a slice of the air transport division. The trouble, though, is the losses coming in there."

"I understand your problem, Geoffrey. Suppose, during the negotiations, we agreed to carve the air transport side so that your slice included exclusively owned, and not leased, aircraft. The bank and its consortium would then be acquiring a tour operator with valuable hotel contracts, a route licence package with sellable or leasable terminal facilities, plus high value capital assets in the form of paid-off airliners. No liabilities. You will, in fact, be getting a major chunk of Orbis Air and its subsidiaries that makes a lot of sense as an entity, as you put it."

Simmington nodded at his port. "That's true. That's true. It sounds rather attractive. Have you had any thoughts on the matter of outstanding favours, Robert?" Simmington glanced at Ruth again, as if wondering whether the discussion should proceed any further in front of her.

"I'm working on something, Geoffrey."

"I'm sure you are, Robert."

Munro sipped his brandy and soda again. He was studying Sylvia Symes over the glass. Everyone here was up to something, and Ruth was the only one who didn't know what it was. At least, she didn't know the motives, the *reasons* for fixing up some sort of deal.

Sylvia Symes sipped her port, and studied Munro. They drank to each other like natural allies. Business has eyes only for business – there's going to be a carve-up, and the people with the knives will profit.

"Orbis Pacific Tours and Desert Life," Sylvia Symes said to Munro. "Michael's sillier image generators. I told him Desert Life would never work. Orbis Pacific Tours is after my time. *Opt* for places unspoiled by pollution, *opt* for Orbis Pacific Tours. What did you tell him about it, Robert? May I call you Robert?"

Munro nodded. "I told him Orbis Pacific Tours wouldn't work."

"But for some unfathomable reason, he didn't listen." She sipped her port again. "This is good, Geoffrey."

"Vintage," Simmington said. "Vintage. Look, I've just seen a chappy through there I have to talk to for a moment." He pointed out of the bar and past the stairs. "Gone into the smoking room, as luck would have it. Bit of a word about those Kuwaiti contracts – rebuilding things for rich Arabs. Robert, can you be a good chap and look after Sylvia for a while? This won't take long."

Simmington left them at the end of the bar, with just the menu for company.

"Actually," Sylvia said, "the salmon really was good. Geoffrey knows his food and drink. How do you like working for Michael, Robert?"

Munro didn't answer.

Sylvia Symes turned to Ruth. "Well, how do you like being

my successor? I hear you're an employee at a junior level –
apart from being this stand-by pilot, as if Michael would ever
let you fly the thing. There's an advantage to being pretty
junior, you know. It means that when Michael decides to
let you go, it won't be because he's afraid you might know
too much. No desk-clearing and office-locking job. In fact
you might not get the sack, as well as the push, at all. The
disadvantage is that you won't take anything with you when
you go. I had shareholdings, severance pay commensurate
with salary. And knowledge." She looked at Munro again.
"I've been hearing a bit about you from Geoffrey."

"Have you?" Munro said.

"You're from Glasgow, aren't you?" She had her arms
folded in cocktail-party style, port glass cantilevered out
between varnished fingernails. "Son of a steelworker from
the tenements in the bad old days. Edinburgh University,
and then the business world. Geoffrey says you're thoroughly
hard-boiled, but that somewhere inside you beats the heart of
a would-be socialist. True?"

Munro shrugged. "You have me at a disadvantage."

"Call me Sylvia, Robert."

"You have me at a disadvantage, Sylvia. I don't know
anything about you."

"Oh come, now. Michael must have told you things. You,
too, Ruth. The people around him as well. My name is
attached to the bad odium which no doubt still lingers at
the top of what's now MT-Orbis. And I bet Pattie Lee would
have something to say about me – if she ever says anything at
all, that is. I assume she is still his PA, and so on?"

What, Ruth thought, does *so on* mean?

"She's still his PA," Munro said. "But I'm sure you know
the way things work better than that. No one ever says anything
about Michael's personal affairs unless Michael tells them to.
Or was it different a couple of years ago?"

Sylvia smiled. "It wasn't different. In fact, it never has been.
Michael has his secrets, doesn't he?"

"If he didn't, we'd all know the trick. We'd all be rich

geniuses, the financial landscape would be flat, and none of us would be better off than anyone else."

"Are you better off? You're divorced, aren't you?"

Munro didn't like that. He lifted his head. He started to use his height to look down at Sylvia Symes, disengaging from the closeness of any oblique conspiracy. Good, Ruth thought. This supercooled bitch has gone too far.

The supercooled bitch gave a slight shrug. "I'll tell you one of Michael's secrets, Robert. You might have worked it out for yourself – but if not, it's worth knowing." She'd noticed that she was treading on toes, and had decided to trade a little something to keep things on the rails. She appeared to know what she was doing. "Michael *isn't* a financial genius."

Munro seemed to accept the offered morsel. "Isn't he?"

"No. He's a computer genius. He's so bloody good at computers and finds them so bloody easy, that after a few years they started to bore him – as a product, that is. So he turned his hand to making money. Starting with the success he'd built up with Siltech, and taking it from there. Michael's an overgrown boy, a sort of seriously rich Peter Pan. Money is his magic dust, and aeroplanes are the way he does the flying thing. He doesn't get the money by being good at business, but by being good at computers – at the *applications*. Do you understand where the difference lies?"

Munro nodded.

Ruth was entirely fed up of being ignored when she wasn't being condescended to. Time to play the only available role, which was the next best thing to Michael's nearest and dearest. "Michael has his limitations. He also knows about them. He isn't good at corporate management. That's why he brought Robert in."

Sylvia Symes shook her head. "The difference is a little deeper than that, dear. Michael has a dark past, you know. That must be obvious, mustn't it? How else could anyone get so rich so quickly?"

Ruth didn't answer. Don't, she wanted to say, call me *dear*.

135

Sylvia Symes was looking out of the bar, past the stairs towards the smoking room, where Geoffrey Simmington had gone. "I don't suppose either of you smoke? I quite fancy a cigarette, and the only thing I have against your lovely club is all the rules you have restricting smoking."

"It saves on redecorating bills," Munro said. "We don't smoke."

"Pity. Well, I'd better see what Geoffrey's up to." She raised her glass. "It's been nice meeting you, Ruth, Robert. You know, it's time someone played Captain Hook to Michael's Peter Pan – but with allies, instead of a crocodile. We'll keep in touch, Robert, I'm sure."

Munro took Ruth into the dining room. She chose chicken *fumé à la crème*, and asked for a Pimm's. Munro chose a glass of wine to go with his veal.

"What on earth," Ruth said, "was that *about*? You're fixing up a deal for Orbis Air – one that cuts out competition between buyers, for God's sake – before Michael's even agreed to the sale. Is it ethical? Is it legal?"

"It's business."

"But what do you get back for it? I mean, you're making it so sweet and sugary for the buyer. What's in it from your side?"

"Money for MT Holdings," Munro said. "And more than you might suppose. The deal is a fix-up, but that has advantages. In its present state Orbis Air is *not* a good acquisition. It requires a massive rescue effort by any new owner, so it's most probably only good for asset stripping. And asset stripping goes through jobs like a combine harvester. However, the deal I'm proposing with Longman Short's consortium has two significant advantages."

"Oh. And those are?"

"If the consortium moves fast enough to pick up the valuable prime cuts in a package, they'll also be moving too fast for the share price of Orbis Air to plummet as its unattractiveness becomes apparent. Leave it to market forces, and it will sink to dustbin prices. By baiting the sale with an advantage so that one buyer wants to move faster than any potential rivals, MT gets more money. I know what I'm doing – it's the way we did things at Bryce McFadden."

"Oh. And the other advantage?"

"They'll be acquiring the new asset in a package form that determines how they'll go on to dispose of it. The way I'm setting it up, the package will be most profitable if its integrity is retained at subsequent sale. In other words, if it isn't treated to asset stripping. The whole will remain more valuable than the parts, in fact. That means the job losses will look more like weeding and pruning than a pass with a combine harvester. It won't be of any help to the hundreds who get kicked on the heap, but it will be invaluable to the thousands who *don't* lose their jobs. It will also make the exercise more bearable for my conscience."

"And what does Michael think about all this?"

"Ah, yes – Michael." Munro paused to sip his wine.

"Are you – " Ruth stopped. Munro was opening a door to a world she'd never even glimpsed before, a secret existence where the mighty pursue their power games. She wasn't sure what she could see there. "Are you – planning something? Against Michael?"

Munro almost smiled, a reluctant expression on the man's sombre face. "At issue is the fundamental health of MT Holdings and its corporate provinces. Let's just say that for various reasons, I'm not entirely confident that Michael is all that interested in the fate of the company. Unlike all the people who work for him, and are entirely dependent on the company for their livelihood, Michael has a sizable proportion of his personal wealth invested elsewhere. So he might see MT-Orbis primarily as a showcase for his own ego, and as a money mine – but not as a coherent entity in its own right, in other words *as a company*."

"But you – um – do see it as a company?"

"I have a fat salary from MT-Orbis, I own some shares in MT-Orbis, and I've spent the last two years of my life exclusively on getting it into shape and trying to keep it in shape. Those two years have seen an accelerating economic disaster in this country, so it's been very hard going. Now we're bumping along the bottom – and that's when our boss decides he isn't interested any more. At least, he isn't interested in doing anything except block every proposal for change. It's only since last week that I've begun to understand why."

Bitterness. There was an undertone of bitterness. The dark henchman who kept the corporate machine running for Michael was turning out to have feelings after all. And plans. Softly, Ruth could hear the sounds of some coming event – an event which might out-manoeuvre Michael. Like the sale of Orbis Air against his wishes, which would involve a massive shift in the balance of power between Michael and Munro . . . "I'm supposed to be on Michael's side. Why are you telling *me* this?"

"So that you'll have time to choose where your loyalties lie."

"Between you and Michael?"

"Between the company and Michael. It's Michael's company, but it comprises thousands of other people, without whose efforts it ceases to exist. It doesn't cease to exist without Michael. The question of loyalty begins to arise when Michael ceases to behave with the appropriate responsibility towards his company."

It doesn't cease to exist without Michael. Munro was hinting at a huge change. Winning the battle over Orbis Air was only the beginning of a war, the first step in moving the power centre. He was talking about cutting Michael down to size, a campaign against the boss, the sort of thing you had to prepare in secret and launch without warning . . . "I'll ask you again. Why are you telling *me* this? What's in it for you if I know? Is it some kind of set-up? Am I supposed to warn him of something you pretend you're doing, so that he's distracted while you in fact do something totally different?"

"Do I seem that devious?" Munro was looking faintly amused. "Tell me what I'm doing – from your point of view."

138

"You're – " What? Laying some hints on the line, voicing some vague criticisms of Michael's attitude? Munro had said that in his opinion, it was better if Michael showed a sense of responsibility towards MT-Orbis. And Munro had let her see him optimising a deal to sell Orbis Air, which was bound to happen in the end. It was no secret that MT Holdings needed to sell something, and that the airline was the biggest loss the company was carrying. Michael had even hinted at an eventual acceptance of the idea. His objection had always been to selling the airline early. After all, the airline and its Trantair subsidiary provided the entire base for the Angel project. No Orbis Air, no solo flight around the world.

"Well?" Munro asked.

"You're letting me know that you feel strong enough to get your own way. Which means stronger than Michael. You're also hinting that Michael is an irresponsible person – isn't necessarily all that much of an asset to the company. Are you trying to turn me against Michael? Or – are you trying to get *me*?"

"Do I seem that naive?" He wasn't in the slightest bit amused any more. "Come on, eat up. We've still got half the meal to go, and there's something I think I should show you."

SEVENTEEN

The reading room at the club was a piece of traditional England full of leather upholstery, broadsheet newspapers and soft conversations. On the chesterfield in the alcove between the fireplace and the brocade-covered windows, they held a very quiet conversation of their own. It was a one-sided talk.

Munro told her about the frauds.

He fetched his briefcase from the porter's desk, and showed

her the reams of figures. They told her nothing, except the reason why fraud is an infernally difficult crime to investigate and prosecute. Ignore the encyclopedias of numbers, listen to the summary from the expert, and hope you can trust his assessment.

The value of the money stolen was impressive – close on three and a half million. Even a company the size of MT-Orbis was being hurt when it lost that amount of blood . . .

As the cab turned into Piccadilly, Ruth hooked her hand in the strap beside the door and leaned her head against her wrist. Munro wouldn't tell her without a reason, and she feared what the reason might be. "I know it's silly, but I wouldn't have thought there'd be so many criminals attacking one company at once."

"All three frauds are related." Munro put his briefcase flat on the floor against the forward partition, and propped his shoe against the briefcase to stop it sliding. "The similarities are crucial. The same type of computer manipulation is involved in each instance. Instead of the computer simply being rigged to run accounts and transfer money, it's been set up so that it systematically hides the fact. Even when asked directly about what it's been doing, it can't provide any information. Something is blocking its output to screen and printer, and somehow it's smoothing over the omissions so that you normally can't even see the gaps. It's the work of an extremely clever specialist."

Ruth nodded as the cab cruised through the window-lit July dusk. The up-market shops, the airline offices and the Royal Academy were icons of a wealthy, trustworthy world.

"The technicalities of each fraud are the same. Pick a subsidiary – or its office – that's in trouble. Sideline funds leaving head office in order to steal interest. Block the closing down instructions when the subsidiary is wound up, and maintain its account together with the supply of funds as originally set up. Hide the entire trick inside the computer. Pocket the results. The only thing that doesn't fit is the sluicing of money through the Siltech Systems Service account in Buenos Aires. It's impossible to hide. Even without the benefit of chance coupled with our own search for more frauds, we'd have found out about that one with the next quarterly figures."

Piccadilly Circus was showing its lights against the cold afterglow of summer. The cab stop-goed its way into Shaftesbury Avenue. "You're suggesting it's one and the same crook each time. Why tell me?"

"Because it isn't any crook. It's a particular crook. It's someone with the knowledge and the opportunity to prepare the ground by being involved in the fate of pet projects – like breaking into the Pacific market with green-awareness tourism, or greening Third World deserts, or breaking into the US-controlled computer market in South America. It's someone who has an excellent overview of the company, and has the freedom to go anywhere and lift information about anything, in order to find the pools from which to drain the funds in invisible trickles. It's someone who has unparalleled computer skills. And it's someone who's totally above suspicion, as any good perpetrator of a fraud should be."

"You mean – " They were passing the theatres, places where deceits are staged, people pretending to be different creatures. The actors worked to scripts. This deceiver was a master of a higher order, ad-libbing his way through years of hidden dealings without making a single mistake. "You mean Michael."

Munro didn't even nod. The cab crossed Charing Cross Road.

"You haven't got any evidence."

"I've got the first piece. It's enough. It starts things rolling."

"And what's that?"

"The sluicing of a quarter of a million – paid in to the Siltech Systems Service account in London quite legitimately, transferred secretly to the hidden account in Buenos Aires, and withdrawn from that account. And all of it triggered to

141

happen simultaneously. Michael's the person who paid in the quarter of a million. It's his money that's been spirited out of sight."

"It could be his money that's been *stolen*. Someone else could have arranged the Buenos Aires withdrawal to exploit the fact that he'd deposited cash with the company."

"The Buenos Aires withdrawal and the London deposit are co-ordinated to the second. How do you think you do that, without controlling both operations on both accounts? It's Michael."

"Well – well – why?" She hauled at the strap, tugged herself tight to its support. The cab nudged her at the junction with St Giles. "Why on earth would Michael do anything like that?"

"I don't know. I understand now why he stalled so long before winding up Desert Life and Orbis Pacific Tours. He was using his position as MD of those companies, and their parent companies, to push through the rescue payments which the frauds were exploiting. I don't know what use the slow money might have been that he was creaming off through the frauds. And I don't know why he decided to go for bigger money once the companies were wound up. And I haven't the faintest idea why he chose to launder money through the company network in a way that was bound to come to light." Munro had slumped in his corner of the cab, a heavy and a burdened man. "It seems more and more like hurried work – something that isn't supposed to show up for the time being, but isn't so well hidden that it's never going to be detected. I'm certain Michael's clever enough to set up an undetectable fraud, if he wanted to. I expect he probably has. But that's one we'll never find."

"Are you going to the police?"

"Not until I can prove it. And not until I'm sure the disclosure won't hurt the company. I might have to simply stop the frauds and let him walk away from it. Most frauds go unpunished, I believe. Companies find them so bloody embarrassing."

142

Crooks go free, some are probably even bought off. There were plenty of rumours about hackers who stole information so sensitive, that the owners made the thieves rich in order to get their property back. It could be just the same with fraud. When you couldn't prove it without spilling a mess into the public domain, you might bribe the perpetrator to give up and go away. It left the culprit with the status of an *alleged* criminal. And sometimes the allegation would hit an innocent who never got the chance to clear his or her name. "I don't believe it. You can't pin it on Michael without a motive. The question stands. Why on earth would someone as rich as Michael stoop to fraud? It's like your own question – why would someone as clever as Michael set up a fraud that can be detected?"

Munro actually laughed. It was a hollow and cynical sound. "I can tell you why Michael threw a fit when he discovered I'd started the special audits of the subsidiaries. It wasn't because I was pushing the issue of identifying Orbis Air as the item to be sold. It was because of the risk of the frauds coming to light much sooner than would otherwise have been the case. A special audit looks at precise figures. And it's the special audit that found the frauds. So I understand some of Michael's behaviour. But I haven't the faintest idea." Munro was looking down at the floor of the cab, staring at his briefcase which held the secret reams of figures. "I haven't the faintest idea why he's done it."

They went through the dimmed-down lobby and took the stairs to the basement garage. At the top of the second flight, where the wall turned to white-painted blocks, Ruth stopped. It was her refrain for the evening surfacing again. At the bottom, Munro pushed open the first door, and waited. As he looked up towards her, the lights on the stair glowed like Svengali ovals in his glasses.

"I still want to know," she said. "Why are you telling *me*?"

The ovals in the glasses stared back at her. "Because he needs an accomplice."

"An accomplice?"

"At some point, someone has to turn up in person at the bank where the money finally arrives, and make the necessary dispositions. That person can't be Michael, because the risk of discovery would be too great. It has to be someone he has reason to trust, and who can disappear from everyone else's sight for a while without anyone thinking anything of it. The bank at the end of each chain could be anywhere in the world, after all. The ideal accomplice might be someone who goes on business trips with Michael."

Or Michael's girlfriend, she thought. Sharing his bed, so sharing his breach of the law. Suspicion of the innocent seems the order of the day. She started down the stairs. "I haven't been on one of Michael's trips for months. He doesn't take me with him any more."

"I know." Munro was still holding the door open for her. "But the dispositions at the banks could have been made some time ago."

Ruth followed him into the corridor leading to the second door. The first door closed itself behind her. "If I'm his accomplice, why are you warning me? So that I'll turn witness for the prosecution, or whatever it's called, and help put Michael in prison? *If* he was the one behind the frauds, that is."

Munro opened the second door at the end of the short stretch of corridor. "I don't happen to think you're the accomplice. Though I could be wrong."

"Well then – *why* tell me?" She got to the final door as Munro went through. She steadied the door, and paused. "I mean to say – you haven't told me anything that *proves* it. I don't believe it. I could go and warn Michael that you've got this crazy idea about him. What would that do to you?"

"It is Michael." Munro was standing in the garage now, where sparse fans of fluorescent light echoed off the ceiling, columns and floor. "I've got hold of the figures before he's had time to shut the operations down. If you tell him I know, before I *can* prove the connection, the worst that would happen is he gets away unpunished. He'd have to stop the frauds, and

I'd require that he retires from all his directorships. That way, the company would be safe in future."

Ruth stepped out of the corridor. Behind her, the door sighed closed on dampened springs and clicked into its lock. The car park was empty. It was cool and concrete-dusty, with a scent of hydrocarbons and rubber. When she moved her feet, the place whispered with hard sounds.

Munro gestured with his briefcase along the empty rows to where Ruth's green Golf waited under one of the lights. "I'll see you to your car."

"No thanks," she said. "And I don't believe it's Michael."

He shrugged. "Then I'll be going back to my club. I can call another cab from reception. Goodnight, Ruth."

"Goodnight," she said.

When he'd gone, she walked between the columns to her car. Echoes and shadows of plots and schemes haunted her progress. As she drove home through darkening, emptying London she was thinking: what does Munro want? *What* does he want?

It could be a bluff, a set-up so she'd tell Michael one thing while Munro was secretly working on quite another plot. Or it might all be lies. The figures he'd shown her could have meant anything at all, and the story he'd told her could be pure invention. Or Munro might have been fishing, just fishing, guessing that Michael might be involved and trying to gauge her reaction.

Or every bit of it could be true. Munro might be hoping she'd take the heavy hint and warn Michael he'd been found out. Then the whole business could, conceivably, be settled quietly without any public fuss. Michael would withdraw and quit the company – and get away with the money he'd taken. It would be her responsibility, not Munro's. He'd have protected everyone from the fight, but he'd have dodged the moral consequences.

Or truth or lies, Munro could be making a play for her. The present protector is weakening and is on his way out – this new dominant male is strong, and is winning. And here came the life-long conundrum again, first her father, then Ashley who took her to Africa, then Michael. Any man powerful enough to protect her also cast a stifling shadow . . .

Ruth was going to take a long time getting to sleep.

EIGHTEEN

The next morning, Wednesday, Michael was all sweetness and light, a Peter Pan of a man on the make. Angel was ready, Wragby, Michaels Field and Mission Control were ready. The charities were drooling, the sponsors were ready, the media were ready to be ready.

And the weather over England and in the Gulf of Mexico was good for the weekend. No Atlantic depressions, no tropical hurricanes.

So on Friday the adventure was going to begin . . .

Michael left Terri Sabuli to direct the eruption of activity inside Mission Control. He took Ruth by the arm and steered her out into the corridor. Window at one end and stairs at the other, with doors to the commandeered project offices on the opposite side, it made a dingy strip of private space.

Michael let go of her arm. He leaned against the wall, jacket pushed aside, hands on his hips. Ruth found herself standing in front of him, waiting to meet his eyes.

"The time is right," Michael said. He was looking down, somewhere between her feet. "The public interest is warm, there are no major distractions in the news. And it's a couple of weeks before the next quarterly figures are published."

Ruth could still feel where his hand had released her arm. It had been the first time he'd touched her in three weeks.

"The figures will be bad." Michael shook his head. "Bad enough to prompt any sponsor who's just a little bit wobbly to do a runner after all."

"Oh," she said.

"Then the project will collapse. There'll be no publicity, no across-the-range promotion, no recouping the costs of building Angel and setting the whole thing up. And my company *needs* the publicity, the promotion, and the payback." He lifted his eyes and looked at her at last. "I have to bring in the money, and the spin-offs. I *have* to. So that's what the rush is for."

He was tired, worried – a weary version of the man Ruth had known for more than two years. He was no villain, no vampire sucking blood out of his own organisation. Those were shadows of the night before, mistakes called into being by Munro.

Michael leaned his head against the wall. "I'm going to have another busy day. Terri's doing a press release, then she'll set up some TV interviews for me. But I've told her to fix nothing after seven o'clock."

"Seven," Ruth said.

"I want a quiet evening. Ruth – I want to make amends for yesterday. My behaviour was – well, it wasn't any good at all. I couldn't do anything about the work, but I should have had the sense to say why. I shouldn't have been off-hand. I'm sorry."

An apology from Michael was rare. He made the world adjust to him. An apology, maybe, was a very personal thing.

"Ruth, could we have dinner tonight? Could we go to your place? I'll be tied here in London all day. But – could we have some time together? Quiet, just for us. Before the whole thing gets rolling on Thursday?"

A last piece of private time before the final preparations at Wragby, the take-off on Friday, the rushed stopover in Florida and the five days of flying round the world. A little bit of personal time after all . . .

So Ruth smiled.

Munro didn't smile. Let Michael play his games, another wilful expedition back into Never-Never Land, where adventure rules and responsibility can be unloaded on other people. Let Michael play his two-faced games, the innocent boy who won't grow up – and who won't own up to a selfishness so intense that it steals in order to serve its endless greed.

Corporate fraud is called a crime without a victim. All it hurts is the company. But a company is composed of people – damage the company and you damage them. To hell with the shareholders: if the company folds the worst they lose is money. But if the fraud erodes the profits, or if it helps kill the company, employees lose their jobs. They lose their personal worlds.

Robert Munro came from Glasgow, by way of Edinburgh University and a degree in economics. Robert Munro was a steelworker's son. He grew up in tenement squalor, he moved to a new estate that decayed into a desert, he saw his father lose his job, land on the heap, and live out a lingering life for nothing at all. He'd spent his own career propelling himself as far away as possible from even the shadow of such a fate. Security, such as it was, lay in the acquisition of financial power. But inside him, he still had a social conscience . . .

He hated a man like Michael Tranter, who had everything – and who used any means available as he slavered after more, and more, and more.

Something would have to be done.

It would have to be done soon, before the company was caught on the hook of complicity, and Michael's chief executive officer became a conspirator in the concealment of crime.

Because there was a fax on his desk, addressed to him in person. It had come from a Mr Peter Cavendish of the Securities and Investments Board. The City's regulators wanted to talk to him, at his convenience, about one or two matters which had come to light.

They knew something, too . . .

Nothing of use had come out of the recordings of Pattie Lee's office phone calls, nor from the tap installed by Smith and

Brown Associates on her private line. Their close surveillance had shown nothing suspicious. She worked long hours at the office, and was still taking business calls from Michael, or making calls on his behalf, hours later each night. Michael paid her phone bill himself. Once a week she made a half-hour call to Hong Kong. Pattie Lee spoke English with her Hong Kong parents, and the expense of a translator could be spared. The concern, in every call, was whether or not her parents could raise enough money to buy their way into another country – before the butchers of Peking were let through the frontier by the oh-so-caring British powers that presently be.

It might make a personal motive for seeking money as a saboteur and a commercial spy . . .

Every Saturday evening she took free from the phone, and went to the cinema, a concert, sometimes the theatre. She went alone, she ate alone at one of several restaurants, she came home alone. No sign of a contact. She went shopping once a week, and bought in enough for breakfasts and light evening meals for one.

On her breaks from the office she visited her hairdresser, she went to the building society where the company paid her salary, and she called at the City branch of the Kowloon Crown International Bank. Smith and Brown Associates drew the line at penetrating the bank's computer, but proposed a burglary of Pattie Lee's flat to copy disks and documents. Munro said no. He didn't like the smooth and far too easily excused slide into outright criminality.

There was, after all, no evidence coming from the trawl through Pattie Lee's life. She'd tipped off Geo-Petro with a carefully placed lie, and that was it. But she was perfectly positioned to play the spy . . .

He called Pierce on the black telephone, his private line. "Do you also investigate fraud, Mr Pierce?"

"Ah – yes. It's our other speciality, in fact. Has, as it were, something come up?"

"Something has indeed come up. Might you be in a position to do some investigating abroad for us? Once again, we can handle the internal side of things, but our means are limited."

"Abroad? Yes – but it would be expensive. I should warn you in advance, Mr Munro, that a fraud investigation rapidly becomes *very* expensive indeed. Matters get so tangled, you understand."

"Could you start today?"

"*Today?*"

"Today, Mr Pierce."

"Yes – I suppose so. At a price. I mean – we could start getting people and things organised, that is. And, well, I'll need a thorough briefing."

"Meet me for lunch at my club. Twelve thirty."

"Ah – twelve thirty. Right."

He didn't like Pierce. He enjoyed giving the young man a surprise. People who exude assurances should be knocked off their feet now and then.

Munro returned to his own latest surprise, the fax from Mr Cavendish at the Securities and Investments Board. For the moment he would acknowledge receipt and express his willingness to set up a meeting at some future date. But the SIB would have to wait.

There were more important things to do, now that Michael was going to be out of the way on his circuit of the world.

NINETEEN

On Thursday morning Michael woke her early and rushed her through breakfast. He wanted to be at Wragby well before lunch. They drove north in Ruth's Golf: Randall Wild would be taking the Volvo and picking up a few things at Michael's cottage before continuing to Wragby.

Ruth drove. Her Golf had no phone, so Michael was

150

isolated from the web of his business world. He busied himself going over yesterday's weather data supplied by Orbis Air. He seemed very concerned about the Indian Ocean.

The night hadn't been so exciting. Michael wasn't interested in games. His mind, after a short interlude, was fixed on other things. Not surprising, really. If Ruth had been about to attempt the first non-stop solo flight round the world, and at the same time raise millions for Third World charities, thereby earning herself a publicity boost that would last the rest of her life – well Ruth, too, would have had trouble concentrating for very long on sex . . .

The resentment was still there, burning inside . . .

The arrival at Wragby Aerodrome was disappointing, with no press horde waiting in ambush at the gate. The whole place was quiet. They should have been shunting a queue of airliners through the maintenance hangars, now that summer and the holiday season were beginning. But a recession year wasn't good for scheduled air travel, it was a disaster for the charter business – and it was even worse for Orbis Air.

The show was inside the hangar where Angel was parked. A dozen men and women from Chester's team were crawling all over the aircraft. Chester, in dirtied white overalls, was running in circles as he checked every piece of work in progress. He stopped long enough to wave Michael into the hangar, then turned and stuck his head back inside the engine bay under the aircraft's tail.

Michael let the smile die quickly. "I believe they've set an office aside for me as a bedroom," he said to Ruth. "So that I don't have to sleep in the dormitory. I'll need a good night's sleep before take-off."

Ruth nodded. He was also announcing a night without her.

"Think I'll find it and dump my things. I want to get my laptop connected up so I'm back in touch with Pattie."

Ruth nodded again. Back in touch with his money, he meant.

John Coates was walking over from the crowd in the hangar,

wiping his hands on a rag. When he stepped into the sun that invaded the hangar door, Ruth could see the grease in his beard. It glistened in the light.

"John," Michael said. "How's it going?"

"Fine." John stuffed the rag in the pocket of his overalls. "Everything's going to be ready on time. The navigation program still has to be loaded into the computer."

"That's what I'm here for." Michael watched the work on the aircraft for a moment. The focus of the frenzy seemed to be following Chester Alby around. "How's Chester holding up?"

"Fine." John shrugged. "He's trying to do everything himself, but things seem to be staying on the rails."

"What mood is he in?"

"Oh, you know – really tense."

"Yes." Michael turned away from his Angel and its attendants. "Right. I'll go and look at my room. Did you lock the car, Ruth?"

Ruth just gave him the key. She watched him walk away towards the Trantair offices and the staff building beyond. Suddenly, she was back on the outside of his life. He lived it for himself. Just for himself.

"To tell the truth," John Coates said.

She looked at him. "What truth?"

"About Chester. In point of fact, he's screwed himself up into a hell of a mess. I don't mean his work's suffering, but he certainly is. Chester's long past having kittens, and well into shitting bricks."

Pierce phoned late lunchtime on the private line. "Mr Munro? I just thought I ought to tell you that the new business is under way. Are you sure it's appropriate to talk on this line?"

"I gave you the number on purpose, Mr Pierce."

"Yes. Quite. Well, the investigations in Buenos Aires and Cairo are on, as of today. We're going to be doing Los Angeles sort of by remote control from Tokyo, to start with."

Remote control. It seemed the taboo against probing the

secrets of a finance institution ended outside the UK. "You mean you're using someone in Tokyo to hack the computer at the Los Angeles bank?"

"Gosh, no! Well – not yet, anyway."

"I see."

"Ah – you do realise, don't you, that it's going to be some little time before we get anything substantive from these new approaches? One has to find the first thread before one can even think about picking it up, as it were."

"I do recognise the problem."

"Yes, I'm sure. Anyway, as to the other matter, I've just got the latest report on my desk. Hot news, as it were. Lee received a call from Tranter at her office at eleven fifty-two. It seems to have been routine business, letting her know his computer is accessible via its modem, et cetera. At eleven fifty-eight, she called her hairdresser and asked for an immediate appointment. She got one for two o'clock. Must say, I wish my hairdresser could be ordered about like that. She left your building at ten past one. She visited the Kowloon Crown International Bank, and she arrived at her hairdresser about ten minutes ago, which is where she is now. No obvious signs of taking up contact with anyone, I'm afraid."

"No. She seems to visit her hairdresser very frequently."

"A lot of women do, Mr Munro."

When he put down the phone, Munro started to wonder about connections that couldn't exist. Michael was a crook, and shipped his invisible money abroad. Pattie Lee was spying for someone else, and maintained close contact with a foreign bank with headquarters in Hong Kong. Michael was in a desperate hurry to fly off on his circuit of the world – almost as if Pattie Lee's hostile rumour, which had sparked off the sudden rush, had really been a blessing in disguise.

But there wasn't any ingredient he knew of that could be added to the mix to make it set into a sensible pattern. Which suggested that the pieces came from completely separate puzzles. There were no connections, behind the scenes, between the Chinese enigma with the seamless disguise, and the man who wore a Peter Pan costume over his supercrook suit.

Ripley buzzed him on the intercom. "Mr Munro? It's your return call from Sylvia Symes at Rowe Spitta Pitts."

TWENTY

Terri Sabuli arrived, and installed herself with fax and phones in one of the admin offices in the Trantair building. Ruth had borrowed Chester's office upstairs, with a view of the perimeter trees, and no sun through the windows while the afternoon was grilling the blank flatness of the aerodrome. She was going over the printed charts marking Michael's course round the world. She wasn't going to fly Angel, her role as backup pilot was a charade – but she should be ready all the same. Just in case God decided not to risk the competition any more, pointed a celestial finger, and Michael suddenly vanished without trace . . .

Michael and Terri walked in, carrying handfuls of faxes. Terri Sabuli was taller than Michael, but he was the one leaning close to her ear and saying something personal. They separated, innocently, when they saw Ruth seated behind the desk. Terri put her faxes on the desk, Michael moved up a chair from the drawing table. Terri smiled at Ruth.

Michael added his faxes to the rest of the pile. "Chester should be here in a minute." He pointed at the A4 chart segments Ruth had been studying. "Any problems, Ruth?"

"No," she said. "Not with the charts."

"Navigation," Terri said. "All great circles and funny angles and lots of sums. I'll stick to sweet-talking and arm-twisting."

Which of those, Ruth thought, would you most like to do with Michael?

154

Terri was wearing a grey checked blouse with great big sleeves rolled up to her elbows, and a tight black skirt that reached to mid-thigh. She decided to sit on the front corner of the desk. Her backside, as she placed it neatly, was perfectly smooth, with no ill-fitting seam underneath to spoil the exactness of the skirt's second skin. She crossed those long legs, wrapped in satin tights. If Michael went for Terri, Ruth wouldn't be able to compete. She wouldn't even try. She might kill Michael, though.

Chester walked in, still wearing his overall. Ruth, caught in possession of his chair, made a move to stand up.

"Want to sit here, Chester?" Michael said, tapping the back of the chair he'd brought from the drawing table.

Chester shook his head. "I'll stand."

So Michael sat down in the chair. He smiled at Ruth – saved you there. Then his gaze settled on Terri's legs where they disappeared, more or less, inside the hem of her skirt. Smiling and smiling at Ruth, but being a villain.

"Are those the forecasts?" Chester pointed at the faxes on his desk beside Terri's knee. The back of his hand was slicked with sweat, his neck and forehead were damp with a silvery sheen. It was a hot walk in the sun across the concrete to the Trantair building. It would be even hotter inside Angel's hangar.

"Just came through," Michael said. "No significant changes since this morning." He glanced at Ruth. "You don't mind if we do this now, do you?"

"No." She waved a hand vaguely over the charts. "I'd finished anyway."

"Good. Well, this is it. The moment of truth." He was staring at Terri Sabuli's stretched hem again. "Do we or don't we? Yes or no?"

"Angel will be ready." Chester sighed, a hot man wishing he could unload some of the heat. "She'll be ready."

"Good. And I can finish loading the program before the afternoon's out. Anything on your side, Terri?"

"Only good news." She folded her arms. The fabric of her

blouse was too loose to press against her breasts. It merely came closer, unbuttoned neck unfolding slightly, suggesting. Her act was a constant come-on, keep-off, and which of the two might I mean? "The local TV are sending a crew to cover the take-off, so there'll be pictures available for the nationals to use and foreigners to buy. Everything we need."

"Good." Michael smiled. He leaned forward, slowly, and lifted the pile of faxes from beside Terri's knee. His smile looked at Ruth for a moment. What did that mean? Don't worry, I'm not going to. Or yes, that's my next bed. Or simply: *I'm* flying, and not you. "Good," he said again, settling in the chair and starting to shuffle the forecast sheets. "Let's just recap this. First of all, Wragby. If I can find it."

"The top sheet," Terri said. "I put them in order, Michael."

"Unfortunately, I've mixed them up. Never mind." He pushed the sheets together again and propped them in his lap. "The essentials are – fine and humid tomorrow, sun in the morning, cloud during the afternoon, light wind from the east. But on Saturday, we're expecting thunderstorms coming up from the south and lasting all day."

"So," Chester said, "no take-off on Saturday."

"No. Sunday will be fine here, but going on Sunday would mean arriving in Florida on Monday, and doing the second take-off with a full load on Tuesday. But central Florida's going to be closed in with some rain and associated winds from Monday to Wednesday, and for the full-load take-off we need absolutely still air to have a chance. So we'd have to delay. But that would get us into the storms that are expected for the southern Rockies before next weekend, and then the following week there's a high probability of storms off the California coast. And what the weather will be like here by then is anybody's guess."

"So," Chester said. "If we don't go tomorrow, how big is the delay going to be?"

Michael shrugged. "Probably two weeks, possibly more. And that won't do."

156

"More sponsor problems," Terri said. "The quarterly figures are due soon, and apparently they aren't very good."

"I know." Chester didn't glare at her, but he let the feeling show. Terri was the perfectly dressed macho-tease mannequin and he was the one wearing overalls, but he had the rank. "I'm a director of Orbis Air and Orbis, as well as Trantair. I've seen the figures."

Terri shrugged.

Michael decided to wind it up. "Right. Tomorrow. That's fixed. Take-off at noon, and no changing our minds." He stood up and handed the faxes back to Terri. "I'll be getting on with installing the navigation program." He started for the door, then paused and turned. "Cheer up, Ruth. Whatever it is, it isn't going to happen."

Then he left.

"Well, then." Terri stood up. One pass of her hand straightened her skirt. It was an elegant gesture, but practical and slick. She didn't feel the need to perform for Chester, and Ruth didn't matter anyway. "I'd better get back to my sweet-talking and arm-twisting. If I've understood the set-up correctly, Chester, it's your job now to get onto Orbis Air and have them file all the flight plans for the American stage."

"Yes," he said.

"Well, I'll leave you to it." She glided in luscious strides to the door.

When Terri had gone, Ruth made a second attempt at vacating Chester's chair. He let her go through with it. Standing, she stacked the charts and moved them to the corner of Chester's desk – where Terri had been sitting. The woman left a lingering presence wherever she went, like a memory of touchable dreams.

A waste of energy to start hating her. Ruth decided to smile at Chester instead. "Could I help?"

"How do you mean?"

"Well – I could get onto Orbis Air for you. The flight plans are ready. I know what they are. Provisional permissions are already in, so – "

"I don't need your help. We don't need *you*."

That hurt her. It was anger, with a naked blade. She hadn't expected it, she didn't know what to do about it.

Chester had lifted his hand, and was pointing at her. "*You* don't have to do anything. Don't get in the way. You're no use. You're a dead weight."

"What? I'm *what*?" She didn't know what to do. She was facing a sudden rush of anger, like a wave about to break. It came out of a calm ocean, without any warning.

"You're a *fake*. You haven't got a hundredth of the skill and experience that's needed for a real backup pilot. You couldn't fly Angel. Nobody believes you could. You're just a dummy backup to cover the sponsor's requirements."

"I – "

"You're a *fake*! Don't pretend to me you aren't! You only got anywhere near the project by way of Michael's bed!"

She didn't know what to say. In Chester's office, standing behind Chester's desk, she was trapped by his stored-up hatred.

"You're *so* proud of yourself. You've slept your way into a cosy little job. All the perks from the boss. All that *heavy* work standing around and being an ornament. A television interview, playing at being somebody. The great Ruth Clifford. The intrepid pilot. The partner in Michael's life." Chester grinned. His grin was like a snake starting to strike. "And all the time. *All* the time. What you don't know about that dressed-up piece of cunt that was in here."

Ruth shook her head. She could feel the blood. The blade was slicing open the lies in her life. Cosy job. Perks from the boss like country cottages and luxury car rides. All that *so* important work in the public relations department, and then on the project. The kick of being on TV. Ruth Clifford, the want-to-be pilot, the isn't-going-to-be famous. Ruth Clifford, Michael's partner in life, his put-down, pushed-around, switched-on-and-off entertainment accessory. Ruth Clifford. So proud. The rich man's little lap-dog.

"*All* the time," Chester said. "Sleeping your way to a clever little life at Michael's side. You're so pleased with yourself you never even notice. All the time, he's also sleeping with *her*!"

"What?"

Chester nodded. "With *her*!" He kept on nodding. He turned away. He faced his own office door. There were sweat highlights on his cheek, on the back of his neck. He had his hands on his hips. There was a stain starting to show through his overalls under his arm. His head stopped nodding, down at the bottom of a movement, staring at the floor. "It's so fucking hot in that hangar. I need a drink. I'm going to get a drink." His head swivelled round to look at her. "Of water. *Just* water."

TWENTY-ONE

Michael disappeared in the evening. So did Michael's car, the Volvo 960 which Randall had driven up from London for him. Randall was still there, killing time with a paperback while everyone else who was free watched TV in the lounge of the staff building. Everyone else but Terri Sabuli. She'd disappeared, too.

Ruth wandered outside, where imperfect dark was coming down. She walked along the lines of cars, while the breeze rolled a perfume of grass, dense as silk, from the airfield. She went slowly past the Trantair block and along the apron to the hangar where Angel lived. Night's soft silence was creeping, waiting, under the trees on the perimeter. The television, the ten o'clock news, came very faintly from the open windows of the staff lounge. There were no lights in the Trantair block, just the security lamps on the corners. There was no illumination, no sound, further down the row of hangars and workshops. Right across the open airfield, a sliding glow too far away to hear, a security patrol was cruising. People, their interrupted work, and all of it isolated on the threshold of a summer night. It should have been one of those magic moments.

The access door, set in the sliding maw of the hangar, swung open and belched light. John Coates came out. Behind him, a silhouette in the doorway, Chester leaned aside – and the light vanished. Then Chester came out and closed the door. From the airfield edge of the apron, where the grass began, Ruth could hear the click of the lock turning. Angel's chastity was safe until tomorrow's flight.

John had started walking. Chester caught him up, and they went on towards the staff building. John said something she couldn't decipher, Chester didn't seem to answer. They were the last of the late team, they'd checked every screw, bolt, weld and resin bond on the aircraft. They walked away through shadow towards the lights, sounds of shoes on hard concrete in a velvet night.

When she looked across the dark arc of the airfield, even the security patrol had vanished from sight.

It came cruising down the approach road, bright headlights ploughing the fragile darkness. The Volvo glided behind the outer line of cars, strobing itself slowly through their windows and their side-panel reflections. It turned, engine whispering and tyres grumbling, and pulled into line at the end. The engine stopped.

After a minute, the headlights went out.

In the light coming across from the Trantair building, Ruth could see Michael in the driver's seat. The woman who got out on the opposite side was Terri Sabuli. Any kiss, any touch of hands, had taken place before the headlights died.

Terri hitched a white jacket over her shoulders. She walked away from the car, long legs, short skirt, jacket almost as long as her hemline. That was the assignation, the stolen fun, the last secret pleasure before the big adventure which began tomorrow. Now it was time to sleep. Terri walked towards the staff building and disappeared inside the door.

It must have been the soft shoe shuffle of the trainers instead of Terri's city heels. He didn't realise she was coming until she put a hand on the wide open door.

He was sorting compact disks. He dropped the ones that weren't stacked in his lap. He looked up at her from under the rim of the door. He got his breathing under control. He shook his head. "Have you been practising, Ruth? That's quite a heart-stopper."

She leaned on the corner of the open door. "Where have you been, Michael?"

"Test-driving the music." He'd sorted the CDs into two stacks between his thighs. "I'll leave the sounds of the moment for Randall, and take the classical with me in Angel." He started to slot half of the disks back in the rack behind the drive control lever.

"Which does Terri go for?" On the half-illuminated back seat, she could see neither condom wrapper nor any forgotten item of underwear. Anything as obvious as a blanket would be back in the boot by now.

Michael started to get out of the car. "In fact," he said, "we went along to the pub in the local village. There are half a dozen gentlemen of the press staying there tonight. Terri thought it might be an idea to warm them up with a nice little surprise."

"Did she?" Ruth stepped back to let Michael escape from the car. He smelled faintly but distinctly of pub. There was no trace of alcohol on his breath, but then he never drank when he drove – or when he was going to fly round the world the next morning. Terri's perfume, leaving the car with him, told no tales, not after they'd been driving together for a while.

They could have stopped on the way back, or taken a detour to Sherwood Forest now the day-trippers had gone. Did Michael pause to warm Terri up with something nice that by this stage in the liaison would be no surprise any more? Hot sex in the deep shadow under trees, back seat or blanket on the ground. She'd seen it all with Michael before, in the good old days two years ago, when their relationship was still new.

As Sylvia Symes had so cynically said, she was going to have nothing of her own to take with her when it was time to go.

The car door slammed gently and the locks clicked.

"I'll stow these aboard Angel." Michael waved the stack of disks in his hand. "Come on."

She followed him past the Trantair building, all the way back to the hangar. He walked in front of her. He was always ahead of her, always in the way.

Michael had a key. He unlocked the access door and swung it open, then stepped through. Heat, soaked up during the day and stored under the corrugated roof, oozed out into the cooler night like breath from a sleeping dragon's lair. Ruth followed him into the heart of darkness.

He switched on the gallery lights, the ones under the catwalk stretched across the far end, and along the underside of the rails for the gantry crane which ran the length of the hangar. The vault of the roof stayed in shadow. Angel, a matrix of high-gloss gleams on brilliant green, stood ready for Michael.

This lightweight dragon, with its foreplane blades and width of wings, didn't sleep.

Michael walked round the foreplane to the crew ladder, climbed two steps and reached in through the cockpit window with the music disks. First he brought the disks with the route program and loaded their data, now he brought the music, too. He and Angel would dance their way round the world.

Michael jumped down from the ladder, lightly. Look – no broken ankle, no possibility of a fall. "I can't resist checking the log. Make sure Chester's done all the last minute things." He turned and walked away under the wing. "Actually, I want to make sure it was all counter-signed by John. Chester's showing excessive signs of overwork at the moment, and I'd like to be certain someone was looking over his shoulder." He went past Angel's tail propeller and strolled to the foot of the stair which climbed the end wall. "We don't want Chester making some little mistake with big consequences, do we? It wouldn't do if I got halfway round the world – and then vanished without trace." He started to climb the steel stair. His footsteps echoed like a stirring of bats under the invisible roof "Well?" He raised his voice, and it bounced back from the walls and focussed on Angel, where Ruth stood. "Are you coming?"

Ruth walked round the aircraft. She walked right around the outstretched wing, avoiding its shadow. It was Michael's fallen Angel. He'd joked about calling it Lucifer. The evil's in the man who's going to fly it round the world for fame and glory. Bright Michael, turning somewhat bad.

There was a workshop at the back of the hangar, and a single office up above. Michael had reached the catwalk across the wall at the head of the stair, and was opening the office door. Ruth could see him from below, barely, through the catwalk grating. He was a hint of a presence up above the blinding lights.

She started to climb. The steep stair had open treads and a tubular handrail on the exposed side. There was no handrail on the side bolted to the bare wall. The climb up the stair was an ascent into layers of heat.

She paused on the tiny landing, halfway up, a break in the stair where one person could wait and let another pass. She looked down on Angel, from the propeller at the tip of the short tail, over the wide shoulders of the wings, past the cockpit roof to the long nose which pointed at the doors. Ruth thought up the idea, the idea was made flesh in GRP and solid state electronics, and Michael took it for his own. Now, in this last private place, before he disappeared for a week and then returned wrapped in an armour of greatness, before he moved on to a new slice of his egomaniac life that extended beyond Ruth's use-by date – now would be the time to tell Michael what she thought of him.

She climbed the noisy and shadow-netted stair, through the ceiling of light and into the darker heat of the roof.

Michael was in the office that opened off the catwalk. It had a curved and corrugated ceiling, shelves and filing cabinets filled the undersized side walls. He was reading the log by the lamp standing on the pair of desks in the middle. The office window in the end wall was open wide. From the vault of the hangar behind her, a silent sigh of air flowed through the door, the office, the window on the night. It was an exhalation of pent-up heat. I've had enough. I've decided not to take any more.

"Everything in order." Michael closed the log. When he turned, the desk lamp divided his face – half bright, and half shadowed with a gleaming eye. The man you see. The man you don't. "Are you going to tell me what's wrong, Ruth?"

She leaned in the doorway, with a darkness behind her which floated on light. "I know about you and Terri. Where did you do it this evening – in the car, or flat on a blanket in the woods somewhere? How does she like it? What does she do for you?"

"Oh, come on, don't be crude." He switched off the desk lamp, and became shaded Michael by indirect light. All of the man you never quite see. "After all, you and I don't do it much any more, so why on earth shouldn't I do it with someone else? And why don't you, if you're feeling frustrated?"

He came towards the door. "There's no pressure on you, Ruth. Your job isn't in danger. I wouldn't dream of doing anything nasty, you know."

He slipped past her in the doorway. So close, and not a touch.

Ruth turned to face the breath of heat from the hangar. It's over. I followed him here to have my say, and he's smothered it at birth with his own announcement. I was going to dump him, but instead he's dumped me. Michael always wins. Clever Michael can never lose.

It's *over*.

She stepped out on the steel catwalk and slammed the door. The sound boomed back and forth in the hollow hangar.

The air under the roof was suffocating. It was thick with the stored-up sweat of the sun, soured by an engineering incense of oils and solvents, lubricants and coolants. It had trapped the rising prayers of preparation. The roof's flat shadow sat like a translucent layer of melted fudge on top of a filling

of light which covered the core of this Angel cake. The
gallery lamps, below her feet and shining downwards from
under metal shades, inverted space and turned perceptions
upside down.

It's over. He told her it's over.

Michael had paced the catwalk gratings to the head of
the stair. He turned on his heel on the first step. Lit from
below, as he looked up at her his face received a footlight
glow of inside-out shadows like a demon king. Below him,
wings spread wide and waiting in the light, was his Lucifer.

He had his hand on the tubular rail. "You're not exactly
a secure, or self-confident, or successful person, are you,
Ruth?"

Precisely, he was slitting her throat with the razor of his
own easy achievement.

Time to open the gate a fraction, time to let out some of the
flood that's choked up inside. "At least," she said, "I'm honest.
I'm not a criminal. Your success makes me *sick*. You've done it
with *lies*."

The lies whispered round the hangar and sank into the
light.

He stood there in his web of darkness on the see-through
stair, and slowly smiled. "The salient point, Ruth, is merely
and simply that I have indeed done it. I'm successful."

She stepped forward on the rattling grids. "You're a
criminal. You're a cheat and a liar and a *fake*. You're an
utterly selfish bastard! You're a *crook*!"

He held up his hands, open and innocent, catching the
flock of echoes. "I know, Ruth. I know. I do know exactly
what you're talking about. But I doubt you know very much
about it. And I'm not going to waste my time enlightening
you." He turned away again and started down the treads of
his steep and shadow-netted stair. "Who's been telling you
things? Is Bob Munro starting to stir at last, my Iago, my
Mark Anthony with his own conspiracy?"

She came to the top of the stair.

"I assume you understand the Shakespearian allusions,

Ruth? Has good old Bob been telling you things? Persuasive little facts he's filtered just for you?" Michael stopped. He half-turned, away from the wall. His right hand came across and joined his left hand on the rail. He looked over his shoulder, up at her. He was standing in a mesh of metal shadow grids. "You know he's setting you up for something, don't you? Not that it matters."

"Doesn't it," she said in a hiss that sizzled like heat under the roof, "matter?"

"No." He turned away, beginning his next step down from the dizzying, tempting height. "From now on it won't matter to me in the slightest, though I'm not about to tell – "

He missed the tread in the sieve of light, and stumbled.

He started to topple.

Ruth stepped down into the criss-cross web.

Michael began to roll against the rail. His left hand came free. The rail sang like a muffled bell. The stair jangled.

Michael's right arm stretched out. His right hand, holding the rail, folded over at the wrist.

Ruth missed the indecipherable treads. She bounced off her backside and skidded down towards him.

The stair clattered and the hangar hoarded the sounds.

Michael was losing. Halfway down to the useless little landing, pivoting on an inverted grip in upside-down light, he was swinging out over the cascade of steel treads.

His fingers were unwrapping and his right hand coming free.

His left arm flailed through the air and smashed into the cement block wall.

She was rushing down the clamouring stair.

His face was staring at her, frozen with a slow panic.

His right hand, wrist upturned, was holding by its sliding thumb.

Hard noise and harsher light waited to swallow him.

The fingers of his left hand, scraping cement, found a joint between the blocks.

He hovered on the shuddering, reverberating stair on the threshold of his fall.

Ruth wasn't going to get to him in time . . .

TWENTY-TWO

Sylvia Symes closed her dessert menu and placed it flat in front of her on the tablecloth. "I know what's wrong. No table decoration. You need a candle for ambience, or flowers for friendliness."

Munro looked up from his own menu. There was nothing on the white cloth except their glasses of wine. "If you recall, this was an all-male club until a few years ago. I think the oldest hands would have viewed friendliness by candlelight with some misgivings. We have to preserve some of the club traditions."

"You have no sense of the romantic, Robert Munro. Talking of which – and do forgive the touch of bitchy glee – should I gather, from something you said in passing, that my successor as Michael's playmate and laundry maid is finally getting the message? Does the little girl know where his attentions are directed yet?"

"I've no idea." He was trying to select a dish. He didn't want to gossip about Michael's sex life. The purpose of the meal was to set something entirely different in motion.

"Oh well, I suppose when Michael chooses to use his charm – and his *disarming* act of private vulnerability – he's capable of running a whole stable of women. I'm sure he'll still be keeping it up with Pattie Lee."

That made him forget the menu. "Pattie Lee?"

"Oh, yes. That had the hallmark of a buzz which thrived on perfect secrecy and a regime of what you might call punctuated abstinence. Business trips, and probably only

167

very rarely between times. I mean, he was doing it with her for most of the five years he was doing it with me, but the opportunities were somewhat limited. With tight rationing, the thrill should last."

"Wait a minute. Are you sure? Michael and Pattie Lee have – or had – something going between them?" He was thinking about the reports Pierce had been supplying. There was no out-of-hours contact between Michael and his PA except for business calls. There had been nothing going on behind office doors, because Michael hadn't been seen at the MT building except for a few meetings since the rush to finish his crazy project began.

Sylvia shrugged. "I caught them in the act. They needed some papers in a hurry, so I couriered them out. I arrived unannounced. Michael and his oriental personal computer were on a trip to Argentina, you see." She glanced over Munro's shoulder. "Here comes our waiter, by the way. When I walked in the room, it wasn't her disk drive he was interfacing."

Simpson, the waiter, arrived. "Are you ready to order pudding, sir, madam?"

Sylvia patted the menu. "The strudel with vanilla sauce – is it really a vanilla sauce, served cold, or just custard by another name?"

"Vanilla sauce, madam. Served cold."

"Very well then. Do you like strudel, Robert?"

He didn't. "I'll have the sorbet platter, Simpson."

"Very well, sir." Simpson removed the menus. "Without biscuits, as usual, sir?"

"Thank you. As usual." He was thinking: Michael and Pattie Lee? It would mean the woman had her hand on his company secrets, his business secrets – and everything else. She had Michael over a barrel. Sylvia Symes was supplying another rope to tie Michael down. "Tell me," he said, "more."

"If you insist." Sylvia twisted round and unhitched her bag from the back of her chair. "You don't mind, do you?

If I smoke. Some ex-smokers get so aggressive about it. It's allowed in the dining room, isn't it?"

"It's allowed," he said.

"Good." She produced a cigarette from her bag. "That was when our break-up row finally erupted. Very cathartic, and very terminal for me." She handled the cigarette with a quick delicacy, sliding the paper through her fingertips and then caressing it between her lips. "That woman just sat there." She struck flame from a silver lighter. "On the bed." She drew the fire into the cigarette. "While I learned from Michael how they'd been running their bloody affair, and how she was going to take over as his business assistant." The lighter disappeared back into the bag. "It's little advancements like that which explain why Pattie Lee is so totally and *hermetically* loyal to Michael."

Except, Munro thought, for the spying thing.

Simpson reappeared. He set spoons and forks, then topped up the wine. The smoke from Sylvia's cigarette streamed thinly towards Simpson's face. Simpson didn't like it.

Sylvia sighed. The merest trace of smoke came back with her breath. "Funnily enough, I'm sure that for some reason Michael is equally loyal to Pattie Lee. Don't ask me what it is. Perhaps they know some secrets about each other. But I'll bet it's still going on, every now and then, behind everyone's backs." She held her cigarette up like an incense stick, and glowered at it. "I got out with shares and a lump sum and a transferable chunk of the pension. I had a good salary for five years – though I earn much more now. But the best thing Michael ever did for me was that he stopped me smoking. It didn't exactly fit his all-green image. I started again when he kicked me out. Never been able to stop since."

Munro sipped his wine. He didn't want to hear about private pain behind Sylvia Symes's tough exterior. That wasn't the point of the plot. "How do you feel about my proposal, Sylvia?"

She drew on her cigarette, she breathed smoke through

her nose. "You're thinking I'd like to take my revenge." She watched the cloud of smoke disperse. "You're right."

"It would also enable me to make the adjustments needed to MT-Orbis before any more damage is done. That's good for your clients, and for you as an investor. At the moment, Michael won't let me do anything."

"I appreciate the point. Will Geoffrey Simmington play?"

Munro nodded. "He owes me a favour. And his consortium gets to do its business this way."

"And you're sure this isn't a bad time?"

"It's a very bad time. But Michael has the company sewn up. It could take me another ten years to get enough of my own people in to break his grip. MT-Orbis might not last ten months if things continue as at present."

"Why is Michael letting his company go down?"

"I haven't the faintest idea."

"I see." She contemplated her cigarette again, a little fire worm trickling smoke. "So you're in a hurry, and this is the only opportunity that's going to come along. While he's out of the way in his bloody aeroplane for a week. Have you got *any* leverage to use against him? How are you going to pull it off?"

"I've got some leverage." He had enough, all being well, to start the process rolling. It should gain him temporary power. Success would depend on making changes fast enough to have forced a standoff by the time Michael came back from his trip round the world – a stunt which he couldn't very well abandon in mid-circuit in order to rush back to his office. Michael's absence at the start of play was the key. "I was hoping you might supply me with more."

"You were?"

"Last time we met, you said that Michael has a dark past. You also mentioned computer applications."

Sylvia Symes smiled. "So you were paying attention after all. I don't suppose you've actually got some evidence that Michael runs what you might call extramural financial activities?"

Munro shook his head. He wasn't going to tell her the

170

cards in his hand. She might already be involved in some move against the company, might be hoping to use him in a scheme to help someone else do the ruining of Michael. "What about his past?"

"Well now, wouldn't it be nice to know?" She paused as Simpson reappeared. He put a little glass ashtray on the cloth beside her place setting. She flicked ash into it. "It's all before my time. Michael only ever had one good business idea of his own."

"And what was that?"

"His marketing strategy with Siltech. He founded the company when he was twenty-two. He managed to get it off the ground so fast because Siltech software came as a full PC and MS DOS compatible range, but it also had something extra. It took *security* seriously, had lots of it, and mostly as a no-cost option. Higher grade customised security was also on offer. Security conscious users lapped it up. Of course, eventually IBM and the other big boys caught on to the need and the advantage disappeared, so Siltech was just running on market momentum by eighty-four, when I got mixed up with Michael. Since then we've had the downturn and collapse of hardware and software sales, and only the big outfits have the fat to survive. Not Siltech."

"You're saying his big idea was to provide systems supplying a high level of security ahead of the competition?"

"Yes. And it was brilliant. All the green stuff he's got into since then is just packaging, but that first idea had substance. It was intrinsic to the product. But the big question." She paused, and tapped more ash from her cigarette. "The big question is, how did a bloke who's really not very good at running businesses – I mean, look at his recent record of failures, which he's been getting away with because of his wizz-kid reputation. Look at the fact that he's had to bring you in to organise things, and has still managed to meddle, obstruct and mess things up."

Munro nodded. "The big question?"

She drew on her cigarette, took it out of her mouth and

sucked in the smoke. "Where did he get the inspiration about computer security? Where did he get the money to set up Siltech? How did he manage to buy his airline? How did he get the personal money he pumped into it until he'd turned it into what was, until recently, the very successful Orbis Air? Where did the personal start-up cash for all his green projects come from? Why is Michael so rich?"

"The conventional answer is that Michael is a financial genius."

"But I've already told you he isn't. I ran his affairs. I know. He has masses of experience, he's expert at running the manipulations involved in deals. But he *doesn't* have the flair to read the market. And if he was relying on luck, half the time he'd fall flat on his face."

"So?"

"So – I'm sure, after five years of watching him work, that he's done it by insider dealing. He's had inside knowledge from somewhere. But it isn't the kind of insider dealing you can trace, with contacts and meetings, and people who'll plea bargain by telling you what they told him in return for a lighter sentence. He's done it all by himself from the *inside* of the inside."

"Meaning?"

"Meaning he hacks computers. He can find out anything another company knows about its own affairs. He was a teenage computer enthusiast when the very first PCs were coming on the market. He started getting rich through share deals while he was still at university. In those days there was no such thing as computer security because no one knew about the risk. For someone like Michael it was an open door. And once he got going, he could crack any Siltech-secured system that he'd sold to anyone else. I *know* he did because of the correlations with companies where he made spectacular share deals. Talk about Trojan horses and that Latin thing – *quis custodiet ipsos custodes*. Michael is fundamentally bent. Oh – and our pudding, as you call it here, is on its way."

Simpson put the strudel in front of Sylvia and the sorbet

selection in front of Munro. He set down a silver sauce boat on a separate plate, and ladled white vanilla sauce over Sylvia's strudel while she was grinding out her cigarette.

"I didn't warn you, by the way, Robert. If you ring me at home the odds are I won't be there, but Malcolm's bound to be in."

"Malcolm?"

"My toyboy." She glanced up at Simpson, but he didn't seem to have reacted. "He eats all my food and I exploit all his excess energy. Thank you, Simpson."

"My pleasure, madam."

Munro watched Simpson leave again, then turned to Sylvia. "You wouldn't have any proof, by the way?"

She shook her head. "I did think of it. When I got back from Buenos Aires I went to the offices to copy any disks I could get hold of. I was a full day ahead of Michael, because he had to stay for the meeting he'd lined up there. But the bastard sent Pattie Lee back only one flight behind me. Before I knew it, my office was locked and they'd relieved me of all my keys. That woman checked every item I cleared from my desk. They gave me fifteen minutes to get out. Not bad, eh?"

"Pretty harsh." The personal hurt was surfacing again. He didn't want to know. He didn't go round crying about the divorce, so he wasn't going to listen to other people's tears. Business was what he'd decided life should be about. He studied his ring of sorbet spheres, trying to decide where to start.

"Michael knew what I might know, and what I'd go looking for. That's why he got rid of me, of course."

Munro nodded. Across the dining room, Simpson was coming back again.

"One of my great regrets, Robert, is that I didn't get any proof. If I'd had anything on him, I'd have used it to nail his balls to the floor." Sylvia glanced up as Simpson arrived. "I mean that figuratively, of course."

"Excuse me, madam, sir. There's a telephone call for you, sir. It seems it's rather urgent. Would you care to come to the porter's desk?"

Munro left his sorbet and Sylvia and her strudel. He left the dining room and went to the desk beside the oak-panelled outer door. The porter pointed to the three telephone booths in the hall. "It's a call from Wragby Aerodrome, sir. You can take it in number one."

"Thank you, Willis." He went into the booth, closed the concertina door behind him, and lifted the phone. Wragby meant the project, some new and infuriating thing about Michael's project. A little click opened the line. "Munro."

"Terri Sabuli," said the voice at the other end. "There's been an accident. A bad one."

TWENTY-THREE

Terri Sabuli hung the phone on its hook. The next step. What's the next step? Stay calm, stay cool, and work out the next thing to do. There's nobody else in charge but you.

Chester came running through the main door. It slammed off the wall and started swinging closed. Chester went careering past her towards the stairs.

"Chester? Is there something new?"

"Blanket!" He was already pounding up the stairs. "I'm getting a blanket!"

So somebody else was thinking – up to a point. The next thing to do is . . . Get identifications, medical cards, anything the hospital might be able to use.

She ran for the stairs and followed Chester.

Terri didn't follow him to the dormitory. She turned the other way, past the toilets. Someone was being sick in the men's. Some people couldn't take the sight of blood. Funny – having the decorum to come all this way back from the hangar and find a toilet before throwing up . . .

She went into the office where Michael was camping out.

174

She couldn't find the light. She stumbled over something yielding and half-empty – his overnight bag. The desk was pushed right up to the window, with the desk lamp silhouetted against the glow from the security light on the Trantair building. She switched on the lamp. The thing she was leaning over was a laptop computer with its screen folded open, a modem plugged into it, and the phone bedded into the sleeves of the modem. A computer was no use.

A bed had been wheeled in from the dormitory and wedged between the door and the filing cabinet. The bed was made, and unused. A mark on the blanket showed where Michael had sat on it. Some clothes were folded neatly on the chair – underwear on top of an Orbis-green flying outfit. Most of Michael's stuff was on the desk next to the computer. The overnight bag lay open where she'd kicked it aside. It had handles, a shoulder strap, and buckles.

She looked at her ankle. There was a hole in her tights. That was the second pair of the evening. The first pair got slightly damaged in the back of Michael's car. Large or small, everything in contact with Michael was suddenly coming to grief.

She checked the desk. Beside the laptop was a stack of high-density disks. The top disk was labelled NAV PROG 1. There were more disks inside a plastic box. She wasn't looking for disks.

The phone rang. Once.

The laptop beeped.

The screen-on light glowed. At the top corner of the LCD screen, words wrote themselves: Modem Port. Underneath, the DOS prompt appeared and blinked. Then it hopped down a line at a time as something came in over the phone.

```
MTPOSTMT: MESSAGE FROM MTPOSTPL
LOAD MICTRAXX
DECRYPT ON
"CONFIRM STARTED WITHOUT TRACE, PL"
KEYLOCK
STORE
```

175

The screen went blank, the light went off, the phone went dead.

Terri stared at the thing. It must have been a message from Pattie Lee, always attached by an informational umbilical to the man at the centre of the universe – all incomprehensible codes and security routines devised by the one-time computer genius to protect his financial secrets. Well the message wasn't going to mean much now. Not without Michael to make sense of it.

She scrabbled through the disks, pens, empty notepad on the desk. She started to poke in the shadowy inside of the bag that had bitten her tights. When she got to the shaver and the Antaeus bottle it began to seem like a dead end. When she found a condom it reminded her of his wallet.

His wallet would still be with him in the hangar. That was where everything should be.

Like Chester, she was thinking right but at panic revs – screeching a gear and then stamping on the clutch before she got very far. The best action had been phoning Munro. He'd be here in the morning, and then she wouldn't be in charge any more.

There'd be nothing left to take charge of, anyway. The egomaniac rationale behind the project had evaporated. The whole thing was off. The showbiz distraction was dead. Economic reality was going to take over. With Munro running things, the clamp-down and the lay-offs would begin. It would have been nice – it would have been very nice – to have not only a successfully set up but also a successfully *completed* circus like this on her record by the time MT-Orbis began shedding staff. Because that's what Munro would start to do. As Michael had said, Munro had a plan.

She left the office. She didn't waste time on the light.

Terri ran easily, all the way from the staff building, past Trantair, to the hangar. She ran past Michael's Volvo at the end of the last line of cars. It shouldn't upset her.

But it did.

An hour ago, under the trees inside the perimeter, she was coming down through a dark glow in the back of Michael's car. It was a private buzz after the professional bonus of her blitz on the newspaper people whiling away the evening at the pub. Michael made a rewarding subject to work for. He was so good at such things – charming the tails off the cynical press, or performing all the way up to a woman's best expectations. He positively invited you to try fucking the boss. An hour ago she was still coming down from her orgasm astride Michael's thighs, eyes closed in self-congratulation, head tipped aside under the roof, feeling him reduce inside her, feeling his hands gently squeezing her hips under her hitched-up skirt – letting her know he was aware, too, of her pleasure, an attentive partner spreading cream on the sexual cake.

She had no trace of an emotional tie to Michael Tranter. She could use him as smoothly, charmingly and entirely selfishly as he would use her. But it was a shock just the same.

She slowed as she reached the hangar. She stopped running as she got to the door where all the light leaked out. John Coates was there, staring past her down the length of the night.

"Have you called an ambulance?"

"I've called – " She heaved at a stabilising breath, the way she would in the gym. "An ambulance."

"There's no sign of it yet."

"It's a long way." She stepped through the door. She tugged her jacket back into place on her shoulders. She marched past the dayglo-green aeroplane. A waste of time and money, now.

Michael lay at the foot of the catwalk stair. Randall Wild was helping Chester tuck a blanket round him. They were a pair of black men tending their fallen god, their injured little Nelson, white of race and whiter of face. Ruth Clifford was kneeling behind Michael's head, holding it in her hands. Those hands were bloody, leaving stains in his hair. Someone else was gathering together the erupted contents of the hangar's first aid box. A Trantair man was holding Michael's lost shoe, not knowing what to do.

"Don't lift his shoulder!" Ruth was yelling at Chester, and Chester was moving out of reach as if his fingers had been burned. "Don't *move* him! In case he's got a spine injury. Don't move him! Leave it till the professionals get here. *Right?*"

Chester went back to patting the blanket in place. Randall got delicate, too.

Ruth Clifford knew what she was doing. She didn't panic. That was a surprise. She must have had first aid training for the fieldwork with World Assist. She'd dealt with Michael's left arm. She'd pressed wads of gauze in place below his elbow, where the bone was sticking out and the blood was running in a bright red flow. Now the arm was smothered in bandages, with a long-handled pipe wrench for a splint. The bandages were red, but there wasn't much more blood on the floor. The blood was starting to soak into the edge of the blanket. It was soaking into the concrete, too.

So, Terri thought. What do I do? I stand out a mile. I'm so tall, I'm so brown. I don't fit anywhere. I make the most of it. I keep myself beautiful, dress myself stunning, make African artwork of my hair. I make a *focus* of myself. Attention, expectation, envy and desire always turn to me. That's power. The penalty is – I stand out a mile. I'm too tall. I'm too brown.

But I'm always better organised. "Chester, get the blanket folded down. Check he's still got his wallet."

Chester stared at her.

"His driving licence, medical insurance, any drug allergies, blood group – it's all going to be in his wallet."

Chester still stared.

"The hospital can use it all. Check his wallet!"

Chester got the message. Chester started folding his loving blanket aside.

"Lucifer," Michael said. His eyes were closed. "Angel. Bloody fallen Lucifer, too."

Ruth moved a hand to stroke his forehead. "It's all

right, Michael. It's all right." Her fingers smeared blood on his skin.

Terri looked at the steel stair, which disappeared steeply into the dazzle of the lights. "He really fell down those stairs? Down *all* those stairs?"

Ruth nodded. She didn't look up. "He rolled over that little landing thing, then he caught his arm between the treads. I heard the bone break. The stair was going like a bell and the whole place echoing. But I heard the bone break."

"Christ." The thought of such a sound closed scissors round her own arm. "How bad is it?"

"Compound. Multiple. Both bones just below the elbow." Ruth was holding Michael's head in both hands again, her fingers reaching under his neck. "But it won't kill him or cripple him. A broken back, broken neck, internal bleeding, a haemorrhage inside his skull – that will."

"Yes." She looked at Chester. He'd got the wallet and was checking its contents. There was another thing she had to decide.

Faintly, a siren sounded. That would be the ambulance, most of a mile away at the gate. The siren stopped again.

Somebody had to go with Michael in the ambulance. It might be going anywhere – Nottingham, Sheffield, Lincoln. Whoever went with him would be stranded. "Randall – you take Michael's car and follow the ambulance when it leaves. Understand? Check with them where they're going in case you get separated on the way."

"Okay." Randall was folding the blanket over Michael's chest again. "Shouldn't somebody be in the ambulance with Mike?"

"Exactly. I'm just sorting out who."

"I'll go." Ruth was watching Michael's eyes as they moved behind his lids. His mouth twitched. The fingers of his right hand tapped Chester's shoe. "I'll go with him."

"You'll stay here."

"I said – *I'll* go."

"No. I've been talking to Munro." It was her own decision,

179

but she'd blame it on Munro. The woman was the type to do what a man said. "He says you stay here."

"I'll go!"

"Bloody end," Michael said. "Angel. Lucifer."

Ruth leaned over him. "It's all right, Michael. It's all right now. It's all right."

The ambulance siren howled again, much nearer and getting louder. "It's here!" John Coates yelled from outside.

"Let me go." Chester was holding up the wallet.

Terri snatched the wallet. "You also stay here. John!" She turned away from their broken Michael. At the other end of the hangar, under Angel's wing, she could see blue highlights flashing on the frame of the open door. "*John!*" The siren was trying to shout her down. "You're going with Michael in the ambulance!"

John waved. The siren stopped. The lights didn't.

"Bloody over," Michael muttered. "Without trace."

Part 5

Florida Sunrise

TWENTY-FOUR

Munro stayed overnight at his club, left at first light for the MT building, picked up his car and drove north. He was past St Albans before the sun blared up over his bonnet to blind him.

He got to Wragby in time for a seven-thirty breakfast. It wasn't much of a meal, though the coffee was tolerable if you didn't pay it too much attention. The rich smell in the canteen helped disguise the coffee: the last decade of the twentieth century, and half the people still ate a breakfast fried in a sea of fat. But the biggest distraction had nothing to do with food.

"I have to know," Terri Sabuli said. She wasn't eating. She was far too busy checking back and forth through a pad full of notes. It was the first time he'd ever seen her looking even slightly less than perfect. "We're scheduled for a take-off at noon. We have to expect the press to start arriving in an hour or two. By eleven the TV people will be here. If I'm cancelling them, I have to start phoning now." She turned to look at Ruth Clifford, who was sitting alone at the next table. Ruth had her elbows on the table and her face buried in her hands. "So – I do have to know."

"I know." Munro pushed his plate out from under his nose. Sliced white bread like floppy sponge rubber, so altogether English and the last thing he expected to find in Michael's green-tinged empire. "Let's summarise. The aircraft's ready?"

"Yes," Chester Alby said. He wasn't eating, either. He was

183

leaning back in his chair, nursing a mug of tea. He still looked stunned, as though his best friend had died. "But so what?"

"And the weather," Munro went on. "It's good, but only today. Tomorrow it's bad, and then there are problems further along the route. The next window won't be for two or three weeks. Right?"

Terri Sabuli nodded. "Now – or who knows when."

Munro nodded. He looked at his coffee, with its last gasp of powdery steam. No new take-off window for two or three weeks. Two or three *days* in which to make an unhurried decision would have been what he needed. But two weeks was too long, and three would leave it too late. By then the quarterly figures would be out, and this time he wouldn't be able to bully Geo-Petro or any other of Michael's sponsors back into the fold. The project would collapse. Coupled with the miserable figures, that might start the ground going under MT-Orbis. Which mattered very much. He glanced at Ruth, head in hands. No one would lose basic confidence in MT-Orbis if they tried the project, and failed . . .

Especially if they didn't have a pilot. At least, not their star pilot.

"She couldn't do it," Chester said. "She never could. She might get as far as Florida, but she'd give up in the face of the real thing."

As far as Florida might do. As far as Hawaii would be even better – it would bring in some money to offset the millions the project had cost. By then they could invent mechanical failure or pilot fatigue. Any excuse for calling it off – just as long as it was too late for a sponsor to quit, and take the confidence with him. Then by the time the quarterly figures appeared, the project would already be a thing of the past.

"John phoned," Chester said. "They're operating on Michael's arm this morning. They're going to have to put pins and callipers in it. It's going to be months. He won't be flying for a year at least. Cancel the whole thing."

Munro didn't answer. Michael was the other matter. Michael was going to be out of the way for a while, after all. Not everything had gone entirely wrong. A big distraction for a few days, for as long as Ruth Clifford could keep flying, might be a help. Most people would be looking in the wrong direction . . .

"Cancel it." Chester put his mug on the table. "Cancel it."

Munro looked at Terri. "Has Michael got any other injuries?"

She shrugged. "Bruises everywhere. Concussion. Too early to say if that's going to have lasting effects. But no skull fracture, no spinal injury, no internal injury. They can't tell us more yet. He went to just about the biggest hospital in Sheffield, but they still run on a skeleton staff during the night."

"I see." He turned to Ruth Clifford at the next table. "I'll leave it up to you, Ruth."

Her head moved. She peered over a tent of fingers. Her eyes looked – angry.

Yes, he thought, I passed the buck. I can, so for once I damn well did. This whole thing is a sideshow – thought up, two years ago, by you – and I'm not going to waste another minute worrying about it. "This isn't the military," he said. "I'm not going to order you to do something which might involve risking your life, if you're not up to it. You're free to decide."

Ruth moved her gaze to Chester Alby. She put her hands down flat on the table. Slowly, she pushed herself upright. All the time, she stared at Chester.

Chester began to have trouble staring back.

Ruth smiled a bitter little smile. Chester, the gesture said, you're beaten already and it's a waste of time staring you down. In a slow movement, she pushed back her chair and stood up straight. She looked at Munro again. "Chester thinks I can't do it. Terri thinks she's taking over from me anyway. And you don't care one fucking bit. It's up to me, is it?"

Munro nodded. "It's up to you."

"Well, then." She looked at her watch. "Quarter to eight.

I think I'll drive to the hospital and check how Michael is. Let's see – here to Sheffield and back, with some time there. I should be back at Wragby by eleven. I'll let you know then." She started to turn away, then paused. "Oh yes, nearly forgot. Get Randall to bring John Coates back from the hospital *now*. If Chester's left in charge of Angel, without John to keep tabs on him – then I certainly won't fly. See you."

Ruth drove west until she picked up the M1, then headed north. One exit later, she'd changed her mind. Going to see Michael was a waste of time. If he wasn't undergoing his operation, he'd certainly be sedated. There was nothing to say to him anyway. The words failed to get said in the heat in the hangar, and then the catastrophe happened instead. The world was a different place now. Talking to Michael wasn't going to matter until there was something entirely new to say.

Looking at Michael – lying in the hospital, cleaned up, bandaged, hooked to a drip – was pointless, too. She'd seen him last night at the foot of the stair. She'd touched his bone. She got his blood on her hands. Looking at Michael wouldn't tell her anything new. The image from last night was always going to be there. Always.

So she stopped at the services. She phoned ahead. If she was going to talk to anyone about a big decision, if she had no lover, no special friends, no confessor of her own choosing – well who else should she turn to but the man who dominated her life from the very start? Never mind his contempt. Forget her own disappointment, turned to hatred. It wasn't logical. It was probably a bad idea. The decision was hers alone. But talking to her father would break the silence of years. And telling him she had the chance to be famous, and after that very probably rich, might earn his respect. At last.

She left the motorway at Catcliffe, and drove the dual carriageway deep into Sheffield's valley, right down to the mounded roundabout that was big enough for a Norman castle and most of its village. She'd missed the morning rush-hour, and the drive up through the city centre was

186

smooth and fast. Uphill all the way. She went past the lower side of the university zone. She went past the great slab of the Hallamshire Hospital, where Michael would be trapped in his anaesthetic dreams. She drove the steep climb to Broomhill, and on up to Crookes. The narrow main road over the top of the ridge was already choked as shopping got under way. She turned right, and drove down into the streets of terraces on the slope of Commonside.

Mellors Road was a dead-end, cut off crudely by a blank brick wall taller than the gutters of the last house in each row. Above the wall were the back yards of the houses in the next street up the hill. Ruth drove to the end and turned round between Skodas and Yugos and rust-trimmed Capris. She cruised down the slope again and pulled in behind an ancient Ford Princess parked with its nearside wheels on the pavement. The pavement still had a flat kerb of real stone, and cracked paving slabs patched with asphalt. She switched off the engine and got out of her Golf. Mellors Road was a silence between two rows of windowed brick, with a warm July wind blowing the morning scent of a dusty, busy city.

The Princess was the car her mother drove. She used to drive a Toyota which was replaced new every year. Her father had driven a Jag, that out-of-date car still seen as a prestige symbol by the risen working class. Now her father didn't drive at all. Hilda Jane and John Thomas Clifford – they went up in the world, and then dropped down again. They fell a very long way.

Terri Sabuli dodged the press at ten forty-five. She left them to the people on her team, and escaped to the secretive area of the hangar. Chester was in charge of the work, exchanging the cockpit seat for the made-to-measure version fitted for Ruth. John Coates had arrived and was following Chester's moves, discreetly. At the back of the hangar, at the foot of the stair, there was a brown bloodstain on the floor.

Terri thought the car might be Munro, too executive proud

to walk the distance to look for her. She went out through the hangar doors and into the sun of the morning.

Ruth was standing by the open door of her green Golf. She looked as though a murder had just been attempted – of her.

Bad news, Terri thought. Very bad. "How's Michael?"

"I've no idea."

That was a surprise. At least it meant Michael hadn't died on the operating table. "Have you been to the hospital?"

"No."

"Oh." Great, she thought. Bloody well joy-riding for three hours while I sweat it out, stalling the press on whether or not we're going ahead now that Michael's had his accident. "Have you thought things over, at least?"

Ruth shrugged. She screwed her eyes up against the light, and tried peering in through the hangar doors.

"John's there," Terri said. "By the way. One thing I never thought was that I'd take over from you. I wouldn't want to be Michael's girlfriend. I don't want to be anybody's girlfriend. I don't define myself by the man I'm with. You and I have absolutely nothing in common."

Ruth stared.

"So." Terri folded her arms. "Has anyone told you what to do yet?"

"What's that supposed to mean?"

"Well – Chester claims you can't do it. Munro isn't going to decide for you. It's clicked with you that Michael's incapable at the moment, and he wouldn't say yes anyway. Have you found anyone else to ask?"

"No! I haven't!"

"My." Terri shook her head. The right play here was amused disapproval. "I've hit a raw nerve there."

Ruth turned away. She stared at the mirages starting to flow on the glassy expanse of the airfield. "Sorry." She shook her head. "I haven't found anyone who'd – tell me to do it. Sorry."

188

"Don't mention it. What does Ruth Clifford want to do, by the way?"

Ruth Clifford, it seemed, wanted to watch mirages.

"I don't like to push, Ruth, but take-off is supposed to be in an hour. We're going to be late as it is, but we mustn't be too late, or we'll have trouble with the weather."

Ruth Clifford lifted her head and stared at the sky, the big, blue Wedgwood glow of a wide open summer sky. Then she lowered her head and blinked at Terri. "Okay. Let's go."

When Munro left Wragby, Ruth was already in the air and he was in command of MT Holdings. The company rules he'd written dictated the fact. Michael, the MD, was unable to fulfil any of his duties, so Munro, the deputy MD, took on all the executive powers until such time as Michael could sit up in his bed, phone the board and tell them he was in charge again. That wasn't going to happen for a week. By then there'd have been some changes.

On the motorway, as soon as there was an interlude with no killers and no incompetents in the traffic, he called the office and told Pattie Lee to book herself a Sheffield hotel, then drive up to the hospital to babysit Michael. He thought she'd protest. But she didn't. At the next safe interval in the traffic he dialled Pierce at Smith and Brown Associates and told him Pattie Lee would be on the move.

It wasn't until he paused at a services that he opened his briefcase to check Sylvia Symes's number at Rowe Spitta Pitts.

When Terri Sabuli strapped herself into the seat as the airliner taxied to the end of Wragby's runway, Ruth had already crossed the coast at Plymouth, had left the cameras and the well-wishing aircraft and the local radio presenter behind, and was heading out over the Western Approaches. She had a head start on the support team, but the team had four jet engines and the use of the stratosphere. They'd be in Florida twelve hours ahead of her.

I did it, Terri thought. I made her make up her mind. God knows what her problem was. But mine is solved. I'm getting to manage a publicity circus that actually runs. When I leave MT-Orbis I pick my next job. And I'll be choosy.

When the sun had gone down into sea and clouds – late, very late, because she'd been chasing it into the west at two hundred and fifty knots – Ruth felt at ease with the machine. Half-loaded, with ballast and twenty-two hours of fuel, Angel behaved perfectly. No tendency to yaw off course, no wobble of the wings. Chester, just possibly, could still design an aircraft after all. The autopilot had done all the flying ever since Plymouth. The adjustments it made in order to hold the course were minimal, flawless movements.

She trusted it, more or less. She even trusted the alarm on the collision radar, because it had worked every time in the bright sky over England. But the dark would feel less safe.

She reached into the locker behind the seat for a drink. She wanted orange, but it took three tries and two false flavours. In Florida she'd supervise the loading of the food lockers herself.

She watched the blood drain from the northwestern sky, out there beyond the tip of the right foreplane. Once in a while the control surface on the foreplane waggled as the autopilot smoothed the ride. Four thousand feet, and all's well. There might be nothing at this height over the entire Atlantic.

She looked at the throttle to her left and the joystick to her right. She watched the coloured glows of the cathode-ray tube displays become the dominant light in the cockpit. Eventually she loosened her lap belt, hung her weight from the assist handle bolted to the ceiling, and cranked the seat down flat. She lay in a narrow box with three dark windows through which the running lights flashed, with instrument screens shining above her knees, and a constant engine noise she could hardly hear any more. She set the alarm for two hours, the longest she dared go without checking the course.

Unexpectedly, she slept.

TWENTY-FIVE

It wasn't dark. It wasn't light. It was a dimness in between. It was quite some time before he realised it wasn't his eyes . . .

The room was blank, with a strip light that wasn't on, with two doors and one tall locker in the corner, with a rail suspended from the ceiling for a curtain that wasn't there. On the wall, over the metal bed frame, was a box with a speaker, a couple of dials and a hooked up set of headphones. Beside it was a compressed air point, an oxygen point, high voltage and low voltage sockets, a set of switches. A cable with a button on the end trailed over the bed frame and dangled above the corner of his pillow. He was in a hospital. He knew that already. But he couldn't remember why.

There was a bedside table without flowers, grapes or cards. There was a chair with no one sitting in it. Pattie Lee wasn't there. He knew she had been, but he couldn't remember . . .

It wasn't day, it wasn't night. Not enough light came through the curtains drawn halfway across the window. First light or last light, the beginning of day or night? And which day?

That tapped the barrel, and out it flowed.

Pattie Lee wasn't there! He had no information! No outside contact! No surrogate set of hands, eyes and ears to act, see and hear! Isolated! At a crucial time! They started the whole careful process running – and now *this*!

The big move was a mistake. It was a terrible mistake.

His left arm refused to move at all. His right arm locked halfway up, and the sheet slipped out of his grip anyway. When the sheet fell back on his left arm, it hurt. Before he collapsed, and before the sheet came down, he saw the right-angle cast lying across his stomach where he thought his arm might be.

191

The pillow *hurt*. His legs hurt. His back and his chest and his stomach howled at him. The hammer-blow from the pillow reverberated as if his head was a vast bell. The bell and the room rotated for a long time – not like a carousel, but like a fairground waltzer, slow and fast and dipping up and down on a track made of stretched elastic.

The rotation wobbled into chaos on a pendulum with two pivots.

The big move wasn't possible.

When the chaos had stopped, more or less, he tried a different tactic. He let his right hand find his thigh, then made it slide over his hospital gown, even though his shoulder and upper arm hated having to move. His right hand nudged fingers sticking out of a plaster rim. He waited. And waited. But there was no scream of pain from the left arm. So he told his right hand to move on.

The tricky bit was getting his arm to stretch up into the nauseous empty air, and then reach diagonally across his face to get at the button hanging from the bed. His left arm was in a cast, so they hung the button from the left side of his bed. It was a trick to keep the patient quiet.

But he beat the trick and squeezed the button.

His arm tried to collapse over the top of his head onto the pillow, but his shoulder couldn't cope with that. It locked.

It mattered. Getting up, getting help, getting contact mattered. If they went ahead without him, then within days the shit would hit the fan in the most public possible way. They got Angel ready for its start because he told them to. Munro said they should bring the project forward and get it going in a hurry, but he fixed the situation round Munro and forced the man's hand. And Pattie Lee had initiated the other thing because he told her to, timed perfectly to begin on the eve of take-off.

Now *this* had happened, and everything had to be stopped. But he couldn't stop it himself. He couldn't even get out of bed!

The door opened. A nurse came in. She shook her head

and marched to the side of his bed. She started extricating his arm from its angle-poise position over his head. "You'll have to be very careful, Mr Tranter. You're a mass of bruises."

"The button's on the wrong side of the bed."

"No, Mr Tranter, it's the wrong arm you've broken." She let his right arm flop on the sheet. "This hospital was never intended for left arm fractures." She reached over him and started unhitching the call button. "Unfortunately, the left arm hospital was full. So here you are."

"What time is it?"

"Five o'clock. Your watch is in the cabinet there beside the bed. Unfortunately, it's broken. You're a lucky man to have got away so lightly, I believe."

I haven't, he thought, bloody well got away at all. It's all gone wrong, wrong, totally *wrong*. He rolled his head and looked at the bedside cabinet again. No telephone.

No telephone!

"So." The nurse hitched the call button on the righthand side of the bed. "Here you are. Now you just take it very easy, Mr Tranter. It's still quite a while till breakfast."

"I need a telephone. What day is it?"

"Sunday."

"Sunday?"

"Sunday, Mr Tranter. You were admitted at midnight on Thursday. Your operation was postponed twice on Friday because they were worried about your concussion. Your secretary was here for several hours yesterday, but you were asleep almost the whole day. Now it's Sunday."

"A telephone. I need a telephone."

"You won't get one today, I'm afraid. Not on a Sunday. And anyway, you have to rest for another day or two before you even think of doing anything."

"I need a telephone!"

"You certainly don't, Mr Tranter. You need rest."

"I need a telephone!" He tried to get his head and shoulders off the pillow again. Hopeless. Not a single muscle wanted to work, and the elastic yoyo started to swing in his head. "Bloody

193

hell. I'm a businessman. I run a bloody *empire*. I need a bloody *telephone*. Look at this room. No telephone. No television. But it's in my insurance. Oh yes. I've paid for it. So where is it? Get me a telephone! Have you any idea how the insurance company will react? When it hears? It'll take you off its list! Your hospital will lose the business! Because if I cancel the health scheme, I'll take sixteen thousand people with me! Sixteen thousand! So get me a telephone! *Now!*"

The nurse, he realised, had already gone. Bloody useless. No telephone, no nurse, no idea how to get in touch with Pattie Lee, and no chance of ever getting out of the bed!

When the nurse returned, she had a woman with her in a white coat. The woman seemed to be a doctor. She had a hypodermic in her hand, and was fitting it to a loaded syringe.

She managed five and a half hours sleep on the way to Michaels Field. The infernal sorcery of silicon and data inputs actually worked. Angel flew itself, and a lone pilot in unpopulated airspace could go to sleep without suddenly waking in a different world. The right technology could hold aloft a life.

Ruth sat on the bed and pulled on a T-shirt – the big white T-shirt with Angel printed across the front. Outside the curtains it was still dark in the middle of the local night. Back in Britain, on the time scheme her body worked on, it would be six in the morning. Four hours to go. She'd just had ten hours sleep. That was all she'd done since they brought her to the hotel in Orlando's afternoon. They'd kept her at Michaels Field all Saturday morning after the press circus was over. She could pass an exam on the layout of the airfield. Angel was going to need every last inch of it.

Terri Sabuli strode to the window and opened the curtain wide enough to peer out. "Typical," she said. "Orlando by night could be anywhere by night. From this floor, you'd think you could see Disney World. Fairytale towers in the moonlight." She let the curtain close again. "I haven't been in my profession long enough. I still believe things."

Ruth shrugged. She started pulling on the pocket-patched trousers in Orbis green.

"The weather's tighter than we expected." Terri sat down in the armchair next to the tallboy, and crossed those long legs. "The front will be coming in from the west before dawn. It's due to reach the Atlantic coast an hour after sunrise. Light winds, but gusts and rain. If you haven't taken off an hour after sunrise, that was it. There are cyclonic systems covering the whole Gulf of Mexico. No hurricanes, of course – but you wouldn't be able to take off in a decent breeze."

"I know." Ruth stood up to hitch the trousers over her hips. "I know about Angel on full load. And before you remind me I haven't actually flown the aircraft on full load, just remember no one else has."

"I wasn't going to say a word."

"Good." Ruth tucked in the T-shirt and fastened the trousers. The best conversation with Terri Sabuli would be silence. She sat down on the bed again and leaned forward to pull on the tennis socks.

"A little ice age," Terri said, "seems to have intervened between us. Hasn't it?"

Ruth pulled one sock on and smoothed it over her heel. "Have you – or have you not – been fucking Michael?"

"Yes. And he's been fucking me. So?"

So, Ruth thought, you're as bad as him.

"Michael has clean habits, Ruth. He always wears a condom. What has either of us got to worry about? Or could it be you're old-fashioned enough to think of him as yours?"

Ruth didn't bother to answer. She smoothed the second sock, then reached for the trainers. Now the woman was going to argue the possessive fallacy at her. To want exclusive access is to impose exclusive ownership, but every human being is individual and free, and all that crap. Every human being is alone and adrift, and helpless in the sea of life. You need company, companionship, someone to cling to you can trust.

"Let me tell you, Ruth. The only *yours* there is for you, just like for everyone else, is *you*. Look after it well and forget the illusions and the traps, the mother and the lover roles. They've been devised to divert you from looking after *yourself*. They're chains the men put on us, but don't put on themselves because they know – look after number one."

But it all came down to what was best for number one. Someone to protect you, support you, run your life for you wasn't too bad. It was so much better than loneliness. Devotion to a dominant man did the trick, though they walked all over you. Her father tied her childhood years to the home, and turned her teens into a constant guilty failure to make the grade. Ashley smashed her university career to pieces because he needed a handmaid to help him save the world. Michael wore her for a while as an image accessory, screwed another woman, and tried to steal her dream. The funny thing was – her father, Ashley and not even Michael. They didn't drop her before she decided to do it to them. And oh, did she do it to Michael.

"Well," Terri said. "There's no news from London, no cancellation. So, are you ready to go?"

She tugged at the laces. "Yes."

"No second thoughts, no last minute doubts?"

"No." She finished tying the knot. "Don't you want me to do it, Terri?"

"Me? I want you to do it. You pull this off, and just think what a boost you give to my career. Are you sure you can do it?"

"I've done the Atlantic solo." Ruth sat up straight. She put her hands on her hips. "Overnight, against the wind, twenty-two hours on my bum. Nothing to it. First I did the Atlantic. Now I'm going to do the world."

"Why? I mean, are you doing it for the charities – the further you get, the less they get peanuts and the more they get cornucopia? Or are you doing it for the record books? Or the fame and glory?"

Ruth shook her head. "Ask me when it's over. At the moment, it's just the thing I'm doing now."

"Fair enough." Terri stood up. "Any last minute requests?"

"No. Well – yes. I've got changes of underwear, but I forgot to bring enough panty liners. I mean, I want more than one for a five-day flight. I don't suppose you've got any to spare?"

Terri shook her head. "No more than I need. But this is the land where they invented the twenty-four-hour drugstore, and I've got plastic. Panty liners are our first priority."

"Right." Ruth stood up, and picked the green blouse of her flying outfit off the bed. "Let's go."

TWENTY-SIX

Ruth was ready, from panty liner to the lightweight, two-piece, Orbis-green flying suit. She was dressed, refreshed from a last five-minute shower; she was alone. After take-off, apart from voices in her ear and sometimes a friendly aircraft in a parallel sky, she was going to be utterly alone.

The last quick media-meet was done. Angel was fuelled up to the lip of every filling cap. Every moving part was freshly lubricated and every tube and air filter replaced and tested for unobstructed flow. Every electrical circuit had been metered, every electronic module had been interrogated by the plug-in maintenance routines. Food, drink, bio-degradable waste bags, two changes of underclothes, hygiene kit, survival suit, life-jacket, ration pack, life raft, rescue beacon – everything was stowed in boxes and pockets in the sides, floor and rear of the cockpit. The tower at Michaels Field was ready. The ground crew were ready. The cameras were ready, and an estimated half million Eastern Standard Time early Sunday risers, and another half million TV breakfasters back home in Britain were ready and waiting live.

Why didn't she have anything memorable to say at the close of Terri's slick little media-meet? Expect me back in a few days – Phileas Fogg, eat your heart out – so long suckers, you ain't seen the last of me? This, she should have said, is for the hungry, the sick, the under-educated, the dispossessed, the commercially exploited in the Third World. Except it wasn't. The entire sponsorship-of-charity angle was nothing more than a device to finance Michael Tranter's self-glorifying stunt. This, she should have said, with an eye to the media public's warm little tears about love and loyalty, is for Michael.

Or she could have hit them with the selfish truth. They wouldn't like that. So she opened the locker room door, and walked out to where the cameras were waiting.

Angel was rolled out in front of the hangar, brilliant green under the sunrise. The sky would have been another perfect bowl of blue, but there were cloud tops coming up in the southwest, pink-brushed palisades starting to rise behind the control tower.

There was barely a hint of a breeze.

The tips of Angel's huge wings drooped under their own weight. The long canoe tank sat flush under the aircraft's belly. The underwing, sprouting from the canoe, made a pair of blunt blades at knee-height above the ground. The suspension of the tricycle landing gear was compressed down to the stops. The high tanks in the shoulders of the main wing were full. The tanks which filled the fuselage from cockpit to the engine in the tail were full. The canoe was full. Angel had never carried so much fuel.

Ruth walked to Angel under telephoto eyes. No reporters and no camera crews were allowed this near. There was just the Orbis video team, and she ignored them. You got used to cameras so quickly. The concentration helped. When you're about to try and fly round the world, it isn't the media you're afraid of.

She climbed the crew ladder with John Coates at her side. He helped her slide in through the cockpit window. She settled in the seat. She'd been here for twenty-two hours already, her one and only previous flight in Angel. It was a quarter of her total air time. One single flight, and Angel was the aircraft she knew best in the world.

She put on the headphones and mike. She cleared to taxi with the tower. John plugged in a jack lead and went to sit on the back of the towing truck at his end of a curve of cable. She switched to the intercom. She released the brake. The truck started pulling Angel southwards, past the tower.

Ruth went through the pre-flights. On the back of the towing truck, John went through the checklist. Choked with a mass of fuel, double-winged and canoe-bellied, Angel wallowed over every slight unevenness in the ground.

She had both side windows open. After the drive down from Orlando, the dawn air had been sweet. Now it brought a perfume of exhaust fumes from Florida's Turnpike just half a mile away on the west side of the airfield. Cheap summer tourists who'd done the overnight drive were heading south to Miami, others were leaving early for the long journey home. Some were going to Orlando and Disney World. Others were coming out to Cape Canaveral's acres of swamp and ancient launch pads. There were a lot of police patrol cars on the Turnpike. They didn't want people stopping along the perimeter of Michaels Field to watch the show.

When she tipped her head to look up at the sky, it was empty and cool and new-day blue. Just the place to be.

Angel rocked clumsily round the turn at the south end of the runway. John said goodbye and good luck, and unfastened his cable. The towing truck uncoupled and drove away. She sat in the silence, with a gentle crosswind from the west drifting through the cockpit. There was nothing in front of her except the instrument board, the windscreen, Angel's long nose and the slender foreplanes, and the undulating ground. Flattened shadow furrows blended together in the distance. The day's new sun, sitting in the branches of the orange groves to the right of the runway, found every fingertip ridge and hollow which blemished the skin of the world.

Far away, at the midpoint of the runway, the Orbis charter with the air camera team took off. It went up in planform, climbing into the brightness of the sky. She took her sunglasses from their clip over the top of the instrument panel and put them on. The glare of the sunrise softened.

Direct in her ears, Chester spoke to her from the tower. "Okay to start up."

She slid the side windows closed. Then she fired the engine in Angel's tail. She checked the window catches.

The engine temperature climbed, then steadied. Oil pressure was steady, fuel flow exactly right. On the navigation screen on the right of the panel, the computer was reporting her position to the metre. Angel vibrated against the wheel brake.

"Engine's fine," she said. "How's the time?"

"We're bang on time."

"Right." She pushed the switch under the digital window up at top left of the panel, the one next to the readout for London time. "Mission clock started. Am I clear to go?"

"You're clear."

"Okay." She peered ahead. Just in sight, to the right of the runway, was the first marker. By then she had to have reached the minimum speed for flaps. At the midpoint of the runway, lost in the level mesh of light and shadow, was the rotation marker. Still further away was the third marker. If she wasn't airborne by the time she passed the third marker, she had to abort while there was still enough runway left to stop in. Stopping before she hit the fence mattered. Angel was a vast incendiary bomb with wings.

She checked the window catches again. Then she settled her left hand on the throttle and wrapped her right hand round the stick. The easy-use side position of the joystick was the best piece of design in the whole cockpit. "Are the press listening in?"

"They are," said Terri's voice.

"Okay. This one's for the hungry, the sick, the under-educated, the dispossessed and the commercially exploited in the Third World. Here goes."

She took her hand off the throttle to release the brake. Then she pushed the throttle through.

The engine screamed. Angel began to roll. The airspeed needle on the repeater dial quivered. The digital readout on the central VSI screen flickered from zero to a tentative number and back. Angel moved, its long nose wavering slightly up and down. The repeater needle lifted off its stop. The main display settled on a number and began to count upwards: 005 knots, 010, 015 ... All the readings on the engine panel stayed safely sandwiched between their superscript and subscript margins. As the throttle went to full, the engine and its propeller screeched appallingly behind her.

"Standby flaps," said Chester's voice.

The marker rolled towards her on the right. She pushed the lever for half flaps. Looking over her shoulder, first right and then left, she could see the underside of the main wing, and could see the flaps angled down from the trailing edge. She could also see the blunt-ended underwing so close to the rushing ground. Over on the left, the tower and the cameras on the adjacent roof went past. Okay world, watch me be famous!

The tips of the main wings had lifted themselves level. They should be curving upwards. Angel was still too slow. The rotation marker went past. She pulled on the stick, and saw the foreplane control surfaces slope down, pushing the nose upwards. The nose didn't lift.

"Rotate. You're supposed to *rotate*."

"I'm trying to rotate." She kept the stick back. The speed crept up. No rotation. She started rocking in her seat. Come on, on, on!

The nose lifted. She eased the stick. Tip too high, and she'd strip the tail propeller against the ground. The nose came up to the rotation angle and blocked her view ahead. No awful sight of the end of the runway rushing near. Angel's shadow sped beside her on the left, a caricature of a would-be bird stretching halfway to the bushes bordering the Turnpike.

The final marker went past on the right. Angel cut through its shadow in the air – nose up, flaps deployed, engine screaming at full, and airspeed ten knots too slow ever to leave the ground . . .

Ruth throttled right back. She applied full flaps for the braking effect. With stick control, she let the nose drop smoothly. The nosewheel squealed at spin-up. Ahead she could see where the tarmac runway turned into grass run-on. Then scrub.

She started applying touches of wheel brake. Angel kept trying to leapfrog the obstructing wheels. She had to waggle the stick to keep the aircraft running straight.

She could see the fence at the far end of the run-on strip, concrete posts and steel wire to catch her before she hit the scrub.

Angel was a mass of fuel with wings, a fireball inferno waiting to erupt at her back. She killed the engine to get rid of the ignition source. She hauled the wheel brake hard and to hell with overheating . . .

Angel stopped with less than twice its own length to go before the rough grass of the run-on strip, and another two hundred yards to the fence and the dusty bushes.

The truck came out and towed Angel all the way back to the start point at the south end of the runway. The sun freed itself from the branches of the orange trees, and the shadow furrows vanished from the tarmac ribbon. The clouds building a wall across the southwest were taller, much nearer, and had dark bases. The breeze had swung from west to southwest and had taken on an unevenness, a little bit of bluster.

Thirty precious minutes had gone by the time they started topping up the litres of fuel lost from Angel's tanks. Forty minutes had gone before the vehicles withdrew and Ruth fired Angel's engine again.

She checked the window catches. She settled herself,

202

left hand on the throttle, right hand on the stick. "Are we clear?"

"We're clear," said Chester's voice. "The camera aircraft is coming round from the south, on your right, to film the take-off. They'll keep their distance."

"Okay." She looked along the rippling, vanishing runway. The first heat shimmers were already floating above it – warm air, less dense air. Less lift. "How many people are still with us?"

"You mean the audience?" asked Terri's voice. "About the same. A million. You're holding people's attention. Things have got a little tense. They're patched in and listening, by the way."

"Are they?" A gust rocked Angel, gently. If a gust hit while Angel was rotated on its two rear wheels, and a wingtip dipped and hit the speeding ground . . . "Well then, this one's for Michael, as well as for the Third World."

She released the brake. Then she put her hand on the throttle and pushed it through.

The engine screamed. Angel moved, the runway began to roll under its long nose. The repeater airspeed needle lifted off the stop. The main display on the VSI screen began to count upwards: 010 knots, 015, 020 . . . All the engine readings stayed within the optimum bands.

The first marker came closer. The airspeed crept higher. Last time it didn't creep high enough. Drag slows you down. You need flaps, and the added lift they generate, to take off. But the flaps cause drag.

"Standby flaps," said Chester's voice.

The marker rolled towards her on the right of the runway. She put her hand on the flaps lever. The marker went past.

"Flaps," said Chester's voice. "Flaps!"

She looked backwards out of the side windows, right and left. The tips of the huge wings were beginning to curve upwards. Lift was coming with speed. The speed was building faster because she didn't have flaps. Out on the left, the tower and the cameras went by. Okay folks, watch me make a fool of myself.

"Flaps! For God's sake, flaps!"

The rotation marker was rushing down at her. She pushed the lever for half flaps.

She twisted her head and checked the flaps were down. On the right she saw the rotation marker whip by.

"Rotate! Rotate!"

She pulled on the stick. The foreplane control surfaces sloped down, diverting the airflow and adding lift to the nose.

The nose came straight up. She eased the stick before the tail and the whirling propeller hit the ground.

The nose blocked the view ahead. She couldn't see how much runway was left. Come on, Angel, come on! Fly. Fly! Why won't you *fly*?

The airspeed indicator was reading take-off speed. She did it. She got Angel fast enough to fly. Come on! Come on!

The indicator crept five knots over take-off speed. The wingtips were curving upwards as they strained against the weight of Angel and its pilot and its fuel. Come *on*! *Fly!* Why won't you lift up and *fly*?

The final marker went past on the right.

Angel was nose up, flaps deployed, engine screaming at full, six knots over take-off speed and still rolling on the ground . . .

Ruth hauled the throttle back. She rammed on full flaps to get the braking effect. She let the nose drop. Angel pitched forward and slammed the suspension against the stop. The nosewheel squealed.

Ahead she could see the end of the runway. It was too close. She'd been travelling faster, and now she was running out of room.

She cut the engine and hit full wheel brake.

The mass of fuel wanted to make Angel somersault. Angel couldn't, and started to veer left. She hit right rudder and let go of the stick to turn the nosewheel guide. She got Angel straight again.

The roll-on strip and the fence were waiting.

She got hold of the stick and pushed it forward. The foreplane control surfaces angled up. They pushed *down*, creating turbulence and drag in the air, adding weight and friction to the nosewheel.

Angel had to stop. It was time Angel stopped . . .

She was going to hit the run-on, and that would bounce the landing gear too hard. No more take-offs until the suspension had been renewed. Two days. Three.

With the rudder and the nosewheel she risked a turn. Angel didn't tumble. The aircraft came round to the right, faced the blinding sun, swung further, scraped its leftside wheel along the edge of the runway –

And stopped, facing back the way it had come.

She took off her headphones for a moment of privacy. She opened the cockpit window. She listened to the silence.

Angel couldn't take off, even with the right speed. Something had her beaten.

TWENTY-SEVEN

Angel sat with drooping wings at the wrong end of the runway, tied down by its mass of fuel. Enough heavy energy to fly round the world, but too much to get off the ground.

Away in the south, where the control tower shone in the morning sun, the towing truck was swimming through shimmering heat pools. Hot air over the tarmac meant thinner air on the runway, meant less lift for Angel's wings . . .

Ruth started the engine.

She put the headphones on again to protect her ears from the noise coming through the open window . . .

". . . think you're doing? You're wasting fuel. Wait for the towing truck. Will you *answer*?"

She released the wheel brake, and turned the nosewheel guide. Slowly, Angel rolled round to the right, away from the edge of the strip. She got this far. She got every obstacle out of the way, and ended up here under the eyes of quite a lot of the world – and it turned into a fiasco.

"Will you *answer*, for God's sake? You're wasting fuel!"

"I know." She turned the nosewheel so that Angel swung south again and lined up pointing down the strip. She pulled on the brake. "If we're going to shout, Chester, it might be an idea to cut the media out of the loop."

"Already done." That was Terri's voice.

Ruth nudged the throttle forward. Angel began to vibrate against the adhesion of the brake.

"Cut the *engine*," insisted Chester's voice. "Save *fuel*. You're only making the topping up take longer."

She glanced at the mission clock. Fifty minutes gone. She should have been up in the air and two hundred miles away. "Angel's too heavy, Chester. I don't want any more fuel. I don't want the tanks topping up. I managed six knots over your critical airspeed, and Angel wouldn't lift. You got your sums wrong. A few fractions of a percent, probably – but a few fractions on the wrong side."

"Look, cut the engine. Let the towing truck take you back to the start point for a final try."

"Stop telling me what to do, Chester."

A gust of wind shook Angel's sagging wings. In the cockpit, it brushed her face with warm air.

"Think of the weather," said Terri's voice. "The front's coming and the wind is worsening. There's only time for one more attempt. You've got to go back to the south end. You've got to take off heading north. You *can't* do it the other way round. There are power lines south of the airfield – "

"I know about the power lines."

"They're far enough away not to trouble an ordinary aeroplane, but Angel doesn't climb fast enough."

"Angel doesn't climb at all, Terri." Down towards the control tower, boating on silver mirages, the towing truck was still too far away. It would take too long. Hot morning sun boiled the air above the tarmac, evaporating the lift clean away. She was *losing*.

"The weather's closing in. This will be the last try. You've got to get back to the start position while there's still time. The weather is bad for the next few days, then worse further down the route. If you don't go this morning, you never will."

"I know about the weather, Terri." The cloud bank closed the entire horizon from south right round to the west. The southwest wind, coming diagonally from the right, was blowing dust across the tarmac, taunting Angel.

The wind was already wrong. Instead of a crosswind from the west, it would be as good as a tail wind if she tried to take off south-to-north. The tail component would be at least ten knots, which would mean a ten knot reduction in Angel's actual airspeed while rolling along the runway. There wasn't a chance of getting into the air. Not south-to-north.

If she tried it north-to-south, she'd have that component as a head wind. She'd have a ten knot airspeed advantage, instead.

The rotation marker was in the middle of the runway. It was the only marker she could use. She wouldn't have a measured-out abort marker to tell her when to give up, and with the nose high, she wouldn't be able to see the end of the runway coming. She'd bounce across the grass run-on like a panicked goose. The fence would cut through Angel like wires slicing cheese. The pieces would stack on the cushion of scrub on the other side. She'd have a funeral pyre which started with a fireball.

There didn't seem to be anything she could throw out of the cockpit. If she got rid of the entire hygiene kit, she'd save less weight than a litre of fuel. She needed the lifejacket, life raft and survival suit – most of the route was over ocean, with no immediate hope of rescue if she went into the water.

She reached down and pulled the intercom plug out of

the portable CD player. She unhooked its retainer strap. She picked it off the floor, tested its weight – then threw it far enough to be sure it wouldn't wreck a tyre when she started to roll. She threw the box of CDs after it. The box broke, the disks scattered, culture spilled on coarse ground. I'm sorry, she thought, for the beautiful music. But it's Michael's. It isn't mine.

The wind hit Angel again.

Ruth opened the throttle a little more. The engine began to scream. She closed the cockpit window. She checked the catch.

"Get the truck off the strip. I'm taking off now."

"You can't!"

"Ruth, *please*? The power lines."

"Get the truck off the strip. Tell the TV. Make sure all the viewers can call their friends in for the big bang. We're fifty-five minutes behind time. So here goes."

"Ruth, do it the right way round. Please?"

"Cut the engine, woman. You're using too much fuel!"

"I'm trying to lighten the load, Chester. I'm trying to correct your design error. So shut up." She wrapped her right hand round the stick. She moved her left hand from the throttle to the wheel brake. "Okay. This one's for me."

She released the brake. She pushed the throttle through.

Angel lumbered into an accelerating roll. The main air-speed indicator started at ten and counted upwards: 020, 025, 030 . . .

The useless abort marker went past on the left. The wind tried to push the three-wheeled, wide-winged, long-nosed aircraft sideways as the speed came on. She corrected with a touch of rudder. She watched the rotation marker coming. Wait for the flaps. Wait.

"The truck's out of the way, Ruth."

"I can see that." She was going past the tower and its buildings and the cameras on the roof. Okay folks, watch the mad Englishwoman kill herself.

She was racing towards the rotation marker.

"Flaps, Ruth. Shouldn't she do flaps? Chester, shouldn't she do flaps?"

The rotation marker whipped past on the left.

Ruth pushed the lever for half flaps. She checked the flaps, left and right. She saw the tower disappear behind her wing. The wingtips were curving upwards.

She pulled the stick. The foreplane surfaces sloped down.

The nose came up. Too fast. She snapped the stick neutral again, then pulled a shade of foreplane elevator. The nose held at ten degrees. The propeller didn't shred its way into the tarmac.

The wind tried to turn the long nose aside and push Angel left off the runway. She corrected with rudder, swinging the nose a shade towards the wind. Angel rushed slightly crabwise down the runway, nose up, tail down, and glued to the tarmac by two wheels.

"Abort, Ruth. Call it off. Call it off. Please?"

It wasn't easy keeping the line. She had to watch the edge of the runway and make sure it didn't drift in or out. There went the original flaps marker. No use now.

"Ruth! Call it off!"

Ten degrees nose high. A bad bounce and the propeller screws itself into the asphalt. Take-off speed. Five knots over take-off speed. Come on, Angel! Fly! Fly! *Fly!*

Ten knots over. The runway can't last forever.

"Ruth!" And other sounds behind Terri's voice. "Go! Go! Go! Go! Go!" Like urgent booster prayers.

Fifteen knots over. Angel! *Fly! Fly!*

Twenty knots over.

The wheels bounced. They came off and she *felt* the hope. There can't be any runway left. Wait for the bounce to end and the wheels to touch. There isn't any runway left –

Wait for the bounce to end –

Angel was drifting left. A touch more right rudder. Still waiting for the bounce to end –

Total silence from the tower. Someone's *watching* me.

Angel was two feet off the ground. There was no more

speed coming on. Too much drag. The wheels cause drag. But you still need the wheels for when you have to touch down. No wheels is a crash that will kill you –

She pulled the landing gear switch. The drives growled and hauled up the wheels. Airspeed went up another ten knots. The runway went down.

Nose high and clean without wheels, Angel climbed as high as a man's shoulder. Not high enough!

She let the nose drop five degrees, easing the angle of attack and the air resistance. Airspeed crept up. "How high am I? How high?"

"Six feet. Eight feet. The fence."

Suddenly the runway was over and it was rough grass underneath. The airspeed kept creeping up.

The wire fence and its concrete posts flashed under her seat.

"Ruth! You cleared the fence! You must be at ten feet! You *cleared* the fence!"

"Go!" started in the background. "Go! Go! Go! Go!"

Forty knots over take-off speed. Over scrub. She couldn't see straight ahead because of the nose. Left and right were approaching ranks of orange trees. Beyond them, the sky was dark under tall white clouds with bastions and turrets . . .

"The power lines, Ruth. The power lines!"

She looked left, trying to find the power lines. She saw the camera aircraft, a thousand feet out and a couple of hundred high, with the line of US Highway 1 in the distance, and behind that the gleam of the sea. Under her were regimented orange groves with new fruits in the topmost branches close enough to pick.

She couldn't find the lines. To the right was Florida's Turnpike, lanes of trucks and cars full of people getting the show of a lifetime. The lines had to cross the turnpike. All those lanes. A very wide span. "Where are the lines highest?"

"Where they cross the turnpike. Go away from the turnpike."

She dropped the nose two more degrees. There were the sunlit masts standing right across her path in front of a darker sky. The insulator arrays glittered down at her. Not a chance of getting over them.

She turned Angel with right rudder and a trace of right roll. She checked over her shoulder to make sure the underwing didn't dip as far as the trees. Angel fought against the stick and tried to roll level. The turn became a sloppy sideslip.

She straightened up heading just to the right of the tallest mast, the nearer of the pair straddling the turnpike. She was going to clear the trucks, just about. Why did the Americans have to drive such huge trucks?

The drivers in the first lanes were heading her way – windscreens full of appalled, amazed, unbelieving faces. She got over the top of the traffic, hoping her left wing would clear the mast. Hoping she'd get under the power lines with their red-and-white warning spheres strung like tawdry technological beads. In a police patrol car going under her, the driver was shouting into a mike held for him by an open-mouthed partner –

The power lines went over the cockpit roof. They went over the tail fin, too.

She was flying over the southbound lanes at truck-exhaust height on a long diagonal, overtaking the traffic. Did it! She *did* it! And every second she stayed in the air burned off a few grammes of fuel, made Angel less likely to fall.

"Ruth! You're mad! You did it! You're mad!"

Right in front of her was a bird. A big bird. A vulture scouting for dead meat along the roadside. The dead meat was going to be it and her. She couldn't make Angel move across the sky –

The bird turned. It flapped wild and heavy, and got up over the top of her.

Got to do something about this. The airspeed was high enough to risk it. She pulled the flaps back to a quarter, trading loss of lift for reduced drag. Angel didn't drop down.

The airspeed crept up. She was out of arm's reach of the orange trees when they swept under her again.

"Chester says turn to the right, to the west. And get some more *height*!"

She pushed on the stick and started coaxing Angel round in a reluctant turn. Angel wanted to wallow on a level keel. The tips of the main wings curved upwards as they generated lift against the mass of fuel hanging from their centre. The curves created an enormous dihedral. As the right wing dipped down, its effective length increased – more lift on the right side. As the left wing went up, its effective length decreased – less lift on the left side. The result was a force twisting Angel back out of the roll.

She fought the roll resistance and managed a slow, clumsy, gradual turn, taking her out over orange groves, scrub, more orange groves and long dirt tracks. She was still in the sun, but the world ahead was dark. She abandoned the turn with the heading due west towards the wall of cloud, and with her wide shadow skimming the trees ahead of her under the foreplane.

The readout on the VSI screen, the altitude reported by the inertial navigation set, said fifty feet. A minimum rise in the ground would kill her. Thank God for a flat country.

She retracted the flaps. Airspeed increased in a slow count. Eventually, reluctantly, the altimeter said one hundred feet.

She ran out of sun. The newest landscape of orange trees was coming at her out of a grainy veil of grey. She took off her sunglasses and slotted them into their clip over the instrument board. Rain started spitting against the windscreen.

She got into the air. She got Angel into the air.

Part 6

Angel Global Solo

TWENTY-EIGHT

Munro drove from Guildford to London's Docklands at the turn of Sunday evening. He didn't like the drive. He didn't like the ghetto of yuppie culture he was heading for. At least the roads were quiet.

Darren Pierce was quiet, in unexpected pauses. You wouldn't think the local car phone users could tolerate such bad reception in the canyons between their designer tenements.

"Can you hear me, Mr Munro?"

"I can hear you again, Mr Pierce." His arm was getting tired from having to hold the phone so long. The conversation would have become impossible if he'd had to cope with a manual gearbox. "Lee has just left Sheffield."

"That's right. She's heading south on the M1. She hasn't checked out of her hotel, so presumably she intends to return. She was at the hospital for three hours this afternoon, though I can't quite understand why. I called the hospital myself on the pretext of inquiring for MT Holdings, and they told me – "

Pierce dropped out of the ether. Munro was driving past a renovated, value-added, apartment-lined warehouse. Wait, he thought, until the shadow ends or a radio reflection intervenes.

"– pretty clear she made extra calls from other phones."

"I'm sorry, Mr Pierce. You faded again. What did the hospital tell you?"

"Oh, right. Ah – that Tranter is still under sedation. I can't imagine why Lee stayed so long. Anyway, as I was saying,

215

on Friday and Saturday she made five calls to her London hairdresser from her car phone. From what was said, it seems clear she made additional calls from other phones – possibly public phones, the hotel, the hospital. It's all quite curious."

"Why?"

"Well – it seems she's been trying to get hold of a member of the staff, her own hairdresser, in fact. Apparently he's taken some free days prior to the expiry of his notice, which he handed in on Thursday. She seems to have known about this. She's been extremely anxious for him to contact her, but the establishment says he hasn't been in to receive her messages, et cetera."

"How do you interpret that, Mr Pierce? A hairdresser couldn't be her contact to whoever's paying her. That's far too much cloak and dagger for the real world."

"I'm sorry, Mr Munro, I didn't hear most of that."

"I said, how do you interpret that?"

"I don't, frankly. A company which was spying on you wouldn't indulge in such a silly subterfuge as building a spy network round a hairdresser. I'm flummoxed, actually."

Flummoxed, was he? That was a quaint word for a private detective. How the modern world was changing. "Could the hairdresser be a boyfriend, and she's having to stand him up because of the emergency with her boss?"

"I'd be inclined to doubt that. I'm sure my people would have noticed any such relationship. Besides, wouldn't she have the chap's home number?"

"I suppose so." Munro turned a corner into a shadowed canyon overlooked by tiers of toybox-coloured balconies. "Mr Pierce?"

No more Mr Pierce.

Malcolm, who opened the door, was a shock. It wasn't his age – no more than a dozen days over twenty. It was his looks. He looked exactly the way Michael Tranter must have done at the same age, though probably less lightly built and almost certainly somewhat more humane – less a sensitive young boxer than a muscular young vicar. Sylvia Symes had landed herself a tame, amenable and much less shop-soiled version of what she had before.

Sylvia joined them in the ultra-modern, brickwork and black furniture living room. She padded barefoot over the rug, she wore a dressing-gown, she had a towel wrapped round her hair. "Sorry about this, Robert. I've only just got back, and really needed a shower. It's been, as I said on the phone, a frightfully busy day." She pointed at the black lace cushions on the black sofa. "Sit down, for goodness sake. Malcolm, would you get Robert a drink? Robert, what would you like?"

Munro shook his head. "I'm driving."

"Not yet, you're not. What we've got to work out before tomorrow is going to take hours. So you're staying for dinner. It's my turn, after all. You dined me at your club. And Malcolm really is quite a cook."

Malcolm smiled. He was the same height as Michael – not an inch taller than Sylvia Symes in her bare feet. "I'm doing bean salad – all ingredients fresh. Then Creole steaks with mango and pineapple plus pistachio rice, and then coconut ice with chocolate sauce. Tempting?"

Munro nodded. He didn't cook like that on his own at home in Guildford. "It's tempting."

"Good," Sylvia said. "Now sit down at last. What are you having, then?"

Munro took his seat on the sofa. "Brandy and soda."

"Right," Malcolm said. "G and T for you, Syl?"

"Please."

Sylvia sat down in one of the armchairs. She watched as Malcolm walked through the brickwork arch to the dining area. She watched him *move*, Munro thought. Some of us are lucky. The veins on the sides of Sylvia's ankles were beginning to stand proud. She was getting older. But she had her younger version to replace Michael. And Michael had arranged a younger model to replace her. Munro had a new, small home – and no one in it.

"Well," Sylvia said. "Is Geoffrey on board?"

"Yes." He'd finally tracked Geoffrey Simmington down at his golf club, and Simmington had insisted he came out to the club for the chat. Munro had spent half the day touring Greater London and the green belt. "He'll bring Longman Short's own shares, and he'll be proxy for every shareholder they broker. What about you?"

"It's gone very well," she said. "I've visited every major shareholder in Orbis Air who's represented through Rowe Spitta Pitts. Quite a few of them are starting to throw wobblies about the state of the company. The wobbly ones were easy to persuade. The others required sober argument."

"And?"

"I soberly argued." She reached up to her head, unhitched the tucked-in towel, and started to rub her hair. "A sell-off will protect the equity they hold in Orbis Air – as well as reinforcing the health of MT-Orbis overall, and therefore protecting the equity any of them hold in other subsidiaries. A rapid sell-off will get a better price, before confidence goes. And if the current board is hostile to the idea of a rapid sell-off, then it's preferable to beat the board so that the necessary preparations can begin. The argument convinced in every case but one."

"And who was that?"

"Oh, just one single shareholder." She stopped rubbing her hair. "Here come the drinks."

Malcolm came back through the arch, a crystal tumbler in each hand. He gave the gin and tonic to Sylvia, and the brandy and soda to Munro. "I'll be in the kitchen, Syl. Cigarettes on the table, by the way." He pointed past her to a glass-topped occasional table with black tubular legs. On it, between an ashtray and a lacquered Japanese bowl, were a cigarette case and lighter.

"Thanks, love." With her free hand, Sylvia unwrapped the towel from her head. Damp blonde hair emerged in tangled strands.

"Who," Munro said, "was the shareholder who didn't agree?"

"Don't worry, Robert." She started lifting the strands of hair with her fingers. "It's only one. If Geoffrey's clients are all in line, we'll have enough."

"I'd like to know." He settled back on the sofa. He crossed his legs. He balanced his drink on his knee. Act friendly, not ready to pounce. "We're talking about important shareholders, not kindergarten capitalists. I'd like to know which shareholder isn't in favour of a move that's obviously good for MT-Orbis."

"It doesn't matter, Robert. There's no need to start reading things into it."

I'm the one, he thought, fighting a very seriously negligent boss, trying to get a battered company back on its feet, coping with a case of espionage and facing a possibly very brutal takeover move. I'll make up my own mind about what things do or don't mean. "I'd like to know, Sylvia. I'll find out when the votes are actually counted, but I'd find it more useful to know now."

She shrugged. She leaned forward and put her gin and tonic on the floor. "Well – but it doesn't matter in the slightest." She twisted round and grabbed the cigarette case and the lighter. She flipped open the case. "It's – just the Bryce McFadden Group."

Munro nodded. He studied his brandy. It seemed like a good idea to sip it. The Bryce McFadden Group. Simmington had said the Group was tipped to be looking for a victim for a new takeover. Now the Group was refusing to support a move which would halt the slide of MT-Orbis shares that was on the horizon, and would stop the value of Orbis Air doing a nosedive. Someone was running a spy called Pattie Lee, who had her finger on the pulse of MT-Orbis. It was the kind of underhand tactic the Group had been turning to when he left. A picture, reflected in his brandy, was beginning to form. Two years ago he left the Group, and now they were coming to get him. "The Bryce McFadden Group," he said. "I didn't realise they brokered their shares through you, instead of running them through their own agency."

"Neither did I." Sylvia wreathed herself in smoke. "It seems the arrangement was made last Monday. And was kept quiet."

"I see." It was a leverage tactic. If the Group wanted something, and if Rowe Spitta Pitts benefited from the Group's business, it put pressure on Rowe Spitta Pitts to encourage other clients with parallel shareholdings to want the same thing as the Group. From his days with the Group he knew what a takeover victim had to do, if it could. Move too fast to be caught. Be too fit to be wrestled to the ground. Be too fat to swallow. Be too tough to digest. To achieve all that with MT-Orbis was going to be hard, even with Michael out of the way.

The unsettling thing was that Sylvia Symes obviously saw the same picture emerging. She was going against it, at the moment.

"What about Michael?" she said. "Once you start things rolling, how do you stop him coming back and snuffing you out? Have you got any aces up your sleeve?"

Munro nodded. That was a safer game. Three aces for certain, he thought. Plus pressure from the Securities and Investments Board. Plus a new prize from Wragby. "Enough."

TWENTY-NINE

Terri was awake again. She didn't like sleeping in an airline seat. It made a mess of your clothes, and marred the muscles down the entire length of your spine. Sleep became a series of uneasy dozes as the air system sighed and the engines whined like a foursome of Valkyries playing shadow hunters in the stratosphere night.

The rest of the team were scattered about the cabin of the

220

cargo aircraft. Segregated among the seats were their restless corpses, worn down by insufficient sleep, too much travel, too much work, and too much excitement. How did Ruth Clifford, in Angel, feel?

Chester Alby came back down the aisle from the flight deck. He didn't seem happy. Nowadays he never did, but the problem with Angel's take-off had made it worse. Exhausted, he looked like a man being hunted by a shadow of his own making. He stopped two rows short, about to turn aside to where his seat waited for him, reclined as far as it would go. In the half-light coming from the strips above the overhead lockers, he scanned the cabin. When his eyes got round to the rear rows, he noticed she was awake.

"Any news?" she said.

Chester nodded. "We're starting London approach in fifteen minutes. Landing in about thirty-five."

"Good." With luck they'd be cleared by two o'clock. An Orbis staff bus was waiting to take them into London, and by the bus and then a night-time taxi, there was a faint chance she'd be home and in bed by three. That would allow time for three hours of real sleep before the media day got under way at six in the morning. "How's the mission going?"

"Everything's fine. The Americans made quite a thing of Angel's departure into the Pacific. Mission Control just reported that Angel's had sunset. Everything's on time and on course."

Angel, Angel, Angel. For Chester, the mission without Michael consisted only of his aeroplane. "How's Ruth?"

Chester shrugged. "All right."

"And any news of Michael?"

"The operation on his arm hasn't thrown up any complications. But they were still concerned about after-effects from the concussion. I hope there aren't any. Concussion can do nasty things." Chester started edging between the seats.

"Don't worry about Michael. He's as hard as they come."

"You," Chester muttered, "should know."

Let the man mutter, Terri thought. Michael – in that

respect – didn't matter any more. She'd been shaken by the mess he was in immediately after the fall, but she was over that now. For the moment she wasn't even fascinated by Michael's egomania. Something else had shown itself to be worthy of study.

The take-off in Florida had been an exhibition of sheer stubbornness, and of a willingness to die in the effort to force something to happen. Chester had been certain the aeroplane would get off the ground if only the woman in the pilot's seat would do the right things. But Ruth had been doing the right things, and Angel wasn't ever going to take off. Then Ruth deliberately decided to do the wrong things. The most insane decision was pulling up the wheels before she'd even hopped as far as the end of the runway. If she'd come down again it would have been no rough landing with a run-on and a lot of damage. It would have been wreckage engulfed in a sliding fireball.

It had nothing at all to do with any belief that the take-off might happen by itself if you gave it the mechanically right chance to come true. It was a sheer refusal to let it *not* happen.

It was a compulsive madness. It produced compulsive viewing for a final total of over a million breakfast viewers, plus tens of millions of bulletin watchers later in the day. Ruth's take-off turned an interest item in the world news into a breathtaking headline story. All media are entertainment. Media news means entertainment with the spice of reality. And you can't beat a real cliff-hanger of a show. Ruth had bought her transient fame, her fragile place at the forefront of the three-minute culture. She'd done it by an insane refusal to let it all fall through.

It put even Michael Tranter in the shade for the present. What was that cryptic message that came through on his laptop shortly after his fall, a message presumably sent by his affairs-supervising robot, Pattie Lee? *Confirm started without trace*. What a rich irony there was in the timing. Michael was a selfish and self-satisfied man who specialised in supplying a woman with good sex, a fat salary, and a pain in her self-esteem if she wasn't careful. And then Ruth, the woman he was doing it all to at the moment, had taken the mission away. The great adventure had started without a trace of Michael Tranter.

The big question was – how would it end?

THIRTY

She started out from Michaels Field so low, and Angel climbed so slowly, that the air traffic controllers cancelled the flight plan and took her straight out west to the Gulf coast – below all the rest of Florida's air traffic, and nowhere *near* Disney World or Orlando or Tampa. The alteration won back half of the delay at take-off.

Out over the Gulf of Mexico, Angel took an hour at a steady grind of two hundred knots to climb to a thousand feet. Ruth could have used more power and climbed faster, but more power used more fuel, and she'd already taken off with litres less than the load needed to complete the flight – not enough to make it impossible, but enough to squeeze the margin for bad winds and diversions.

It took Angel another fifty-five minutes to get to two thousand feet, and another fifty-two minutes to make three thousand. By then Ruth began to believe there was a reasonable chance the whole effort wasn't going to end in a long splash in the waters of the Gulf. She didn't believe Chester's calculations any more.

She spent most of the time after the start in cloud, with nothing to see but shades of grey. The weather ruined the send-off from Florida, making an early morning rendezvous with private aircraft impossible. More of the same complex cloud roof had closed in the Texas coast near Galveston. No mid-morning flyers did impromptu aerobatics around her, providing photo opportunities and free publicity. Even the local Orbis camera aircraft was cancelled. A collision in cloud wasn't the way to circle the world.

The weather, though, brought winds that helped. By Galveston she'd made good another fifteen minutes of the delay. The only penalty was turbulence, which jolted her as she sat in the taut sling of Angel's upcurved wings.

They got glorious pictures as she flew across the divide from New Mexico to Arizona, north of the Pinaleno Mountains. She'd coaxed Angel to six thousand five hundred feet, and needed all of it on the way over the continental spine. They had thunderstorms. The camera aircraft, coming up from Douglas, paced her through interlacing canyons between vast mesas of cloud.

Angel liked to fly straight and level. Angel lumbered through the turns. The vast dihedral of the overloaded wings produced a leaden roll resistance which defeated all but the shallowest angle of bank. It was complicated by the long nose and short tail. When Ruth applied rudder and twisted the aircraft round its vertical axis, the extended nose got a slight sideways push as it began to slant into the air ahead. The force acted with the rudder and tended to twist Angel more vigorously into the turn. It was the exact opposite of what happened with a traditional aircraft, where the side force on the longer tail worked against the rudder and tended to stabilise the machine. In Angel's case, there was a constant need to counter the aircraft's perpetual desire to roll level but at the same time tighten the turn with increasing yaw. Left to itself, a banked turn would develop into a spiralling sideslip and eventual stall and tail spin – curtains for Angel and for every woman on board.

The handling wasn't going to become smooth again until Angel could roll normally, and that wasn't going to happen until the canoe tank was empty and the canoe and underwing had been thrown away. Angel would then be thirty percent lighter. Angel would also be on the other side of the Pacific.

Ruth flew over upland desert, then lowland desert. She

went past places with names. Pecos, El Paso. South of the Pinaleno Mountains and the San Pedro River were Tucson and Nogales. At the mouth of the Gila valley was a little town called Sonora. It was like flying through a world from childhood. She watched the scrolling, scruffy desert. There was no ranch house with a sleepy guard on the roof. No greasy old brother Buck with his flat, black, battered hat raised to shade over-the-hill eyes as he stared idiotically at a fantastic flying machine. No legend came limping out of a television fantasy land, where father figures were tall, and strong, and kind . . .

The Arizona air traffic authority kept her far away from Phoenix, taking no chances with her clumsy flying bomb. Ruth would have liked to see Phoenix from the air by day. She saw it once while flying over on a clear desert night – a vast valley of lights. That was when she still went on trips with Michael. He was on his way to Los Angeles to inaugurate the new Pacific routes to Australia and Malaysia. *Opt* for the natural world. *Opt* for life untouched by industry. *Opt* for places unspoiled by pollution. *Opt* for a better experience. *Opt* for Orbis Pacific Tours. The US carriers didn't want a newcomer in the Pacific. They opted to strangle the operation. It finally died in November 1990. By then Michael didn't seem to mind in the least . . .

The show came up to meet her at the California coast between San Diego and Oceanside. A buzzing gaggle of every kind of aircraft waited to see her arrow steadily through the evening and out into the empty Pacific Ocean. She overtook their circles and left them all behind – Ruth, and Angel Global Solo, the ones who were chasing the sun . . .

Michael sank backwards, downwards into the light. His right hand, reversed, slithered on the rail, forearm sliding on polished steel. His left arm flailed and his left hand bounced off the cement block wall. His feet stumbled backwards in a desperate race to catch his falling body. He descended deeper into the light, while his eyes stared upwards out of a shadowed face that was very much afraid –

He hit the little landing halfway down the rattling stair, and the landing finally defeated his heels. He toppled backwards with the full rushing momentum from his tantalising fall. His right hand lost the rail. When his back hit the landing, the gush of his expelled breath was even louder than the reverberating metal –

His left arm went full length up and over and took the lead, like a backstroke swimmer leaving a ledge in a pool. Over he went in a backwards roll, legs still kicking and trying to tread air. Over he went, rolling on his shoulder to begin a new foot-first pitch down the remainder of the stair and into the depths of the light. But his left arm had disappeared between the second and the third tread –

Michael, the bouncing man, suddenly jerked like a falling puppet whose string had been snatched. His arm, for a fraction of a second while his body whirled in illuminated space, refused to come free. And clear through the clattering steel and rattling stairway and echoing whiteness of noise which filled the light – clear, clean and quick enough to escape every sense but memory – was the snap of bone fragmenting like old wood.

And where, in all this, was Ruth?

Ruth was up above the light. Ruth was out of reach. In the dark . . .

Silver painted the pockets on the back bulkhead. Flashes, faintly, lit the padded roof, a syncopation of co-ordinated colours. The assist handle divided the alternating spectrum, red on the left, green on the right. The noise was the cockpit alarm.

She got up on her elbows. She grabbed the assist handle. She started to crank the seat upright. The alarm, which blinked bright amid the soft illumination of the instrument panel, was just the wake-up bell. Not the collision radar. Not a system alarm.

No danger in the dark . . .

226

A low moon was beating her to the rim of the night. A boulevard of wave-textured light ran out under the root of Angel's foreplane and met the moon at a horizon picked out as dark sea against misty, backlit cloud. The only colours were silver, and reflected flashes under the wings of red and green running lights on the wingtips.

The autopilot was in control. Angel's heading was south of west, taking a direct line to the Hawaiian Islands. Mission time was 21.30, UK time was 07.30 on Monday. Ruth would be passing Honolulu in three-quarters of an hour at just about local midnight, and in those three-quarters of an hour in England, the armies of commuters would be on the move, heading back to work after their survival weekend at home. How many of them knew? How many of them cared, or shared in her escape from the constant cycle of the everyday, as they checked the TV or listened to their car radios or read a paper on the train? What did fame feel like?

Fame was far away. It could wait. Nearby was a back which couldn't twist, shoulders whose bones seemed to have been replaced with rigid steel, thighs and calves which throbbed just short of the pain threshold, and a backside which was trying to make its owner believe it had been been bruised black and blue. Nearby also was a radar screen which was blank, and a VSI screen which said Angel was level at four thousand feet, on the correct heading, nose trimmed three degrees high in the attitude required with the canoe and its underwing. The throttle was at the planned setting. Airspeed was two hundred knots, true ground speed was two hundred and twenty-five as Angel rode the unceasing trade wind into the west. The ground was restless ocean swell . . .

Inside her mind, biding its time with a patient plan to ambush her eyes, was a heavy darkness which ebbed away with the slowness of reluctant tar. She needed a drink. She broke out a quarter-litre carton and sipped orange juice through a straw. The dense darkness still drained stickily out of her mind. Bedded in it and shrinking, an image in a pearl trapped in pitch, was Michael disappearing downwards into light. Enclosed inside the pearl, the clamour of a hangar choked with echoes vanished into silence.

The only sound was the engine. But it was such a constant noise that she didn't hear it any more.

Time to do something, time to uncouple her thoughts from the guilt that surfaces in sleep. The trouble was that Angel did everything itself. The next position update was due in thirty minutes, and would happen automatically. The aerial, enclosed in front of the cockpit inside the nose, was trained steadily on the most convenient communications satellite by a slaved computer. The computer knew where to point the aerial because it remembered the exact locations of the orbiting satellites to the second, it was told Angel's position every ten seconds by the INS, and it could work out the pointing angle from the data. The heart of the INS was another computer. Combining the technological tricks with the route Angel was destined to follow was a further mathematical task under the control of the central computer. The genius who made all the wizardry work together was Michael. Ruth flew Angel instead of Michael, but exclusively because of him.

The guilt wasn't going to go away.

She put on the headphones, pressed a switch on the communication panel at upper centre of the instrument board, and opened the two-way link to Mission Control. "Anybody there? This is me watching the moon go down."

"Hello, Ruth." The voice belonged to Mandy Rees. "Sleep well?"

"Three hours straight. Is everybody back from Florida?"

"They've all got home safely – though none of them have showed up here yet. Terri's due soon. You've made the early editions of all the papers, Ruth. The tabloids are putting you on the front page with headlines like 'Flying to Fame', 'Angel Away' and 'True Brit Grit'. The television's been showing lots of pictures. I counted fifteen reprises of your take-off yesterday. The sponsors are jumping up and down."

"Good. I'm glad they're happy." She was happy, too, but in a second-hand sort of way. At the moment the flight was enough reality. Its repercussions and lasting consequences could wait for her attention. "Any news of Michael?"

"He's okay, though I heard it's supposed to be months before his arm will be out of plaster. It's a really nasty break. The hospital have been sedating him to make sure he rests and gets over the concussion."

I know it was a nasty break, Ruth thought. I heard it. I handled it to staunch the bleeding. I want to know, in a sympathetic sort of way, how he feels about me taking on his glory. But if he's sedated, he won't care.

"Ruth, it says on my plan here, that you should call Honolulu, and then report back to me that they've accepted you."

"Right. I'll do that. Back in a few minutes. Bye." She switched off the satellite channel, then she poked a button beside the navigation screen and got a menu window. She selected *frequencies*, then paged down until she could press for *Honolulu*. The computer set the radio channel automatically. On her headset, in RT mode, she had to use the transmit button. "This is Angel Global Solo calling Honolulu. Do you read me? Over."

She sounded lonely, a little voice lost in the night.

THIRTY-ONE

Geraldine Trayhorn was wearing her grey checked jacket again, with a grey skirt. She wore a white blouse and a black bow tie. She still looked a little Monday morning sleepy. She was twenty-six and single, according to her file. Perhaps she lived lively weekends. She smoothed her blonde, bobbed hair behind her ears, and scanned the sheets in front of her on the conference table. "That's it, I think. That's the state of progress. I've traced some of the internal sources for the

229

money being stolen by way of the three frauds we've actually identified, and I've found a further three million missing from accounts." She shook her head, still looking at her papers. Blonde hair escaped again from behind her ears and swung strands beside her eyes. "I've no idea where the additional three million is going."

Curtis Gupta nodded.

"Three and a half million stolen through identified frauds," Munro said, "and a further three million disappearing in directions as yet unknown. It's becoming an impressive crime."

Curtis Gupta nodded again. He was born in Britain of Bengali parents. His hair was black, his suit was black with a grey pinstripe. His white shirt had a red collar and cuffs, his tie was red, his glasses had red metal frames. He was a yuppie with a B.Sc. and an M.Sc., and a lot of skill with computers. He was Munro's own appointment into MT's security department. "Do you assume the additional three million are being stolen by the same person?"

I do, Munro thought. I know it. But he glanced at Trayhorn to pass the question over to her.

Trayhorn shrugged. "It's being bled out of the same sources used for the first three frauds." She tucked her hair behind her ears again. She leaned back in her chair. "The path the money takes disappears immediately behind blocking programs operating inside the computer. I think it's the same person."

Gupta looked at the sheets on the table in front of Trayhorn. "And the problem at every stage is that the computer hides everything. You can only trace the path through any account by making a pen-and-paper analysis of every single movement on the account over months at a time."

"Exactly. It takes ages."

"So." Gupta looked at Munro again. "You want me to try unlocking the blocks in the computer system."

Munro nodded.

Gupta tipped his head and glanced at Trayhorn's briefcase,

which was stuffed so full of documents that it wouldn't close. "Who knows about this?"

"Me," Munro said. "And Trayhorn. And you."

"No one else?"

"No."

"Security," Trayhorn said. "If our investigation leaks to anyone at all, the fraudster might find out. Then he or she will just fade out of contact with the crime. We'll never trace the criminal."

"True." Gupta folded his arms. The red shirt cuffs poked further out of his sleeves. "I suppose I'm quite good at computers. But I'm not an accountant. I'm no good at fraud."

"You'll work together," Munro said. "Your cover is that Trayhorn is working out the costings of my restructuring for the company, she's putting it on the computer, and you're on the team to ensure that very sensitive data is properly protected. We have, after all, the espionage problem in the background."

Gupta nodded. "Is that getting anywhere, incidentally?"

"The in-house investigation is stalled." And the out-of-house investigation was Munro's personal secret. So was its interim result. "Before you ask, there's no reason to believe the two matters are connected. This is financial fraud, and has no relevance to any attempt to damage, dismantle or take over MT-Orbis." Munro looked at his watch. Eight fifteen, and still ahead of the mainstream office day. "Right. That's the brief. You're on the team. And like Trayhorn, you're answerable exclusively to me. I'll clear it with Stallybrass. For the moment we can end this here, and you start work." He stood up. Gupta and Trayhorn hurried to stand up as well, instantly obedient to the new week's acting absolute boss of MT Holdings. "I'd like to thank you both for coming in so early. And I don't want either of you to leave the building today without checking with me first."

They nodded. Trayhorn started to collect her papers from the table.

"Trayhorn," he said, "I'll want to coach you later on a

briefing you're going to make on the Orbis Pacific Tours fraud. We'll have to edit the facts to avoid giving too much away. By the way, do you own any shares in Orbis Air?"

"Shares?" She lifted her briefcase onto the chair and eased the papers inside with the rest of the documents. "No."

"Do you own shares in MT Holdings? Or any other subsidiary?"

"No. Why?"

So much, he thought, for popular capitalism – or worker participation, for that matter. "We'll have to change that." He started ushering them from the table towards the door. "I'll get back to you."

"I don't want to buy shares." Trayhorn clutched her overfull briefcase under her arm. "I can't afford to."

"Don't worry about financing it." He nodded towards the door, which Gupta had already opened, to hint that all discussion was over. "I'll get back to you later."

Geraldine Trayhorn just shrugged, took the hint, and left.

He gave them a minute to clear Ripley's outer office, then he crossed to the door himself and opened it. Mrs Anne Ripley looked up from her desktop screen. "I've checked with the hospital. There's no phone installed for Mr Tranter yet, but it's on their job list for this morning."

Munro nodded. So by noon at the latest, Michael would be able to start making a nuisance of himself – unless someone was helpful enough to sedate him again. "I want you to call an extraordinary shareholders meeting of Orbis Air – here, in this building, in the Orbis Air boardroom, at four thirty this afternoon. If anyone argues, remind them that MT's twenty-four percent gives me the right to call the meeting. Let the Orbis Air people downstairs do all the running round, but make confirmatory calls to Geoffrey Simmington at Longman Short and to Sylvia Symes at Rowe Spitta Pitts."

"Very well." Ripley pushed a couple of keys and saved her screen. Then she looked at him again. "Mr Munro, would it be of any help if I knew what's actually going on?"

"Yes," he said. "In fact it would be of enormous help."

She'd be able to cover for him, double his attentiveness, and take some of the organisational load. "But I'm not going to tell you."

"Oh." She thought about it for a moment. "Why?"

"So that you're less likely to get the sack if the whole thing falls apart. Call my broker as soon as his office opens, please. I want him to transfer some shares."

THIRTY-TWO

She half sat, half lay, squeezed in the front of the glider cockpit as Icarus lurched to the tug of the invisible tow. It was darkness without sun. It was the nightmare version of past reality, the one where there would be no escape unless she stopped it happening, unless she clawed her own way out . . .

It fooled her. She thought that this time, at last, the catches were locked tight. Bouncing on the ground, lifting into the night, soaring steeply upwards into midnight pitch nothing –

In the infinitely elastic moment, the catches slip free. She can't fasten them in time. The canopy starts to lift. Her fingers bend against the Perspex as she tries to press down on the rim. But the suction of rushing night-time air is too intense –

The canopy rips up and back and bursts. The explosion of eggshell shards happens in a bulb of silence, outside which the night wind rushes. As the fragments, spinning, reach the envelope of sound they vanish into it with hisses like white hot glass flung into black water. The canopy frame, armed with jagged remnant teeth like some obscenely dislocated jaw, bounces up and down over her head. Behind her, Michael tears at the controls while his words say it won't work. It won't work.

In the infinite elasticity of time, the crash is happening again. In the desperate awareness of the endless last moment,

233

she's failed. She always fails. The glider is falling backwards like a streamlined stone. It will stab the invisible earth with its tail. The tail will disintegrate, its skin will splinter into razored plastic shards which will find Michael, then the back of her seat, then her flesh.

This is all, this is every bit of it. No miracle of escape. This is the onset of the ultimate moment, the vast void of terror and despair when life is torn to pieces. Bones snap, skin flays, muscle shreds, and the mind, the *you*, inside a capsule of purest agony, is refined in one freeze-drying instant of dissipation into nothing . . .

The glass cascade has advanced along the splintering tail as it plunges itself against the anvil of earth. It has entered the shell of silent blackness. It drowns Michael's curses. Michael dies first in this drawn out fractional moment. Michael knows her hands have let him die because she didn't hold that gaping jaw closed –

But the voice she hears over the porcelain crescendo is her father's. He waits on the ground and is now inside that falling envelope of terminal hell. *Fall*, says his voice. *Fall back where you belong.* And while she's falling back out of dreams, out of an attempt at independence, backwards against the unforgiving truth of pointless ending and death, she sees him. He wheels his chair round with a deft flick of practised arms. The chair stops with a brief wobble, the slight resilience of tyres locked on a hard surface, and he stares right at her. *Fall. Fall!*

Fall.

Falls break arms. Falls break backs. Break lives. Where was Ruth when her father fell?

In the dark . . .

With colours that flash. Red, and green, and then brighter white. When she pushes down her chin and looks over her chest, a box of green symbols and lines glows back at her. The glider doesn't have a display like that. Not even Michael's glider.

But Michael's aircraft did.

She lifted herself on her elbow. She reached up and

grabbed the assist handle. Her hand was painted in alternating time steps – red from the left, on the back of her hand, green from the right, on her palm. White in between. Red and green were the running lights on the wingtips. White was the strobe reflecting off the underside of the high wing. The sounds were windrush, and the steady whining roar from the engine which was pushing Angel through the night.

She sat up. She cranked the seat into its upright position. Icarus, the glider, was still splintering to scythes and knives in the blackness waiting behind her mind. If she closed her eyes, or if the lights stalled in their standoff traffic light argument, red and green, stop and go, if she went back into the blackness it would enclose her in the fall . . .

The repeater instruments were blurred, the screen displays were too busy in detail but static in their messages. Flight level. Attitude level. Altitude steady. Heading steady. Airspeed steady. Ambient temperature, engine temperature, fuel rate, engine revs, generator voltage, avionics power – all steady. Nothing to reward her attention, and nothing at all out there in the night.

She checked the catches on the side windows were closed.

A voice. She needed a human voice. She pushed the switch on the up-front panel on the instrument board. Blue words in the communications window told her the satellite transceiver was ready and the antenna correctly aligned. She put on the headset. She tightened the safety strap more firmly round her hips. An image in her mind with an impact that killed, the fall still waited. She needed a human voice to keep it at bay. "It's all right. It's all right. The dream's gone."

Terri Sabuli yawned at her handset. "What did she say?"

Mandy Rees shrugged, listening to her own handset with the mouthpiece covered. "Search me. She sounds half-asleep. I'll wake her up. Ruth, this is Mandy. How's it going?"

Terri hung up her handset on the sloping desk. She needed waking up as well. It was midday. She should be alert. She lifted her coffee off the front edge of the desk, and swung her chair to look at the rest of the control room. Four of Michael's Orbis-image young women waited, wearing their uniform of jeans and trainers and the project T-shirt, with the crazy green aeroplane slung by its wingtips from tit to tit. They sat on their chairs or on their desks, attending to the rank of phones which at the moment weren't going to ring. Media interest was quiet as Angel winged the vast Pacific. Ruth was supposed to be asleep . . .

Mandy covered her mouthpiece again. "No problem. Just difficulty sleeping and feeling lonely, I think." She uncovered the mouthpiece. "Why not cancel the alarm, Ruth, and wait a bit longer before having another shot at sleeping? You've still got four hours until sunrise."

Terri sipped her coffee. She should be awake. Outside the windows at the back of the room was the back-alley view of grimy Soho brickwork, lit by a summer sun which was soured yellow by London's breath. She'd taken a risk and allowed herself several more hours of sleep than would have been wise – if, for instance, something had happened while Ruth was passing the Hawaiian Islands at local midnight and eight fifteen in the UK morning. But nothing had happened. The Pacific night had been empty.

She sipped the vending machine coffee. She was slow and uneasy, stuck in a body that was stubbornly jet-lagged after only two days across the Atlantic. Must be the first sign of getting old. Everything was firm and supple and free of sag or cellulite – a sound diet, regular swimming and low-weight workouts saw to that. But the internal mechanics were getting less flexible and less accommodating to change. Early thirties and no need to worry yet, but age was lurking beyond the future's horizon. You can get a new outfit of clothes, but your live-in machine is built for a single occupancy on a limited lease . . .

The Mission Control door opened. Pattie Lee, of all people, walked in. She wasn't in the slightest bit tall – but she managed to look down her little Chinese nose at everyone and everything in the place. She was wearing her dark-blue summer cotton suit over a white blouse, all carefully creaseless and perfect. Her hair was brushed without a strand loose. Her stockings were straight and her shoes were spotless. She gave the big map on the long wall a bare glance. She scanned the tables with their telephones, the communications desk with its two occupants, the trio of computers on a table piled with map sheets, meteorology plots and concertina printouts of the mission's schedule of pre-timed events. She walked up to the communications desk.

"Munro," said Pattie Lee, "isn't here."

"No," Terri said. "He isn't."

Mandy hung up the handset, consigning Ruth to the Pacific night. "He hasn't been here all morning. Shouldn't he be over at the MT building?"

Pattie Lee's mouth twitched. "Apparently he isn't."

Terri balanced her coffee on the edge of the desk again. "He's supposed to be extremely busy at the moment. Is it important?"

"I have some urgent things to take care of for Michael." Pattie Lee's eyes gleamed down at her. Contact lenses – the woman wore contact lenses. "I need some data from his laptop. He had his laptop at Wragby."

"I remember."

"Munro brought it back to London. I need it."

"Munro brought it back?" There was something slightly odd about that, but she couldn't put her finger on it. Too much lingering jet-lag. "We'll tell him if we see him. Come to think of it, where's Chester? He should be here by now. He's our best expert on Angel, just in case."

"He might not turn up just now," Mandy said. "Unless there's a problem. There's this big flap on over at MT, isn't there?"

"Is there?"

"At Orbis Air." Mandy looked at Pattie Lee, then back at Terri. Mandy was obviously surprised to see she'd had first pick at the grapevine. "Munro's called an emergency shareholders meeting."

"Has he?"

"I didn't know about this," Pattie Lee said. She said it with a trace of real surprise.

"And Chester's on the board of Orbis Air," Mandy said. "Isn't he? So he's involved."

"Ah yes." Terri reached for her coffee again. "Michael's token black."

"Pardon?"

She shook her head at Mandy. "I notice these things. Just look at my skin colour. Tell me, does Michael have any other black, or Asian, or Chinese – or even an Irishman – on any other of his loads and loads of boards? Does he have a single woman director? It all fits, believe me."

"Fits what?"

"Michael being a white middle-class English male."

Mandy seemed puzzled. "Don't you *like* Michael?"

"Oh, he has his good points. And he's a brilliant showman. The trouble is, he's terribly bad at going down stairs."

"You know, jet-lag's tangled your brain, Terri. Where's she gone? Pattie Lee, I mean."

Terri looked round. Pattie Lee had left without even saying goodbye.

THIRTY-THREE

Michael lay in his solitary room with the weight of his plastered arm distributed between left shoulder and midriff. The heaviest pressure was concentrated on the ribs over his spleen. The cast was what they called lightweight, but embedded in it along the outside of his right-angled arm was a metal brace. His hand had been bandaged so tightly to the stirrup at the end of the brace that it was completely impossible to twist his wrist. Metal bolts, heads standing proud of the cast, went through

238

the brace and into the bone. The arrangement permitted no movement at all of the fragments of bone broken apart below his elbow. It was a very bad break. But if he would go trying to lever treads out of a steel staircase with nothing more than his arm plus the force of his somersaulting body . . .

Traumas, he'd been led to believe, are masked forever by shock amnesia. Unfortunately, he could remember every exact extended detail of his long fall – including the *sound*, and the pain – until unconsciousness and a concrete floor intervened.

The trick was to try not to think about it.

Since mid-morning he had a television – which, without a computer and keyboard attached, was useless – and a telephone. The telephone sat on top of the table, which had been moved very considerately to the righthand side of the bed. He could call people at last and put fire under some arses – except that a little task like remembering phone numbers required unwarranted effort, and the concentration involved was proving too elusive. An effect of the concussion, the doctor said. Nothing to worry about. Fade away in a few days. He must have been feeling better since lunchtime: when the doctor looked in, he was polite to her.

A very bad break. He was never going to forgive Ruth Clifford. If she managed by some miracle to complete the flight, then the second the media fuss died down after her return he'd strip her of job, salary, pension, everything. The fall could have killed him. Or broken his back, or his neck, and crippled him for life. Ruth Clifford would never be forgiven. Out on her ear, instantaneously, with no compensation. Thank God for foresight and the ability to learn by experience. It wouldn't be like getting rid of Sylvia Symes. Ruth held no shares, ran no brokering interests – and knew no secrets. A clean break.

Unlike his arm. The bolts would be in for months, and an operation would be needed to remove them. Where he was planning to be, months ahead, he'd need a lot of money to get the job done right. Money, though, wasn't the problem. It

239

was already on its way, automatically, in very ample quantities. The problem, out of the blue, had become: how was he going to arrange to follow it? Things weren't supposed to turn out like this. It had been a very bad break indeed.

The phone rang. And kept on ringing. It took him a long time to twist round and pick up the phone with his hand reversed. He dropped the receiver, retrieved it by the cord, landed it next to his head on the pillow – and eventually got it round, righthanded, to his left ear. The doctor said he'd need at least a week of complete rest before the bruises eased enough for his muscles to move again. He could allow himself one day. Two at the absolute most. "Hello."

"Hello, Michael," said Pattie Lee's voice. "This isn't a secure line, is it?"

"No. It goes through the hospital exchange."

"Right. Two things. Munro won't surrender your laptop. He's avoiding me and his PA is obstructing me. He's up to something."

"I'm not surprised." Munro had, after all, been dropping some sort of hint to Ruth Clifford. She'd yelled at him about it at the top of the stair.

"Munro's also called a shareholders meeting at Orbis Air."

"Has he? When?"

"Now. George Connor has arrived from Oxford, and they've just gone in. I can't discover what it's about, but Munro's taken someone called Trayhorn in with him. She's from accounts, and accounts tell me she's been preparing material in connection with Munro's restructuring plan. I think Munro might be planning to bounce the Orbis Air board into a sell-off. He's taking advantage of your absence."

Bob Munro should be smarter than that. From Munro's point of view, with no knowledge of the game actually being played, it should be obvious that Michael had only been stalling a move on Orbis Air until the flight with Angel was safely under way. After that, Munro should realise, he wouldn't oppose a sale. The real truth, of course, was totally different. "Never mind Orbis Air. You have to get the laptop."

"How, Michael? Call the police and say he stole it?"

"Don't make jokes about involving the police."

"Then how do I get the laptop?"

How indeed? How could she get the laptop, and get hold of the data inside it? The plan had been that she'd acquire it after the take-off at Wragby, and much later Michael would be able to unlock the contents of the machine. No data – no future.

"I haven't got an answer, Michael. And it matters. Have you got an answer?"

It was about the *data*. The same data was security locked on the hard disk inside the computer at his home. "Yes. You'll have to go to my place in Oxford. I've got copies of the data there. You'll need a key. You'll have to come back here and get mine."

"Can't you send it down? Red Star it? There are main line trains from Sheffield to London."

"I'd need staff to send it out. I could *post* it from the hospital, but it wouldn't even go out until tomorrow. You wouldn't get it before Wednesday."

"Can't I just access your computer over the phone?"

"Not for the stuff we need. It won't accept modem input. You'll have to come and collect the key."

"Right. Then I'll see you in a few hours."

"Yes. Wait! Wait a minute. Did you think of cancelling the other thing – the pickup?"

"I tried to cancel it. But the contact's been withdrawn, as planned. Some people are going to find they've gone fishing, but there's no fish. They won't be pleased."

"Can't be helped. They won't be able to trace us, anyway. For now, just make sure you get up here before they close the hospital for the night. Don't get stuck in any traffic."

Robert Munro ran the meeting. The opposition never had a chance.

The opposition consisted of shareholding directors of Orbis

Air led by Andrew Carlyle and George Connor. Carlyle was acting MD of Orbis Air in Michael's absence, and was backed up by the company's finance director, Neil Curthoys, as well as John Stallybrass – who headed up the airline's security in addition to MT's – and Chester Alby. Connor was acting MD of Siltech in Oxford, and had a seat on the Orbis Air board. Michael Men, every one of them, fitted out with multiple directorships and salary upon salary. Michael had bought his courtiers handsomely.

None of the other directors of Orbis Air were present. They'd been caught out, as intended, by the short notice Munro had given for the meeting. A mere half of the seats in the airline's boardroom were filled. It would have looked even more sparse, even more obviously contrived, without the outside shareholders.

Geoffrey Simmington was there for Longman Short, and Sylvia Symes was proxy for the clients she handled at Rowe Spitta Pitts. No other outsiders had made the meeting in time.

The only stranger at the table was Geraldine Trayhorn. Munro brought her in to take minutes, and to present the basic facts on the fraud at Orbis Pacific Tours.

Trayhorn coped with the task smoothly. No one asked a question during the presentation, so she didn't have to interrupt herself to take specific minutes. She was greeted, at the finish, by silence. She sat beside Munro and lifted her pen, ready to make notes. But the silence continued. Some of them were probably worrying about boardroom liability in cases of fraud. George Connor and Andrew Carlyle would be wondering about the purpose of the meeting.

Time, Munro decided, to put them out of their misery. "The fraud is big enough to be damaging, and so sophisticated it's unsettling." At his side, Trayhorn's hand jerked into motion and started taking notes. "It would appear to have been perpetrated by a well-informed insider in a position of responsibility, not to say trust. It's extremely serious."

Andrew Carlyle tossed his head, a sudden movement of

solarium suntan and sweeping white hair. It drew attention. It was the equivalent, in Michael's boardroom classes, of putting up his hand when he wanted to speak. But Michael wasn't here today, so Carlyle went ahead without waiting for permission. "I think, Robert, that the seriousness is self-evident. Which leads me to ask – why call an extraordinary shareholders meeting to inform us? Why haven't you taken this to the board first? Or me, dammit?"

"For the following reason, Andrew." He glanced at Trayhorn's newest note: *AC asks reason for bypassing board.* Far too explicit, too undiplomatic. "The fraud has been running for some time. However, it was not detected by Orbis Pacific Tours, nor by Orbis Air – despite the direct involvement of Orbis Air finances in the mechanism of the fraud." Neil Curthoys, the finance director, looked unhappy at that.

Carlyle shrugged tennis-trained shoulders. "That's hardly fair, you know. It sounds pretty well undetectable to me."

"It was detected, Andrew. At MT level. Miss Trayhorn found it. The computer has been manipulated to massage the data it's supplying, but that doesn't hide the actual movements of money. As soon as you take the trouble to compare real movements with the computer data, the discrepancy becomes apparent."

Fraud detectable, Trayhorn wrote.

"I'm afraid I don't see your point, Robert. Are you implying – well, some sort of failing on our part?"

"I'm stating the obvious fact that Orbis Air failed – over some considerable time – to police its own financial affairs adequately. The responsibility for such a failure rests with the board."

"Good God, man!" Carlyle's suntan began to burn. "Some little bugger fiddles the computer, and you as good as say *we're* to blame!"

"You're to blame when you let someone steal the company's money." Munro paused long enough to look across at Connor. George Connor was shaking his head. The man from Siltech had seen what was coming, and was saying it wouldn't work.

He wouldn't let it. We'll see about that, Munro thought. "I repeat, Andrew – the fraud was not undetectable. Adequate checks would have found it. But there were no adequate checks. You failed in your duty to protect shareholders' money. I therefore move that the board of Orbis Air be dismissed, and a new board appointed. The new board can then pursue the matter and consider steps necessary to recover the stolen resources and prosecute the perpetrator."

Carlyle looked aghast. So did the other Michael Men. All except George Connor.

"But – " said Stallybrass, the security overseer with a blind spot about computers. "The board can't dismiss itself. Can it?"

"This is a shareholders meeting," George Connor said, quietly. "He needs an absolute majority to dismiss the board."

"But – " Stallybrass looked round the half-empty table. "There are so *few* of us here. Are there enough?"

Connor shook his head.

Come on, Geoffrey, Munro thought. You're missing your cue. You're an inattentive conspirator.

"I second the motion," Simmington said. "The negligence of the board seems sufficient to call the company into disrepute. It risks damaging share values."

"Dismissing the board," Stallybrass said, "won't affect share values, I suppose?"

"Dammit!" Carlyle slapped the table in front of him. "This is totally out of proportion!"

"Orbis Air is turning in a severe loss," Munro said. "It's teetering on the brink of becoming everyone's bad investment. Very decisive action is required before the last shred of confidence goes. So." He looked at Connor again. "I vote MT's twenty-four percent holding for the motion to dismiss the board."

Connor nodded. "I vote Siltech's twenty-four percent against."

Carlyle turned from Connor to Munro. In the absence

of the king, the courtiers had to hold things together. No change without Michael's say-so. Carlyle glanced at Geoffrey Simmington and Sylvia Symes, the only representatives of outside investors. "You haven't got enough votes."

Munro shrugged. "I vote the cross-share stake held by Orbis in Orbis Air."

"You can't, man!"

"For the motion, of course. That's another twenty-four percent."

"You *can't*," Carlyle repeated. "George – *can* he?"

"No." Connor was almost smiling. You're an outsider, Munro, he seemed to be thinking. You're not one of Michael's chosen few. We're defending Michael, might and right. You can't beat us.

Connor's got the self-satisfied advantage of a paid-up English education, Munro thought. I'm an upstart from the Glasgow slums, vanished accent or no. But I've got the better grasp of the company rules. I wrote them myself – the job Michael hired me to do. I never imagined they could be used like this. If Michael bounces back too soon, the experiment will turn out fatal.

"If you like," he said to Connor, "we can convene an Orbis meeting here and now. You're present for Siltech, Andrew's here for Orbis Air, and I'm here for MT. That's ninety-six percent of the Orbis shares. The company has no outside investors."

"Michael's four percent," Carlyle said. "You can't leave out Michael's stake."

"Michael's shares," Munro said, "are suspended while he remains unable to vote them himself. A proxy is forbidden. It's in the rules."

Carlyle just shook his head.

"Well," Connor said. "Let's vote Orbis shares. Since you enjoy full executive control of MT during Michael's absence, I assume you're voting MT's forty-eight percent for backing you in dismissing the board at Orbis Air?"

Munro nodded. "I am."

"And I vote Siltech's twenty-four percent in Orbis against."

As expected. Munro glanced at Trayhorn's minutes. She'd given up. Two separate shareholders meetings happening simultaneously, one inside the other, in the Orbis Air boardroom was too confusing.

"Ah!" Andrew Carlyle looked triumphant. Connor had shown the way, and now he could settle the business and sink the usurper. "I vote Orbis Air's twenty-four percent against, too. That makes our combined forty-eight percent against your forty-eight. You're blocked at Orbis. You can't use the Orbis holding at Orbis Air. You're stuck, Robert Munro."

Munro shook his head. The fool didn't understand the rules. "You can't vote Orbis Air's shareholdings in any other company. Not while the Orbis Air board is under a motion of dismissal."

"What? I can't *what*?"

"You can't vote Orbis Air's stake in Orbis. At Orbis, the vote is MT's stake against Siltech's. So, Orbis goes my way."

"Are you – ? Can he – ?" Carlyle turned to Connor. "Is he *right*? Can't I vote at Orbis because of his bloody little trick?"

"I think – " Connor had just lost his self-satisfied smile. "We might have to check, but – "

"Do you want me – " Munro raised his voice. "Do you *want* me to order a copy of the company's charter in here? Am I supposed to read it out to you? Do you want me to pull in legal advice? Do you think I don't know what I'm *doing*?"

Silence.

Carlyle stared at Connor. So did Stallybrass, Curthoys and a devastated-looking Chester Alby.

Connor, slowly, lifted his eyes and looked back at Munro. "Oh, you know what you're doing. How long have you been sitting on this fraud, waiting for the opportunity to use it?"

Not long, Munro thought. It turned up just in time. "Back to the Orbis Air meeting," he said. "The vote now stands at MT's twenty-four percent and Orbis's twenty-four percent

246

for the motion of dismissal. That's two percent short of the absolute majority required. Siltech votes against." He turned to look at Geoffrey Simmington and Sylvia Symes.

"My bank," Simmington said, "votes with the motion."

"Sylvia?"

Sylvia Symes smiled. "My clients are in favour – with the exception of Bryce McFadden, who decline to vote. The motion has a comfortable majority, Robert."

Munro nodded.

"Perfect." George Connor folded his arms. "You've set this up perfectly, haven't you? With Geoffrey and with *her*." He glared at Sylvia Symes. "*You're* taking revenge on Michael, I suppose. Munro has plenty of time to discuss our finances with *you*. He just can't find the time to discuss them with *us*. A very neat set-up."

Sylvia Symes just smiled at Connor.

Munro tapped Trayhorn's writing pad. Time to resume the minutes. "Motion carried," he said. "Board dismissed."

Andrew Carlyle slapped the table with both hands. "Well! That's it. First the rules give him full executive power at MT Holdings. Then he uses the rules like a bloody hatchet on us at Orbis Air. Failing to protect shareholders' money. Jeopardising confidence. All over a piddling little fraud. This is the first time I've seen anyone cut off a puppy's head just to stop it pissing on the carpet!"

George Connor was studying Munro. "This is about more than just pissing on the carpet, Andrew."

"I know, George. I bloody well know. He wants to sell off Orbis Air while Michael isn't looking."

I want more than that, Munro thought. You might be bright enough to see the picture by this time tomorrow. He looked at his watch. Five twenty. It had been short and vicious so far. One last job before closing the meeting. "I move that I be appointed to head an interim board."

"Seconded," said Simmington.

"I'm in favour," said Sylvia. "Munro is appointed."

"I need a specialist in Orbis Air's day-to-day finances to

keep the company running. I propose reappointing Neil Curthoys."

Curthoys looked surprised.

"Seconded," Simmington said.

"Just a minute!" Carlyle pointed a suntanned finger at Curthoys – suspecting a traitor, perhaps. "You've just had us all sacked for not running the finances properly – then you put our finance director back on the board."

"Carried," Sylvia said.

Munro waited for another protest. None came.

"Finally," he said, "I need someone with special responsibility to cover the investigation into the fraud." And someone whose fate is tied to mine, he thought, so I get a two-to-one majority against Curthoys and can keep full control of the token board. "I propose Miss Trayhorn. She does hold shares in the company, by the way."

Trayhorn had dropped her pen.

Sylvia Symes opened the cigarette case inside her purse, brought out a cigarette, and lit it with her silver lighter. She looked round the all but deserted scene of swift blood-letting. Trayhorn was still seated at the empty boardroom table, slotting papers back into her briefcase. Simmington, cigar in hand, was wandering along the windows, apparently looking for one that opened. He had enough sensibility not to want to smoke a cigar in an unventilated room in the green-aware MT building.

"Well," Sylvia said. "That didn't take long."

Munro looked at his watch. Five thirty. One single efficient hour. Now he'd launched his move against Michael. The first victims still thought it was about selling Orbis Air – a purging of all the people who'd supported Michael's objection to the idea. They thought the fraud was nothing more than an excuse to clear the way for a sale. They hadn't seen the half of it.

Sylvia folded her arms in her cocktail pose, cigarette cantilevered out in the fingers of one hand. "What's your next move?"

"I'm waiting until Connor's on his way back to Oxford. Then I'm calling a meeting at Orbis for nine tomorrow morning."

"I see." Sylvia watched her cigarette smoulder. "You won't be needing us, then."

"No." Munro had Orbis sewn up. He wielded the stake held by MT, plus the cross-shares held by Orbis Air. Connor's control of Siltech's final slice of Orbis wouldn't be able to stop another boardroom coup. And another shocking morning for George Connor in London would steal all the time he might have used to throw some sort of defence together at Siltech in Oxford. Something like a blitz on the accounts to clean up the act. Because Siltech would be the final castle to fall.

Sylvia nodded towards Geraldine Trayhorn. "You surprised your little protégée, Robert."

"Did I?"

"When you bounced her onto the board. She wasn't expecting that, was she?" Sylvia paused to draw on her cigarette. "Tell me – have you got your eyes on her? Or indeed, have you already got your hands on her? She's quite pretty, after all."

"She's a good accountant," he said. He needed the loyalty of an accountant adept enough to spot an exceptionally clever fraud. He didn't need idiotic ideas about entanglements with a woman half his age. He'd just launched a war. At fifty-two, a hardened business player, he shouldn't feel so excited, so agitated, so fluid inside. He shouldn't feel so frightened by what he was doing. He should be as ice cold as the image he was projecting. He lacked, perhaps, the killer instinct. Well, this was Monday afternoon, and by the end of the week he was going to find out, one way or the other.

"Look, Robert – I'd better go and rescue poor Geoffrey. He does so want his cigar. I'll invite him to share a taxi." Sylvia smiled. "Very nice work so far. Bad day for Michael. Keep me up to date, won't you?"

In the lift, on the way up to MT's executive floor, Geraldine

Trayhorn finally decided to speak. "I thought – " She tucked her briefcase tighter under her arm, and started again. "When you transferred those shares to me, I thought it was something to do with spreading the vote for some reason or other. I mean, a dozen shares in a company the size of Orbis Air is neither here nor there, but I thought that was what it was about." She turned her head and looked up at him across the lift. "Now I'm a director."

He nodded. "For a few weeks."

"Well – why? What's going on? What are you *doing* to me? What are you getting me into?"

Into my tiny army, he thought, for this war. I'm tying you to my side before you even know what the fight's about. "I'm getting you into deep water," he said. "Stay on board the boat."

"And what do I get," she asked, "if I stay on board?"

A fighting chance against the sharks, he thought. "The best job I have to offer, once the dust has settled."

Trayhorn nodded at the doors. "If you win, you mean."

THIRTY-FOUR

The sun came up behind her left shoulder, between the underwing and the vast scythe of the main wing, and poured crimson into the cockpit window. Long minutes later, it brushed the ocean below, creating an infinite corrugation of gleaming wave crests and rouge-shaded troughs. She sat suspended in brilliant light.

The sun rose at Mission Time 30.30, while Angel was riding southwest on the trade wind. The sun came up thirty and a half hours after the clock started in Florida at the first sunrise. Ruth, in Angel, had advanced six and a half hours on the sun. It went round the planet faster than she could fly, but she was chasing it just the same.

Three-quarters of an hour later she had her sunglasses on, the ocean was dazzling, and the empty sky above was a blinding blue. She crossed the International Date Line, a fiction drawn down a longitude in the middle of nowhere. Local Monday changed to local Tuesday in the transition of an Angel's length. The mission clock read 31.15, the UK clock read 17.15 and was still stuck on its faraway yesterday. Here, the time zone date had flipped and a day had disappeared.

Two and a half hours later still, she crossed the equator. Not a change to be seen on the ocean below, just waves rolling diamond carpets under the sun. The Gilbert Islands went past on the sliding map, Abemama and Aranuka to the north, Nonouti to the south. They were atolls, rings of coral jutting just far enough out of the sea to give a few palms a foothold above the breaker line. They captured no cap of cloud, raised no jungle-clad mountain peak. She thought she could just about see two smudges on the northern horizon. She saw nothing to the south. The peoples of Oceania were scattered thinly. They didn't have many aircraft, and they had more useful things to do with them. No one came flying out to watch her go by. She saw no human life – it was amazing what a rarity ships could be on the open sea. The world is vast.

It was hot in the cockpit. She rubbed cream into her left hand and forearm to prevent a burn: white-skinned redheads turn angry scarlet in the sun. Her left leg cooked inside the cotton of her trousers. She had the ventilation wide open and the cooler on. She was at four thousand feet, and the air was very warm. The sweetest thing to do would be to sleep . . .

Stiffly, a skeleton wrapped in aches, a prisoner strapped to a seat she couldn't leave, Ruth flew on for another three hundred air miles, three hundred and thirty-seven ocean miles. Life had reduced itself to an extreme of simplicity. Sit – and watch the instruments as they reported the gradual passage of emptiness outside. No ship, no aircraft, no expectation of land. Angel flew itself along a predetermined course, a great plan which had come from Michael's head and was written down as tiny islets of magnetism spiralled on a computer disk, concepts constructed to suit the ego of a very arrogant man. Well, it was Ruth who was here after all. She had nothing to do but sit, and ache, and wait as time went by and the sun slowly lapped her again, a blazing hare to her flying tortoise. In the contest of time zone paradoxes, it was the tortoise which would catch the hare.

She found two things to do. She ate a low-fibre, high-energy snack and washed it down with orange juice. And she switched to internal fuel when the last leftover litre was used up in the canoe tank under Angel's belly.

At 35.00 on the mission clock, it would be time for the canoe tank and the underwing to go.

The blue lights lit in the little window on the communication panel, and Mandy Rees's voice started to squeak out of the headset hung on the hook beside the seat. Ruth put the headset on. "Start again, Mandy. What did you say?"

"Are you ready to change to internal fuel? It's thirty-five hundred."

"I'm already on internal fuel. And I've done the system checks. I can think for myself, you know."

"Good. Then I suppose you're ready to dump the canoe and stuff, too?"

"I'm ready. I'm fed up with toddling along at two hundred knots. I want to get up to speed." Speed was two hundred and fifty knots, the optimum cruising speed for a clean, underwing-free Angel.

"You're getting to like this, aren't you?"

"Well – actually I'm a little nervous about the next bit."

"Nerves," said Terri Sabuli's voice, "are for stage fright, Ruth. You know – all those spectacular travelog pics with a nice green aeroplane overhead. This next bit is just the technology, the nuts and bolts stuff, the way it actually works. No one's ever interested in that part. No one's watching. So no nerves, okay?"

What was Terri Sabuli trying to do – adopt her? "Is anyone from our aircraft team interested, at least?"

"John's here."

John Coates was good news. "And what about Chester?"

"Oh, he went home."

"He *what*? Doesn't he give a *shit* about me?"

"He isn't quite with it at the moment, Ruth. Munro called some sort of meeting at Orbis Air this afternoon, and sacked the entire board."

"*Sacked* the board?"

"And Chester's in the majority who weren't reappointed. He's still got his department to run, but I don't think he knows if he's still got his salary."

"Michael. Does Michael know about this?"

"If he didn't know, I'm sure either Chester or Pattie Lee has told him by now. The word is, Munro is acting on Michael's wishes for the good of the company."

Munro had told her – if Munro had been telling the truth – that the good of the company had nothing to do with Michael's wishes any more. "Do you believe that, Terri? That Michael instructed Munro?"

"Interesting question. We've got exclusive use of the satellite channel, so it's a private line, Ruth, but there's half a room full of people listening at this end. Let's get on with the job, shall we?"

She gave her status report: speed 200 knots; altitude 4000 feet; course 225 degrees; position 170 degrees east, 3 degrees 20 minutes south. Visibility was perfect, the sky was empty, and there was no one on the sea below who might get hurt by a piece of falling GRP. Ruth was ready to let the canoe assembly go.

The procedure was simple. She just flipped a switch down on the left side of the instrument board. That activated an electrical circuit which opened four clamps. The clamps held the ends of four metal pins which protruded from the top surface of the flush-fitting canoe, and passed a few centimetres through the hull to locate into the clamps. She had to flip the switch, the clamps would open, the pins would be released, and the canoe and its underwing would drop free. Easy. No need to be nervous.

But she wasn't dealing with a simple drop tank. The canoe assembly was a boat-shaped semi-fuselage with wings of its own. When it fell away, Angel would lose three things at once – the weight, the drag, and the lift from the underwings. The loss of lift would tend to make Angel fall. The loss of weight – even the empty plastic shell, minus its tons of take-off fuel – would make Angel climb. The loss of drag would make Angel gain speed, and therefore lift from its own wings, and would also make the aircraft climb. On balance, the immediate response when the canoe was jettisoned should be more height and more speed.

If Chester had got things right. He got things wrong with the take-off conditions. He wasn't infallible. Ruth would have liked a dress rehearsal in safe airspace within immediate reach of rescue, rather than trying it for the first time over the deserted western Pacific. Well, that option wasn't on . . .

She took hold of the stick, and then cut out the autopilot.

She felt the faint pressure of feedback on the stick as Angel cruised straight as an arrow through smooth air. She put her feet on the rudder pedals. With her left hand, she tightened the lap belt holding her in the seat. She wouldn't want to think she needed the shoulder straps, too.

"Okay. I'm on manual and ready."

Her hands and feet were automatically nudging the controls, making fractional adjustments to keep Angel's trim steady, course true and rate of climb zero. She didn't know how to anticipate the kick when the canoe fell away. Her reaction would have to be automatic, too.

Her left hand, in sunlight, unlocked the switch at the bottom left of the instrument board. Its telltale light came on, an overwhelmed amber eye. Next to it, the clamps-open warning light was off.

"Okay. The switch is unlocked and the circuit live."

She rested her thumb above the switch. She checked heading, trim and climb. She turned to look over her right

254

shoulder, on the shadow side, so that she could see the underwing drop away. She flipped the switch.

"I've jettisoned the canoe assembly."

Angel didn't even wobble. The underwing took forever to begin to fall. The fall was imperceptible.

It didn't fall at all.

She looked back at the instrument board. The clamps-open warning light had come on. The clamps were open. The pins were free to slide.

The underwing was still there.

"Ruth? Is anything wrong?"

"It hasn't gone. It didn't drop."

"What do you mean, it hasn't gone? John, get that other handset. Ruth, you said you'd jettisoned – "

"It didn't *drop*. It's still there. I threw the switch, but it's still *there*."

"Ruth, this is John. Did the clamps-open light come on?"

"Yes. It came on. It's still on."

"Has the underwing moved at all? I mean, can you see if it's tilted, or if it's dropped?"

"It hasn't moved. It hasn't *moved*."

The underwing flew on, untroubled, a stubbornly loyal part of Angel. It wouldn't fall, it wouldn't go, it wouldn't remove itself and its weight and its drag penalty. Angel had to get rid of it, and get up to clean and efficient cruising speed, to have a chance of flying round the world. But the thing wouldn't *go*!

"All right," said John's voice. "Let's stay cool, and let's get systematic. The circuit telltale or the clamps-open warning light could be misreading. The circuit might not be powering up – or it is powering up, but it's failing to move the clamps for some reason. Are there any lights on the alarm panel?"

She looked at the alarm panel in front of the throttle, down by her left knee. She looked at it carefully, because she was peering through sunlight into shadow. "No."

"All right. Then let's call up the self-test menu and check. Close the clamps again, switch off the circuit, and go back on autopilot."

Ruth pushed up the switch to close the clamps, which hadn't opened anyway. She twisted the switch to lock it and kill the circuit. Then she put the autopilot back in control.

It picked up her handling with the barest nudge.

She poked at the keys arranged round the rim of the navigation screen. The navigation display disappeared, and she got the self-test opening menu instead . . .

For a moment the panic, conjured by the unexpected, the wrong event, took charge. She was staring at a pale cathode-ray screen made meaningless by a cascade of sunlight, its dim details legible but bleached of all momentary sense. She was sitting in a seat suspended four thousand feet too near to the sun, with nowhere left to go but down . . .

"Ready, Ruth? Select *auxiliary systems* on the menu."

THIRTY-FIVE

Terri Sabuli phoned him at nine thirty to say there was a problem with the aircraft. At nine thirty on a Monday evening, he would have thought he'd be left in peace in his office to get on with the work. The problem meant that at worst Angel wouldn't be able to fly the full course, and would have to abandon the mission and land early – in Africa, probably. It would still bring in a large slice of the sponsorship money, and he wasn't an aircraft engineer anyway. Let Michael's little experts look into it.

Munro had very different worries. He picked up the black telephone, the outside line, and called Darren Pierce at Smith and Brown Associates. Pierce was there. He damn well should be, for the money the investigation was costing.

"No, I'm rather afraid nothing's come through today on the Buenos Aires, Cairo or Los Angeles things, Mr Munro. But then those parts of our investigation were only set up on

Thursday, and we've just had the weekend, of course, and it isn't easy to do much in the banking world then."

"Mr Pierce, the Los Angeles connection is being run from Tokyo, and it's already Tuesday in Tokyo. I've made it clear that cost is not the controlling factor. Results, however, are."

"Yes. Quite. I do understand. But it doesn't alter the fact that, regrettably, nothing's come in on that area as yet."

Regrettably, that was the area where he needed results. The espionage thing was secondary. Pattie Lee was conveniently occupied away from her office, and her boss was anything but fully informed of the latest events. Pattie Lee was no longer in a position to pass crucial secrets to her hidden employer and cause a collapse of Munro's restructuring plans. The employer was probably the Bryce McFadden Group, since it was definitely the Group which was getting ready to raid MT-Orbis shares – judging by its stance on the Orbis Air manoeuvre. Well, that didn't matter this week.

What mattered was Michael. As soon as Michael surfaced, Munro's control of MT Holdings would evaporate. If he attempted a fight before he'd had time to dig in, he might delay Michael for a day at best. After that, Michael would be able to reverse the voting of MT shares in the three main subsidiaries, and throw in his own four percent stake in each company. With his personal stake added to MT's, he'd have an instant majority at Orbis. And then with the cross-shares held by Orbis, he'd also have Siltech and Orbis Air. It was, after all, the arrangement Munro set up to protect Michael's control of MT-Orbis. He'd set it up all too well, and presented himself with an almost impregnable set of defences. If Michael came back into the game too early, Munro would be beaten, broken and instant history, a man of fifty-two with nothing left but some personal shares and not even a ghost of a career.

What he needed first was time. He had to consolidate his control of the three subsidiaries, so that Michael wouldn't be able to evict him straight away. And then he needed proof – enough evidence either to convict Michael, or at least to discredit him so thoroughly that no board of directors in MT-Orbis would ever obey him again.

The proof, if he was going to need it quickly, would have to come from Pierce's investigation. The trouble was, he couldn't risk telling Pierce which name he was trying to nail. Not yet. It would provoke too many questions. First of all, Pierce would have to find some independent evidence of who the suspect might be.

"Mr Munro? I've just been checking my screen here. I've got an update on the other business. Lee left London at approximately four thirty this afternoon. Our man in Sheffield picked her up arriving at the hospital just before eight. She was allowed in because of the more open visiting hours for private patients, I imagine. Anyway, she left again at eight thirty, but she didn't go to her hotel in Sheffield. She took the M1 south."

"Was Tranter with her, by any chance?"

"No. Our Sheffield man followed her, but unfortunately he lost her a little while ago at the turn-off to the M69. It's still daylight, of course, but it isn't all that easy to follow a car on a motorway without sitting on its tail and giving the game away, you understand."

"Wouldn't it have been helpful to put a radio tracker on her car, Mr Pierce?"

"Gosh, no. That can cause *serious* trouble. Imagine the mess if the police – or especially the security services – picked it up in passing, as it were."

"So you've lost Lee."

"Well – not forever. I've just dug out a road atlas. She could be heading for Birmingham or Coventry, or she *could* be intending to pass Coventry and pick up the M40 to Oxford."

Michael's home was near Oxford. Siltech was in Oxford. George Connor, the chief of Siltech's Michael Men, was also there. Michael, through the agency of Pattie Lee, was already making his move. It wasn't the one Munro was waiting for.

He'd been expecting Michael to stage a sudden reappearance at MT Holdings, all plaster cast and smiles, and take back control in one swift fight at the top – before the top had been decapitated, had been functionally isolated, from the body of MT-Orbis. Instead, the man was making a move at Siltech. Michael, damn him, was a streetfighter. A tactician like Munro couldn't predict what he was going to do.

"I think Oxford's the best bet, Mr Munro. Suppose, for instance, that Tranter's entrusted Lee with the key to his house so that she can get hold of some files, let's say, and keep up with his affairs. She might take the opportunity to do some snooping of her own, and we *might* be able to prove it. Best of all, we might even be able to observe her passing information to her contact."

Chester Alby drove a Saab 9000, and he made the journey from Reigate to Soho in rapid time. Terri had waited twenty minutes before she called him, but he still managed to arrive a bare hour after things had gone wrong. He came through the door with momentum on his side, looking like a man moving in to take charge of a crisis.

He strode past the communication desk to where John Coates was sitting at the aircraft data computer. His reflection, slipping from window to window in a ghost control room suspended in a darkening alley, was less substantial. "What's the situation?"

"We're keeping her on course," John said, "and we're keeping her at two hundred knots. The canoe's still attached. The clamps are set closed again – just in case a faulty connection decided to connect, and the canoe suddenly dropped without any warning. The self-test routines indicate no faults, and Ruth has changed the fuse on the circuit on the off-chance that it was dead but wasn't reporting properly. But it still doesn't work."

Chester nodded. "Have you tried any manoeuvres?"

"Absolutely not. Straight and level until we know what the problem is."

"Good." Chester nodded slowly. In the window, its back to the problem, his reflection nodded, too.

"Any thoughts?" John asked.

"Well – I've been thinking about it on the way in. I think I know what might be wrong."

John nodded. And waited.

The women at the press desks waited. Mandy Rees waited, and turned to Terri. Mandy, it seemed, had also noticed that Chester wrote off women as irrelevant in a crisis. He'd asked if John had tried any manoeuvres, not if Ruth had done so.

Chester put his hands on his hips. "Have you heard from anyone else about this?"

"Munro," Terri said. "I told him, but he hasn't bothered to call back."

"And Michael?"

"It's late, Chester. Michael's in hospital. I haven't told Michael."

"No. No one wants to tell Michael anything." Chester hung his head, disappointed at the world. "Well, I told him what happened this afternoon."

To hell, Terri thought, with Munro's and Michael's power game. "The problem with the aeroplane, Chester. The mission. The thing that's putting Ruth through the mill. What do you think might be causing the problem?"

Chester turned his head and looked at her. His expression could have been borrowed from his ghost in the window.

THIRTY-SIX

Mission Time was 36.20, UK time was 22.20. Ruth had been waiting for eighty minutes.

Angel was still stuck with an extra pair of wings like a butterfly pinned in the sky. Somewhere in a vaguely

Christian schooling, she'd heard that God's angels were ranked according to the number of wings on their backs. Angel didn't want to lose half its wings. Angel wanted no demotion in heaven.

The show of pride was going to be self-defeating. With four wings and all the drag they caused, Angel wouldn't be able to fly round the world. There wouldn't be enough fuel left to make the last stage across the Atlantic and back to Florida. And it would be Ruth who'd failed to do it.

"Ruth?" said Terri's voice. "We're still waiting."

"Yes." Well so was she. "Let me talk to Chester."

"Chester's checking his sums on the computer at the moment."

"Let me talk to John."

"John's checking distances and times to populated land, Ruth. You want to be doing this where help's available, just in case."

Just in case Angel was damaged, and went down, and plunged her into the sea. "All right. You give me the explanation again."

"Me? I'm no engineer."

"Give it to me again. My mind isn't at its best at the moment. If you can follow it, so can I."

"Oh. Thanks for the faint praise, Ruth. All right, then. Excuse me while I take a deep breath."

Ruth waited. She was getting used to waiting. Even though it made her want to scream.

"Right, here goes. The canoe thing is held flush against the underneath of the aeroplane. That's so that the airflow is smooth and efficient and so on. It means there's no gap between the canoe and the aeroplane, like there would be with any ordinary drop tank, so there's no turbulence in the airflow. If there was turbulence, it would push the canoe away the minute the clamps were released. As it is, the only thing that's going to move the canoe down and let it drop clear is its own weight. Am I making sense so far?"

"Perfect sense."

"Good. Well, the trouble is, the canoe has wings of its own. And they were designed to carry most of its weight when it was full to the brim with fuel. Now it's completely empty. To put it simply, the canoe's wings are producing more lift than the canoe has got weight. It *can't* fall. You open the clamps, the canoe doesn't drop, the pins stay firm in their sleeve things inside the aeroplane, so the canoe keeps on moving along at the same speed as the aeroplane, so the wings go on producing too much lift. So the canoe stays glued underneath you. Right?"

"Exactly right."

"Good. Then why are you making me tell it to you?"

"I want you to tell me *how* it's happened. I know who designed the aircraft. I know he designed this mess into it. But I don't understand how such a gross error was never *corrected*. I mean, they must have tested the procedure for dropping the canoe."

"Apparently they only did static tests."

"*Static* tests?" A static test meant a test while the aircraft was standing on the ground. No airflow, no aerodynamics, no lift generated by the underwing.

"It seems the canoe thing was too expensive to throw it away in a real test."

Unlike Ruth, the potentially throwaway pilot. Be calm, be very calm. Do the yelling at people later. First, get on with trying to solve the situation. "All right, Terri. Let's go through what we're going to do about it."

"Well, first of all you have to fly to a safer location. There's a risk involved in the process. You need an island with an airfield so that you can land. If there's even the slightest suspicion that the fuselage has been damaged when the canoe drops, then you can't take the risk of going on. You also need a place with smooth water – a lagoon, or a natural harbour. I mean, if you lose the propeller or something, and have to come down fast. Or if the landing wheels are damaged. You don't want to do a crash-landing on dry land with all that fuel on board, do you?"

"Ditch in the sea, you mean."

"Well, you could circle to use up fuel. But you've got enough for about eighty hours on board. That's more than three days."

"Right. Let me talk to Chester about it."

"He's still busy with those sums of his."

"I don't care about his sums! Calculations! His calculations got me into this mess in the first place!" Be calm, she said to herself. Be very calm. "Put Chester on, Terri. I won't mention the fuck-up he's done on the design, on the testing, on everything. I won't mention it. Believe me, I'm not interested in recriminations at the moment. I want to know how I'm going to get out of this mess. And I want to know *now*."

"Right. Hold on."

Ruth waited. She sat in her seat in the sky, staring down at glistening ocean left and right of the cockpit, her little prison, her customised torture chamber. The real cruelty was the existence of a way out. All she had to do was abandon the mission, the solo non-stop circuit of the world. Then she could forget the need to throw away the canoe assembly. She could keep the clamps safely closed. She could land, risk-free, at the nearest airfield. She could get out, get her picture taken, and then disappear into a life of obscurity. Ruth Clifford? Never heard of her.

The torture stopped the minute she gave in, like a woman confessing to heresy at the hands of the Inquisition. All she had to do was lie about herself, deny her own ambition.

"Ruth? This is Chester."

His voice was shaky. He sounded slightly scared. It made her feel strong. "Tell me the procedure."

"Okay. Step by step. First you trim the nose down level, getting minimum angle of attack. Ease off the throttle so you stay at two hundred knots. You'll start to lose a little height with a full internal load, but that doesn't matter. The key thing is not to build up speed, so you don't increase the lift from the underwing. Right?"

"Right."

263

"Then you wait a few seconds to make sure Angel is stable. Then you hit the foreplanes and pull the nose up high. If you were trying to climb, you'd apply throttle. But *don't* apply any throttle with the nose up. If it works first time and the canoe drops, you'll pick up speed and you'll start to rise anyway. If the canoe doesn't come free straight away, you have to bring the nose down level again before you get into a stall. Then you just keep repeating until it works. Right?"

"Right. And how does it work? What happens?"

"Okay. When you pull the nose up, the canoe will be slightly slow to respond. The front of the canoe is literally going to get left behind for a fraction of a second. Then – "

"You mean *if* I've opened the clamps before I pull the nose up high. Otherwise the canoe comes, too."

"Yes. I mean – yes. You have to open the clamps before you do it. Pull up the nose. You have to open the clamps first."

"Yes. I open the clamps, Chester. I pull up the nose. The canoe is slightly slow to respond. What does that do?"

"Well – it opens a gap at the front of the canoe, between the top surface of the canoe and the underside of Angel. It breaks the smooth airflow. You get turbulence between the two surfaces, and you get a pressure wave pushing backwards into the gap. The effect will be to prise the canoe far enough away for the pins to come out of their sleeves. Immediately the pins are free, drag will slow the assembly, the underwing will lose lift, and it will start to drop. It should all happen in less than a second. The assembly will still be stable at release. It won't tumble. It won't damage the propeller or the fuselage. It should be eight to ten seconds before it stops doing a glide descent and starts just falling instead. By then it won't be anywhere near you. Right?"

"Right." She started hauling the straps out of their reels in the shoulders of the seat. She clicked them one at a time into the lap-belt clasp. Then she took hold of the stick, switched off the autopilot, and put her feet on the rudder pedals. Now, she thought, or never. Because I'm scared.

With her left hand, she twisted the release switch to unlock it and activate the circuit. Then she flipped the switch and the clamps-open light came on. The underwing stayed put.

"Right. Open the clamps. Then get the nose level."

She nudged the stick forward. The nose came down three degrees and settled level. Airspeed started to rise. She eased the throttle slightly and got it back to 200 knots. Altitude started to bleed off gently – a slow hundred per minute down. She had four thousand feet in reserve.

"Right. Now, I just pull up the nose, and the canoe should separate. Let's see if it works."

"What? Don't do it *now*, woman."

"Why not, Chester? Are you afraid you've got the wrong answer to the problem?"

That shut him up. She got ready to pull the stick. Just remember to get the nose back down again before the aircraft stalls. And hope the canoe doesn't tumble the instant it comes free.

"Ruth," said Terri's voice. "*Wait*. Don't try it yet. You're in the middle of nowhere. The nearest land's four hundred miles away. If anything goes wrong – if you go down – there's no one to help you. You'll be in the water for hours."

"Shut up, Terri. I'm busy. Chester, let's see if you can put right what you got wrong. And if those turn out to be my last words, I hope people never stop reminding you I said them."

She checked the clamps were open. She checked Angel was straight and level and losing height at a leisurely hundred per minute. She looked over her right shoulder, away from the sun, at the stubborn underwing riding smoothly in the main wing's shadow.

Then she pulled back the stick.

The nose went up and her seat tipped. The underwing dropped a fraction. Through the engine noise and the slipstream, clean through the shells of the headset enclosing her ears, she heard a scraping sound –

The underwing was still there.

She looked over her left shoulder instead. It was still

there, displaced a little downwards. There was too much slipstream noise.

She looked forward. Airspeed was rolling off. 180 knots, 170, 160. The stall warning started to flash in the corner of the VSI screen. She pushed the stick. The foreplane surfaces tipped from angled down to angled up. The nose dropped level.

The stall warning disappeared.

Airspeed 150 knots. *Far* too much noise. A coarse slipstream noise. And vibration.

The underwing was still there!

140 knots. Three hundred per minute down. Altitude 3200.

Something's gone wrong.

She added throttle. She kept the nose level. She kept adding throttle. The noise and the vibration got worse. She kept on adding throttle until the airspeed was back at 160.

Altitude was 3000. Rate of descent was one hundred per minute down. That wouldn't do!

She didn't want to add any more speed until she knew what was wrong. Pieces of Angel might tear loose. But she needed more lift. So she pulled the stick gently and lifted the nose slightly. She added more throttle to maintain airspeed.

The noise became a screech even louder than the engine. The vibration began to bounce her in the seat. Pockets in the cockpit sides started to wave at her.

She got the rate of descent to zero, and kept the airspeed at 160 knots. By then the altitude had slipped to 2700 feet, and she was running out of sky . . .

"Chester! What have you done to me?"

266

THIRTY-SEVEN

Pattie Lee found Michael's house easily, even in the streetlight-free, designer-appropriated villages of the Chilterns. The July dusk was still bright enough at ten thirty to read the signs at the ends of narrow roads, and the names on white-barred gates which signalled gravel drives hidden behind herbaceous-topped walls. In the tree-shadow twilight overhanging the lane, Grove House Cottage had a stone wall crowned with a parapet of alyssum and veiled with a web of speedwell. Michael's housekeeper looked after the garden. Michael just paid for the result.

Pattie Lee rolled the nearside wheels of her Renault up on the grassy bank at the foot of the wall, switched off the engine and got out of the car. Sweet country quiet made a space for her. Michael never invited anyone but his girlfriends here, guarding his privilege. It seemed something worth guarding – this wasn't a bit like arriving home in dirty, congested, dangerous London.

The gate swung back against its stop with a soft, empty sound. There was no breeze, so she didn't bother to stamp down the bolt which held the gate. She walked back to her car, and as she got ready to open the door, she could smell the Renault 19's aroma of metal and petrol. In London, the air was never fresh enough to tell an individual car from the surrounding stink. Closing the door was like shutting out the breath of life. She started the engine and coaxed the car into the lane. She swung wide, then came back on full lock and rolled through the gate on hollow grinding gravel.

In Sheffield, at the hospital, Michael gave her the key. He also gave her the news Chester Alby had phoned through while she was hurrying up the motorway. Munro had discovered a

267

fraud at Orbis Pacific Tours, and had used it as a pretext to dismiss the board of the parent company, and to install himself as caretaker. Munro had seized Orbis Air. Chester said Munro was trying to get rid of Michael. He said Munro claimed he wanted to clear up the fraud before it caused a final collapse of confidence in the company. He said Munro didn't seem to know who had perpetrated the fraud.

Michael knew. Pattie knew.

Michael was worried. It wasn't the fact that Munro had begun a coup. In different circumstances, Michael would have walked out of the hospital, had Pattie drive him to London, and by the time everyone went home from work tomorrow, he would have secured MT Holdings, Orbis, Siltech and Orbis Air, and thrown Munro out on the street. The attempt at a coup didn't matter. Not even the discovery of one of the money mines mattered. It was the timing that was the trouble. Time, for Michael, was crucial – and there was an awful lot of the plan to put back on a new set of rails.

So Michael handed over the key, but he didn't like it. He *really* didn't like parting with the passwords which would give Pattie access to some of the contents of his very personal computer. Perhaps he wasn't quite worried enough.

For a cottage, Michael's house was large. A civilised man, he'd refrained from knocking out most of the interior walls, so that the rooms remained close and cosy, but were interconnecting round a core of kitchen and steep little stairs. The place had central heating and secondary double-glazing behind security locked casements. Pattie went from room to room, switching on the lights – ceiling lights, spotlights, indirect lights tucked between beams – and closing the Sanderson curtains. She turned on the heating: no need to be caught out by the cool of the eventual night. She checked the kitchen. The fridge was well-stocked. In the freezer was real food, cooked and frozen and ready to revive into real meals. Cooked by whom – Michael, his housekeeper, or Ruth Clifford in the recent past? There was also a yuppie tray filled with ready-made microwave snacks. Given the lateness of the hour, and the low-calorie total of the toy-sized portion, one of those would do.

She drank apple juice. She ate. Then she went upstairs. The computer was in the study at one end of the house, distributed over a desk under the sloping ceiling. The computer could wait until morning. She put fresh linen on the double bed. Sylvia Symes and Ruth Clifford had played queen of the night there, Terri Sabuli hadn't made it as far as the house. Now it was Pattie's turn.

She started the bath running. Michael was far too sophisticated to have installed a Jacuzzi. If he wanted his body massaging underwater, he could get a woman to do it. His bath was white, large, and set in a tiled surround in a four-piece bathroom done in Tuscan red. Pattie undressed, then took her underwear down to the utility room behind the kitchen. She put the minuscule load in the machine and programmed it for whites, and drier, then walked out and closed the door: clean underwear in the morning matters greatly to a well-brought-up woman.

She checked the wine. Like all the English, Michael judged wine by its price, and was a prisoner of the choice offered by importers who maintained a market based on exclusivity. Pattie Lee, daughter of Hong Kong entrepreneurs, knew more about wine. When it came to spirits, however, Michael knew what he should. She poured herself a giant Glenlivet and added straight water to encourage the taste. She switched on the CD. She selected Debussy's *L'Après-midi d'un Faune*. Music trickled from speakers all over the house, like dappled light in a sun-green, summer-struck wood. At a quarter past eleven she padded up the steep little stairs. A hot bath, full to the brim with a meringue of glistening bubbles, a good whisky, beautiful music, a dream of a house.

Michael had never let her see his home in the country. Well now she'd changed that. She'd got one more of the things she wanted.

Tomorrow, early, it would be the turn of the computer.

*   *   *

Terri walked along the corridor like a diver wading through sleep. Failure, and a smell of fear felt for someone far away, takes all the strength out of a tired woman. It means you have to stretch yourself up straight before you go through the door to a Mission Control, where all the phones and their night-shift attendants are waiting to tell the story.

The fallen star of the story was Chester Alby. He sat in front of a computer screen. The screen showed an exploded drawing of one of the carrying mounts for the canoe assembly, overlaid by a window full of stalled calculations. Chester's mind had stalled, too. He was staring at the screen, his hand clutching the edge of the table beside the keyboard. Chester hadn't come good in a crisis. He'd come to a stop. The entire mess was his fault, and he didn't know what to do about it.

The canoe assembly was stuck. Ruth had opened the clamps and then pulled the aeroplane's nose up hard, just as Chester had told her to. A gap had opened over the top of the canoe, and the canoe and its underwing had started to prise away from Angel's belly. The forward pins had started to slide out of their sleeves while the rear pins were still held in place by the lift from the underwing. The front of the canoe dropped a couple of inches, the pins tipped slightly inside their snug sleeves . . .

And jammed tight.

Now the narrow gap between Angel and the canoe was imitating an airbrake and creating as much drag as all the rest of the flying machine added together. Ruth was having to use almost full throttle to keep Angel flying at a mere two-thirds of the intended cruising speed for the rest of the mission. That alone meant the mission was over. Using too much fuel at too little speed, Angel couldn't complete even half of what was left of the course.

That, though, wasn't the real disaster.

The effects of the skew canoe – the aerodynamic accident – were being tested for the first time. There was no way to predict what would happen if Ruth tried even the most gentle manoeuvre, such as a slow change of course towards help and rescue. The only way to find out was to try it. The result might not be nice.

Worse, the half-detached canoe assembly couldn't be locked home again. The pins in the rear sleeves had tipped and were holding the clamps open, the pins in the forward sleeves had slipped down out of reach of their clamps. If the force of air became too great, if the pins suddenly slipped, if the GRP composite round the pin housings cracked – the canoe would come free without any warning. The forward pins might go first. Then the front of the canoe would drop, the air rushing against its upper surface would push it down, and would rotate it about the rear pins and grind them into their sleeves. The canoe might not come away smoothly, if it fell. It might rip the bottom out of Angel's fuselage.

Ruth was using fuel at almost twice the planned rate. The fuel would last until round about midnight on Wednesday – two more days. The canoe might slip at any moment. Ruth would have only a minimal chance of being fully alert, with both hands and both feet on the controls, in the instant when the catastrophe happened . . .

She would have to head for the first airfield she could turn towards in a long and gentle curve.

Unfortunately, Angel couldn't land.

It was impossible to lock the canoe again. The canoe assembly was held in place by a balance of friction on the pins, massive drag, and lift from its underwing. After Angel touched down and started to slow, the lift from the underwing would vanish. The whole assembly would finally drop. According to John's figures, Angel would still be rolling along the ground at a speed of at least sixty knots. The canoe assembly would hit the runway and start to break apart right underneath the rushing aeroplane – with its underwing still spread in front of Angel's main wheels. The crash would be instantaneous. The vast load of fuel on board would make a fire which would rage until there was nothing left of the fragile machine or its flesh-and-blood pilot.

A landing was out of the question. Even if Ruth could have

withstood the stress of juddering through the sky for two days until the fuel was used up, even if she managed to come in safely for a glider landing with the engine shut down – the canoe would still drop, its underwing would strip Angel's wheels away at speed, and the aeroplane would cartwheel itself and its pilot to pieces.

With one single mistake, Chester had written off the mission, Angel, and Ruth.

Terri leaned over John's shoulder. He was still communing with his own computer, stabbing keys and toggling back and forth between diagrams and columns of calculations. He was trying to understand how Angel was flying at the moment, in the hope of finding out how to change it. "Getting anywhere?" she said in his ear.

"No. This computer can't crunch the numbers. I'll have to get the whole team on it at Wragby."

"I notice you don't say *we*."

John's fingers paused. John turned his head and looked across at Chester, staring catatonically at his screen. "No."

"So – how long would it take to get them started at Wragby?"

John stopped trying to do the impossible with the computer. He rested his hands on the desk each side of the keyboard. "If I start ringing round now, I suppose some of them could be ready at Wragby by about two in the morning. But I'd have to get up there as well to set up the work. Who's going to be on hand here, if anything happens?"

Not Chester, she thought. Even if he managed to snap out of it in time, no one would trust a word he said. "What's your best suggestion?"

"Get an aircraft to go and meet her – so that someone's there to see exactly where she hits the water, if the worst happens. Then get her on course towards land, somewhere with helicopters, boats, and everything – including a good hospital. She'll have to ditch in front of the shore. The aircraft will be wrecked. She might be killed in the landing, or she might drown in the wreckage. But at least there won't be a fire."

"Better than nothing." Terri stood up straight again. I'm the tallest person in the room, she thought, even in flat heels. I'm too brown, too exotic, and I stand out a mile. Everyone's waiting for me to take the lead. But I don't know the first thing about flying. The ins and outs of an emergency like this are not what you learn in public relations.

Mandy was watching her from the communications desk. Terri walked across towards her. "Any luck?"

Mandy shook her head. "I can't find Munro. He isn't in his office, he isn't at home, he doesn't answer his car phone."

"Never mind." Munro wasn't a flying expert, either. All he would be able to do was confirm the obvious – put Ruth's life first, and do whatever was necessary to protect it.

It just wasn't fair. Terri was the victim of the thing that had really gone wrong with the mission. Faults on the aeroplane weren't the worst problem – not even this fault, which meant the end of everything. The real trouble was that there was no one in command. The boss would have been Michael. He'd built the mission as an extension of his ego, and everyone else was there just to help carry it out. Now Michael wasn't available, and the mission was a headless enterprise. There was no one left to say yes or no to anything.

Except, she thought, for me.

You wouldn't have known, to look at him, that Chester was even breathing. But the light of his screen was reflected by the tears which were filling his eyes. Now wasn't the time to start feeling sorry for Chester. Ruth was imprisoned in a booby-trapped aeroplane on the other side of the world. Ruth was waiting to see if she'd live.

It was time to give her some decisions.

THIRTY-EIGHT

The canoe and its underwing made a cross which Angel had to haul across heaven. Ruth didn't want this aerial calvary. She wanted to escape this crucifixion.

She had her feet on the rudder pedals and her right hand on the stick, ready just in case the thing suddenly tore free. With her left hand she flipped the release switch up and down, off and on. Closing and opening the clamps. The telltale said the circuit was live. The warning light insisted the clamps weren't closing. It burned dimly, defiantly on the lower left of the instrument board, protected by a skin of shadow from the climbing, advancing sun.

The clamps wouldn't close. The forward pair should be able to, because the forward pins had slipped down and pulled almost free of the sleeves. But the rear clamps were hitting uselessly against the steel of the rear pins, which had tipped just too far for their notches to engage. So the clamps couldn't close.

Off, on, off, on. The clamps had to be hammering against the rear pins. *Hammering.* Off. On. Hit. Retreat. Hit. Hit. Hit. She couldn't hear or feel any hint of the impacts. The engine was making an infernal noise, the slipstream was screaming, Angel was vibrating like a cart careering over cobbles. Why wouldn't the pins *shake* loose? Angel's vibration couldn't do it, so she hammered them with the clamps. On. Off. On. Off. Hit. Hit. Hit.

Her father said she couldn't do it. Now she sat imprisoned in her flying chair, entombed alive in a crippled aircraft that could never land. He sat in his wheelchair, half-alive, trapped in its mechanical embrace, walled into his tiny house, his world shrunken to a fragment, his body broken in two. She wanted his *advice*? After all these years disowning her mother and him, she *wanted* something? After walking out, turning her back, running off with her education. After leaving him to manage his firm *alone*. After leaving him to work his fingers to the bone, trying to keep the firm going while the steel industry was wiped out and no one needed furnaces maintaining any more. After deserting him when he needed her most. After what happened . . . Her father sat in his wheelchair and spat fury at her. After all of *that* she wanted his advice about flying round the bloody world for her poncy smart-arsed boyfriend? Well she couldn't do it! Never! *Never!*

She couldn't do it. Hit. Hit. Hit. No response. The thing was still there. The clamps-open light still burned.

She tried to check altitude, course, speed. She couldn't see the figures. Her eyes were blurred. She turned aside to look down at the sea which slid steadily across the long morning. The smears moved with her as she turned her head. It was her sunglasses as well as her eyes. She let go of the switch and removed the glasses. The lenses were splashed and spattered. She blinked in the blazing light, and tears overflowed on her cheeks. Clumsily, with one hand because she didn't dare let go of the stick, she folded the glasses and slotted them into their clip. She wiped her cheeks with her fingers. Her father – just – didn't manage to reduce her to tears. But this did.

"Ruth? We're not getting any quick answers at our end. John thinks he needs the whole aircraft team, and the big computer at Wragby. But that will take hours to set up, and then we'd still have to wait for the results. By that time you'll be long past the Solomon Islands and over the Coral Sea. You might even be over Australia. I suppose at your present speed it's something like nine hours to Australia. I've just been checking. By then it would be dark there, and you'd also have nothing but dry land to come down on, if the worst came to the worst. Dry land is bad, with all that fuel on board. I also don't think you'd have much fun flying Angel for nine hours without being able to use the autopilot. I mean – that thing might come loose any second. I don't think you could cope with that, Ruth."

The engine roared, the slipstream screamed like a troop of Valkyries harrying Angel through the air. She couldn't cope. She couldn't cope with *this*. She wasn't born to be brave. She was *frightened*.

"Ruth?"

"No!"

"Okay. No. So I've got a decision for you. The mission is over. Only a lunatic would want you to carry on. In a moment I'll give you a new course to the Solomon Islands. John's working it out. We're sending you to Honiara on Guadalcanal. They've got a real airport there, and facilities. You'll get an instant rescue when you ditch. You're absolutely clear, aren't you? The only way down is to ditch."

"Yes!" Unless the whole assembly prised itself loose and dropped its front end like a huge, cross-shaped airbrake. The tail end would splinter its way out of Angel's fuselage under the force of the slipstream. Tumbling and tearing, it would collide with the propeller at the tail. Then Angel, out of power and out of control, with a gash torn in its fragmenting belly, would take Ruth down.

"We're going to ask them to send an aircraft out to meet you. I mean, there's always a chance that the pilot of the other aircraft might see something that helps. *If* we could find a way to get rid of the canoe thing after all, you could land on *wheels*. You could come down safe on *land* at Honiara."

It sounded like a run-of-the-mill miracle.

"It's about four hundred and fifty miles, Ruth. Getting on for three hours at your present speed."

Three hours. Rattling down a tunnel of time, with the cross underneath her lowered like a vast scoop, a jaw trying to swallow air. A jaw about to gape, to dislocate, and tip Angel into the sea. Three hours was too long.

"I'll have the course for you in a minute, Ruth."

Any course change meant a turn. The stress might prise the thing loose. It would rip away front end first. The consequences would kill her aircraft. And kill her.

It was the pins at the tail she had to dislodge. Then the

276

tail would drop, all the pins would come free, and the canoe assembly would fall away horizontally, harmlessly. She'd be safe. She'd have her mission back. She'd have her life back.

At the moment she was sitting in the middle of a spring-loaded explosion on a hung fuse.

Three hours was far too long.

"I'm going to try something." Altitude was 2700 feet. Speed was 160 knots. That was way over take-off speed, but still slow enough to use half flaps without ripping the flaps out of the trailing edges of Angel's wings.

"Ruth, just wait a minute for the new course."

Flaps directed the airflow downwards, producing upthrust. The additional upthrust from the flaps acted at the trailing edges of the wings, and the wings were well towards Angel's tail. The upthrust from the flaps would lift the tail and tend to tip the nose down. With the stick pulled back, the foreplane control surfaces also directed the airflow downwards, pro-ducing additional upthrust at the nose. Using the stick alone would make the nose lift, as if Angel was trying to pull into a climb. Used together, flaps and stick gave the configuration for take-off. Except that on take-off Angel was storming along with the nose pitched high . . .

This was level flight. Upthrust at nose and tail together should push Angel bodily upwards. The manoeuvre was called vertical translation. No aircraft is stable in flight in that configuration. The latest agile combat aircraft needed computers to keep them from catastrophe while trying a vertical translation – while rising up the sky with the fuselage still level.

Angel was as agile as an airborne cow. Angel had no flight computer to assist in super-tuned manoeuvres. But a heavy, wallowing thing might survive whole seconds of vertical translation before a stall, pitchover or turbulent roll took hold . . .

During those seconds Angel would go up, staying level, because of the extra lift on the foreplanes and from the flaps on the main wings. There would be no extra lift on the underwing, because the underwing had no flaps. As it started to slide forward and upwards through the air with Angel, the underwing would effectively be dipping its leading edge into the airflow. The aerodynamics of the underwing would be spoiled. Its lift would be reduced. The canoe and underwing couldn't fall away from Angel in level flight, but in a vertical translation Angel might be able to lift itself off the canoe. If the pins came free.

It was what Chester should have told her to do in the first place.

"Ruth, John has the new course for you. The heading – "

"I'm going to try a vertical translation. Tell John. A vertical translation."

"Ruth! For goodness sake don't try to do anything."

"I can't stand this any longer and I'm the only one with an idea! Tell John. A vertical translation." She switched off the channel. They knew where she was and what she was trying to do. The accident inquiry would know where to look for the pieces.

She checked. The clamps weren't closed, the release switch was set to open. Nothing but friction to stop the pins sliding free. She kept her right hand on the stick, she moved her left hand to the flaps lever. If she knew any prayers she might try one, though at two thousand seven hundred feet she wasn't near enough to God. She pulled half flaps and tugged the stick. She could hear the flap motors grinding through all the noise. In front of her, the control surfaces on the foreplanes tipped down –

Airspeed rolled off. She put her left hand on the throttle and pushed it up to the stop. Airspeed held at 150 knots. The rate of ascent was three hundred per minute. Angel shuddered crazily as it lunged upwards into the sky. Over her shoulder, the underwing was still there. It was juddering like a tuning fork.

But it was still there!

Angel was lurching left and right. The stall warning flickered in the corner of the VSI screen. Angel was about to go. The underwing was going to stay attached. She wanted to hit the thing, hammer it loose!

The clamps. Go frantic with the clamps. Off. On. Close. Open. Hit. Hit. Hit!

Angel was going to go. The stall warning burned steady on the VSI. Here came a tail spin in a cow of an aircraft which could never recover in so little sky. Still less than three thousand feet. No chance at all. Here came the fall. The final, terrible, terminal fall!

Hit! Hit! Hit!

It happened. Angel failed. The jolt from the seat bounced her so hard she lost hold of the stick. Flaps off. God help me, get the flaps off. You have to *try*. Life doesn't give up. Hand on the stick. At least you have to *try*. Go down fighting.

Down, down, down.

A tail spin. Try to turn into the spin and get the nose down. In a tail spin the controls are reversed. Kick the rudder *away* from the spin, pull the stick *back*. Which way am I spinning? Left or right? There isn't enough height to pull out of a vertical dive, even if I get the nose round and down. Nose first into the sea should be quicker than tail first. It might hurt less.

Which way am I spinning? No clouds on the blue. The sun should be swirling circles in the cockpit. The heading should be ripping round the scale –

The heading was steady.

The rate of ascent was positive. Two hundred per minute. It was two hundred per minute upwards. The nose was nine degrees high. Altitude three thousand one hundred. Coming to three thousand two hundred.

Angel was climbing. Straight and nose high and vibration free. The screeching came from the engine at full throttle. No slipstream scream. The howl was coming out of her mouth . . .

Her voice knew before her mind caught on.

It's gone. It's gone! No underwing to the right, no underwing to the left. No underwing at all. *It's gone!*

Father forgive me, but I knew that you were wrong.

I can do it. I can do it! I hit the pins and the thing fell free.

I can do it!

Get the throttle back.

Stop wasting fuel.

Part 7

Master of a Higher Order

THIRTY-NINE

A near disaster left a sour taste. Coffee from a vending machine was even worse. The seasoning to a sauce of despair came from falling asleep slumped over a desk, and then waking up with no toothbrush this side of Kilburn.

It didn't help, either, to know what a luscious publicity opportunity had been missed. If Terri had been told in advance that Ruth would get out alive with the mission back on course, she'd have let it go out real-time on every channel in every medium across the entire world. What a story to miss! On the other hand, perhaps it was better to hide the fact that Michael's Angel had been designed as a deathtrap. Civil aviation authorities take air safety very seriously indeed . . .

The silent telephones agreed. So did the lights. So did the darkness before dawn in a four o'clock alley outside the window at her back. Mandy was there, musing. Two press-desk girls seemed to be playing chess. John was missing. Chester hadn't come back.

Chester finally decided to leave after midnight, and he went very quietly. He kept his catastrophe to himself. Bloody fool of a black man, fouling up so fundamentally. On the whole of Michael's team that left her, Terri Sabuli, out on a prejudiced limb trying to prove dark-skinned deviants are as good as anyone else in a white man's world. Chester thought he had the discrimination bad, and he was male. But a woman, and a black as well, had two crosses to bear. Specially when some other nigger let the side down.

No forgiveness or sympathy, then, for Chester Alby.

Mandy was walking over. "With us again?"

"Parts of me are." Terri stood up and started tugging her clothes straight. A skirt was the worst thing to wear if you wanted to stay up all night. It got tighter and tighter until your stomach started to sting. Sleeping at a slump didn't help. She hadn't planned to stay. Canoe assembly jettisoned at nine in the evening, then hurry home for a shower and half a night's sleep, then back shortly after four to oversee the Australian circus. Oh well, there was always the chance of a break in the afternoon.

Now it was Tuesday and the clock said 04.10. The mission clock said 42.10. On the wide wall map, the arrow representing Angel was parked on the course line where it crossed the Queensland coast.

"Bang on time," Mandy said. "Ruth says she's got a posse of Aussies flying with her. They seem a lot more friendly than the Americans were."

"Americans only get excited about Americans. The Australians are a lot less parochial. A posse of Aussies. Write that down. We can use it. Has Ruth been getting lyrical?"

"I think she's still on an adrenalin high. After-effects. It was pretty scary back there."

"It was." Terri started lifting her hands to her face, then stopped herself in time. Massaging away some of the sleepiness would be fine, but it would mess up her makeup – which she was going to need for the new media day. Apart from a lipstick in her handbag, everything else was with the toothbrush, on the other side of Kilburn. "Where's John?"

"He's in one of the offices across the corridor. He's asleep on a desk. Look, what about something to eat? We should be able to find something, even at four in the morning. This is Soho. I'll see if anyone has any ideas."

"Do that, Mandy." Food would be a lifesaver. There was work to do. CNN were already buying pictures from an Australian crew in an aircraft over the coast, and using the shots in evening news shows across the United States. The heat of the action, though, would be all native Australian for the next four hours. The climax was due at eight in the UK morning, when Angel flew past Ayers Rock at sunset. Time to get the team working. Up and at 'em.

It looked like a smooth mission from now on. For most of the rest of the week. Sleep was going to get precious.

By eight, Pattie Lee was dressed, and was sitting in front of Michael's computer, sipping tea. The computer faced her from the desk under the sloping ceiling at the end of the house. The ceiling was white, everything in the room was white except for the curtains, which glowed with translucent autumn colours. Outside the casements of the dormer, a sunny morning strolled breezily through lime branches overhanging a little back lawn. The grass was cut, was free of dandelions, and was terraced in steps away from the house. Edging the bottom of the garden were rose and herbaceous borders faced with stone. Very pretty, very tidy. Michael's housekeeper and gardener seemed to be very good.

Pattie would have to be nice to Mrs Kenton when she turned up mid-morning. A strange car, with a strange Chinese owner who's obviously made herself at home in Mr Tranter's house, would be a surprise. Mrs Kenton would want to telephone the hospital to check that the visit was all right. To save embarrassment, Pattie would leave for a little while.

She would drive to the nearest petrol station, which Michael said was two villages away. There was no school this side of the M40. Everywhere had been colonised by yuppies and carved up by country life executives, and the native rural world had become a shredded little community of farmers without heirs and villagers without amenities, jobs or children at home. It was a long way from the English country idyll she grew up to love in Hong Kong. It was in the books, in the school, in the world view of her parents – who felt themselves citizens of the Crown Colony first, and Chinese a long way second. Anglophiles and enterprising, they built a business from scratch. A very good business, quite a large business. But not big enough.

The English country idyll was a lie, and the English were busily erasing its last echoes at home. It wasn't the only lie. Loyalty, honour, trust – all those unique British virtues were lies. Be loyal subjects, die in our wars, and we will honour you. Be trusting subjects, work all your lives to promote our wealth and influence across the world, and we will indemnify you. That is the essence of the British way – our uprightness.

When she was a little girl, Pattie's brother was killed while serving with British forces in Malaya. When she was a grown woman, the British finally stopped stalling on their pledge of precious democracy, their promise of effective protection, and decided instead to hand over Hong Kong wholesale to the People's Republic of China. The single measure of security offered against the butchers of Tiananmen, the inventors of the Cultural Revolution, the most enthusiastic users of capital punishment in the world, the eradicators, wherever it suited them, of bourgeois thought and polluted bourgeois brains – the sole concession was a list of top executives and Crown servants who would be granted the dubious shield of a British passport.

Pattie's parents weren't Crown servants and weren't top executives. They were manufacturers, and what good are those? So they weren't going to get the new passports. They weren't going to get into shining white Albion, the pinnacle of self-important racist nationalism. Their business, meanwhile, was disintegrating as confidence collapsed and capital drained away from a colony about to be pushed down Peking's throat by its sanctimonious Whitehall masters. The breakdown of their business meant the evaporation of their wealth. With the wealth went the purchasing power which could have bought them entry into some other country willing to take Chinese – provided they could pay their way.

So Pattie's parents were facing imminent ruin, followed by the purifying thought police of Peking totalitarianism. Perfidious Albion, somebody said. The sun never set on the British Empire because God couldn't trust an Englishman in the dark. Loyalty will be honoured, trust will be repaid.

Lies.

Pattie parked her laptop on the desk in front of the laser printer, and switched on Michael's machine. She was here, among other things, to port files from desktop to laptop using commands and passwords Michael had given her. He'd hated parting with any of the passwords for his private machine, but this was an emergency, and they needed copies of the same data that was securely locked in Michael's laptop, which Munro had spirited away. So Michael had passed to Pattie most of what she wanted to know.

But not all of it.

SILTECH-32 40 Mbyte. 08.10, Tuesday 16th July 1991.
Last used 21.03, Wednesday 10th July

Michael had last used his computer to load data into his laptop while he was here with Ruth Clifford, before they left for Wragby the next morning. The data was the point of the plan. Pattie had been going to take the laptop, and the data, with her. Michael was going to take the data's internal security passwords with him in his head. Pattie couldn't have used the data without those internal passwords, Michael would have needed Pattie because of the data she held. Neither could have cheated the other.

Right now, according to the mission plan, Angel should be sailing majestically past Ayers Rock, a green machine against the burning ochre of Australia's favourite landmark. Michael hadn't wanted to miss the splendid photo opportunity, waving from the cockpit as the last sun levelled the vast outback. It would have been a fitting final image, flying intrepidly into the sunset, of the last hero on earth.

Oh well, Michael fell down some stairs and Ruth Clifford, the red-haired and under-confident bimbo, was doing the flypast instead. Let her enjoy it. By this time tomorrow the mission would be over, and they'd be trying to choose an airport in Africa for the defeated heroine to land. It wouldn't do her any harm. It wasn't as though there was a bomb on board . . .

Michael's very personalised software was being polite as it waited somewhere inside its 40 megabyte hard disk dataspace.

Good morning, Michael.
How do you want me this time?

Conceited, cocksure Michael. Pattie typed in *SLSS* and pressed *enter*. The screen blanked and responded.

Silsys Systemizer ST DOS 4.0
Copyright Siltech Systems 1989
Customized: Tranter
Please select a directory or file

No fuss, no graphic, no title screen. Just the title notice and a prompt for an entry command. Efficient, like the mean man beneath the flamboyant surface. She typed a directory path, right down to a parcel of files specified with a wildcard.

PRIVATE\PROJECTS\HUSH-USH\WT*

The path instructed the computer to go from the root directory through three subdirectories and pull out all the files with the Without Trace data.

The directories you specify are keylocked
Please enter the correct password

Pattie typed *BUGOFF* and pressed *enter*.

Please enter the second password

She typed *TRESPA-W, enter.* She didn't even need to

check her notes. Up popped a menu crammed with WT files, and a window offering management options. Into the business in one.

Porting to the laptop for Michael could wait. The first job was to make her own copies of everything. Two copies, in fact, in case the files were booby-trapped with logic bombs to prevent further copying from disk. She reached into her briefcase and pulled out a handful of 3½ inch disks, and stacked them on the table like high-tech gambling chips.

But Pattie Lee was being methodical.

Pattie Lee never gambled.

FORTY

Andrew Carlyle, formerly of Orbis Air and still a director of Orbis and Siltech, was present at the meeting. George Connor, deputy MD of Siltech, was there. Two loyal Michael Men turning up to be slaughtered again. Chester Alby was the only Orbis director who didn't put in an appearance. Alby's boss was in hospital and was taking hits from a traitorous general, and at the same time Alby had built an aircraft for his boss which had almost fallen apart in midair. Too much disaster for a third-rate man to take.

Geraldine Trayhorn gave her briefing on the fraud involving Desert Life. Neither Desert Life's immediate parent, Orbis Foods, nor Orbis itself had noticed the theft of so much money. It had been left to Trayhorn, an accountant in MT Holdings at the top of the corporate pyramid, to find the fraud. Failure to safeguard the company interest. A case for dismissing the Orbis board.

Munro wielded the half stake in Orbis owned by MT Holdings, plus the quarter stake owned by Orbis Air. No contest. George Connor voted Siltech's stake against the motion, but that was just a gesture of blind defiance. It would be Siltech's turn in Oxford in the afternoon.

Munro appointed himself caretaker of Orbis, reappointed the finance director to keep Orbis running, and voted Trayhorn in to give him a majority on the three-seat board. Her vote belonged to him, whatever happened. If he lost, she was ruined. It was cruel, but it was a necessary preparation for Michael's counter-attack.

When it came, Michael's counter-attack was going to count for everything.

At eleven thirty, Munro and Trayhorn went down to the car park beneath the Orbis building. When they got to Munro's Mercedes, he unlocked the doors, gave Trayhorn the key, and told her to drive. Trayhorn looked, for a moment, aghast. But as late as Monday morning she'd still been dealing in an investigation into serious fraud. Now, before noon the following day, she'd been appointed to her second directorship, she'd become a conscript in a campaign against the boss, and the frauds she'd discovered were figuring prominently in the fight. She was intelligent enough to understand the crisis. By comparison, a big and unfamiliar car with an automatic transmission was no challenge.

She got into the Mercedes and kicked off her high-heeled shoes. She adjusted the seat and the mirror, checked the controls through once, then started the engine.

The car park was too cramped and too full. Trayhorn had to reverse all the way out into the street. She paused with the car swung half out of the entry to the Orbis dungeon. "Which way?"

"Take Wardour Street." He reached down into his brief-case between his feet. There was the problem of the fax Ripley had given him as he was leaving the office to come over to Orbis.

"Why am I driving?"

"You'll see." He got out the fax. It came from Mr Peter Cavendish of the Securities and Investments Board. It was a follow-up to the one he'd received on the previous Wednesday. His reply didn't seem to have been adequate. At least it had provoked the man from the SIB into being slightly less vague. Cavendish wanted a meeting about irregularities in the past dealings of a company owned by Michael Tranter, and now incorporated within MT-Orbis.

If they knew something about Michael at the SIB, Munro would certainly be happy to talk to Cavendish. But not yet. Not this week. Irregularities in past dealings would cast a shadow over the boss of MT-Orbis, but it would be a shadow that unfolded itself slowly. It would be the kind of suspicion that could be denied by Michael. It wouldn't throw a stick between his legs. It wouldn't defeat his counter-attack. This week, Munro needed a much sharper and much swifter weapon – or at least a hastily erected defensive wall. There wasn't time for background measures.

He put the fax back in his briefcase. Geraldine Trayhorn was coaxing his Mercedes into the jam of one-way Wardour Street. "Pull over opposite Film House. The corner where the taxis are waiting."

"Are we picking someone up?"

"Yes." Darren Pierce was there, teetering on the kerb and anxious to make his connection without connecting with a taxi driver instead. "That's the man."

"I don't think I can stop with all this – "

"Just pull over and let him get in."

Trayhorn eased the Mercedes across the front of a taxi and against the kerb. She got confused about the handbrake, which was foot operated, and decided to rest on the footbrake with the drive selector in neutral.

Pierce, meanwhile, slipped hastily into the back seat. "Good morning, Mr Munro. Nice timing."

"Good morning," he said without turning round. He checked that Trayhorn chose the right setting to drive off again. "Have you found Pattie Lee?"

"Ah – is it all right to talk?"

"Miss Trayhorn's on the case, Mr Pierce."

"Yes. Good. Well then, our operative in Oxford has indeed found Lee. She's at Tranter's house, as we suspected."

Trayhorn pointed ahead at the imminent arrival of Oxford Street. "Turn right?"

"Turn right. Can you deduce, Mr Pierce, whether she's there with Michael Tranter's knowledge?"

"His daily doesn't seem upset."

"I see." The seat rammed his back as Trayhorn let the car leap into Oxford Street. Once they were out of the junction, the traffic pulsed them along with its stop-go thrombosis. Michael wouldn't have sent Lee to his house for fun. It could only be part of the preparation for the counter-attack. But if Lee was also working for a third party, would she have instructions to help Michael retain control, or to hinder him? "What about the other matters?"

"Well now – I'm afraid the Desert Life thing isn't looking very hopeful. The Cairo bank, where the money's been making its first stop, is turning out to be a tough nut to crack. Their security is first rate. We really need to know where the money's ending up, so that we can trace the chain back from there. I don't suppose you've got anything that might help us find the end-user account?"

He wasn't up to date on the investigation. He was in the middle of a coup. "Do we?" he said to Trayhorn.

"No." She was concentrating on the traffic, which was only too willing to help demolish the car entrusted to her. "We won't find that from the inside."

"Buenos Aires," Munro said. "Anything there?"

"Ah – that's a bit, well, tricky."

"Why?"

The lights stopped them opposite the pedestrian-unfriendly frontage of Centre Point and facing towards the narrower maw of New Oxford Street. "Straight ahead?" Trayhorn asked.

"Straight ahead. Why, Mr Pierce?"

"Well, we've had a bit of superficial success. The date you gave me for the start of irregularities coincides with a stopover in Buenos Aires by two company employees."

"That's quite useful, Mr Pierce. Who was it?"

"Ah – Michael Tranter." Pierce's voice had taken on a tone of slight anxiety. No one points the finger at the MD and principal shareholder of a company being parasitised by fraud. "Michael Tranter was there, with Pattie Lee. Of course, it doesn't actually tell us anything about either of them."

But it helped. Oh yes – it helped. "I don't suppose they were in Cairo at a suspicious time?"

"No. I mean – actually, you're in a better position to check on Tranter's movements. But we *have* got something that might be useful on the Orbis Pacific Tours thing."

The lights let them cross into New Oxford Street. All the lanes were stop-and-go full. "Do you want me to go down Covent Garden, or head through Holborn?"

Munro passed Trayhorn's question to the back seat. "Mr Pierce?"

"Oh – I can get a cab anywhere. No problem."

"Holborn. What might be useful, Mr Pierce?"

"Well – to be brutally honest – working by remote control from Tokyo does allow us to be a little more relaxed about legalities."

"So you really have been hacking someone's computer."

"Well, people are sometimes temptingly lackadaisical about security – even in America. Starting from the Los Angeles account, we've been looking for the holding account the fraudster was using to finance speculation or whatever on somebody's stock exchange. By that I mean, the money diverted on its way from Orbis Air to Orbis Pacific Tours would be held long enough to be used – "

"We're fully aware of the mechanisms of the fraud."

"Yes – of course. Anyway, our chaps have discovered that the money was coming through to Los Angeles from an account at the Hong Kong branch of the Kowloon Crown International Bank. Unfortunately, they haven't been able to pursue it further. The Hong Kong banks are definitely not careless in matters of security."

The Kowloon Crown International Bank. Pattie Lee had

been doing a lot of business at the London branch of the bank. Had she been doing things for Michael, or trying to track down things done by Michael – in order to blackmail him, perhaps? The mess had connections as fluid but as impenetrable as London's labyrinth of one-way traffic. Was Pattie Lee the real fraudster, working for someone else and trying to frame Michael? Confronting the questions was almost as bad as negotiating London's road junctions.

Trayhorn was doing fine in the driving seat of his car. He looked at her hands on the wheel, he looked at her knees, he looked down her sheer nylon shins to her feet . . . She was working the twin pedals of the automatic in her stocking feet, while her shoes were tucked under the seat. Her flat driving shoes – if she drove to work – would be in her own car in the garage at the MT building. He should have thought of that before making her drive.

The traffic stopped-and-went in chunks into Bloomsbury Way. The sticky flow of vehicles moved like a slow packet-switching network in some vast mechanical computer. Michael Tranter was the man for computers.

"There's a rather interesting connection, Mr Munro." Pierce's voice had adopted a kind of confidentiality. "Lee has dealings with the Kowloon Crown International Bank."

Munro nodded. Whatever Lee and Tranter were doing, together or independently, he was going to find out. But he might not like the answers when they emerged. "It seems we're starting to get somewhere, Mr Pierce. You're earning your fee."

"Well, we do aim to please. Of course, this kind of problem is notoriously *opaque*. But we try our best."

"I'm sure you do."

"Yes. Ah – is that it for the moment? I have to be off to the doctor, actually. Just a check-up, but these appointments are rarer than a personal organiser without a peeper."

Rarer than a personal organiser without a peeper? Pierce was a very poetic private eye. "That's it for the moment, Mr Pierce." He was watching Trayhorn's feet on the pedals again. Nylon seemed to be slippery. She curled her toes over the profiled rubber.

"Where shall I drop you?" Trayhorn said at the traffic in front of her. "I'm going down past Red Lion Square. Will that do?"

"Yes. I can get a cab there. Thanks."

Trayhorn turned into Drake Street, and then changed lanes. As she manoeuvred into parallel traffic she glanced over her shoulder, past Munro. Blonde hair – and blue eyes. She had blue eyes. She turned left and went round the near side of the square. Pierce hopped out, waved vaguely, and was scanning for a cab before they'd moved off to turn back towards High Holborn.

"I didn't know," Trayhorn said, waiting at the turning out of the square, "that you'd put a private detective on Mr Tranter."

"About half the private detective's firm, as it happens. It began as surveillance of Pattie Lee."

"His PA?" She started the car moving again and nudged back into the traffic. "Why?"

"There were reasons to suspect her of commercial espionage."

"A spy?" Trayhorn slowed the Mercedes to join the end of a tangle trying to get out of Procter Street. Her toes curled over the brake. "*Were* good reasons?"

"Now it's getting complicated. The Pattie Lee case and the frauds are beginning to converge."

"And the common factor is Michael Tranter." She put the drive in neutral, then applied the parking brake with the pedal at the side of the foot well. She rested her feet on the mat. Her toenails were varnished, ghosts of red hidden inside layers of nylon. The colour was the same as her fingernails. And her lipstick. How many women actually varnished their toenails? "You never told me in so many words that he's the man behind the frauds. He is, isn't he? You're just looking for firm evidence."

Munro nodded. She understood the picture perfectly.

"How did you find out?"

"The Siltech Systems Service fraud in Buenos Aires. Whoever sluiced that chunk of money through the company had to be able to co-ordinate the pay-in at the London end and the withdrawal at the Buenos Aires end. Michael Tranter paid the money in."

"I see." She watched the vehicles ahead, searching for signs of movement. "Scary, isn't it?"

"It is. I'll buy you a pair of tights, by the way."

She stared at him.

"Don't worry, I'm not trying to get personal." He pointed into the foot well. "You're ruining the soles of those, so I'll buy you a new pair." She was still staring at him. "I know it isn't much, but it's fair."

"They're stockings, actually." The car ahead began to move. She turned her attention to the road, released the brake, and started the Mercedes rolling. "But when we go to Oxford this afternoon, please give me some warning if you want me to do any more driving, Mr Munro."

That sounded like a rebuff, careful and polite, from junior to very senior colleague. He watched as they swung slowly past the participants in a nose-to-tail which had been blocking the end of the lane into High Holborn. Hazard lights blinking, a big five-door Rover was crowded behind a Metro against the kerb. The pin-stripe at the wheel of the Rover was calmly writing on a notepad. The teenager from the Metro was kicking glass fragments of her car towards the gutter. Colliding with Michael still felt even softer than the knock the pin-stripe had given the Metro. There had to be something going on he hadn't seen yet.

Traffic on the main road moved at a speed less like a transport clot about to cause an urban infarction. Trayhorn relaxed a little as the separation between cars increased. "Are you going to kick out the board of Siltech this afternoon?"

"Yes."

"And what then?"

"I'm going to start a shares trade between MT and the subsidiaries."

"I see. So that the MT stakes in the three main subsidiaries go down, the cross-share holdings between the three go up, and Mr Tranter can't regain control of them even if he gets back in command of MT Holdings. Correct?"

"Correct."

"And how long will that take?"

"Two or three days." Which was too long. He needed some kind of real progress on the frauds. "I'll be driving this afternoon. On the way to Oxford we'll go through your briefing on the Buenos Aires fraud. On the way back, you can brief me on any progress you and Curtis Gupta have made. I'm immensely grateful to you for your skill in finding the frauds, by the way."

"I had no idea it was going to turn into anything like this. I happened to notice that things didn't add up – literally. It's my job. I just do the numbers."

Me, too, he thought. I've done the numbers all my life. I did them so well that I ended up at Bryce McFadden, and then Michael poached me to set up MT-Orbis for him. And I did that so well, I've put Michael in a fortress and myself in the moat – just the way he wanted me. I do the numbers. But at the moment I can't find all the numbers I need.

"Mr Munro – I don't mind if you get personal."

He looked at her for a long moment, sitting in his driving seat and allowed to drive his executive car. She wasn't supposed to think he'd been organising her into a compartment of his life. "I'm not expecting you to pay me for these temporary directorships you're getting. Not in any kind of way. You do realise they're temporary?"

"Yes. I haven't got the experience to last long at board level."

"Exactly. I'm not trying to buy you, for God's sake. I'm expecting you to work." Work very hard, he thought, and very fast – and come up with a miracle for me.

"I know." She had her eyes on the traffic, she was in control of his car. "I still don't mind if you get personal."

FORTY-ONE

After lunch they gave him a sling, a vast triangle of cloth which spread the weight of his immobilised arm across both his shoulders. It made sitting and standing bearable, so he decided to practise getting dressed and ready for the big bad world.

It wasn't too bad. Buttons can be managed with one hand, so can a belt. His jacket, hitched after several attempts across his shoulders, was likely to be kidnapped by any moderately lively breeze. Going to the toilet one-handed wasn't the elaborate degradation he'd anticipated – except for separating the toilet paper from its roll. But shoe laces? Impossible.

The phone was taking a pause. Perhaps they were all getting drunk in a midday restaurant. The phone hadn't stopped ringing since mid-morning, and it was alarm calls they were sending him. Munro had taken Orbis Air! Munro had taken Orbis! If nothing was found to stop him, Munro would take Siltech! What a surprise. What else did they expect Munro to do? The depressing thing about loyal hirelings was that they had no imagination. They couldn't think creatively. Munro could. That was what made him useful, and also dangerous.

Not, however, to Michael.

There was some old saying that the best swordsman in the land doesn't fear the second best swordsman: he knows everything his opponent will do, and knows it sooner. Munro was the second best swordsman in MT-Orbis. Every move he was going to make was inevitable, predictable – and defeatable.

The excuse Munro had been using to slaughter boardrooms

298

was negligence in the face of fraud. That's what would be happening at Siltech during the afternoon. He obviously knew about some of the scams. Their discovery had been inevitable ever since trading losses led Munro to propose a major revamping of MT-Orbis. The detailed costings required for such a restructuring were bound to reveal the steady drip of money falling out of sight. The trick had been to hold Munro back long enough, until it wasn't going to matter any more when he found out.

The interesting question was, did Munro know who was responsible?

He probably did. Munro had notions of acting for the good of the company. Such ideas made a man take risks with his own self-interest, and led him to strike as soon as possible – while the boss was out of the way – in the hope of saving the company before the boss mounted a counter-strike. If Munro had simply been seeking personal power, he would have waited patiently for proof. Then he would have had a quiet chat with Michael – and taken complete and permanent control.

Instead, he was taking out all three subsidiaries in the first tier in less than two days. Impressive. Efficient. His next move would be to swap shares held by MT in those three companies against shares they held in their own subsidiaries in the lower tiers. The trade would leave the value of each company's portfolio intact, but would reduce MT's stake in Orbis, Siltech and Orbis Air. Then, once Michael was back in the driving seat at MT Holdings, he wouldn't be able to regain control of the three big subsidiaries. Munro's intention would be to block the income flowing upwards through the pyramid of MT-Orbis. MT Holdings would gradually weaken, would lose value, and eventually Munro would expect to buy Michael out in an amicable settlement. Clever.

Except that he wouldn't get that far.

The share swap would take until the end of the week. Michael wasn't going to give him that much time. Munro probably knew it. He couldn't be hoping that Michael was going to fall down another flight of stairs, so he had to be banking on finding proof of who did the frauds. How many of the frauds, come to think of it, had he found?

It didn't matter. Munro didn't know the half of what was going on. The original plan would have fooled him as surely as it would have fooled everyone else. The new emergency-plan-B version was still going to come as a surprise. The game was very different from the one Munro thought he was playing.

Michael could rely on Pattie Lee. He didn't trust her, but he could depend on her because she had to depend on him. He couldn't do plan B without her help – not with a broken arm – any more than he could have carried out the original version alone. And she couldn't get to the final reward without Michael, because he was the *only* one who knew the key. It wasn't written anywhere except inside his head, and on the program guarding the files and waiting for the password.

He and Pattie needed each other, which was the only guarantee of any honour among thieves.

Meanwhile, it was almost time to track down Randall Wild in London, and get his fat backside in gear. Mobility was called for, and you couldn't drive a car with one arm in a cast.

Michael tried his shoe laces again, stooping to attempt the one-handed trick. Any change of posture and weight distribution made his left arm, his broken, bolted, bound-up arm, throb ferociously. The rest of him merely ached and burned. He'd like to get his own back on Ruth Clifford – he really would!

Oh well, not to be. She was heading for her own little surprise, and that would have to be revenge enough. She deserved worse, but it didn't matter. Only money mattered.

FORTY-TWO

You've seen one ocean and you've seen them all, even by night. The Indian Ocean was a dark parchment of waves, with a moon river reaching down from the horizon on the left of Angel's long, night-lit nose. The heading was north of west, onwards round the great circle, away from Australia and back up towards the equator again. The equator was waiting in Africa.

Ruth decided to sleep. She'd had half her normal ration in the past fifty-three hours, and she was doubly exhausted by the fear which came with the near disaster of the canoe assembly, and the elation which took over once the thing was gone. Sleep was the thing she needed most.

The Indian Ocean was an emptiness, with no island on her route and no weather waiting for her in the long darkness. She was protected by the radar alarm and guided by the autopilot and the central computer's navigation program. The computer worked with the INS system, and that was updated by satellite reference every two hours. The position accuracy after each new update was ten metres, the drift in accuracy between satellite fixes was one hundred metres – three hundred and thirty feet up, down, backwards, forwards or sideways. As an added safeguard, the barometric altimeter was recalibrated at each update against atmospheric pressure, and provided the autopilot with a second opinion about altitude. And anyway, the watery plain below was very, very flat. There were no mountain ranges to snare Ruth while she slept. Besides, the program in the computer knew the elevation of every piece of land it was due to meet. Michael had thought of everything.

He always did think of everything.

Except he ignored the fire he was igniting when he took

from Ruth her dream of the crazy mission – her secret belief that she might be tough enough to do it, if someone gave her the chance. He fanned the flames by dropping her from his private world. He set light to a pit filled with tinder-dry resentment, the harvest of Ruth's thirty-one years of life.

Michael failed to think of that. So he argued, missed his footing, and ended up on a concrete floor at the bottom of a flight of stairs.

There were other fires in the Indian Ocean night. There were fires which flickered through cramped muscles, which charred bones and welded joints into immobility. They smouldered while she loosened the strap across her lap. They crackled when she tried to hang some of her weight from the assist handle with one hand while she cranked the seat flat with the other. They engulfed her back and legs when she started to lie down . . .

She dropped full length on the levelled seat. Angel didn't even waver under the impact. The autopilot held the aircraft steady while its human passenger lay helpless in her invisible cocoon of flames. Too little movement, for more than fifty hours. It was a terrible thing she was doing to herself. Slowly, clumsily, she tightened the strap again. She wouldn't want to bounce round the cockpit if Angel hit turbulence while she slept. She'd love to walk round the cockpit, but there wasn't an inch of room. A lazy stroll across the wings would be the thing. If only she could *stand*!

Munro drove his car along the motorway, gliding with the five-thirty traffic that was cruising towards London. A dense armada of cars was heading back the other way. The lanes on this side were easy.

Siltech had been easy. George Connor wasn't able to mount a defence of his control of the company, and Michael obviously hadn't intervened. The absence of any counter-attack was disconcerting. Michael wasn't shy about interfering in corporate affairs in any other way. Specially not in secret ways.

Geraldine Trayhorn, now a director of Siltech, sat in the

passenger seat and briefed him on the internal investigation. In the time she'd managed to spend since Monday morning working with Curtis Gupta, a lot of little pieces had come to light. The picture was still a broken jigsaw, bits of edge and isolated elements with vast gaps in between, but its scale was becoming evident. Once he'd started drinking the blood of MT-Orbis, Michael Tranter had done it in style.

Gupta knew how to use computers. Where Trayhorn had been extracting data and doing the endless calculations by hand, Gupta could set up a program to sift information and scrutinise it for arithmetical errors. He could also isolate the work from any snoopers by running it on a machine disconnected from the network, without having to transfer raw data by printout and keyboard. What he couldn't do was identify the accounting input that was needed, or interpret the results. That was Trayhorn's job. Gupta's contribution was a revolution in the speed of the work.

When Munro brought Gupta into the investigation, Trayhorn had been searching for three weeks, and had found a total of six and a half million missing from accounts over the years – listed as still in the pot, of course, but vanished just the same. One day later, they knew about another three and a half million. Michael's fraud was massive.

Trayhorn had cracked the pattern by which Michael Tranter tapped and imperceptibly drained resources, or sidelined interest from investment funds. Gupta had streamlined the process for screening accounts data. What they hadn't solved was the problem of how the tricks were actually done. It was all there inside the computers connected into the MT-Orbis net, but the network wouldn't tell them anything at all. It kept its programmed secrets. Gupta, according to his references, was good. But Michael was a master of a higher order.

"That's it." Trayhorn closed the file in her lap. The file was full. It slid on her skirt until the edge of its card folded against her stomach. "That's where we were at two this afternoon."

I'm getting old, he thought, with his eyes on the road again. I'm getting pathetic. I'm envying a file, for God's sake.

"Mr Munro?"

He had his right hand on the wheel. With his left hand he lifted his glasses slightly and rubbed at the bridge of his nose. Tiredness has no place in the executive lifestyle. There's too much else to be done.

"Are you going to get personal?"

"No." He let his glasses drop into place again. "I've just started a war, and I'm very busy with it. We're going back to the MT building. You're going to your office, I'm going to mine. We've got work to do. A very great deal of work. Is that clear?"

"Your tone's turned a little bit fatherly."

He put both hands on the wheel and practised crushing it. Be calm. An executive has no time for temper, either. "What do you expect? I'm old enough to be your father."

"Actually, my father's younger than you."

FORTY-THREE

She had the desk light on under the slope of the ceiling. Dusk was beginning to lay down layers of shadow in the little garden outside. She was pausing to turn down the brightness of the screen –

Downstairs, the door opened.

Pattie held her breath for one second. Then she hit *control* and *escape*. The software unloaded itself through seven levels at once, while she swept disks and notes into her case. The DOS prompt reappeared, and she switched the machine off. Then she went through into Michael's front bedroom and looked out of the window.

The gate was open. The Volvo 960 stood on the gravel drive.

She went past the bathroom to the stairs, and started down towards the footsteps and the voices.

304

"Ah, there you are." Michael was in the little hall between the openings to the dining room and the living room. Behind him, the front door stood wide. He had his jacket in his right hand, and his left arm in a sling. Bumps on the sling marked the positions of the bolts penetrating to his bone. He was a sorry sight, weary, wrung out, with his hair plastered flat in unwashed rat-tails.

"Is anyone else here?" She looked past him, through the open door. She could just see the front wing of the Volvo. "I mean, you can't have been driving with one arm."

"Randall." Michael nodded towards the door behind her, beyond the foot of the stairs. "I've sent him to the kitchen to grab something to eat. Then I'm sending him back to London with the car. By the way, the BMW is still here in the garage, isn't it?"

"I've no idea." She was looking round at the kitchen door. She couldn't see Randall through the glass, but the light was on and she could hear him opening and closing cupboards. "I haven't looked in the garage."

"Well, if you haven't moved it, nobody has. How's the work going?"

"All done," she said. The data copying for Michael had been dealt with in no time. The additional copying she'd done for herself had taken a little longer. The slow and careful search through his programmed world for a clue to a very special password wasn't finished, but had just been cancelled by his arrival. "Why are you here this evening? I was expecting you tomorrow afternoon."

"Change of plan. I want some extra computer time."

"I see."

The kitchen door opened and Randall Wild came out. He had to stoop to get his flat-topped haircut under the frame of the cottage doorway. "All right if I make some coffee, Mike?"

"Have anything you like, Randall."

"Right. Hello, Miss Lee." Randall went back into the kitchen. He left the door open.

Michael backed into the living room. Pattie followed him. He smelled of hospital disinfectant, an entirely wrong aroma for his English country idyll. "Apart from everything else that needs to be done," he said quietly, "I've decided to give Bob Munro what he deserves."

"I see."

"Also, I couldn't wait any longer to get out of that bloody hospital and back to civilisation. I need to have a bath – and wash my hair." He pulled at his hair with his fingertips. "First a bath, then some food, then the computer."

Pattie didn't want him looking inside his computer. The first thing he'd see was the record of when it was last switched off. He'd know she'd been doing extra work. She didn't want him to switch on the screen until he had too much to do and too little time to start wondering what she'd been up to. "You're tired." She moved closer. She pressed her hip against the back of his hand which held his jacket. "Food first." She lowered her voice to a whisper. After so much time, there was no need to let Randall Wild in on their secret. "And then – I'll wash you."

Michael didn't say no.

Munro didn't leave for his club until after ten. He lived there, and at the office, almost permanently now. He wasn't expecting to see his Guildford home again until the weekend. Work, worry and corporate politics had taken total control of his life.

Geoffrey Simmington was there for the evening. He took Munro to the bar and bought him a brandy and soda. "Get that down you, old chap, and I'll buy you another. You look as though you need it. Working all hours?"

Munro nodded. He drank half his brandy and then put the glass on the oak bar. He leaned on the leather-upholstered rail and let the warmth of the alcohol melt some of the tension inside. For a moment, Simmington seemed like a pin-striped streak of ministering angel. "There's rather a lot to do, Geoffrey."

"I can quite imagine there is, Robert. How's the business of securing control going? Ready to cut off MT Holdings at the neck?"

"If necessary. I'm putting the mechanisms in place."

"I'm sure you are." Simmington sipped his port. His eyes, hard as glass inside their rays of friendly wrinkles, hid business plans and busy thoughts. Geoffrey Simmington, senior banker, played nobody's side but his own. "Been a peep out of Tranter yet?"

"Not yet."

"The quieter the better, eh? Sylvia's very pleased with the turn of events, by the way. And the consortium's ready for the Orbis Air deal as soon as the dust has settled. The only cloud on the horizon, it seems to me, is the Bryce McFadden Group. Those chappies have been playing it rather shady, I'd say. Any progress on that spy thingy?"

"Some. We've found the spy." Munro picked up his brandy again. "But I'm starting to change my mind about who the spy's working for."

"Really? Come on, empty that glass. I promised you another one." Simmington started trying to catch the barman's eye.

Willis, the porter, had come through to the bar from the entrance hall. He made a handset and dialling mime for Munro. "Excuse me a moment, Geoffrey. Telephone. I'll be back."

"Of course, old chap. The drink will be waiting."

Willis led him to the telephone booths. "Number two, sir."

"Thank you, Willis." He went into the booth and closed the concertina door. He lifted the receiver and listened for the click which opened the line. "Munro."

"Darren Pierce, Mr Munro. I do hope I'm not disturbing you this late in the evening, but I thought you'd want to know. Tranter has just turned up to join Lee at his Oxfordshire house."

That was too soon. That was far too soon. It meant the real business was about to begin. "I see. Thank you."

307

"I felt sure you'd want to know. Should there be any further developments, will you be at the same number?"

"I'll be here until seven tomorrow morning, Mr Pierce. Then I'll be at the office." There was going to be a lot to do – fast. He couldn't start it now because the department staff wouldn't be there at MT to initiate his arrangements for the share swaps. The best thing he could do for the moment was sleep. But first he needed Geoffrey's drink. He needed it quite badly.

FORTY-FOUR

Sometimes the strap round her hips woke her up when she turned. She loosened it. Once Michael was holding her down and driving her insane. But it was the strap again. When her head lolled off the edge of the seat, that woke her, too ...

This time Michael had already gone – flown suddenly from the back seat of the glider, dream in dream, sailed down his stairs and shattered at the bottom in thundering light. Shattered into furious Michaels, agonised Michaels, disappointed Michaels, and Michaels with pieces of a self-satisfied saccharin smile.

The glider was splintering on its anvil of earth. The wings were coming off, great angel arms rotating up in a broken windmill whirl. And while she was falling out of independence, out of Icarus freedom, backwards against the undefeatable reality of ending and death, her father swerved his chair round with a single flick of his arms. The wheels locked with the slight wobble of tyres on a hard surface. *Fall*, he said to her. *Fall! You could never do it!*

The wings were gone. Stripped. Melted. In the infinite elasticity of this last of all moments, as the seat began to break into her back, he leaned forward, bent like a crucified man, like a crow, like a cobra spitting. *Never could do it! Never! Never!*

Never –

Fall –

Falls break arms. Falls break backs. Break lives. Where was Ruth when her father fell in the pit of his furnace? In the dark –

Where the flames flashed red, then green, then brilliant white. Left, then right, then all around.

She lifted her head. 60.49 glowed the mission clock. 22.49 shone the UK time. A red flash. A green flash. She'd slept for so long. She never intended to sleep for so long. If anything had happened – she'd have consummated her fall in a place called the Indian Ocean.

A bright white flash. She started to haul herself up. Angel was lurching and bumping. Hanging from the assist handle, she got her eyes level with the windows. A red flash, then a green flash from the running lights. Then a bright white burst from the strobes, a snapshot of a capsule of misty illumination like the eggshell of silence surrounding Icarus as it fell . . .

She got herself into a sitting position. She managed to crank the seat upright before her back gave way. Her eyes had cleared enough to study the VSI. The heading was constantly drifting and correcting as Angel lurched and the autopilot restored the course. The computer, when she asked it by punching the keys, confirmed that the routine satellite fix had been done at 60.00 hours, and the position data transmitted automatically to Mission Control. Angel was still on course.

Seven hours. She'd slept for seven hours. You can't do that alone in an aircraft which is cruising through the night. It isn't possible. Michael's mastery of computerised technology kept her alive, just as his skill kept her from dying when Icarus . . .

Now she was in cloud, tracing a route through it with momentary bubbles of light. It wasn't retribution for all her lingering sins. Her father cutting everything to the bone in his desperation to save the firm, going broke as Thatcherism ripped the steel heart out of Sheffield and the furnaces closed, as his daughter failed to come back and help him work money miracles with the university education he'd paid for. Her father, shedding staff, working round the clock, doing the jobs himself, falling from his ladder to the furnace floor where a bed of bricks waited for his back. Michael descending his steep steel stair, first like a dancer, then a cartwheeling acrobat, then a flapping and bouncing thing . . .

It wasn't retribution. It was cloud. Turbulent cloud on a weather front, pitch black between Angel's flashes of light. They let her fly into weather, cloud, turbulence. They didn't wake her, didn't warn her. They weren't even there for the endless Indian Ocean crossing. They shut down Mission Control and went home! Left her all alone!

John answered. "Hello, Ruth. I've just taken over from Mandy as your babysitter. You've had a really long sleep. Bet you needed it, too."

"I'm in cloud. I've just woken up in cloud. The turbulence is pretty strong. Why didn't anyone push the alarm at your end and tell me?"

"Cloud? Wait a minute. Let me just check. No. There's no cloud and no weather front predicted for your position."

"Well there is cloud. My position is fourteen degrees forty minutes south, sixty-three degrees thirty minutes east. And I'm in cloud!"

"I've got the latest chart here. And satellite pics. The infrared pics for night. There's no cloud where you are. Your position's exactly right for the time – sixty fifty-five. The nearest cloud formation doesn't come closer than five hundred miles to the north of you. The data's an hour or so out of date. It could have moved. But no weather system moves that fast."

"Well this one has!"

"No, Ruth. It must be some local cloud that's formed since the pic was made."

Was it, now? It was solid cloud full of energetic movement, just like a weather front. Angel was bouncing about like a billiard ball inside a giant bingo machine. "Well what do I do? Go over it? Under it? Round it?"

"We don't know how big the cloud area is. And we don't know the height of the cloud tops, or the cloud base. It doesn't make any sense to try avoiding it. But stay awake, whatever else. If you hit a major convection cell, you'll have to take over from the autopilot and fly out of it. You don't want to go down. And you don't want to go up suddenly inside a thunder cloud because Angel hasn't got de-icing strips."

"I know that, John."

"And cheer up. It's going to be daylight in about an hour."

"Good." She took off the headset. She resigned herself to bouncing about inside her strobe-lit crystal ball in a blind bowling alley. She was thirsty, and her bladder was full after so many hours, but she didn't want to risk either a drink or a urine bottle. Too much lurching about. Too much chance of a spill in her solitary cockpit cell.

She switched off the maddening strobes and left the softer running lights to alternate their colours alone.

The cloud was past after fifteen minutes, leaving just night with starlight. Behind her, to the right of Angel's blunt tail, the dawn finally began.

At 62.00 the computer ran its routine position update again. The world in the west was green, the sky behind was bright, and the ocean below was an expanse of gloomy grey. Ahead, a little to the left and well down from the horizon, a point of light blinked on, and then off.

It persisted. It came closer, making a slow diagonal towards the interruption of Angel's foreplane. The single point resolved itself into a tiny cluster of pinpricks blinking in unison. Down on the empty ocean, a ship was flashing its lights.

Could it be signalling to her, after seeing Angel approach as a pinpoint silhouette with scintillating running lights, flying towards it out of the empty dawn? The ship was well informed

311

if it knew that it happened to be where she was going to pass by. That provided a measure of fame, in a world which was watching and listening. What kind of ship could it be? One with good lookouts and an air surveillance radar – Royal Navy, US Navy, Indian Navy? Or just keen-eyed local fishermen, or a tanker or a freighter crossing her route at the end of the night?

The ship, just a cluster of slowly flashing lights on a sombre sea, disappeared behind the foreplane.

Then it sent up a trio of signal rockets, tiny firepoint dancers dying in an empty world.

She didn't know her maritime codes or the law of the sea. She didn't know whether they were distress rockets or friendly fireworks. She called John and told him what she could see. She confirmed her position, then switched off the satellite channel. She changed to the distress frequency, then cut out the autopilot and throttled back so that Angel lost height.

There were no Maydays and nothing but static to hear. The lights had stopped flashing and were burning steadily. They were too many and too bright to be riding lights. The signal rockets seemed to have been an extravagant hello. She decided to answer with a fly-past in the dawn. There would be some channel on which she could talk to the ship, but she didn't bother to search. If they'd greeted her on approach, they knew who she was.

She levelled at five hundred feet and one hundred and eighty knots. The waves were faced with light reflected from the day coming up behind her, were topped with blue from the sky above, and backed by deep green from the retreating night ahead. Like the sun, she was chasing darkness round the Earth.

The ship was small. It was an ocean tug. The high bow and the block of superstructure were turned half away. There was a pair of side-by-side funnels, and an open, flat and desperately low stern deck crossed by ribs over which steel hawsers could slide. All the tug's working lights were on,

312

brilliant magnesium points which stuck like migraine seeds in her eye.

She aimed to overtake the tug on its port side. Someone was watching from the bridge wing. Near the stern, figures were lowering an inflatable into the water. They held on to ropes, but they paused to wave. No wake boiled from the stern. The tug was lying stopped on a calm sea. There was no sign of distress or damage. Diesel exhaust plumed thinly from each funnel. There was power on board, or the lights wouldn't have been burning. They waved and she waved back, hoping they could see. She'd heard nothing on the shortwave they would have used to call for help. Nothing at all, just silence and a waving tugboat crew with an inflatable dinghy halfway over the side.

The tug fell out of sight behind her wing. She added power, trimmed the nose slightly high, and started Angel in a slow climb.

Angel wasn't the kind of aircraft to climb in a hurry. Ruth took it easy and spent twenty minutes bringing Angel up to four thousand feet and two hundred and fifty knots, back on course for a landfall at the northern tip of Madagascar in another three hours.

She felt good. A salvage tug, or an opportunist who'd stopped to pick something out of the water, had seen her coming over wide open ocean, had recognised her aircraft and had decided to say hello. It was a moment of contact with strangers, it had given her half an hour of active flying instead of sitting there forever as the autopilot's passenger. Now she was high over a crinkled seascape painted pink by the sunrise blossoming behind her. She was stretching out the glorious beginning of the day as Angel slowly raced the sun round the girdle of the world. She believed at last that she was going to make it. There were no more canoe tanks to jettison, no mountain ranges to cross, just Africa and ocean and another forty hours to Florida, then a few more back to Britain. The electronic controls which flew Angel made the aircraft a safe, reliable, easy machine. Ruth was going to succeed.

She checked that altitude, course and speed matched the autopilot's pre-set expectations, then she switched it on and let go of the controls.

On the VSI screen, the autopilot cue came on. Then vanished.

The autopilot's own window requested inputs for altitude, course and speed.

The autopilot wasn't flying Angel. The aircraft was still on manual. Ruth switched the autopilot on again.

The same thing happened.

The autopilot wasn't working. Or at least, it suddenly didn't know what the pre-set course was supposed to be. Either there was a fault on the autopilot, or a fault in the navigation computer which was programmed to feed it with data.

That was bad.

FORTY-FIVE

Terri had dressed herself in black Lycra leggings and a loose red-checked blouse, with a gold chain belt that dipped at her hips. It was a waste of good taste at Mission Control at two thirty in the morning, but this was another emergency and she might be here forever. She'd intended to get a long night's sleep – she'd had next to no sleep the previous night and less than eight hours added together between Michaels Field and the canoe assembly crisis. She managed another six hours, then John called her in.

"That's very bad," she said. "Isn't it?"

John nodded. "The autopilot is out and the INS is out. They aren't getting input from the navigation computer. The computer is the culprit. We can't get it to give a read-out, and it failed to run the routine update half an hour ago. On the face of it, either the navigation computer has failed or the course program has gone down."

"Ruth can't fly solo without the computer. Can she?"

"No. And another problem is the satellite channel. It's getting fuzzy. The pointing system isn't receiving updates, so it's drifting off line as Angel moves. We'll lose it soon."

And then they wouldn't even be able to talk to Ruth. An alternative chain of communication would be needed. "So – how's she flying Angel at the moment?"

"The VSI screen is down, but she's still got the repeater instruments – gyrocompass, roll and pitch indicators, and the barometric altimeter. The altimeter was calibrated at sixty-two hundred, when the computer did its last fix, so the setting won't have drifted too badly yet. It's still fairly accurate."

"And where is she?"

"Here." John placed his finger on the chart he'd unfolded over the commandeered press desk. He was using the telephones to flatten awkward folds. "About one hundred and twenty-five miles east of Cap d'Ambre, here on the tip of Madagascar. That's by dead reckoning, using the last accurate position we had – the one she read through before she switched off the autopilot and went to look at that ship."

"So – what do we do? Let her fly on to Madagascar?"

"I think that's the best idea. The weather's excellent, the visibility goes on forever, so she'll see Cap d'Ambre no matter what the dead reckoning error is. Then we'll take her right over the cape – there's a little peak – and use the map position to re-calibrate the INS. Once the INS is up and running, we should be able to bus position data through to the computer pointing the aerial, and get the satellite channel working again. But it's going to fade before then."

"And what do we do about that?"

John paused for a while to rub his beard. "The only thing I can think of is to open a satellite channel to Dar es Salaam, and get the people there to patch us in to a local transmitter so that we can talk to Ruth by radio. That would cost a fortune."

Terri nodded. "MT-Orbis has got a fortune. Okay, we'd better set that up before the direct channel fades completely. Otherwise we won't be able to tell her what frequency to use. Am I right?"

"Absolutely right. By the way, Chester Alby isn't answering his phone."

To hell, she thought, with Chester Alby.

Ruth only had the repeater instruments mounted below the blank VSI screen. The gyrocompass would stay accurate for longer than the fuel lasted, but the barometric altimeter would become increasingly unreliable as she flew through zones of varying air pressure. Once she got to Africa she'd have to resort to pilotage, zig-zagging from landmark to landmark – until night intervened and she was forced to land. If they didn't come up with something at Mission Control, the mission was over after all.

She needed the INS, so she needed a precise map position to set it up. Visibility was excellent and from four thousand feet she could see over the haze for scores of sun-drenched miles. So where was Madagascar?

"Ruth? Haven't you seen it yet? Over."

Terri's voice was faint and scratchy. Dar es Salaam was only seven hundred miles away, so the signal should have been stronger. Perhaps they had cheap transmitters in Dar es Salaam. She pressed the transmit switch on her headset. "No sign of it. Over."

"You *can't* miss Madagascar. It's five hundred miles long. Over."

"Well it isn't here. I must be a bit too far north. What do you want me to do, keep going until Africa? Over."

"Wait a minute. John's got an idea."

She waited. The mission clock said 65.00, bang on time for Cap d'Ambre on Madagascar's northern tip. Madagascar should have filled the horizon from dead ahead right down into the vanishing haze of the south. Instead, the only thing in sight was sea.

"Ruth, this is John. Tune your OBI to the Antananarivo beacon. Antananarivo's slap in the middle of Madagascar. If you pick up the beacon and fly towards it, you're automatically going to meet the coast. Once you've hit the coast, you turn north, and then we'll get you to Cap d'Ambre and that INS fix. Okay? Over."

It sounded like a good idea. She pressed transmit. "What's the beacon frequency? Over."

The Antananarivo beacon was very faint. The Omni-Bearing Indicator picked it up all right, but the distance measuring equipment couldn't read its range. She turned towards the beacon, almost due south, and waited. She was obviously coming down out of the north straight towards Cap d'Ambre.

But Madagascar stayed stubbornly out of sight.

The beacon's signal didn't get any stronger, either.

Angel's navigation computer had gone crazy and shut itself, the INS, the autopilot and the satellite system down. The imaginary data-world of the course program was no longer available. Which left just the real world. But she seemed to have slipped sideways into fantasy, and the real world had vanished. The magical realm was made of blue sky, blinding sun, bluer ocean – and nothing else. It was a place where five-hundred-mile islands could disappear. Real life lay elsewhere. It used to talk to her by way of a sharp, clear, two-way satellite. Now it crackled and wheezed in her ears. It came from outside, through a radio filter, stripped threadbare by an intervening shell which enclosed the emptiness where she and Angel flew. Perhaps the silent ship hadn't been saying hello. Perhaps it was trapped, and had been trying to warn her. Turn back, before this Sargasso of reality ensnares you. Turn back!

She knew where that train of thought was heading – into a siding which got steeper, and darker, and rolled you down into panic. Ruth panicked easily. She'd learned that when the canoe wouldn't fall. She'd also learned what to do about it. Initiative. Do *something*. And do it, for best results, before you've already lost control.

She couldn't wait for them to think it through in London. She had to short the circuit before it burned her up instead. The problem threatening her was that of being *lost*, having no position at all, in the middle of a circle of nothingness. Flying down one faint radial towards infinitely distant Antananarivo wouldn't tell her where she was. A second direction would.

She pressed the transmit button. "I'm going to triangulate. I need the frequency of a second beacon. What about Dar es Salaam? Over."

The first pair of press-desk women arrived to get ready for the scheduled African landfall, due at six o'clock in the UK morning. Mandy had come in, earlier than planned, and took them aside for a briefing on the new situation. Telling the press could wait.

Terri put down the telephone. Chester still wasn't answering. Perhaps he wasn't even at home. Who cared, anyway? Who said he'd be able to help?

John came back from the communication desk to the temporary map table. "I've asked her to check with the Mombasa beacon. It's two hundred miles from Dar es Salaam. The separation's big enough to get a useful result." He tapped the map. "That result's wrong."

Ruth's OBI bearings to the Antananarivo and Dar es Salaam beacons crossed at a position which put her slap on the equator at forty-nine degrees east. That was impossible. That was eight hundred and fifty miles to the north of her course. Three hours ago she'd been on course. Angel's navigation computer had run a routine satellite position fix and relayed the result automatically to Mission Control. That was at 62.00, Mission Time. At 62.05 Ruth read her position through, still on course, then switched off the autopilot in order to descend and take a look at her ship. At 62.28 she called to report that the autopilot and the navigation systems were down. Since then she'd maintained the gyrocompass course, exactly as planned, expecting to fly into the northern tip of Madagascar.

Now it was three hours later. Ruth couldn't possibly have travelled eight hundred and fifty miles off course, even if she'd headed due north by mistake – in which case she wouldn't have come so far west from her last accurate position, anyway. And even if she had turned due north, she'd have noticed because the sun would have been coming in through the side window of her cockpit, instead of being behind her.

The position was completely impossible.

John shook his head. "I'll see if she's got the bearing." He went back to the communication desk.

Terri pulled one of the meteorology charts across the map, and leaned on her elbows to study it. The chart had been faxed through by the weather people at Orbis Air. She couldn't read meteorology symbols, but someone at the other end had scribbled useful names on everything, like *cloud* or *front* or *rain*. The time entered on the chart was Tuesday 22.30, about half an hour before Ruth, according to the entry John had written in the log, complained of being woken up by cloud and turbulence. There was nothing called *cloud* anywhere near her course. But there was an awful lot of cloud a long way to the north.

John came back. He started marking up the bearing line from Mombasa. The pencil line went straight through the impossible position, forty-nine degrees east on the equator. He looked at the position, he looked at the dead reckoning course plotted towards Madagascar far to the south. "That's wrong," he said. "Angel couldn't get there. Either the OBI has crapped up, as well as all the computers on the aircraft, or Ruth's too tired to read the OBI properly. That position is impossible."

"No." Leaning on her elbows, Terri looked up at him. As she tipped her head, she could feel her African plait curl against the collar of her blouse. "Angel was already off course four hours ago. That's when Ruth said she was in cloud. That was hundreds of miles north of where she was supposed to be."

"Where she *was*." John poked at the map. "Here. On the

319

course. The position reports confirm it. That's the sixty-two hundred hours update, one single hour after she hit the cloud. She was down here, not up there where that weather system is."

"No. She was up there where the weather is. That's how she's got where she is now – by following her gyrocompass course. She started out too far north, so she's ended up too far north."

"She *can't* have been there. The computer was still working. It was calculating its position all the time, and it was keeping its calculations up to date by correcting them with the satellite fixes."

"Well then." Terri decided to stand up straight again, so that she could look John in the eye. "It must have been getting its sums wrong. For quite some time."

By five in the morning there was dingy brick-coloured daylight sinking dustily into the alley outside. A quarter of a world away, down on the equator, Ruth was flying through burning sunlight, still an hour away from her new East African landfall.

The planned course would have brought her in through central Tanzania, then over Rwanda into Zaire. Instead, she was going to cross the Kenya coast at the island of Lamu, one hundred and fifty miles north of Mombasa. There was an airfield at Lamu. Ruth could fly right over it and get an exact geographical fix to feed into the INS. The airfield could also give her a sea-level pressure reading as she went overhead. She could use it to set the barometric altimeter, could read off the precise altitude it gave, and feed that into the INS as well. She'd have an inertial navigation system which was set to an acceptable accuracy in all three dimensions. Then she would merely have to keep it up to date with geographical fixes and beacon triangulations for the rest of her transit of Africa, and the INS would allow her to navigate safely along the course they gave her from Mission Control.

A reliably set INS, feeding its position data to the computer which pointed the satellite aerial, meant that they'd also have the direct channel in operation again. Everything would be halfway back to normal.

The improvised course segment was going to take Angel south of Nairobi and through the Kenya Rift Valley, then across Lake Victoria and Uganda on the way to Zaire. The flight permissions had come in instantly – no one in the countries concerned was going to refuse a windfall tourist promotion. Ruth would have to push her aeroplane to seven thousand feet to clear the mountains west of Nairobi, but Angel was carrying only half its maximum load of internal fuel, and would be able to leap the barrier. Everyone should have been happy.

But there was no autopilot. It was blocked. The navigation computer wasn't sending it any instructions any more. It had no imaginary world to fly through.

Ruth was flying Angel, holding the course and keeping the aircraft steady. She'd have to fly Angel all the way across Africa. She'd fly into darkness, over Nigeria, in twelve hours. She'd reach the western coast at Dakar in eighteen hours, eleven o'clock on London's Wednesday evening. At that point there would still be another fourteen and a half hours of empty Atlantic to go before she reached Florida.

Ruth couldn't fly Angel for that length of time. She had no autopilot. She wouldn't be able to sleep during the Atlantic crossing. If she fell asleep, she'd crash in the sea. If she stayed awake, she'd be so tired she'd probably kill herself while attempting the landing in Florida.

So at eleven in the evening at the very latest, at Dakar airport, the mission would be over. No circumnavigation back to Florida. No bonus stage to Britain. No permanent entry in the history books for Ruth. A lot less money for MT-Orbis and the benefiting charities.

Well, there were still eighteen hours left to solve the problem.

John was looking at the Mission Control copy of the course program on his screen. It went on smoothly past the point where it had crashed in Angel's computer, and it looked exactly the way it was supposed to be. John sat there and spread his hands, defeated by its apparent perfection.

"I can't see why it shouldn't work," he said. "The whole thing's crazy. Why should it go wrong on Angel, take Angel off course during the stage from Australia – but keep telling us it's holding exactly on the correct course at each update, and tell the pilot it's on course with the cockpit readouts? Why should it hide its own error when the satellite fixes would tell it how far it had strayed off the course?"

Terri shrugged. "Ask a specialist."

"Michael's the only specialist for this program, and he's in hospital. Have you tried Chester again?"

"He isn't at home, or he won't get out of bed, or he's unplugged his phone." Terri shook her head. Angel's designer had disqualified himself, anyway. "Do you suppose the error might be only in the copy of the program in Angel? If you could compare the two and look for the difference, that should be easier, shouldn't it? Easier than trying to take apart the way the program works, I mean." John was just looking at her – what did she know about computers, anyway? "Print it out, for God's sake, in programming language, or machine code. Whatever's best. Put the two copies one on top of the other and hold them against the light. Spot the difference. It must be possible."

John shook his head. "Can't do that. There's no facility that would let us read out the program from Angel's computer, or transmit it through to us here so we could print it out. Or put it on screen. There's no way to get at Angel's copy."

"Isn't there, now?" On the Thursday evening, at Wragby Aerodrome, when Michael fell down his stairs, Terri went to look for his wallet and his personal details to send with him to the hospital. She looked in the wrong place, because his wallet was with him in his jacket pocket all the time. What she found instead was his laptop computer and a message coming in from Pattie Lee. And beside the computer was a pile of disks. Among those disks would be the ones Michael had used to load the course program into Angel's computer. Where might those disks be now?

Pattie Lee had been looking for Munro. Pattie Lee said Munro had taken the computer. He'd have taken the disks, as well.

How early in the day would a rebellious executive get to the office?

FORTY-SIX

Michael was using the keyboard fluently and fast, toggling between two windows, one managing the way his computer was interacting, the other running the program in development. Even one-handed, he was a miracle to watch. No wonder she spent all the previous day, but still failed to find the key she was looking for.

Well, she had copies of a lot of things Michael wouldn't like. With enough time, and the future help of a computer expert, she would find it in the end.

Pattie was bringing him his breakfast in instalments. She put a coffee cup down on the desk, out of the way of his notes scattered beside the keyboard. Michael was working with notes to keep track of the levels he was in, and the locations. He was on the modem and deep inside a fiction – the dataspace within the computers at the MT building in London. He paused to change his access route. He got out of the Newcastle exchange and set up a hop via Amsterdam, Liège and Dublin – a precaution to keep himself hidden, just in case something went wrong at the other end.

While the program was breaking, changing and restoring the telephone connections, he sipped his coffee and eyed his scribbled notes. He put down the cup and picked up a sheet. "Put that in the shredder for me."

She didn't try reading the notes. Michael was watching her. She switched on the machine and fed in the sheet. Methodically, the shredder sliced the paper into confetti strips. Michael was mean, suspicious, and extraordinarily careful. That was why he got rich, why no one else got near enough to demand a cut of those riches, and why he'd got away with it for so many years.

Sylvia Symes *nearly* found out, but Pattie took Michael in hand herself, and got rid of the woman in time. Only Pattie Lee ever succeeded in getting to the truth. They worked out a deal. Michael didn't trust her and she didn't trust him, but the partnership went well. When it became clear that the health of MT-Orbis was deteriorating too fast, and that Munro would be going through the figures before the grand plan had come into effect, Pattie was able to do what Michael couldn't have managed with any credibility. Michael thought up the rumour, but it was Pattie who placed it with Geo-Petro – which forced Munro to move in and stabilise things by bringing the Angel project forward. Munro thought there was a spy working in secret for an outside company. Let him think so. The real secret was right under his nose.

"What," she said, "are you in fact doing?"

"Something Bob Munro won't expect."

She watched while he sipped his coffee again, still waiting for the phone connection to clear. "Are you going to wipe the records of the frauds? If he got more, Munro would use it to sink you."

Michael shrugged. "Too complicated. The data's far too scattered. It would take weeks to erase and replace it all. Anyway, there's no need to bother, is there?" The screen reported it was ready to continue. He put down his cup, then typed an instruction and sent it through the modem. A machine code line appeared in reply. "This barrier's easy. I put a hole in it myself at installation. I wouldn't have wanted Munro trying to hide company accounts from me one day, would I?" He looked over his shoulder. "Go and turn on the radio. Eight o'clock news. See if they've cancelled poor little Ruth's flight round the world yet."

At eight o'clock, Ripley arrived. By then Munro had been at work almost an hour. His computer screen was on, the printer was still warm, and his desk was covered in tabulated sheets detailing the share blocks owned by Orbis, Siltech and Orbis Air in the lower-tier subsidiaries. Those shares had to be swapped, value for value on a moving market, against some of each block MT Holdings owned in the three major subsidiaries. It was going to be infernally complicated to set up. He wouldn't have it ready to go before tomorrow.

Terri Sabuli arrived at eight fifteen, and Ripley showed her through. Sabuli looked tired, but perfect. She moved silently, a slowly stalking focus of long-limbed, dream-dark, disallowed desire. Did Michael ever move in on her, and if so, who would have been using who?

She stopped where her perfume could skirmish on the border of his desk. "Did you find the disks I was asking for, Mr Munro?"

He turned to get his briefcase, which he'd propped under the window sill behind him. "I found them." He took out the stack of 3½ inch disks. They were labelled NAV PROG 1 to NAV PROG 5. "I assume these are the ones you need."

She took the disks from his hand, and checked the labels. "They look like it, don't they? There were quite a few more disks, if I remember correctly."

"Not with a relevant label." The rest of the disks were locked in the boot of his car. So was Michael's laptop. They were going to stay there. "Make backup copies of those, by the way, before you start doing anything with them."

"First thing I'll do," she said. She opened the bag at her hip and dropped the little disks inside. "Let's hope these give us the answer. If we don't get it solved, we won't be able to transfer all that lovely money from the sponsors to the Third World."

He looked at her, a living icon for the meeting point between industrialised West and developing Africa. A striking and very beautiful icon, a synthesis of exotic hope. "Are you concerned about the Third World?"

"To a certain extent. I'm also concerned about doing a good job. We're all going to need our successes, aren't we, when the company slims down."

He didn't answer. It could have been an observation about keeping the best, or about the need for those who were sacked to have good records if they were going to get other jobs. It could also have been a request for information about her personal fate. Or it was a hint to Munro about what would happen when Michael came back. Sabuli didn't seem to be on anyone's side – but he certainly didn't want her recruiting herself for Michael. "If you can spare a few minutes," he said, "I've got something here that might interest you. You handed the sponsorship deals to Michael to finalise, didn't you?"

"Yes. I bullied them into naming the sums they'd spend, then I moved on to manipulate the media. Michael tied things up."

"So I thought." He opened his desk drawer and lifted out a springback binder. He put the binder on the shareholding printouts in front of her. "Those are copies of the individual deals. You'll see the pattern is the same every time."

She picked up the binder and opened it. "Everything's in order, I assume?"

"Oh yes, it's perfectly in order. I've added a summary of the effect of the deals. The gross sponsorship income is first used to offset the mission costs. Fuel, licences, communications, airfield rental and so on."

She nodded, turning pages in the binder. "I know."

"But the mission costs are so defined as to include the setting up, staffing and running of Mission Control, even though existing MT-Orbis staff and facilities have been used."

"Really?"

"Costs also include camera aircraft and the preparation of the video film which will be used as an Orbis promotion – and the project office, which has been in existence for months."

326

"Are you sure?"

He nodded. "The net will go to the charities, as agreed. However, the money is to be held in what amounts to a trust, and then made available to the agreed charities in the agreed proportions, once they've decided what projects to spend it on over the next few years. The cost of administering the holding trust will be deducted from the net. Further, the interest earned by the money in the fund will not be paid into the fund, but will go to Orbis as cash income. Since the Orbis income is negative at the moment, it won't even be taxed."

Terri Sabuli looked out of the windows for a moment, then back at the binder, then at Munro. "Didn't the charities query any of that?"

"Apparently not. I assume they're grateful for what they can get. They're big, but they're still beggars in the market-place. If you check the totals, and don't forget the interest, and if you assume a steady pay-out rate from funds over three years, the figures on the bottom line are quite surprising."

"Are they?" she said, looking for them.

"If the aircraft completes the circumnavigation back to Florida, the total raised will be thirty million, plus four million interest. Eighteen million will remain with Orbis."

"*Eighteen?*"

"Whereas, if the bonus stage is completed, with the doubling of a large number of the sponsorship pledges, the total raised will be fifty million, with six million interest on the net over the ensuing three years. The net isn't as big as you might think, because if the bonus stage is flown, then the development costs of the project are also offset."

"What? The *development* costs? You mean designing and building Angel? But then it won't have cost the company a *penny*."

Munro shook his head. "In point of fact, the company will be heavily into profit on the venture. Under those circumstances, Orbis would retain thirty million."

"*Thirty?*" Sabuli slammed the binder closed. "*Thirty million? Is that even legal?*"

"It's perfectly legal. All the parties are agreed." His intercom buzzed. "The contracts are watertight." He held down the switch on the intercom. "Take a seat over there at the table and look through one of the contracts. It's an object lesson in self-interest and the use of financial power. Michael obviously believes very strongly that charity begins at home."

Terri Sabuli crossed over to the conference table, opening the binder again as she went. Got her in one, he thought, on a very sensitive spot. The glorious boss of MT-Orbis is in fact utterly selfish, even when working within the law. Michael takes from the world's poor, as well as the rich. He released the intercom switch. "Yes?"

"I've got a Mr Peter Cavendish on the line," said Ripley's voice. "Are you available?"

Cavendish of the SIB. Bloody hell, couldn't they leave him in peace for the rest of the week? He didn't want to talk about past messes with Michael. He had a live one on his hands. "No. I'm in a meeting. Tell him I'll call back later today. But block any further calls he makes until tomorrow."

He had no time for Cavendish until the shares swap was done.

FORTY-SEVEN

Terri put her feet up on the front edge of the communication desk. It wasn't good manners, but she was in charge, so there was no one to tell her no. She spooned yoghurt slowly out of a tub, thoughts drifting away from the notepad problem propped on her knees.

Sometimes things aren't what they seem. The charity deals – she set up the sponsorship arrangements, but Michael took over and handled all the contracts with the benefiting charities. He'd taken every legal advantage. The whole adventure, now that Ruth had got more than halfway round the world, wasn't going to cost Orbis or its parent organisation a penny. If the mission could have been completed as planned, Orbis would have made a huge profit, and at the same time MT-Orbis would have enjoyed an increase in sales, trade and turnover right across its products and services range. You had to be clever or lucky to come across a chance to get rich – but you had to be the meanest bastard to actually manage it.

Michael Tranter made it look easy . . .

The notepad slipped. She slid it back up her leggings to her knees, and returned to eating the yoghurt. Thinking about the charity deals could wait. That was background. The foreground problem was still flying steadily across Africa with neither autopilot nor course program. It was noon, Mission Time 74.00, and Ruth was passing Libenge as she crossed from Zaire to the Central African Republic. Up until now, they hadn't been much help to her.

Things aren't what they seem. Something was waiting there to be discovered, but she couldn't quite see what it was.

John was working at one of the screens. He had both programs, the Mission Control version and the Angel version – Michael's Wragby version – loaded into the computer's memory, and was stretching his skill to the limit in an attempt to understand the mess. Chester might conceivably have been some use, but he didn't answer from home and he hadn't been seen at any of his places of work. Michael, amazingly, had disappeared from the hospital, so he couldn't give them any help. Munro could have sent over some experts from the computer department at MT, but Munro was refusing to return calls sent to his PA. John was on his own.

The five disks from Wragby were distribution disks for setting up the course program in Angel's computer. John had copied the disks, then loaded the program into his own machine. Then he compared files from the two versions. He didn't have time to read every line of machine code, but he could match file length. File for file, the Wragby version was exactly the same as the Mission Control version – except that the Wragby version had no course data files for any part of the planned route after 62.00, the point in the Indian Ocean where the system went down. The program had crashed because it ran out of data in its imaginary midair.

Now John had started with the executive and command files, and was matching them line by line, hoping to find a difference, a clue, a hint of the fault. It looked like a waste of time. The program in Angel's computer stopped, and that was that.

The notepad propped on her knees had little names and numbers scribbled in columns. John had written down all the file lengths and the disk capacities during the copying process. She flipped the pages – endless lists of files, plus the spare capacity on each disk. Something didn't make sense. There were so few files on disk five that they could have been fitted into the spare space on the first four disks. Why use a fifth disk? The easy answer was that the disk was supposed to be filled with all those missing course data files, but something had gone wrong when Michael copied them to disk, and they hadn't copied. Then, in the last minute rush at Wragby, he didn't notice the error while the files were loading into Angel's computer. No mystery.

Except that the spare capacity on the fifth disk was no greater than the spare on the other four. With so few files on the disk, the space left over should have been huge.

There was no fault on the disk. The computer would have reported any fault to John during copying. There were just those course data files, NAV-C-26 to NAV-C-31, one file for each two-hour segment from leaving Australia to that last and final position in the northwestern corner of the Indian Ocean. John had already looked at the files. They were just the way they ought to be, mapping the course along the planned route. There was no sign at all of a northward deviation of over eight hundred miles.

But if the spare capacity on the disk was so small, and the

files were too few, there had to be something else there. It didn't show, it wouldn't copy. But something was there.

John wasn't interested. Nobody wrote files which didn't copy. To do so would be a waste of work. And it wasn't a mistake. A programming master like Michael wouldn't make such a stupid error.

John was close to an explosion. He was extremely tired, overloaded, out of his depth, and he was doing the very best he could. Terri didn't press the point.

But things certainly weren't what they seemed. Legal but outright immoral charity deals, an inexplicable course failure, phantom data filling space on a disk. The nothing it added up to seemed not at all nice. And it was all connected directly with Michael Tranter.

Terri lowered her feet to the floor. She balanced the yoghurt tub and spoon on the communication desk, then she stood up and took the notepad with her across to the nearest telephone. She picked up the phone and dialled Munro's number over at the MT building.

"Mr Munro's office. Can I help you?"

"This is Terri Sabuli again. I suppose Mr Munro still isn't available?"

"I'm afraid not. I'll be giving him your message as soon as he's free."

The message was that there was something wrong with the course program and the computer on Angel. It wouldn't sound all that interesting to Munro, the big bad man who was busy trying to get Saint Michael by the balls. Understandably, he had other things on his mind. "Let's forget the message. We need help now. We need a computer expert."

"Have you thought of calling the computer department? I'm sure if you explained your requirement to them, they could get permission from Mr Munro to send someone over."

"I don't think it's something that just anybody should be looking at. We've got some disks here which Mr Munro gave us. They are Michael Tranter's disks, and there's something *very* strange about the data they hold. Isn't there someone Mr Munro would trust who could look at them?"

There was a pause from Mrs Ripley at the other end. Pushing the conspiracy button – whatever the conspiracy might actually be – seemed to work. "Miss Trayhorn is liaising with a computer expert on Mr Munro's behalf. Do you know Miss Trayhorn?"

Trayhorn was the sidekick Munro had been appointing to boards on the basis of her skill at finding frauds. "I know of her. Could you give me her number?"

FORTY-EIGHT

John gave her a string of command lines to enter into the computer through the keys arrayed round the navigation screen. The process didn't unblock the course program. The procedure unloaded it. The navigation screen stayed blank, but she got the full VSI display back on the screen right in front of her. That made life easier. Pity about the autopilot . . .

She flew across semi-desert, grassland, and equatorial mountain vegetation. She crossed Lake Victoria and then Lake Edward. Most of the time there was at least one aircraft filming as she went by. Over Zaire, from Kisangani to Libenge, she was escorted by an Orbis charter aircraft and a TV consortium machine. Angel, in bright eco-green, traversed an endless flatness of diseased and dying forest. The disease that was killing the forest was called humanity. Its infective agent was the local broken-backed economy, its source was the wealth and greed of the West, its consequence was tracts of ruined and barren land. Above it all, eco-conscious, self-promoting sightseers, Angel and the media aircraft slid endlessly between billowing heaps of rain cloud which sat a thousand feet off the forest floor, on nothing . . .

Angel was handling much better as the fuel load drained away. The wings were no longer bowed upwards like a sling, and the aircraft was prepared to roll in a turn. The tendency to yaw was still there, but Angel's weight of remaining fuel damped it down. Enough fuel to cross half of Africa, the equatorial Atlantic, and then onwards back to Britain. Such a pity.

The INS was safely back in service, though with a positional error that it wouldn't have suffered if the satellite fixes had been available. The navigation computer was supposed to handle those, but now it wasn't handling anything. Updated by the INS, the direct satellite link was back in operation, too. But the autopilot was blocked. It depended on the computer, which needed the course program – and it seemed there wasn't any course program at all after Mission Time 62.00. There was no virtual world for the autopilot to fly through.

Ruth couldn't fly Angel all the way to Florida. She was tied to the controls, she couldn't move in her seat, she couldn't lie down, she certainly couldn't sleep. Her eyes were behaving as though they'd seen enough of the world, the cramps kept taking hold and tearing her. It looked like Africa was the end of the line.

They hadn't told anyone yet.

Broken jungle gave way to savannah and scrub, with vegetable plots and scrawny cattle and lots of little huts. There were waterways and irrigation ditches. Africa was changing.

In front of her, the sun was halfway down the sky. It was so hot on her chest. It made her sleepy, but at least it baked some of the pain out of her shoulders.

Mission Time 75.00, London time 13.00. She opened the channel and put on the headset. "Hello, it's me again."

"Hello, Ruth," said Mandy's voice. "Are you *still* on the line? What about giving someone else a turn?"

"Oh, I asked the little green men to pop over, but they

were afraid to leave their flying saucer. Any progress on the problem?"

"No, I'm sorry to say. Terri's off looking into some sort of hunch about it, and John's still hard at work and is going positively cross-eyed. We're all trying."

"Anything from Chester? Or Michael?"

"Not a sign of them. Would you be happy with anything Chester had to say, Ruth?"

"Not really. I might enjoy shouting at him. Look, it's going to be dark in another four or five hours, isn't it? Here on the course, I mean. A landing in the dark isn't impossible, but I'm a bit tired, so daylight would be better."

"I understand. You're right. Looking at the route, there's an airfield at Ibadan. That's where you'll get sunset. And there's an international airport no distance away at Lagos. Do you want to land there?"

"I want to discuss it with Terri."

Terri brought in a canteen tray loaded with coffees and sandwiches. She pushed the door closed and started looking for a place for the snack. Trayhorn's office was a mess. There were printouts everywhere, falling cascades of fanfold paper covered in black pinprinter lines, all overlaid with scribbles in red, blue and green. But that wasn't what they were working at now.

Trayhorn pushed paper on top of paper on her desk, and cleared a corner for the food. She stood up, offering the desk chair to Terri. There were only two chairs. Curtis Gupta was seated on the other one, confronting the computer screen. The disk labelled NAV PROG 5 was in the drive. It wasn't co-operating.

Terri sat down. She was tired, and the office was too warm. Sunlight, sliced by the blind, laid burning bars across the piles of paper on the desk. It was far too warm to start on the coffee, even though the coffee had cooled on the long ride up from the canteen. She nodded at the piles of paper instead. "Are these the frauds you're looking into?"

"No." Geraldine Trayhorn leaned past her to take a sandwich. "That's the stuff the frauds are hidden inside. We can't persuade anything to come out. The computer's obviously a prisoner of instructions that prevent some things printing, appearing on screen, copying or anything." She started to unpeel the wrapper from the sandwich. "It's all in there, or the frauds wouldn't have worked, but the programs controlling it won't let it be seen."

"Like the stuff on the disk."

"Exactly."

"Bugger it!" said Curtis Gupta. "Bugger the bloody thing."

He was Indian. He was sitting there in his shirt sleeves, with his tie undone. The tie was red, his braces were red, his white shirt had a red collar and red cuffs, the frames of his glasses were red. He was shielding his racial distinction with an overload of conforming clichés. Terri did it differently.

"The bloke who did this," he said, "is ace. Absolutely ace. The sly bastard. If this is Michael Tranter's work, then he's the best."

"Does that mean," Trayhorn asked, "that you can't crack it?"

"Who knows?" Gupta reached up and stretched his arms, fingers folded together. "If it's sitting there, it's got to be there for a purpose. There *must* be a way of calling it up." He brought his hands down slowly and started massaging the back of his neck. "It must be sitting there with a little program that comes out first every time you cue it. The program reads up into the computer's RAM and looks for some sort of password or instruction. If it doesn't find it, the program immediately blocks the read-from-disk instruction, erases itself from RAM and ensures that nothing gets out to printer or screen. It's *completely* read-protected. I can't get at the hidden data through machine code or anything."

"You need the password," Trayhorn said. "Have a sandwich."

Gupta was too busy massaging his neck. "I wonder if I could set up a buffer to catch the program. If I could trap it on its way to the main RAM, perhaps I could get it to write out before it's done the search and erased itself. If I could see it, I'd be able to find its template for the key it's looking for. Then I'd know what the key was. It would take a lot of time, though. Meanwhile, the stuff on the disk has disappeared without trace."

The stuff on the disk had gone invisible. Michael wrote it to the disk, and it disappeared. Without trace. Terri saw a message come in on Michael's laptop at Wragby, a meaningless message. No one sends a meaningless message – you just have to know what the bits of it refer to. Cryptic codes sent from Pattie Lee to Michael Tranter, hidden secrets on Michael's disk. "Without trace," she said. "Try that."

Curtis Gupta stopped rubbing his neck. "Why?"

"It was in a message I saw come over the modem at Wragby." She looked up at Trayhorn. "Michael Tranter's laptop was at Wragby, with these disks. I saw a message come in from his PA. It might have been code words. It might be relevant. Try it. Without trace."

"From his PA?" Trayhorn said. "From Pattie Lee?"

Gupta shrugged. He called up the macro he'd been using to try command lines, and typed in *without trace*, then *enter*.

The light on the drive came on, then went off again. Nothing appeared on the screen.

"Oh well, let's permutate a bit." He tried *WT*, then *enter*. Nothing.

"Could be part of a filename. Wildcards." He typed *WT*, *enter*.

The light came on. And stayed on. A screen full of columns appeared. Every entry in every column was the same except for the number at the end. NAVWT-01 to NAVWT-42.

Curtis Gupta swung his chair towards Terri and beamed.

At 77.00 by the mission clock, Ruth was flying across savannah towards the border where Cameroon ended and Nigeria began. The sun was deep down on the western sky and blaring heat in her face. INS okay, fuel okay, engine okay, pilot whacked, autopilot useless.

The blue satellite channel light came on. She was wearing the headset, and heard everything Terri started to say.

"Ruth, we've no answer yet on what we've found. Some of it is data for a kind of ghost course Angel wasn't supposed to fly. Have you any idea what Michael could have been thinking?"

"No." Unlike some people, she hadn't been what you might call intimate with Michael by then. "What kind of ghost course? It's in the computer, and I don't want it suddenly coming out and doing things with Angel without asking me."

"It's a course that runs from two hours after Australia – that's at Mission Time fifty-two hundred – to a position two degrees south, fifty-eight degrees east. That much we've managed to sort out."

"Two degrees south, fifty-eight degrees east? At sixty-two hundred, by any chance?"

"Yes. Sixty-two hundred. Does it mean something, Ruth?"

"It means it isn't a ghost course. It's the course I actually flew. Check the displacement northwards. Project back from when we finally found out where I was. Use the gyrocompass course I was following. Work out where I must have been when the autopilot failed. I tell you, that will be the course I actually flew."

"Well – we'll check it. I don't suppose *without trace* means anything to you, by any chance?"

"No."

"Pity. John can't make head or tail of the rest of the stuff we've found. Anyway, we've got something else to discuss, haven't we? You'll be getting sunset in ninety minutes. After that, it's six and a half hours to the last opportunity to land, at Dakar on the Senegal coast. And then it's another fourteen and a half hours to Florida. That's a total of twenty-two and a half hours, and no reason to believe there's the slightest chance of getting the autopilot up and working again. So – don't you think it's time to call it off and land?"

"Before I've seen Ghana? Your father comes from Ghana, Terri. I was looking forward to seeing the place."

"It will be dark, Ruth."

"I know." It would be dark in her heart if she failed. A fire in the engine, a fuel leak, a complete instrument failure – none of those would be her fault. But if she gave up, merely because it had turned tough, turned into real flying instead of simply babysitting an autopilot . . . Sitting, sitting, sitting for three unbroken days so far. If she gave up because she wasn't good enough, her father would be right after all.

Ruth didn't want him to be right. Not this time. Not ever again. She got away from her father. She got away from Ashley. She got Michael out of her way. She was chasing the sun. She didn't want to go down in the dark. "Terri, I'm going on."

Terri Sabuli made her wait.

"Oh, Ruth. I might have known. All right, I'd better make sure we're here all the time to talk to you. We'll have to keep you awake all night."

FORTY-NINE

The four o'clock news said that Ruth Clifford was continuing on her way across Africa. No report yet about abandoning the round-the-world bid. Michael said that with the autopilot out, there was no way Ruth could continue across the Atlantic. After more than three days of non-stop flying, with probably no more than twelve hours' sleep, she'd be in no state to tackle the stage to Florida. Over the dark, blank Atlantic, sleep would be inevitable. And sleep, of course, would kill her. If they hadn't announced the end yet, then obviously they were milking it for as much sponsorship money as possible. Wait until Dakar, late in the evening. It was an interesting little sideshow.

338

At least, Michael found it interesting. He found the wrong things interesting. He wasn't flying Angel, so what happened to Angel was of no concern. What did matter was the alternative moves they had to make, now the original plan had collapsed. But he was delaying. He was playing his stupid spoiling game with Munro.

Pattie wanted fresh clothes from home, she wanted her own style of breakfast, she didn't want to be sitting about at Michael's house killing time. Being here was useless, now that Michael was here as well and she couldn't snoop inside his computer. They'd copied all the data they needed, so they could leave. Michael should have been setting that up. Instead, he had to spend the day preparing his secret surprise.

Michael came in through the kitchen door. He carried the patio chair, folded, in his good arm. He propped it in front of the dishwasher. "No announcement about little Ruth yet?"

"No." Pattie switched off the radio before the request records could get under way. "Enjoyed your nap in the sun, Michael?"

"Actually, I've been wandering round the garden. I'll miss it, you know, though I can't say I've ever spent that much time here." He shook his head. "I shouldn't devote all my time to aircraft and computers – it gets you into bad ways. Anyway, I've been wandering round the garden. And I've discovered we're being watched."

"What?"

"Oh yes." Michael smiled. "There's a little shady corner of the side garden where you can see across next door's property and through their gate. There's a car parked up the lane, a blue Honda Accord. Been there all day, actually. I noticed this morning."

"You didn't tell me."

"Slipped my mind. He's parked quite cleverly. You can't see him from any of our upstairs windows, but he can see our front gate. That Bob Munro's a resourceful bugger. He's having me tailed. Or he's been having you tailed until I showed up. Perhaps he thinks I'm going to do a runner."

Pattie folded her arms. "It isn't *funny*, Michael. If he knows enough about the frauds, he might have told the police."

"No, not Bob Munro. If he had enough to prove it, he'd also have enough to get me thrown out of every directorship I hold. He'd do that, instead of trying a coup and damaging the company. He's very company-fixated. Too big a trace of the group ethic. Too much socialist pollution." Michael grinned. "Not enough self-interest."

It was the perfection of self-interest that she hated most about Michael. He'd never done anything in his whole life for anyone else. He wasn't quite human.

"So don't worry," said the less-than-human Michael. "Munro's the one who's put a tail on us. How about a Pimm's, by the way? Might as well make the most of a sunny afternoon."

"If someone's watching us," Pattie said, "it's still going to make life very difficult. Isn't it?"

Michael shrugged. "I can do logic bombs, Trojan horses, viruses, worms, raiders, fishing lines, read-protectors. I think I can slip a tail when it suits me."

At five, Trayhorn returned with the disks. She was followed from the outer office by Ripley. "Mr Geoffrey Simmington," Ripley said, "is on the phone."

Munro was already standing up and lifting his briefcase onto the desk. "Ask him to call back."

Ripley's expression suggested Simmington wouldn't like that. "He's extremely anxious to talk to you."

"This doesn't have to take long," Trayhorn said. "Really."

"Ask him," Munro said to Ripley, "to hold."

"Right." Ripley went out and closed the door.

"Well?" Munro opened his briefcase. "Anything?"

"These are straightforward." Trayhorn put the boxes of disks in his hand. Her fingers touched his palm. "Most of it looks perfectly innocent – memos, notes, shares portfolio stuff. Some of it's protected by what Curtis calls safety-pin passwords. It doesn't seem to contain any secrets."

"Pity." He put the disks – all the disks from Wragby except the course program disks – in his briefcase. "What about the laptop?"

"Ah, that's different. Curtis says there's several kilobytes of stuff in its RAM, but he can't get it out. It won't answer to the *without trace* trick, so it's read-protected in some other way. He was hoping the protection program might be the same as on the navigation disk, but with a different password. Then he could have tried dismantling the program on the basis of knowing how it works." She shrugged. "But it doesn't seem to be the same."

Munro nodded. Michael was too clever to lock up his real secrets with a single kind of key. Sylvia Symes had said that Michael got Siltech off the ground, years ago, by being first in the field of computer security. It seemed he was still leading everyone else by the nose. "Where did Sabuli get the *without trace* idea from?"

"She saw a message come in over the modem at Wragby. Just after the accident, I think. She says it was a message from Mr Tranter's PA. It contained the words *without trace*, but Curtis hasn't found any message like that logged in the laptop's post file. All the stuff we can see in the post file looks clean."

He nodded again. It felt bad, snooping about inside Michael's notes and messages. Yes, Michael was a crook – but stealing a look at his private affairs made you dirty, just the same.

Trayhorn tucked strands of blonde hair behind her ear. She had her head tipped to one side, looking up at him from across the desk. With blue eyes. Twenty-six years old, half his age, and she'd propositioned him, gently, twice. Did she have a father-figure fixation? Was she a power groupie? Was she after a lonely middle-aged man's buckets of money? If things went wrong before the end of the week, he'd be lucky if he was left with a pension.

The intercom buzzed. He leaned across his desk and pressed the button. "Yes?"

"Mr Simmington is still holding. He's getting rather angry."

"In a minute, Ripley." He stood up straight again. Geraldine Trayhorn was standing straight, hands folded in front of her hips. "Anything else?" he said. "Any progress on the frauds?"

"Oh, another couple of million missing in bits and pieces here and there. I think we're at twelve million now, but I'm starting to lose count. Has there been anything new from the detectives?"

"A little. Pierce's hacker got into the Kowloon Crown International bank, and found the account for the Orbis Pacific Tours fraud before the security trace intervened. The date the account was opened ties in with a visit to Hong Kong by Pattie Lee."

"Would that make her his accomplice? I mean, are we getting enough to win now?"

Are *we* getting enough, she said. "I think we're getting enough to hold him off. It buys time."

She bit her lower lip. Part of the way up shit creek, her expression seemed to say.

"If you want to," he said, "you can pull out."

She shook her head. "If I stay with you and you win, I've still got a career. If I change sides and you win, I'm out. If Tranter wins I'm out, because I found the frauds. There's a recession on. Nobody's hiring people. I'll stay with you. Besides – there's a crook to catch."

"Yes, there is."

"Also," she said, "it's exciting." She made a first move towards the door. "I'll get back to my office."

After Trayhorn left, he checked with Ripley on the intercom. Simmington was still holding, and was fuming. What could be troubling a man who would soon be earning his bank a fat commission on an over-value sale of Orbis Air? Munro picked up the internal phone. "Hello, Geoffrey. Sorry to keep you – "

"What the *devil's* going on, Robert? Bloody hell, man, your outfit's just suspended *all* repayments on our loans to *all* your divisions."

"What are you talking about, Geoffrey? We certainly haven't suspended any repayments."

"Don't treat me like an *idiot*, Robert. It became clear after the close of the bank's business this afternoon. You've stopped your damned repayments! You haven't even had the decency to send us a same-day notification. It's bad manners, bad business and bad debt all in one. Good God, man, we were having a *chat* last night, and you already knew you were doing this to us today!"

"Geoffrey, there's a mistake. We have *not* suspended repayments to you or to anyone else."

"Robert, I said don't treat me like an *idiot*! I've just rung round the other banks who've given MT-Orbis credit. It's the same everywhere. All repayments stopped without notification. What the *hell* are you playing at?"

"Geoffrey – " What? Don't tell me things that can't be true, and would be a catastrophe if they were?

"And why – for God's sake, man – *why* didn't you tip me off that your company was broke before you got me mixed up in this backdoor deal with Orbis Air? The deal – and the motive behind it, let me tell you – *stinks*. Using me like that, as a last throw to raise cash – without having enough decency or trust to tell me. That sort of thing isn't on, Robert. It really isn't on!"

Munro didn't answer. He didn't care about Simmington's sensibilities. He was stalled by the impossible. All regular payments servicing all elements of the corporate debt run by all the bits and pieces of MT-Orbis – cancelled.

He hadn't ordered a suspension of payments. No one else had tried to. No one could even attempt it without the alarm being raised. No one besides himself had the executive power required to make the company machine carry out such a step. But it had happened, and it had happened *unnoticed*. All the automatic payouts run by all the computers . . .

To do that would involve a spectacular trick, a hidden miracle, a computer coup carried out by a master of a higher order . . .

Michael!

Part 8

Lucifer

FIFTY

Angel was leaving Ghana to cross the southern edge of Upper Volta. Underneath was grassland in an African night. The sky hid a moon behind high clouds, the horizon still had the green of the old sunset she was chasing round the world. The grassland had no light at all. There were people down below, but they didn't show themselves. The African night was dark.

The last green glow was leaving her behind. She was an Angel with its own flashing colours, red, green and white, a Lord of Light in the sky. But she couldn't defy or drive away the dark. She was an Angel falling backwards into night . . .

No. Stop before it even begins. Bad enough as a dream. The advantage of the long hours to Florida would be the lack of sleep. No sleep meant escape from the dream. You didn't want the dream while you were awake. Not awake . . .

She called Mission Control.

"Hello, Ruth. This is Terri. How's it going?"

"Painfully. My bum hurts. I didn't know a bum could hurt so much. I didn't know it could hurt for so *long*."

"Well – try to imagine its afterglow."

"Afterglow? I don't know what *you* do, Terri, but – well. How are things at your end? Um – if you see what I mean."

"I see what you mean, Ruth. Let's see. There's a big flap on at the moment. All the computer people have been pulled in for the evening. Major glitch in the company network. All the money's frozen or something. There's far too much reliance on technology these days."

347

"You're telling me."

"I know, Ruth. As for the other business, I'm afraid there's nothing doing on the autopilot. And we still can't make sense of this Without Trace program. John's all on his own with it – there'll be no help from the computer people while this new panic lasts. Between you and me, though, I don't think it's going to be of the slightest use with respect to the autopilot. I think it adds up to something else entirely."

"Adds up to what?"

"I'll tell you when I know."

He had the desk lamp burning under the slope of the ceiling, though it was still bright evening outside. An early moth had strayed in and battered itself on the bulb, but now it was more interested in the window panes. It whirred against the casement, trapped like a piece of data under scrutinising light.

Michael typed in the disconnect code. He said goodbye, silently, to Swansea and disappeared without trace.

Behind him, Pattie came into the room. "Well?" she said.

"Oh, that went fine. It's spooky in there."

Her hand appeared at his shoulder with the glass of beer – real German beer from the fridge. "Why?"

"Well, it's quiet in their computer." He sipped the beer through its cold froth. "There's just the overnight file-keeping going on, without the daytime input and output. But I wasn't the only person looking round inside."

"Hackers?"

"No. There was the on-line vehicle trace for the police. And other people." Presences, probing, which he tiptoed round. The security and anti-terrorist services, perhaps. "You know, that's the first time I've ever cracked a computer which didn't belong to a private individual, company or institution. It isn't the same. The security barriers are much easier – I mean, they aren't protecting anything important, like data about money. But the watchers in there have the power to hurt you, if you make a mistake. I don't like it." He sipped the beer again and put the glass on the desk. He tapped his notepad. "Anyway, I've checked the car. Can you get me the Registry of Companies disk, R to S? Over there in the corner. Top shelf. The car, believe it or not, is a *company* car registered to Smith and Brown Associates. They must be very posh. There can't be that many private detective agencies which supply company cars for their sleuths."

"No." Pattie handed him the disk.

"So Bob Munro's spending all our profits, what's left of them." He put the disk in the drive and told his desktop software, one-handed, to read from it. Smith and Brown Associates was listed as being run by R. A. Smith (Mrs) and C. C. Brown (Ms), and as specialising in the investigation of fraud and industrial espionage. Very appropriate. He cleared the screen again.

"What are you going to do next?" Pattie asked. "Hack their computer?"

"No." He took the disk out of the drive. "I'm getting a bit tired of that at the moment."

"In that case, since we've got the data we need – are you finally going to tell me when and how we'll be leaving?"

He liked the impatience in her voice. Pattie manipulated him. She found him out and bounced him into taking her up – into his running program of money mining, and into the secret background of his private life. He liked manipulating her in return. It took a lot of work to bring her off – but the reward, when it arrived, was like an earthquake. It took so much to break her patience that he'd never seen the final result. It would probably be very vicious, something to avoid. But needling her was fun. He looked up and smiled. "We'll be leaving some time tomorrow."

"And why wait until then? We could have left today. We *could* have left yesterday evening."

"Oh no, that wasn't on. I couldn't let Munro get away with it. I had to make sure he gets what's coming to him."

She didn't shrug, or nod. She merely blinked her contact lenses at him. "And *how* will we be leaving?"

Michael looked at the sling that was hiding his arm so ineptly. The only things below his left shoulder which could move were the last two joints of the fingers. He looked up and smiled at her again. "Flying. How else?"

By ten thirty London had clouded over, and the July dusk had turned to dark. Munro's reflection sat at its own desk in the window glass, and turned its back on him.

No business ever ran on zero debt. Borrowing money is a smart thing to do. A high-geared outfit like MT Holdings used heavy borrowing to reduce its vulnerability to a takeover – and apart from anything else, if you organised things right, debt helped minimise the tax liability. The total debt of the MT empire was composed of a vast raft of loans from a long list of institutions. The repayments were chopped down, salami style, into monthly and weekly instalments. At MT-Orbis, for accounts simplicity, it was always Wednesday for the weekly instalments, and this particular Wednesday for the monthly ones.

Stop the repayments – *all* the repayments – without notice or negotiation, and you were instantly a bad business partner, a bad debtor and a maximum credit risk. From the moment the news broke, everyone would know that the crisis in your company was serious enough to be fatal. If at the same time you lost every incoming penny from customers, and if every drawing from every single one of the corporate empire's own accounts vanished into thin air because the credit-shunting mechanisms had gone into an impossible loop – then you were insolvent.

It cracked confidence asunder.

And it was no use wailing that someone had fiddled your computer. It was no use wailing at all.

He didn't even hear the knock on the door. Geraldine Trayhorn was already walking across the eco-green carpet before he realised anyone had arrived.

She didn't look fresh and bright. Her hair was a little astray after a very long day, her face was sagged and tired. There was a ladder in the shin of her tights – stockings, she said she wore stockings. She had her bag over her shoulder and her briefcase in her hand. She looked in need of a long night's sleep. And what, he thought, do I look like?

"I'm going home," she said. "I can't do any more tonight. It's half-past ten. I'm up against a brick wall. I'll be in early tomorrow morning. Very early. Promise."

He nodded.

"And – well – how's the computer system doing?"

"Badly." He settled back in the comfort of his executive chair. Until the receiver came he still had the trappings of office – but none of the power. The chief executive officer, finance director and acting managing director of a company which cannot pay, move or earn a single penny, is the overlord of nothing at all. "The entire computer department has been recalled. They're even hauling people back from holiday. They're setting up a roster so that they can work round the clock."

"Sounds hopeful. Have they got anywhere yet?"

"They've done the easy bit. They've identified the parts of the program which have been interfered with. They can see where the intrusion is because of what it's doing. At each location where it's taken hold, they have to read out all the working data to preserve it, and then check it through to make sure it's free of any intrusive programming – the thing that's done the damage, in other words. At the same time, they isolate and then wipe all the computer memories, disks and tapes associated with that point of attack. After that they have to take out a chunk of replacement program from the backup library, install it, then bring it up to date with all the information they read out in the first place. Then they have to make sure the isolated chunk of the network is clean and works properly. If it doesn't, they have to do the whole thing all over again."

"Oh," she said. "That sounds pretty bad. And I suppose they have to do that at every single location in the network where the attack has taken place."

"Yes – and every single subsystem, large or small, where no attack has taken place." He nodded towards the screen on the corner of his desk. "That includes my desktop, and every other screen in the whole of MT-Orbis. Not one of them can go back on line until it's been checked and proved clean. Whatever's been put into the network might be capable of hiding, waiting, replicating, and then attacking as soon as we start things running again."

"You mean a virus."

"Yes. And if just one copy escapes the cleaning process, the whole catastrophe will begin again from scratch."

"I know." She tucked a strand behind her ear. The strand didn't want to stay. "Do we know where it came from?"

"It's a present from Michael Tranter, and he's clever enough to make sure no one will ever be able to prove it."

"I see. And how long will it take to clear the network and get things running again?"

"Through the weekend and into next week. Tuesday at the earliest. It would be much quicker if they could see what they're dealing with, because then they could search for it and destroy it wherever it's hiding without having to cleanse everything line by line – literally one program line at a time. However, it seems to be very well protected."

"Like the stuff on the disk was. And the stuff in the laptop."

"Exactly."

Trayhorn nodded, thoughtfully. "And the consequences?"

"Massive loss of confidence," he said. "Wild and very destructive rumours, scared investors, loss of sales, disinvestment, share collapse. All very logical."

"That can't happen overnight."

"It hit late in the afternoon, so London didn't have time to react. However, New York hasn't closed yet, and all MT-Orbis shares are trading twelve percent down. Tokyo is expecting to open with us at least ten percent down, and falling."

"Oh. London will be worse tomorrow, I suppose." She

352

shrugged, a powerless gesture from someone unable to help. "Perhaps something will turn up by morning. We're attacking the same kind of computer wizardry on so many fronts, it's only a matter of time before something actually gives."

He shook his head. Time was one thing he didn't have.

"Are you going home?" she asked. "It's very late."

"No." Please, he thought, don't make any kind of pass at me. Not when so much is happening. Not when I'm in this state.

"You can't sleep in the office."

"I've got a room at my club. It's handy in a crisis."

"I see. Well then." She backed off a step, and started moving towards the door. "Tell me – why do you wear glasses? Long-sighted? Don't see things clearly when they're close up?"

"No. Astigmatism. I don't see things clearly at any distance."

"Oh – I think you do." She smiled. "Goodnight."

"Goodnight," he said.

He didn't see things clearly. He couldn't fathom people. He still had no idea whether Geraldine Trayhorn was a misguided casting couch careerist or a top-man groupie – or what? And he would never have believed that Michael Tranter could destroy his own company out of sheer spite. But then he would never have thought Michael was a crook, either. He didn't see clearly.

He never saw it coming.

But now, by listening carefully in what seemed to be a silence, he could hear the cracks which were opening in the foundations of the MT building. The cracks were beginning to reach upwards, splintering walls and ceilings, pillars and beams, on their way to engulf his floor.

FIFTY-ONE

At ten minutes to midnight there was no one about. John's screen still glowed, his computer table and commandeered desk were covered with capsized stacks of printout. He'd found out what the Without Trace program did, but he hadn't discovered a reason for its existence.

The light came on at the communication desk – Ruth calling in from the Atlantic west of Dakar. Terri picked up one of the handsets. "Hello, Ruth. How's it going?"

"I'm sleepy. What about you?"

"Me? I'd put matchsticks in my eyes, but they wouldn't go with the makeup. Mandy's having a nap. And I sent John to get some sleep. He's been at the screen non-stop since about five this morning, and he's been here at Mission Control since ten yesterday evening. His eyes were so red, it hurt to look at them. I'm not sure I've ever seen anyone work so hard."

"Have you told the world my autopilot's broken?"

"Yes. We got that out in time for the late evening news. Didn't I tell you? It should cue up the British and American audiences to want to know what's been happening overnight – make it topical breakfast news – and it's great timing for the early editions tomorrow. *Everyone* will be paying attention when you get to Florida."

"Florida seems a long way away. What about the reason why my autopilot's broken?"

"Ah, now – that's the question, isn't it? I told you that six of the Without Trace files program a course from Mission Time fifty-two hundred to Mission Time sixty-two-oh-four – most of the way across the Indian Ocean from Australia. Right? The course marks a steady divergence from the planned one, and stops at two degrees south, fifty-eight degrees east. That's

354

the course, the hidden course, which Angel actually followed. With me so far?"

"That's what you told me last time."

"Right. Well, John's sorted out the rest of the Without Trace files – all thirty-five of them. And they are, believe me, clever. They override the planned course – by which I mean the course that Michael let everyone believe he was going to fly, the course we've got in our copy of the program here. Without Trace cancels that course, and substitutes its own instead. It also points the satellite dish, controls the autopilot, interacts with the INS, runs the position fixes and sends the routine reports back to Mission Control. But the thing is, Without Trace intercepts and massages all the output to the cockpit instruments, like your navigation screen and your VSI screen, and the reports it sends back to us. It fakes all the readouts so that it looks as though Angel is flying the publicised course, the one we were all expecting. Okay?"

"No. It takes Angel off the planned course and puts Angel on its own course, and then it lies about it the whole time. It pretends to you – and to me, the pilot – that it's really on the correct course. That's crazy."

"Isn't it just? No one here would realise the course had diverged. No one in the rest of the world would, either. Both the planned and the substitute course go over open ocean without even coming close to any islands. The only people who'd see Angel go by, either on their radar or by seeing Angel's lights, would be ships or another aeroplane, perhaps. In the middle of the night they wouldn't see *who* it was. They wouldn't know it was Angel, but in the wrong place. The point is, Without Trace runs a totally *secret* divergence programmed in by Michael."

"Why? What did Michael want with a secret diversion?"

"Not a *diversion*, Ruth. It doesn't go back to join the main course. It's a *divergence*, and it stops at two degrees south, fifty-eight degrees east – eight hundred and fifty miles north of where Angel was supposed to be at that time, and where the program had just reported that Angel was. It sent us a perfectly normal position report at sixty-two hundred, remember? And then at the end of this divergent course – it stops. There's no more program, neither Without Trace nor the official course program. The navigation computer and the autopilot block, and the INS is useless until you can reset it with an independent position fix."

"That doesn't make sense, Terri. Never mind *why* Michael programmed in a secret course. It doesn't make any sense that if he put the course in the computer – if he knew all about it – that he should program it to put fake readouts on the cockpit instruments. I mean, he expected to be sitting here himself, didn't he? So why fix the instruments?"

"Ah, well – John thinks that was just a case of programming simplicity. If the thing was sending fake data to us, it was easier to let it do the same for the instruments than to make it divide the data and massage some of it, and so on. After all, it wouldn't confuse Michael. It would give fake readings on your screen, but the gyrocompass would show the true course, wouldn't it? The gyrocompass repeater, I mean. John says that gives a direct reading without going through the computer."

"That's right. The repeater wouldn't have been affected."

"So Michael would be able to check where he was really going. Incidentally, it's a pity you didn't look at the gyro-compass."

"I was *asleep*, Terri. I was very tired. And I had the VSI – and no reason to suppose it was lying to me. I didn't look at the gyrocompass until after the autopilot went down."

"No. I'm aware of that. I wasn't suggesting anything's your fault, Ruth. Everything is exclusively Michael's fault. No one's in any doubt about that."

"No. Okay. So Michael programmed this secret course, and Angel flew it automatically. He hasn't been unconscious since the weekend, has he? He could have *warned* us."

"Well, nothing was going to happen which would harm you. The program would end, the autopilot would go down, you'd keep flying until you'd fixed your position again – and then if you were a sane person, you'd have landed in Africa.

Three-quarters of the way round the world isn't exactly a bad achievement, and it would mean quite a lot of money for charity. Well – a bit, anyway. I'll tell you about that some other time. The point is, warning us would blow the secret, so he wouldn't want to warn us."

"Okay. But *why* did Michael program a secret course?"

"Million dollar question, Ruth. I'm still working on it. By the way, it's just turned midnight here. You're an hour out into the Atlantic. You've only got thirteen and a half hours until Florida. It's your last day. How do you feel?"

"Lonely."

FIFTY-TWO

Angel cruised through a slow nightscape above ocean, with only the moon to look at as it descended on the left of the aircraft's nose. She could stare at the moon until she was night blind. Clouds were cream-rimmed, shadowed-faced fantasy castles, mountains, islands, continents, changing their aspects and sliding by.

It's like moving, she thought, through a world created inside a computer and played on a dim screen. *Things* float above thinly rippled ground, which is totally flat. There are no inhabitants.

Until a little hopping demon comes bouncing in from out of frame, bounding up and down between ocean and cloud bases, making no mark, but marking each rebound up or down with a musical beep. A chummy little demon – who suddenly swerves towards you.

The name of the game is to waggle the stick, swoop left and right, and avoid the demon. But the demon bounds wherever you swerve. And comes nearer with each bound. So near you can see the smile on its chummy face. So near you can see the teeth inside the smile. So near you can see the nails on the claws at the ends of the arms dangling from its cantilevered shoulders.

So near – that it reaches out and grabs at the wing. Its claws crunch through composite skin. Your aircraft lurches.

The demon swings itself up on the wing. It squats there, grinning its rows of teeth at you. Then it turns, dips its head, and bites the wingtip clean away. It chews GRP skin and bonded airframe pieces into its mouth and out of sight. It gives a musical gulp. It wipes its mouth. It burps. It turns, dips its head, and bites off another chunk of wing. It chews. Your aircraft lurches.

The name of the game is to shake the demon loose. Hit the rigid ocean floor, and you're dead. Hit a cloud thing and the demon enjoys darkness total and dense. In darkness a demon will grow . . .

It gulps and wipes its mouth. Keep flying. It burps. It shuffles nearer along the stunted wing. Your aircraft shudders. The demon dips its head and takes another bite. Your aircraft wobbles and you're losing control. The demon holds on with ease. It chews and gulps and wipes its mouth. Your aircraft wants to spiral down. The demon wants to eat it. The demon burps and shuffles nearer.

The game has changed. The demon is growing wings. They sprout from its back as it consumes your aircraft. It dips its head and bites. It chews and gulps. Its wings grow. It wipes its mouth, quickly, and burps. It dips its head and bites.

The game has changed. The demon must fly before the aircraft crashes. To fly it must grow bigger wings. There isn't much time. When the aircraft crashes it will kill you and the demon. The demon shuffles nearer. Bites. Chews and gulps. Burps without wiping its mouth. The plastic aircraft provides poor sustenance. The demon shuffles nearer. It needs wings. The crippled aircraft is spiralling down. The demon must grow wings quickly. It needs richer food. It needs flesh and blood.

The game has changed. There's no way out. The aircraft

crashes, and you die. Or the demon reaches you first – and you die as it chews you and pumps the pulp of you down its throat. It's a no-win game. Except for the demon. And the demon knows it . . .

"You've never given us a message for your family, Ruth. Won't they want to hear from you?"
"No. I don't think so. Let's talk about something else."

The moon has gone. It's gone and left me. Now I have darkness, some stars, my instruments, and the epileptic flicking-flashing of the running lights and strobes. I need sleep. Sleep brings dreams. Wakefulness, with a brain run right down, brings hallucinations. In darkness a demon will grow . . .
    There's nothing on the wing. I can see in the flashing of my Angel's coloured lights. Even the shadow above the wing is swept by the light on the tail. But I can't see the tail. Something might be clinging to the tail, ready to file away at the disk of the spinning propeller. Something might be crouched between the wing roots, just behind the cockpit roof. Check the catches of the side windows. They're locked. No claw can enter when it reaches down. Unless it smashes its way inside . . .

"You're sounding really drowsy, Ruth. I'm feeling rather drowsy, too. I know, I'll tell you something to stir your indignation and get your adrenalin up a notch or two. Something Munro showed me yesterday. Let me tell you all about the way Michael's rigged the charity deals. Every bit of it legal, too. Listen to this."

Something black, huge, with wings like a dragon. She senses it seconds before it comes out of the high clouds. It bursts down into sight, leaving turmoil. Its wings are folded – or broken. It's a night thing, burned, a meteor extinguished and streaking out of heaven. It's a Lord of Light destroyed by its

359

own glory. It plunges into the dark, deep sea. The splash is like a mountain, but it makes no waves.

The presence passes out of higher light into deeper night. But the moment of its passing leaves a trail, a stain, a bubble track where the bubbles are otherness pumped into the world it passed through. When she closes her eyes, it was Lucifer alight. When she opens her eyes, it was a monstrous cinder near the end of its Fall.

"The weather looks good at Florida. As sweet and calm as you could wish. There's a front due in the afternoon, but you'll be landing at Michaels Field in the morning, local time. Exactly when depends on the winds you meet. You're looking fine for this, Ruth."

Michaels Field. Michael's name. He couldn't name his Angel after himself. Not Michael. He couldn't name it Raphael or Gabriel. If he did name it after himself, the name would have to be –
"Lucifer."

"Look, Ruth, you're starting to worry me. You're wandering. The day's beginning here. There's a bit of light out in the alley. Not that it's going to be much of a day – overcast, with rain forecast later. I know it's still dark where you are. You're a long way further west. You're ahead of the sun. But the night isn't going to last forever. A few more hours and you'll be there. Think about that. You'll be *there*. It won't be a temporary thing. No time record. Not the *fastest* – until someone comes along and does it faster. You'll be the *first*. The first person to complete a non-stop flight round the world *solo*. You'll be the one and only *first*. That stands forever! Think about it, Ruth. Think about it."
"Michael said – "
"Never mind about Michael. It's going to be yours, and nobody else's. Look, let's talk about Michael's tricks with the charity money again. That really got you going last time."

360

"I don't want to talk about the money."

"What do you want to talk about?"

"My father – I thought, I'll go and tell him I've got the chance to fly the mission. *I'll* be the one being famous and earning lots of money. That should show him once and for all, I thought. It might even let us make peace again.

"The problem's old. My father thinks a daughter is second best to a son, and my mother agrees with him. I knew I wasn't good enough for my father. He forced me to get on at school with a sort of moral blackmail, really. *Prove* you're not second best. I mean, a child senses that sort of attitude. And I *wanted* to prove it. I didn't realise how sick it was.

"Of course, I rebelled. I mean, every teenager does. My God, I wanted to get my hands on some *boys* – and fall in love, and run away, and be rich and famous and all that crap. I didn't see why I couldn't eat when it suited me, do my homework when it suited me, go out, come home . . . No chance. No chance of getting the key to the door, and *hell* to pay if my father had to wait up to let me in. And all the time I still needed to do what they told me was right, make up for what was supposed to be wrong in me – because I didn't know, you see. I didn't know anyone could possibly think daughters *weren't* second best. My family was the only one I knew, wasn't it?

"Anyway, smashing exam results, great A levels, and off to university to study economics, believe it or not. I don't own shares, I've never had a managerial job, but I did two-thirds of a degree course at – get this – the London School of Economics. Oh, was *that* a mistake on my father's part. He could have controlled me, all right. He was working class and honest and proud of his big income, so there was no question of fiddling the figures to get a grant from the local authority. My father had to pay my keep and meet all my fees. He could have made me go to Sheffield University and live at home and stay under his thumb, but he wanted to get the very best for his money. So off I went to London and the LSE. Oh dear.

I mean, the LSE still had the leftovers of all that political and radical stuff, and London had, well, everything Sheffield doesn't have, except decent countryside and anywhere you could breathe in deep without coughing your lungs out.

"I didn't tell you my dad's business. He started out at a steelworks. He got to be a foreman on the furnaces. He learned all about furnace maintenance, and decided to go it alone – one man with a pneumatic drill, big gloves and steel-toed boots. By the time I was in secondary school we lived in Dore – that was a very posh part of Sheffield, though it's come down a bit since. My dad drove a Jag, he owned a firm with forty people, enough machinery and stuff to fill a five-acre yard, and the choice of the best contracts going on furnace work.

"He built it all up himself. The trouble was, he had no education. Left school at fifteen and all that. He needed someone inside the firm who could do the finances, so that's where I came in, even if I was just a girl. I was going to get a proper education, then proper business skills. Then I was going to come back and be his manager, then his successor, and stay in Sheffield until I was buried in the family's plot. That was his plan for my life. But he sent me to the LSE, and London . . .

"Everyone was talking about the Third World then, as if it was a place they'd just discovered – you know, where there used to be dragons on the map. And about environmental disaster and silent springs and so on. It was very radical, very different, very *concerned*. And a world away from my father's gangs of men, covered in clinker and dust and sweating themselves half to death inside the bellies of these filthy great steel-making machines. And most of all, no one was breathing down my neck, protecting me from sex, parties – from people, for God's sake. It was *freedom*.

"I got in with this bloke Ashley. What a name. Dad would have shot him on sight. I got in Ashley's bed, and Ashley's books, ideas, politics, social theory, alternative program – you name it, all of it his. Thought control, you'd call it, and I loved

362

it. Well no, I suppose I *expected* it, because that's what I grew up with – my dad telling me what to do, how to do it, and my mum always saying that's right dear, that's right. The thing about Ashley was, he didn't tell. He let mc know what he wanted, and let me get on with it. So different from the tyrant waiting for me at home. God, I thought, this is *liberation*.

"I dropped out. All my father's years of training, all his money – all of it up in smoke. They didn't even get the chance to throw me out. For the first time in my life I said what I thought – your contempt, I said, makes me hate you even though I want to love you. Then I took my things and left.

"I won't go on about Ethiopia. The famine isn't the point at the moment. We were out there with World Assist, *doing* something, saving the world. I was in a tent at the airfield, clerking the supplies that came in, and Ashley was farting about doing things that someone else did properly afterwards. He organised stuff into batches and what have you, and then the drivers came and just put everything they could carry on the back and drove off. Ashley never realised that if we didn't have enough blankets for two loads this time, it didn't matter because the other charities had blankets, too. Ashley was all bloody theory, and he was there for the experience of saving the planet – but only at base camp, where we had toilets and a doctor. He didn't give a toss for the real people up country who were *dying* just to prove his theory of what was wrong with the world.

"I got rid of Ashley. I realised he was smothering me. I took a turn running the Africa desk at World Assist's London office. But Ethiopia got worse, and I went back on field work. But it wasn't safe any more, because there was a very nasty war by then. There always had been a war, but now it was very vicious, and the government was in retreat, and sometimes both sides seemed to pick on us. Our drivers got shot at, our trucks got blown up. It wasn't very nice at all.

"And then along came Michael Tranter with his Orbis Airship. Remember that? He sold it a few months later. Along he came doing his grand tour of the Sahel like some bloody pop star splurging out milk powder instead of megawatts. And I thought, look at that conceited, publicity-hungry bastard, staging sound bites in front of unpaid, starving extras.

"Well, we had to get a load to a camp up in the hills, but an air raid had taken out the bridge over a ravine, so we couldn't do it, though the people up there had nothing left at all. So he said pop it in the back, and he told me to hop in at the front – and off we went, him flying, his crew to push the stuff out, and me showing them which way to go. Well I was hooked. Here was this bright young businessman pioneering something good, namely responsible capitalism, and proving it could work, and promoting the new green philosophy. At least – at the beginning I thought he was promoting it, not just using it as a sales gimmick. So anyway, I ended up with Michael and with a job at Orbis.

"About my father, though. It all happened after I'd left home. Thatcher was in command and they were massacring heavy industry. Sheffield was steel and alloys and not much else – and almost all of it went. With it went my father's business. He sacked his staff, he sold what he could of his machinery, he practically had to give away his yard. Steel City – it looked like a war zone from the east side right through to Rotherham. Towards the end he was trying to keep the bank at bay by doing the work himself. He was a one-man business again, but over his head in debt. The thing is, he *knew* I'd have been able to help. He *knew* the stuff I'd learned would have worked a miracle – if I'd been there. I suppose he had to blame somebody, so he picked me. He couldn't blame the government because he voted for them.

"But that wasn't the worst of it. He was cutting every corner and working round the clock, when there was work. So one night he was in this furnace, up inside the bottom end of the flue removing damaged lining bricks. The furnace was still hot – so hot he had to keep his chisels in a bucket of water, and change his chisel every ten minutes, up and down the ladder, when it got too hot to hold from digging into the bricks. My mother says it must have been his own sweat on the ladder. He fell. And he landed on the pile of bricks he'd been chopping down, and broke his back. Nobody came until the shift changed the next morning. The doctors said it was when he'd tried to drag himself out of there that did it. The fracture pinched his spinal cord, but it was the movement that tore it apart.

"He's in a wheelchair. They've sold everything and got rid of the debts. No more posh house in Dore. They live in a little terrace with a front step that opens straight on the street. He's got one of those electric lifts on the stairs, but he can't get in or out of it without my mother's help. He doesn't get a mobility allowance because he's got my mother to do the shopping. And because he had enough common sense to rescue what he could, so he doesn't have a mortgage and doesn't pay any rent, he doesn't get any other allowance or assistance or anything but the basic disability thing. And he *hates* the politicians who've got rid of what they call dependency culture and made total victims of independent people like him. And he loathes the new kind of businessman, like Michael, who did so well out of the eighties. And – he didn't ever say it. But I knew.

"He didn't say it until last week when I went to see them. Mum said I shouldn't mind his outbursts. He gets so bitter, and who wouldn't, and so on. There I was. All I wanted to do was get in the car, take my hurt and my anger, and *go*. I was on the pavement in front of the door and the window and the lace curtains, and he was inside, and all I wanted was to *go*. But she closed the door and said I shouldn't mind. And then she looked at my car. It's just an ordinary Golf with a cat. And suddenly she says, it's quite a nice little car, but she'd have thought I'd get something a bit posher from a rich boyfriend such as I've got. I mean, it's my own car. I *told* her – it's my car bought with my money. But for her the idea's impossible. It means a woman with a mind of her own, a job of her own and a bank account of her own. Nothing like that exists in the world she lives in. The stupid *cow* – betraying me with that attitude all my life! You'd think a woman would take a woman's side. So it's just as much her fault – his contempt, his fury. My hate . . .

"It's her fault he thinks like that. And what he said. What he said. I knew he thought it. But at last he finally said it. My fault. He said it was *my* fault. He said I did it. He said – he said – I *crippled* him."

FIFTY-THREE

The light outside looked dull and sticky, as if Thursday was only reluctantly awake at seven in the morning. Mandy had organised half a dozen breakfasts for the Mission Control crew. Bacon sandwiches – fattening, but much better than nothing. Terri washed it down with vending machine coffee. It had been a long night of vile vending machine brew.

It had been a long night of confusions and confessions. What a sad little mess to be in. Terri didn't have any hang-ups hiding inside her. She didn't need any such luxury. She had racism, sexism and a touch of heightism to contend with – quite enough to keep her busy. She could attack all her problems with Shiseido makeup, Mondi clothes and a bright red throbbing Corrado. No such easy option for Ruth – her hang-ups were too tightly woven into her personality.

It was time, just about, to call Ruth again. Leave her in silence for more than a few minutes, and there was a real risk she'd have gone to sleep, plunged into the sea, and would never be heard of again. Silently, between one rambling talk and the next, she would have disappeared without trace. Without trace.

"Terri?" Mandy called. "BBC Today want you at seven twenty and again at eight twenty. Okay?"

Terri turned to where Mandy was tied to one of the phones, and nodded. As she turned, she saw someone coming in through the door who didn't belong in Mission Control. Geraldine Trayhorn.

Mandy spoke into the phone again, then put down the receiver. "And they're sure to fire a question about whether, without an autopilot, Ruth is going to take on the bonus stage back to the UK."

"Not a chance," said John from his computer table.

"Obviously. But keep them guessing, Terri. Say it depends on safety. What Ruth and our experts decide."

"Right." Experts, Terri thought. I'm the only expert I've got left. She turned her chair to face Trayhorn. "Morning."

"Morning." Geraldine Trayhorn had finished looking round the room by the time she arrived at the communication desk. She dressed unadventurously but neatly, just like an accountant should – blue shoes, shortish red skirt, white blouse with blue pocket trims, blue bow tie, no jacket on what was going to be a warm day. "I'm on my way to the MT building, but I've been thinking something through. We've got an awful lot of stuff in Michael Tranter's laptop which we can't get to read out. I was wondering – "

"You've got Michael's laptop? Munro's given it to you, the fraud specialist?"

"Yes. I was wondering if you could remember anything more about that message you saw come in via the modem. We can't find the message, you see, and if we could discover what releases it, we might release other things as well. Your *without trace* idea was brilliant, so I thought I'd ask if you can remember anything else about what you saw on the screen."

Terri shrugged. Trayhorn and partner – Curtis Gupta – got the Without Trace program to show itself, which was a great help. No harm in returning a favour. Except that Trayhorn was helping Munro fight Michael Tranter. On the other hand, there was Michael's selfish carve-up of the charity money, and there was the other thing – the very big thing – she was trying to sort out herself. "Well, the message said something along the lines of *started without trace*. There was an instruction of some sort, then it said *key* and *store*. I didn't really pay that much attention. MT POST MT and MT POST PL – that's how I knew it was a message from Pattie Lee to Michael."

"Was there an encrypt command?" John asked from behind her. "Or decrypt? Anything like that?"

"I think so." Terri looked back at Trayhorn, and Trayhorn was looking at John as though he might be somebody's spy. "Don't worry – John sorted the program stuff you unlocked for us. He's as much in the know as I am."

Trayhorn nodded, reluctantly. "Was there a command like that?"

"Something like that. MICTRA or MICTRAX, or with a double-X, perhaps. M-I-C-T-R-A."

"Right. Thanks – I'll give that a try."

"My pleasure. By the way," Terri tipped her head slightly. Here comes my clever question in return. Nothing's for free. "Is there a connection between the frauds and the tangle we've been in with Michael's course program?"

"Why?"

"Because I'm looking for a reason why Michael Tranter might be afraid of getting into very deep trouble."

Trayhorn took time to look round the room. Nobody seemed to be listening, not even John. "There's a connection. Tranter did all the frauds, and we're trying to prove it."

Terri decided to make eyes, show suitable surprise. Funnily enough, it wasn't really all that surprising, now that she'd learned her own little bit about Michael. "And the big mess with the computer and everything?"

"Tranter sabotaged the computer network. It seems an extreme move to stop Munro taking control."

"Wow." Sabotaged his own firm? A wizz-kid from the eighties was very different from the old school, although crimes like burning down your own warehouse to claim the insurance had a long tradition. "And how does it look? Is Munro going to win?"

"If Tranter's too interested in wrecking MT-Orbis to fight for control – yes, I think so."

"Why would he want to wreck MT-Orbis?"

"That's the question, isn't it?" Trayhorn shrugged. "Anyway, we'll see how bad things are when the Stock Exchange opens."

When Trayhorn had gone, Terri called Ruth. "Good morning! It's dull and dreary here. How's it look down in the tropics?"

No answer.

"Ruth? Answer me, please? Ruth? Ruth! Are you still there?"

"Wait." A pause. "I'm juggling with a bottle, damn it." A longer pause. "It isn't easy, you know. It's pitch dark."

"Ah well, drink less, pee less and remember it's sunrise where you'll be in two hours. You've got about an hour to daylight, and you've got six and a half hours to Florida and fame. Ninety-three hours in your flying machine so far. Are you going to be ready for the cameras?"

"God! Oh God! I must look *awful*."

"Have fun anticipating the great event. Meanwhile, I want to ask you about that boat you saw. Remember? Just before your autopilot gave up the ghost."

Everything but Orbis Air opened fifteen percent down, and fell steadily. Orbis Air opened twenty percent down, and plummeted. By nine thirty the trend was speeding up.

In the United States, the Federal Aviation Authority was threatening intervention to protect customers on domestic flights against a total collapse of Orbis Air. In Britain, the Civil Aviation Authority called to warn of a possible suspension of Orbis Travel's operating licence if things continued. Holiday-makers who hadn't yet left for their summer paradises had to be protected against the risk of being stranded. Orbis Air's operations on its scheduled routes would be frozen for the same reason. And when would they intervene? When they decided things were bad enough and heading for even worse.

Munro told the Orbis Air and Orbis Travel managements

to prepare for a voluntary freeze on all flights. A move of their own, suggesting some vestige of control, would be marginally less damaging than the ultimate thumbs-down from the regulatory bodies. An enforced closure to protect customers would precipitate Orbis Air's final sluice into oblivion. That would take the whole of MT-Orbis down the toilet, too. It was no longer any secret that the sale of a viable and valuable Orbis Air was what the rest of the company needed to survive.

"Sounds bad," Trayhorn said, sitting in the chair she'd pulled in front of his desk. "I know you don't expect to get any proof about it, but do you know why Tranter's done this? If he'd wanted to stop you taking control, all he had to do was take charge of MT Holdings again before you'd completed the shares swap. Which is off, I suppose, under present circumstances. Was he just trying to spoil that?"

Munro shook his head. Michael had dealt too much of a blow to the company to want to breeze in and pick up the pieces afterwards. "He's been out of hospital since Tuesday evening. He could have moved in and taken charge, if he'd wanted to."

"Perhaps," she said, "he's hoping that if he wrecks the computer network and the data in it, and if he also destroys the company, then he'll have removed all evidence and all risk of prosecution."

Munro shrugged. "At least that's a rational explanation. Have you been getting anywhere? I've started accounts on setting up a pencil-and-paper system for receiving and holding income, so that we can crawl our way out of insolvency. I can use you there at the moment, if you're still stalled on the frauds."

She folded her hands in her lap. The colour of her fingernails didn't quite match the red of her skirt. She looked down at her hands, then at the mess of update sheets on his desk, and finally at him. "Don't give up on getting Tranter. You don't want him to get away with fraud – the theft of *millions* – and with attempting to wreck a major company, do you? Think of all those jobs going down the drain."

370

All those jobs, those thousands and thousands of jobs. Robert Munro, you're supposed to care more than the average capitalist. "Have you been getting anywhere?"

She nodded. "I called in to see Terri Sabuli on my way to work. She remembered some sort of instruction she saw on the screen of the laptop at the same time as she saw the *without trace* message. I tried a few variations. The right one is MICTRA-double-X. M-I-C-T-R-A-X-X. It lets a lot of stuff read out of the computer, though by no means all of what's in there. Some of the stuff it releases is clearly message stuff, including the *without trace* thing. I think MICTRA-double-X encodes output and decodes input before locking it away. It's supposed to stop anyone being able to intercept and read stuff while in transit from computer to computer, and it also stops them getting it out of the computer where it's stored. But we'll have to ask Curtis Gupta to see if I'm right. Which brings me to the other thing."

"Yes?"

"I need him back, if we're going to get any further. I'm not skilled at computers. I've just had a good hunch and a bit of luck, and I've no idea where to take it from there."

"Right," he said. Progress was progress, no matter how small. "I'll have him paged to go straight to your office. He's in the building somewhere. Everyone who knows anything about computers has been here all night."

"Thanks. And there's one other thing. I'm fed up of calling you Mr Munro, or Munro. What can I call you? And don't worry – it won't be Daddy."

It took him a second or two to get over that one. She'd fingered the middle-aged man's nightmare. Being wanted as a father substitute instead of for yourself would be even more depressing than just being wanted for your money. She'd also made him trip over his own thoughts: he would like her – he very much would. But now wasn't exactly the right time. "Robert," he said. "In private only. And don't call me Bob."

"Right," she said. "And I'm Geraldine. In private only, if

you wish. And don't – " The intercom interrupted her. "And don't ever try shortening it, either."

He just glowered at her on the way to switch on the intercom. It seemed the best way to play the game.

"Mr Munro? Miss Sabuli's on the line. She wants to speak to you urgently."

"I decided to tell her," Trayhorn said, "that Tranter sabotaged the computer and did the frauds."

"Did you?" he said. "Put her on, Ripley." He picked up the internal telephone and listened for the click. "This is Munro, Miss Sabuli."

"Good morning, Mr Munro. I thought you'd want to know about this. If I'm right, I've sorted out what Michael Tranter was planning to do during the mission."

FIFTY-FOUR

Michael bought two tickets from Gatwick to Buenos Aires for the late afternoon. To preserve credibility, he decided not to book with Orbis Air. He paid by plastic, so the booking was instantly firm. He was paying first class, so he asked the airline to phone a reminder call to his MT office at one o'clock.

He also filed permission for a low-level from Wragby Aerodrome to Schiphol, using Wragby's air taxi codes instead of his own name. He booked two tickets for early the next morning, Schiphol to Oslo. Last of all, he hacked the Wragby computer and set it to timetable a Trantair Solomaster fuelled and ready at 19.00 hours.

After that, he wiped all his disks, and then set his computer to erase its hard disk – forty megabytes biting the quantum electric dust. No erasure of addresses and labels, this, leaving all the data behind for the enterprising to recover: it was a total elimination of everything in the store. Last of all would be the one megabyte RAM and the battery-backed RAM. He wasn't proposing to leave any information behind.

He stood up – carefully. His entire body still ached, still yelled at him every time he made it move out of any position of rest, and his arm hated it if he as much as breathed deeply. He blamed that on the bolts, poking their heads against the inside of the linen sling. He blamed it all – including all the hasty re-planning it made necessary – on Ruth Clifford. Such a shame she was going to escape retribution. She'd even been mad enough to attempt the Atlantic crossing without an autopilot, and according to the ten o'clock news she'd survived to see another dawn and was bang on time for Florida. Ruth was going to write her name in the history books after all.

Hitting Munro so hard that he was dead in the water would have to be justice enough. A pity there wouldn't be enough time to stay and watch the shareholders abandon Munro and the regulators scupper him. A company the size of MT-Orbis heading for receivership, Monday at the latest – what a shock.

The erasure program terminated itself on the screen. He checked the procedure by entering a couple of directory paths. Not a thing. He asked the data retrieval routine to search the disk. It found nothing.

"Pattie!" he called. "It's time to pack your handbag."

Then he switched off the computer. That did for everything in the main RAM as well. Just the battery-backed RAM left. He needed Pattie for that. He couldn't lift the monitor aside to remove the batteries without the aid of a second arm.

Back in the good old days he didn't need Pattie, or anyone else. Everyone thought he was a financial genius. They all bought it. They didn't know. Not one of them realised they were really dealing with a computer freak who'd grown up and developed some hard-headed ideas about getting on in the world – someone who happened to make and sell computers and software, who sold them to companies complete with security packages of his own devising, who knew precisely how to get in and out of those systems unnoticed, who'd been doing it for fun, then money, since the day the first modem fell into his lap.

It was all so easy, speculating against the shares of companies when you knew exactly what they were planning to do, how healthy they were, and how their investors were preparing to react to any changes. It was a great way to make money. It was the best. It got you rich, and it got you a hot-stuff reputation in the City. But like everything else in business, the lucrative fires had to be fuelled with start-up money, meaning debt acquisition and cash . . .

The downturn at the end of the eighties squeezed his personal shares income, hurt MT-Orbis turnover and profits, and cut his return from the company. It meant less money coming in. It meant a risk of repayment delays which would lead to questions – which would lift the lid on half a lifetime's work, the entire unexpurgated story of a brilliant businessman's true career.

So to keep the train on the track, he drained off a little of the MT-Orbis blood. It was a temporary trick, which would have vanished without trace once the economic good times returned. It would have worked out perfectly – except for the unspeakable idiocy of a government-driven recession, the inevitable follow-on of Munro's corporate rescue plan, and the detailed scrutiny of finances to which it would lead.

So it was suddenly time to take the money and run.

Pattie Lee was already on board. She liked the idea. She ran all the contact work to Hong Kong in order to find suitable operators and arrange the pick-up end. She also provided his life insurance. It wouldn't do for a lone man, loaded with personal millions, to land unprotected in the lap of a secret welcoming committee: it might turn into a fate not worth contemplating. They set it up so that Pattie had access to a fraction of the money in order to buy him out, while he had no access at all until she'd rescued him. But she had to rescue him, because he was the only one in the world who knew the key which unlocked the data about the rest of the money. Pattie had the data on disk, Michael had the key in his head.

He'd needed Pattie, and the chain of contacts which started with her hairdresser, in order to set it up. He would have needed her to get the data out, because it might be more than his life was worth to have it with him when certain people fished him out of the sea. He would have needed her to free him from those certain people on the way to a life of extreme luxury in anonymous exile. But under the original plan, one thing he hadn't needed Pattie for was to help him get out of the bloody country.

Now, thanks to Ruth and a steel stair at Wragby, he needed her for that, too. At the moment he wouldn't even be able to drive a car with an automatic transmission round a sharp corner. He certainly couldn't fly an aircraft without someone to do exactly what he said with the throttle and the flaps lever, while he rode the rudder pedals and guided the stick. Pattie had confident little hands, and wasn't the sort to show a flutter of nerves just because she'd never touched an aircraft's controls before. So he needed her as much as ever. At the moment.

The tempting thought, though, was that with the original plan ditched and the rescue stunt erased, he wasn't going to need her any more, once they'd landed in the dusk at Schiphol . . .

Pattie was standing in the doorway, watching him. "I'm ready, Michael. Are you?"

By shortly after ten, the shares slide was well under way and showed every sign of accelerating. That's when Geoffrey Simmington phoned. He was all apology, embarrassment – and very bad news.

"It's our clients, Robert. And the bank itself – against my advice. They're requiring me to disinvest immediately. They are all *adamant* about pulling out and rescuing what they can."

"Are they?" Rescuing theirs, destroying ours, Munro thought. Holding on, halting the slide and the collapse in confidence, thereby rescuing ours as well as theirs –

it's no option. The interest most sacred to a capitalist is self-interest.

"I'm terribly sorry, old chap. I know what it means. I've done what I could, but in the end we have to obey the instructions of our clients. I thought I ought to tell you personally, Robert, as soon as it was definite. Before the news comes through from the Stock Exchange, I mean. I thought – well, I ought to tell you myself."

"Yes, Geoffrey." A rat with a lot of influence, and a lot of friends, has decided to leave the ship. Down we go.

"I realise, of course, that this scotches the whole business about getting an exclusive cut of the cake when Orbis Air is sold off. Always assuming you still get round to selling it, that is. I'm awfully sorry, Robert, but our clients absolutely *insist* on pulling out. And besides, the buyer consortium is falling apart anyway."

"Pity." They were missing the bargain of the decade. Orbis Air was getting cheaper by the minute.

"One other thing, Robert. I really must apologise for, well, railing at you yesterday. I realise it was damned obnoxious of me. That's a rum do, you know, a really rum do – someone sabotaging your computer like that. I hope they catch the blighter."

"So do I, Geoffrey. Apology accepted. Goodbye, Geoffrey. I'm quite busy."

He couldn't tell Simmington what he thought of him. He'd been in the jungle long enough to know that. Saying what you think is a luxury you can only enjoy once you've gone down into ruin – by which time you're of no importance, so your opinion doesn't count. If he did, by some miracle, survive, he would need to keep doing business with Geoffrey Simmington and all the other sharks, leeches, rattlesnakes, vultures – all those hordes of any-second enemies.

FIFTY-FIVE

Something dark, huge, with wings like a dragon. She sensed it seconds before it came out of the high clouds. It burst down into sight, leaving turmoil. Its wings were broken. It was a thing of blackness, burned, a meteor extinguished and streaking out of heaven, a Lord of Light consumed by glory. It plunged into the aquamarine sea. Brilliant in the sunshine, the splash rose in a mountain of cascades which tumbled in on themselves for long seconds. But it made no waves.

When she closed her eyes, it was Lucifer alight. When she opened them, it was a monstrous cinder near the end of its Fall.

In broad daylight?

Out of sight, going down into darkness, Lucifer's corpse was streaming soot and bubbles through the deep.

She needed help.

"You amaze me, Ruth. I had no idea you knew about the frauds."

"Munro told me. I didn't know whether to believe him. You say he's getting the evidence – he's going to be able to prove it?"

"So it seems. The picture's fitting together, more or less."

"What picture, Terri?"

"Ah, yes – what picture indeed. I think I've got an answer for you about the Without Trace program. You'll like it."

"Will I? Just tell me, Terri. I'm much too tired for guessing games."

"Right. Here goes. Michael did the frauds. Michael must have decided he was going to get found out. So what does he do? He rigs the course. Here, at Mission Control, we get

377

a perfect course, all the way round the world and back to Britain, so that we don't see anything funny going on. What he gives us is exactly according to the *official* plan for the mission. But he puts a different course in Angel's computer. It's the course Angel flew, it diverges from the official course after Australia, and it ends in the Indian Ocean. And all the time after Australia, Angel's computer was reporting to us that it was really on the official course, so when the last update came through, we'd think Angel was eight hundred and fifty miles south of its actual position. Okay? Then four minutes later Angel reaches two degrees south, fifty-eight east, runs out of course – and sees what?"

"A ship. The tug."

"Exactly! Flashing its lights so it can't be missed, sitting there with its engines stopped, lowering a boat over the side. And what's Michael going to do? He's going to ditch in the water next to the tug. You've got a life-jacket and everything in the cockpit, haven't you? Michael goes into the water, the boat picks him up and takes him back to the tug, they make sure Angel sinks, they fish any broken-off bits out of the sea so they aren't found floating about and giving the game away. It's broad daylight – perfect for the trick. But the sun still hasn't risen, so he'll have no trouble seeing the lights of the tug waiting for him, and they'll have no trouble seeing him approach. And the tug, if you remember, wasn't using its radio, so there'd be no transmissions that anyone else could hear. *No one* would ever know."

"But – Michael would have disappeared. He'd never report in. He wouldn't answer you. You'd know he'd disappeared. I can't see what you're getting at."

"One out of ten, Ruth, and that's generous. You are tired, aren't you? Obviously Michael would have disappeared. He *intended* to disappear. But the thing is, we wouldn't realise for a while – not before he was safely on board the tug, Angel was sunk, and there was nothing for anyone to see if they just happened to be alert and interested. And, most important of all, when we realised something was wrong, we'd be absolutely certain it had all happened eight hundred and fifty miles away to the south."

"Oh. I see."

"You're getting there, are you? We'd raise the alarm, the search would concentrate round the last position – totally reliable, on the basis of our super navigation program and constant satellite monitoring – and they'd never find a thing. No Michael, no wreckage. Tragedy, tragedy. The last hero in his magic aeroplane, more than halfway round the planet and giving his all for charity and the Third World. Suddenly an unknown mechanical failure or something. Not even enough time to put out a distress call. Plunges straight into the sea and disappears without trace. Hence the name of the program, incidentally. World in mourning. Pursuit of Michael, the naughty business thief, called off. Prosecution of a corpse pointless. End of story. Apart from the films and books and the mini series about magnificent Michael Tranter chasing the sun, getting too near, burning his fingers on too much money, and coming to a tragic end while trying to do one last good deed to make amends for his wicked little sins. Talk about a showman. It would be the most magnificent last exit since Lazarus."

"Lazarus?"

"Well, pick your own comparison. Because the whole time, Michael's safe and well. He probably hides out for a while in the Seychelles – those are the nearest islands to the place where he was going to meet the tug. Then one day he turns up with a new identity in South America or somewhere, and lives out a life of luxury and ease with all his stolen millions."

"And how is he supposed to get the money? He couldn't carry it with him in the cockpit."

"It's scattered in banks all over the world. He gets it with the help of his accomplice."

"And who's that supposed to be. I remember Munro said he didn't think it was me."

"Michael's accomplice is – wait for it – Pattie Lee."

"*Pattie Lee?*"

"His ice-cold, butter wouldn't melt PA. I thought that one would get you wide awake. Nice timing for Florida, eh?"

Pattie drove Michael's white BMW out of the garage, along the drive and through the gate. Michael closed the gate one-handed, taking his time and making sure the detective in the car up the lane didn't miss the fact that they were both leaving together. Then he got into the car beside Pattie. It wasn't all that easy closing the door – not with his left arm immobilised. Pattie started the car accelerating smoothly between the hedges and walls and exclusive country gates under the trees. Pattie drove the BMW, of course, as if she'd never driven anything else.

"My door's closed," he said. "But just round the corner up there, stop the car. Come round to my side and pretend to close the door for me."

She nodded. She didn't ask why. Pattie was a smart woman.

She stopped halfway down the straight stretch after the corner, halting with the car in the middle of the lane. She even switched on the hazard warning lights before she got out. She started to walk round the bonnet in the sieve of sunlight filling the lane.

In his door mirror, Michael watched the Smith and Brown company car come round the corner. The driver had no choice. Reversing out of sight would give the game away. The blue Honda Accord rolled slowly closer through the lazy, hazy splashes of sun.

The view vanished as Pattie opened his door. He heard the tyres of the Honda creeping to a halt. Pattie slammed the door closed again and started to walk back round the bonnet. She waved a little apology to the car behind. In the door mirror, all he could see of the Honda was its nearside wing.

Pattie got in, cancelled the hazard lights, snapped the seatbelt home, and drove off again.

At the next corner, briefly, he could see the blue Honda following at the distance adopted by a driver who isn't pushy and doesn't want to overtake. He couldn't see the driver's face for the scrolling windshield reflections of dark tree shadow and bright sky. "How did our man take it then?"

"Calm and collected," Pattie said. "It's a woman, actually. She's got a car phone."

"Shouldn't be without in that trade." He decided to play a CD. Pattie was also calm and collected – worth her share of stolen millions. But he wouldn't need her once he was safe on Dutch soil. A piece of music about cheats, deceivers and unfaithful lovers would be appropriate. He started checking the rack for operas.

This time Terri had made sure that not everything was on the other side of Kilburn. She'd been at Mission Control in the Orbis building, it seemed, forever. She went to the loo to change her underclothes, brush her teeth and renew her makeup. She stood in front of the mirror, half-heartedly trying to convince herself that she was rock steady and the world was the thing that was seesawing and slowly rotating. To think you could get to the point where you'd kill for an hour of sleep.

Carefully, she negotiated the stairs and then the corridor back to Mission Control. Look smooth, she thought, look in charge.

She felt herself wobble as the noise washed over her. Mission Control had never been so lively. Lots to do, all of it good. Ruth was going to land in time for the midday news in London.

"Terri!" Mandy was down at the far end of the room, holding a phone surrendered to her by one of the press-desk staff. "Another sponsor! Knickers in twist about company crash!"

Nothing but fuss and noise getting in the way of the simple task – make sure Ruth lands safely, and make sure the whole world hears about it for at least a solid week. "Tell them the same as the last one! We have a contract to fly, they have a contract to pay! We're flying! They're paying!"

Mandy nodded and spoke into the phone. You could tell by

381

the gestures she wasted on the conversation that she was being much more diplomatic. After all, she'd had a bit more sleep.

Terri steered herself to the communication desk and picked up the clipboard full of pending notes. A lot of interest had flooded in since breakfast, most of it requiring a follow-up, like when would Ruth be ready for an in-depth TV, and so on. She flicked to the sheet listing bids from the Sunday papers for Ruth's life story. Terri's eyes didn't seem able to focus. All the zeros were running together. The long one couldn't really be a hundred thousand.

Oh yes, it was!

Darren Pierce phoned at eleven fifteen. It made a change from the non-stop disaster reports. Michael Tranter and Pattie Lee were on the M40. They might be heading for London, or they might intend to turn north or south on the M25. Pierce wanted to wait and see.

"I'm not happy with that, Mr Pierce. Don't you think it might be time to involve the police?"

"Well, the evidence we have is still a touch shaky. The frauds are solid, but we've only got circumstantials to tie them to Tranter. It provides grounds for an investigation, et cetera, but not for an arrest. And the very fact of a police investigation would guarantee that he ducked out and disappeared."

"What about the possibility of him disappearing before we've unearthed more evidence?"

"Ah – yes. They *could* be heading for one of the airports, or even the Channel. I don't suppose you might have *any* kind of indication that they're going to do a runner?"

That was what he was waiting to hear – Pierce cueing himself to be receptive to a wilder idea. "We know Tranter was planning to disappear aboard his aircraft. We've got compelling proof of that, as of this morning."

"Gosh! That would make all the difference. Mr Munro, are you *absolutely* sure you've got *compelling* evidence? There isn't much time, you see, if he's now trying to skip the country. I haven't got the option, really, of stopping off at your office

and going over it in detail. Firm and compelling evidence he
was going to disappear?"

"Firm, Mr Pierce, and compelling."

"In that case – in that case – yes, that makes grounds for an
arrest. Should he actually try to leave the country, that is."

"So you do think it's time to alert the police?"

"Let's see. The whole process takes a few hours. You
can't just phone the Met and order them to arrest someone.
You have to persuade them of the urgency and seriousness et cetera, and of the need to get a warrant pretty
damned quick."

"Which is better? Do I approach the police, or do you?"

"Oh, I'll do that, Mr Munro. They know me at the Serious
Fraud Office. If I pick up a phone and say I've got a fat
fraudster about to hop the country, they'll listen all right. Ah
– have I got your permission to go in with the full story? The
legal bits of what we've been doing, I mean."

FIFTY-SIX

At eleven thirty he got a different phone call. Mr Peter
Cavendish of the Securities and Investments Board. Outside
it was a cloudy, sticky, inner city summer day with the
intermittent beginnings of rain. Inside his executive floor
office it was air-conditioned coolness. But Munro had his
tie loose and his jacket over the back of his chair, and he
was sweating just the same.

Cavendish didn't waste time on pleasantries when there was
an execution warrant to pronounce.

"MT-Orbis shares have stopped sliding and started dropping. The push came when Longman Short began getting
their clients out. In our capacity as regulators, we have to
take account of investors. Your investors are in a terrible

plight because their shares are falling faster than they can find buyers. If this continues, we'll be forced to suspend trading – unless you do it voluntarily."

That would be the final curtain. The company's reputation would be dead. Suspend shares. Then sell up, wind up, and goodbye. "You're aware that the calamity which has triggered this collapse is nothing more than a bloody great piece of sabotage?"

"I am."

"And that our computer system is literally infested with copies of the program which has crippled it? These copies can't be found except by the most time-consuming work, and they *all* have to be found before we can get even a single subsystem back on line. That's going to take until well into next week. Tuesday or Wednesday. In the meantime, we should have some hand-run accounts for income and outgoings set up before the end of the afternoon. We can limp along – if the bloody shareholders will let us!"

"I'm aware of that."

"And that, in short, this collapse isn't our fault. We're the victim of one single saboteur – a criminal, no less. And you're not only supposed to have a responsibility towards shareholders and market players, but also a primary interest in going against such criminal activity every chance you can get!"

"I'm aware of all that, Munro."

"Well then, why do you want to help the bastard sink us?"

A pause at the SIB across the City.

"The bastard in question, I suppose, is your boss?"

"Why would you come to that conclusion?"

"Last week, Munro, I contacted you about certain irregularities which were bothering us. I asked for a meeting. You said you were willing, but failed to take it any further. I've faxed you again this week, and tried to reach you by phone."

"I've had my hands full. By now you should be realising why."

"Quite. However, the fact that we didn't meet is to be

regretted. It might have given you some measure of warning, which could have been helpful in forfending the present turn of events."

"Cavendish, would you like to tell me what you're talking about?"

"It's unsupported. Does anyone else happen to be listening?"

"No."

"Very well. I presume you know that when Tranter acquired Orbis Air there was a rival bidder. An American corporation. Do you remember hearing how the contest ended?"

"I remember. The American outfit pulled out, and Tranter got the airline dirt cheap in the end."

"Can you remember *why* the rival outfit withdrew?"

"Because they were doing a geared takeover – borrowing heavily to finance the bid. And then their debt servicing came apart, their shares took a hell of a dive . . ."

The corporation had stopped paying back as it should. Its shares had gone through the floor.

"Yes, Munro?"

"They had a sudden problem with repayments to creditors. Their bubble burst. They lost a lot of money and it took them two or three years to recover. You're not suggesting – you're not suggesting there's a connection?"

"The basic cause was an apparent error which occurred in the corporation's computer. Our American colleagues have thought for some time that it *might* have been sabotage. If so, the person who most obviously stood to gain was Michael Tranter."

"Do you mean to say – there are grounds for suspecting that Tranter has done this before?"

"So it seems. *Vague* grounds, I should stress. There's no evidence. But the Americans have been in touch, and in a nutshell, they've been wondering if we might know anything else about Tranter that could be made to stick a little more effectively."

Damn Cavendish, Munro thought. Damn him to hell. If

only the man had been more specific right from the start! "I know of something else that can be made to stick."

"I'm afraid any sabotage of your computer is bound to be prosecution-proof. There'd be no way of tracing it back to the culprit. At least, that's the expert advice I've heard."

"I'm not talking about his attempt to destroy the company. I'm talking about frauds against the company totalling several millions. I think at least twelve million at the latest estimate."

"Twelve *million*? By Tranter? Can you prove it?"

Wait, Munro thought. Don't tell him everything. Don't hand it to him on a plate. Buy thinking time. "Yes, I can prove it."

"Well, then – why don't you bring me up to date on this?"

"Wait a minute, Cavendish. You've just told me the Americans know Michael Tranter is a criminal, even if they can't prove it, and we've been wrecked by something that could have been predicted and avoided. But a couple of minutes ago you were threatening me with a suspension of shares. You know Tranter's the crook, but you're ready to kick his victims down the chute."

"I don't think bitterness helps, Munro. We're talking *real* money, *real* losses, *real* personal bankruptcies if this goes on."

"I know. How much money do you think I've already lost on MT-Orbis shares? Let me get my thoughts together." He pressed the secrecy button on the phone.

He kept it pressed.

Munro gasped. He was asphyxiating in the absence of hope. He wanted more room to move, and more time. He needed the oxygen of action, of *doing* something to fight back against catastrophe. On the accelerating way down in the whirlpool of total defeat, he wanted one single chance to draw breath.

Suspension of shares. Receivership. Ruin. Sell off the assets at hopeless prices to pay back the creditors, then close up. All of it gone. Everybody sacked. End of the world. End of thousands of personal worlds . . .

Grasp the straw that's spinning past you.

He lifted the receiver to his ear again, and released the secrecy button. "It looks as though I can deliver Michael Tranter to you, and give you a fat favour for the Americans as well. What do I get for it?"

"Are you trying to open a bargaining session?"

"Suspension of share trading will be followed by credit withdrawal and compulsory receivership. My God, we won't even get the chance to wind up voluntarily, and cut ourselves to pieces in a relatively humane way. I need you to hold off the suspension of share trading *and* the threat of receivership."

"I *can't* do that, Munro. I can't tell people you're liquid when you're stony broke."

"Other people have had a better deal than that."

"Ah. I see. You want me to give notice of a deadline to show adequate cash reserves. That won't work here. You're falling far too fast."

"You want proof against Tranter. It's in our finances. Wipe us out. Wipe the proof out, too."

Cavendish didn't answer.

Munro pressed the secrecy button again. He thought it was a moan of sheer despair building up inside – this one chance isn't going to come off! Then he realised he was holding his breath. When he broke the spasm, the gasp nearly sucked in his tongue. If this didn't give him a heart attack, nothing would.

"You're proposing a stay of execution, on the basis that we think there's still ground for hope. We – and you – would then be gambling on that being enough to halt the slide in confidence."

"Yes."

"Munro? Are you still there?"

The bloody secrecy button. He had to prise his finger off it. The end of his finger was white. "Yes. That's what I want."

A brief pause at the SIB. The trade was already made. It was just the price they were settling. Done it. Done it!

"It would have to be a very short period of grace, in the circumstances, Munro."

"Then the amount of money would have to be commensurately small, despite the size of MT-Orbis."

Another pause. "All right. I think we can risk that. Midday on Monday."

"Tuesday. It's the *weekend* at the close of business tomorrow, damn it. I can't raise money at the weekend."

"All right. Tuesday. Let me see. Thirty. Demonstrate by midday on Tuesday that you have thirty million cash reserves, and we won't have to close you down. Not at that stage, anyway. I'll have a fax to you in five minutes. It will be public knowledge in fifteen. Good luck, by the way."

He was going to need more than luck. He was going to need a miracle – or a very dirty trick. Wiped clean out, MT-Orbis wasn't going to scrape together half of thirty million by Tuesday.

Munro grabbed his jacket and went down to the finance floor. All hell was loose in the open plan section. He marched through bedlam to get to Trayhorn's office.

Inside the office was a sticky air of choked-up work. There was no space left – even the floor was disappearing under tumbled piles of paper which had avalanched over everything. Curtis Gupta was at the screen, jacket off, sleeves rolled, tie nowhere in sight. Geraldine Trayhorn was seated, bending forward and examining fanfold paper which was draped in a cascade from her knee. Her blouse, tight on her spine, outlined the back of her bra. No sign of a catch – it must open at the front. My God, Munro thought, I know about her bra. I know she wears stockings which have elasticated tops, because there's no place for suspenders under that skirt. I already know almost everything about her underwear. It's ridiculous.

"The size of the frauds," Trayhorn said, "just went up again. I've found some more figures. Over fourteen million and rising."

Munro nodded. All the better. More bait for the next

negotiation with Cavendish. He pointed at the screen. "What about that? Is this computer safe to use?"

"You mean because of the worm in the works?" Gupta shook his head. "No problem. This machine's been isolated from the net since before the attack. We were keeping our work safe from interlopers."

Munro nodded again. Pity it wasn't the kind of number-cruncher you could run corporate accounting on. "Progress?"

Gupta shrugged. He lifted a jumble of paper to reveal Michael Tranter's laptop and the cable connecting it to the office machine. "There's still stuff in here that won't read out. Not with any trick. It's well and truly keylocked. So I've set up a routine. All the bits and pieces of passwords he's used that I've found so far, plus a permutation rule to try them in all combinations, plus another rule to try each combination with a full set of command lines. Saves me hours of work. Days. It runs through and applies each permutation to the stuff in a couple of seconds." Gupta shook his head at the writing, wiping and rewriting screen. "But it won't get anywhere unless the password we need really is a mix of elements he's used before. Where do you start? I've tried Rosebud, by the way. I've tried them all."

Munro watched the self-defeating screen. Heads against a brick wall. He turned to Trayhorn. "Geraldine, I don't know why, but you've decided I'm one of the good guys."

Trayhorn shrugged. Gupta's eyebrow went up. Geraldine?

"You don't know anything about me." Munro had his jacket. He started straightening his tie. "So come with me. I'm going to do something despicable, and I want you to see me do it."

Slowly, Geraldine Trayhorn shifted her cascade of paper to the desk, and stood up. Both of Gupta's eyebrows were in the air.

FIFTY-SEVEN

One of the press-desk women was slipping round the back of the crowded room with what looked like bottles of champagne tucked under her arm. She dumped a bottle, plus plastic cups, on each of the telephone and paper-strewn tables. The occupants glanced at the goodies, but kept talking to the media on the other end of the lines. It couldn't be real champagne – not from the treatment it was getting. Just cheap, sweet fizz.

The engineer called Coates was rubbing his beard. "Yes, there's still enough fuel, though I wouldn't like to calculate the reserve. Depends on how much help she gets from the wind."

Munro nodded. "Weather?"

"Let's see. There's a system of troughs in mid-Atlantic, moving towards the UK. And we've already got this front over the south of the country. But there's nothing bad on its way."

"Crazy," Terri Sabuli said. She was staring at him. "You're crazy. You can't ask for this."

Munro pointed to the communication desk. "Let me talk to her."

Sabuli picked up a handset and gave it to him. Then she picked up the second one and got ready to listen. Geraldine Trayhorn moved in and helped herself to the third.

Here goes, he thought. They'll hate me for this. But not as much as when I sack them, if I have to do that in the end. "Hello, Ruth. This is Robert Munro. How are you?"

"Buggered. I mean, that's really what it feels like. After

390

they've lifted me out of this cockpit and stood me up straight, I'm never going to sit down again."

"How do you feel about the flight coming to an end?"

"Devastated! I've run out of world! Just when I felt like going on for another week."

"That's what I'd like to talk to you about."

Silence. Sabuli was trying to kill him with her eyes. Trayhorn was watching the busy press desks, her face blank.

"Look – I've done it. Well, in another hour I'll have done it. Flown round the world, all by myself, non-stop. Despite what Chester did with the aircraft and what Michael did with the course program. I *did* it. What sort of – what kind of – I mean, what more do you want?"

"Do you know what's going on here, Ruth?"

"You mean with MT-Orbis? Michael's a crook, just like you told me. He's zapped the computer and it's all fallen down. Shares have gone through the floor. Investors deserting in droves. Creditors baying for money. Commentators baying for blood. The regulators probably thinking about closing you down. Terri's been telling me. I'm *really* sorry Michael's done that to you."

"Not to *me*, Ruth. Do you know how many people world-wide work for MT-Orbis in one subsidiary or another? Sixty-six thousand three hundred and seven. That's me, and you, and sixty-six thousand three hundred and five other people. When we collapse, the receiver will be sent in, and the whole structure will be carved up and sold off. A tiny fraction of our present employees are going to find themselves re-employed by the new owners of some of the best bits picked out of the debris. The rest, about sixty thousand people, are going to get *nothing*. There won't even be enough money left for proper redundancy pay. The regulators are going to move on Tuesday at the very latest, the receiver will be in on Wednesday, and a week today the sackings will begin. Sixty thousand lives ruined. Where are they going to get jobs today?"

"It isn't my fault."

"Nor is it my fault. The SIB has given me one single option. By midday on Tuesday – that's three banking and trading days from now – I have to demonstrate thirty million in cash liquidity, or the receivership commences."

"Thirty million? That's not a lot."

"Isn't it? No one's going to lend us a penny. All we've got is our regular income. We're setting up accounts outside the computer system to stop Michael's bloody virus, or whatever it is, grabbing the financial data and dumping it down a black hole. I've just gone through the figures. By midday on Tuesday we'll have ten million. That isn't enough. We need another twenty."

Ruth didn't answer.

He hung on, a patient beggar on a long distance call. From the outside, he thought, I must look like a monster.

Terri Sabuli seemed to think so. She covered the mouthpiece of her handset. "Ruth's much more exhausted than she sounds. She's losing concentration. She's in no state to carry on. Or to make a decision about it. *Don't* do this to her."

"Now," said Ruth's voice in his ear. "Where were we?"

"You *see*," Sabuli hissed.

"The twenty million shortfall," he said. "And the sixty thousand ruined lives."

"Yes. Well – the sponsorship money's coming, isn't it? I land in Florida in less than an hour from now, and the money pours in. Michael's rigged the deals, hasn't he? Funny that he bothered, if he was planning to disappear. Force of habit, I suppose. Once a bastard, always a bastard. I can remember the figures, I think. Terri told me the figures. Thirty million comes in, and about fourteen million stays with the company, not including interest. So you've got your ten, plus fourteen, so you're only six short. Am I doing my sums right?"

"Six million short is sixty thousand people out on the street."

Sabuli turned away in disgust. But she kept listening to the handset. Ruth Clifford was sending silence.

Geraldine Trayhorn was listening in silence, too.

"Tell me, then. If I did fly the bonus stage, how much money does the company get?"

"Twenty-four million," he said, "not including interest."

"Twenty-four and ten is thirty-four."

"Exactly."

"And what's in it for me, apart from the fame and the glory? I'm going to get my interview fees, lecture tours, book deal, film rights and everything, whether I go round the world, or go round the world and then pop up to England, too. What's in it for me?"

"I can't think of anything but the fame and the glory."

Munro waited. He waited in a space of his own. The people at the press desks were too frantically busy to pay him any attention. Sabuli, Coates, and Sabuli's deputy, Mandy Rees, stayed where the end of the communication desk butted against the computer table. His isolation was the only genuine thing in the room. Its cause, the power he was driven to wield, was verging on the imaginary as the corporate source of that power dissolved.

Everything here was substitute. The champagne, the news-of-the-moment story which was pure entertainment, the spon-sor donations which were really advertising, the creamed-off expenses which were in fact operating costs plus return on capital, the benefit for the Third World – a few millions thrown at the problem, instead of a fundamental rethink of the attitudes that caused it. Michael's bid for self-glorification was a fake, since he'd planned to disappear in the floodlit glow of that glory. Even the pilot actually going for that glory, in the end, was a stand-in.

Trayhorn moved into his field of vision, looking up with blue eyes as unemotional as a cat.

"Well," he said. "Has that revised your opinion of me?"

"It depends whether you meant it about the sixty thousand jobs. Putting them as the priority issue, that is."

He shrugged. "I say it. But how do you propose to know if I mean it? Rather a lot of my personal wealth is on the line. I hold shares in MT and some of the subsidiaries."

"I know. You're on the list of lesser investors – you're not a pension fund or a Michael Tranter. I know how much your holding was worth. And I know how much you've lost since yesterday."

"Well don't tell me. I haven't had time to work it out." He noticed that Mandy Rees was nudging Sabuli's arm, and pointing past him towards the door. "I can wait for the surprise."

"Hey!" Mandy Rees yelled to the rest of the room. "Look who's here!"

Ruth was pinned to her seat with nails, spiked and barbed and vibrating nails which went clean through her flesh and into the bone. There was a cord of pain from her right shoulder, down to her elbow, along her forearm and into the hand which held the stick. Her left hand, which for the moment didn't have a job to do, wanted to punch its way through the cockpit roof and wave wildly at the empty sky. *Anything* just to make a movement – any movement – as long as it belonged to that infinite category of things her muscles hadn't done for almost one hundred hours.

Florida was less than a hundred miles in front, with Cape Canaveral a little to the right and Palm Beach way off to the left. She couldn't see it yet because the horizon was haze. At least, she hoped it was haze. Air traffic had already warned her to watch out for the first of the light aircraft coming to escort her in. There were going to be quite a few. The haze had better be in front of the horizon, and not in front of her eyes.

She had to be crazy. Absolutely crazy. She couldn't take another seventeen hours of this. She couldn't possibly do it.

Couldn't do it.

Terri watched as Michael Tranter, arm in a sling and jacket over his shoulders, advanced into the room. He was wearing the good old Michael image, the boss who smiles and knows names, who dispenses oodles of feel-good like an emperor in casuals on Peasants' Day.

Most of the people in Mission Control had been off-shift during the night-time conversations with Ruth. The ones who'd been there, like John or Mandy, were too busy and had too little spare energy to pass the information on. Most of the people in the room still didn't know about Michael the crook, the deceiver, the course saboteur, the unimpeachable and untraceable destroyer of companies. But real life haunted the fringes of their attention, as they waited for the imminent moment when Ruth brought Angel back to its starting point after circling the world. They knew the company was in a sudden and very nasty mess.

So the whole room went down to silence.

Michael strode into the middle. He wasn't a tall man. Even standing barefoot, Terri had been able to look down into his eyes. The things she let him do to her. If only she'd known.

"Thought I'd pop in," Michael said, "to congratulate Ruth. I only just got out of the hospital in time," he added for the majority of his audience. "I wouldn't want to miss this."

Some of them, Terri thought, must know something by now. The rest should be asking themselves why he isn't over at MT helping pull the fat out of the fire. She looked at Munro. It would be worth half her redundancy pay – if there was going to be any – to know what Munro was thinking at that moment.

Munro just stared.

A runner, she thought. He's supposed to be doing a runner. I worked it out, pieced it together myself. It was obvious. It still is obvious. I thought he was trying to cut and run. Munro thought so, too. And then in he walks like a host with a good excuse who's arrived late for the party. He can't be real. He must be a mirage, a figment of my tired mind conjured in the humid lukewarm fug of drizzling summer London.

Munro couldn't believe it, either. But Trayhorn did. She was eyeing Michael like a cat wondering whether to kill. Trayhorn had been far too neutral in face, voice and body posture to be true. It gave the game clean away. She wanted to get her neat and tidy hands on Munro, and would tear apart his enemy to prove it.

The apparition, untouchable, turned. "I realise this is a busy time, Terri, and I'd have been along earlier if it could possibly have been arranged – but I would like to offer Ruth my sincere congratulations."

Come on, move. Speak. The man can't cast spells. "I'll tell her."

"In person." He started towards the communication desk, his only free hand already reaching for one of the handsets.

Terri moved. "She's got her hands full." She squeezed between Michael and the desk, looking down at him. "And I really don't think she'll want to talk to you at the moment."

"Oh." Michael smiled. "I *see*. Have you and Bob been telling her things about me?" He backed off a step and turned to look at Munro. "Nothing too awful, I hope?"

Munro didn't answer. Trayhorn's mouth twitched. It was the constrained beginnings of a snarl.

One of the phones started to ring. But everyone was watching the central tableau.

Mandy Rees moved through the statues. She walked to the press desk and picked up the phone. She listened, then parked the receiver on her shoulder. "Mr Tranter, it's reception over at MT. They've got a message."

Michael's smile changed its shade, from affable to amused. During the change, Terri saw the fierce darkness waiting behind it. "Well?"

Mandy spoke into the phone, listened, parked the receiver again. "It's just a reminder call from Gatwick about your flight this afternoon."

"Ah, yes. Thank you." Michael glanced at the wall clock. "Well then, I'd better be off. Still got quite a few things to do. Terri, don't forget to tell Ruth – magnificent performance. Can't beat the unexpected for bringing out the best in someone. Can you, Bob?"

Munro blinked. He shifted his weight, a heavy man in a

top-priced business suit getting ready to dodge a punch in a brawl.

"That reminds me. Don't forget to check for messages on your computer, Bob. Your office machine, I mean. You keep the one at home disconnected from the phone, don't you? Infuriating habit, that. Makes a person so difficult to get at."

Munro nodded. Barely.

"Well." Michael started to walk towards the door. He knew how to take an audience with him when he made an exit, and leave them staring disconsolate at the wings once he was gone. Michael was a natural born star. "I'd better be running along. Keep up the good work, as we say when we can't think of anything original."

FIFTY-EIGHT

"Ruth," Sabuli said. "She wants to talk to you."

Munro didn't move.

Snap out of it, he said to himself. Michael isn't the innocent boss with a broken arm, whose chief executive tried to take the company away from him. He isn't the victim of persecution, with private detectives put on his tail. He isn't a hero cursed by the jealousy of lesser mortals, one of whom has set out to wreck his company, while all the mean minds choose to pin the blame on him. He isn't a good man in a corner, who's being fitted up with a fake charge designed to bring down the law on his blameless neck.

He's a thief. He's a liar, who walks in brazenly after having planned a spectacular escape into oblivion, leaving no trace except buckets of hoodwinked tears. He's a spiteful destroyer willing to sink his own company and the futures of all his employees – out of revenge at the legitimate intolerance of his theft and his lying. He's the real Michael Tranter. And he's gone.

"Ruth. She wants to talk to you."

Munro took the handset. He waited to make sure his voice was going to work. "Ruth?"

"I've been thinking about it. I still can think, just about. As long as I do it slowly enough, but not so slowly I forget what I'm thinking. I've been thinking."

"Yes?" He had to wait, patiently, while she got ready to deliver her lovingly crafted elaboration on *go to hell*.

"I've been wondering. How much would it cost to buy some land on the outskirts of a city? Big enough for a medium-sized detached bungalow, and a decent garden."

"Pardon?"

"How much do you think it would cost? And the house – how much to build it? There's the architect's fees, because it would be a one-off house built to suit the occupant. Wide doorways, an entrance without steps, and so on. What would it cost?"

"What are you talking about?" He looked at Terri Sabuli, but she didn't seem to know.

"Guess. What would it cost?"

Good God, he thought, humour her. He pulled out one of the chairs and sat down. "At a guess – a wild guess – a hundred and twenty thousand. You did say a bungalow, didn't you? No upper storey. And nowhere in the southeast at that price."

"Nowhere near the southeast. But a hundred and twenty's a little low. It has to be a *nice* house."

"All right. A hundred and fifty."

"And what does a car cost fitted out for a disabled driver? A paraplegic. Not one of those three-wheeled things. A proper car with passenger seat, back seat, and plenty of room in the boot. How much would that cost?"

He shook his head. Sabuli appeared to be starting to understand. He wasn't. "Depends on the car."

"It wouldn't have to be a posh car. Just roomy."

"All right. Say twelve and a half for the car, and perhaps as much again for the conversion. Twenty-five thousand."

"And a specially fitted bathroom in the house, lifting handles for the bedroom, a home computer with a modem for banking and so on. How much?"

"My God, how would I know? Say another twenty-five."

"That's two hundred thousand so far. What investment sum would produce a pre-tax income of at least fifteen thousand a year?"

That one was easier. He didn't need a wild guess. "Cleverly invested, something like one hundred thousand."

"Good. Your sums look like my sums. That's three hundred thousand. Now, I'd have to pay tax, wouldn't I? So that means I'd need five hundred thousand to clear three hundred thousand net."

Terri Sabuli understood. She wasn't laughing at his confusion. She had her eyes closed and her hand over her mouth. "Ruth," he said, "will you tell me what this is about?"

"The price. I'm on the payroll. If you want me to fly the bonus stage for the company, pay me a salary bonus. Five hundred thousand. That's the price."

Munro lowered the handset and cupped the mouthpiece. He held the thing in his lap. It made a symbolic phallus, frozen at the beginning of its collapse, for a man out to have his exploitative way – and then caught cold. Ruth Clifford had decided to bargain. He should have known. It was what he would do, in her position. She wasn't quite the innocent abroad. She'd been learning.

He looked at Sabuli. Her eyes were still closed. He turned to Coates. "How far is it from Florida to the UK?"

Coates shrugged. "From Michaels Field to the UK coast at her proposed landfall – four thousand eight hundred. Nearer five thousand to London."

Five thousand miles for half a million pounds. Not bad. But not impossible, either. She might have asked for the entire difference between the twenty million he needed from the bonus stage, and the twenty-four it would bring in. He lifted the handset again. "All right, I'll pay you a bonus of one hundred pounds per completed mile. The more you do, the more you get."

"I need provisions. It isn't paid with my monthly salary. The company might not exist by the time that's due. It's transferred to my bank account at noon tomorrow."

"That can be arranged."

"And it's paid even if I'm dead."

Sabuli's eyes opened.

"All right. Salary due to a deceased employee normally goes to their estate or nominated heir, unless there's no provision."

"My father. Pay it to my father."

"Right." The background noise suddenly disappeared. She'd cut the connection at her end. Slowly, he put the handset back on its hook. He looked up at Terri Sabuli. "Now," he said. "Would you care to tell me what that was about?"

Pattie Lee was still waiting in the BMW, blocking the car park entrance where the building gave some shelter from the drizzle. She wouldn't dump him, of course. No Michael, no password. No password – no money. He got in quickly to escape the rain, and twisted to close the passenger door. "All's well so far. Is our tail still parked down the street?"

"She is. She's parked illegally."

"Pity no one's clamped her. Oh well, off we go."

Pattie drove them through the midday traffic towards the City. A few cars behind them, the woman from Smith and Brown Associates kept pace in her blue Honda Accord. Once she jumped the lights so as not to lose them. You took your life in your hands when you did that in London. A dedicated private eye.

They arrived at the MT Holdings building and took the side entry. The entry was a dead-end providing access to MT's car park, and the parking for the merchant bank next door. As Pattie was swinging the nose of the BMW round to the right to descend the ramp, Michael looked past the back of her head restraint, through the rain on the window, and saw the detective's Honda crawl past the entry in the grip of the oh-so-slow, oh-so-busy stream of cars. Perfect.

The entrance gate wasn't working. Nobody's personal plastic was going to open it while the computer was down. Instead, one of the security staff was waiting at the bottom of the ramp to open the gate manually. He was standing under the shelter of the overhang. He was already pushing the button as Pattie was winding the electric window down in order to show her pass. The barrier swung up, a yellow and red clapperboard lifting across shadow. "Good day, Miss Lee," the security man said. "Good day, Mr Tranter."

Pattie started to drive through. Michael ducked his head to see out of the closing window. "Good day, Colin."

Colin smiled. Michael smiled. Make 'em love you to the end.

Pattie drove through the concrete labyrinth to the executive area behind the services core. She swung in beside the Volvo on the wide space reserved for Michael. She switched off the engine and they got out. Michael took the BMW key from her, and handed her the new one. They got into the Volvo. Pattie adjusted seat, mirrors and steering column height in the huge car. She'd never driven a Volvo 960 before, but to look at her face you wouldn't know. She started the engine.

They drove out of the car park. The exit barrier had a pressure strip activator, and was still functioning on automatic. It opened, and they left. Colin saw them drive up the ramp, of course, and waved. Michael waved back. It didn't matter. If anyone thought of asking Colin, he wouldn't know where they went, either. The private investigator certainly didn't.

Ruth went round Michaels Field, out over the turnpike in a lazy loop, safe and secure at six hundred feet. No stunt flying this time. An air armada went with her. There aren't that many moments when a horde of people can see someone actually making a little bit of history. Round the world. Solo. Non-stop. Not bad.

Now for the hardest bit.

Someone sitting in this cockpit must be absolutely mad. And there doesn't seem to be anyone here but me.

Angel liked leaning over gently and looking sidelong at the world. Such a change after all those thousands of linear miles. When Ruth straightened up the rudder and let the pressure off the stick, Angel just stayed there, right wingtip down a little, left wingtip up, with the artificial horizon askew in line with the real one. At the heavily laden start of it all, Angel had refused to roll. Now Angel liked it a lot. Had to be a result of the load coming off as the fuel burned away. The huge take-off weight had caused a lot of upcurve on the long, flexible wings. That had produced a lot of dihedral and made Angel far too stable against roll. Mile for mile, pound for pound, the weight had gradually drained away. Now the dihedral was gone.

Oh well. She pushed the stick slightly left to roll Angel level, then centred the stick again. Here came the first mile. Here came the first hundred pounds into the kitty. She was going to make her father pay for this. Her mother, too. She'd build the house. She'd buy the car. She'd send the big fat cheque. But they would never see her again.

The corks kept popping. Smoky condensation kept curling out of gun-barrel bottlenecks. Overwarm fizzy stuff frothed wastefully over the rims of plastic cups. People got delighted, changed hands, shook bubbles off their fingers. Even John joined in, trying to be a cheerful zombie. Even Mandy joined in.

Terri walked towards the door.

A stupid party streamer zipped over her shoulder and uncoiled down her blouse. Its corkscrewed end bounced purple between her thighs. Insulting little thing.

She turned, sweeping the streamer away as if it were some cobweb wrapped round her hair. "We're not celebrating." It was lost in the collective joy. "I *said* – we're not *celebrating!*"

Mandy turned. More of them turned. The noise died down. All the Angels slung on all the T-shirts hung motionless, borne up by bated breath.

"It's a world first. Great. Wonderful. Hooray. Hoo-bloody-ray. But we're not celebrating. Not yet. In seventeen hours, when Ruth is safe. In seventeen hours."

She turned away and went out of the door. She headed along the corridor for the stairs to the loo. The happiness resumed very slowly in the room she'd left. That spoiled it for them good and proper.

Munro arrived at his office and dumped his jacket over the back of his great big executive chair. He went to the window and looked out. Drizzle on the window pane, drizzle on the traffic far below. A great day to go down in the world. Behind him, Geraldine Trayhorn turned to close the door –

Ripley followed them in. "Mr Pierce is on your private line. He says it's urgent."

Munro turned from the window and trudged back to the desk. The clean-green carpet was too soft. It took too much work to walk across it if you were tired. Ripley went out and closed the door. Geraldine dropped into one of the conference chairs. She was long past being an ill-at-ease subordinate in his office.

He picked up the phone. "Mr Pierce, what news have you got?"

"Good news and bad," said Pierce's voice. "The good is that the Serious Fraud Office are getting into very high gear about this. They're going to move exceptionally fast, considering they've only known about it for a bit more than two hours."

"Good." He parked his free hand in his trouser pocket, standing at his desk in his shirt-sleeves, tie undone, grimacing manfully into the phone like some magnate in a sex-and-money soap opera. There was no sex in his busy life, and before much longer there might not be any money, either. "And the bad?"

"Ah – we've lost Tranter and Lee."

He closed his eyes for a moment. "You've *lost* them?"

"Our employee tailed them to the Orbis building, and then to the MT building. She saw them drive into the car park. They were in Tranter's BMW, which apparently is still there."

"Yes. I've just seen it myself."

"However, they don't seem to be in the building."

"I know that, Mr Pierce. I checked on my way up. Didn't your employee see them leave?"

"Unfortunately not. Traffic and all that. They switched cars, I believe."

"So they've given you the slip."

"I'm rather afraid – yes, they have."

"So Tranter's making his run for it. Before the police get out after him."

"Yes – he is. I don't suppose you have any idea where he might be likely to go?"

South America, South Africa, Hong Kong, Singapore – who the hell could know? "Wait a minute." He looked at Geraldine. "What was that message he got while he was doing his jack-in-a-box act?"

"Tickets. I mean a flight. Gatwick. This afternoon."

"He might have booked on some flight leaving Gatwick this afternoon. It won't be Orbis Air. They're going to be grounded any minute."

"Right. That's what we need. I'll get on to the police straight away." The phone went dead. No ceremony, not even from nice young Mr Pierce. He must be getting worried about MT's ability to pay his fee.

Munro put the phone back on its cradle. He put both hands in his trouser pockets and stared at the hopeful green carpet. "Well? What do you think of things now?"

"I'm hungry." She stood up. "I'll fetch something. What do you want?"

Two minutes later, reception asked if he'd accept a visit from Sylvia Symes. He said yes. Three minutes after that, she arrived at the executive floor. She came in with a cigarette in her hand. She parked herself in the middle of his office.

"Can't stay for more than a minute or two. Lunch break. Only I haven't got time for lunch." She had a wild look – a conspirator caught in a bigger trap, losing loads of her personal money and unable to do a thing about it, and high on the fascinating fear of it all. "Had to see you, though." She drew on her cigarette, and then sucked in the smoke.

"What's the assessment?" he asked. "In the dealers' rooms."

"Toilet time." Sylvia extended a varnished thumbnail, turned it down, and poked it at the floor. "At Rowe Spitta Pitts they want me to sell and protect the clients. The clients want to sell. I've been saying wait for the recovery, instead of selling at the lowest price. After Simmington's lot pulled the plug, I couldn't have held them if the SIB hadn't come up with the period of grace. Everyone was screaming to get out – except the Bryce McFadden Group. They've sent constant instructions not to sell."

"I see." The Group was so big it could afford to lose a few million on MT-Orbis – if it had a good enough reason for hanging on.

"Don't worry about the Bryce McFadden Group, Robert. Worry about the slide. It's a natural pause in the trading day at the moment, and they're catching their breath and getting ready to pass the buck to New York. But if New York, Tokyo and Hong Kong merely go down to parity with the London levels overnight, that will be seen here as confirmation of the worst. When trading opens tomorrow, the whole lot will go." She looked at her cigarette, which was growing a stalk of ash. She looked round for somewhere to get rid of it.

Munro shrugged. "There are no ashtrays at MT."

"Damn. Forgot." She held the cigarette vertical to retain the ash. "This smoking's getting worse. Every time I tangle with him, Michael buggers me up even more." She started eyeing the plants.

"You could put it down one of the loos," he said.

"Suppose I'll have to. Toilet time for everything. Look,

Robert – the thing is." She risked another drag on the cigarette. The ash stayed put. "It might be tomorrow. It might even be today. When I can't hold my clients any longer, and one of them *insists* – well, they have lots of shares in all levels of MT-Orbis. When they start to sell, it will help clinch the end. When my clients sell – I'm going to sell my stuff, as well."

He nodded.

"But I'll phone you." A fragile phallus of ash broke free and dropped to the eco-green carpet. "Bugger it! Sorry." Sylvia started treading it into the carpet with her shoe. "I'll phone you when I'm going to sell. Then for God's sake, sell what's left of your stake, too."

FIFTY-NINE

Mission Time 101.15, UK time 15.15, one and three-quarter hours from Florida. The last of the lingering escorts turned back thirty minutes ago. Ruth had the world to herself – ocean and sky, and no abode for the eye. Four hundred and forty miles flown already, and forty-four thousand pounds earned. Easy.

But the sun's antics were disconcerting. It was going to climb on the right, go up over her shoulder, and come down behind her on the left. She wouldn't see the sunset without straining a neck too stiff to turn. She was no longer chasing the sun, but going against it. Chasing the sun had been good. But this seemed ominous.

The heading was off – eight degrees. It shouldn't be. The rudder indicator said the thing was centred. The trim tab was centred. She hadn't put her feet on the rudder pedals for fifteen minutes. The heading shouldn't have changed. It had never happened before. Not in one hundred and one non-stop hours.

She put her feet on the pedals and tickled the heading back on line. She took her feet off the pedals. She started shuffling round in the seat in an attempt to get some food from the storage behind her. If the stiffness got much worse, she'd starve.

Ocean and sky, no abode for the eye. Emptiness, Angel and me.

Time Lucifer did his dive again.

Outside the window, fine rain was going past on its way to play with the pedestrians below. Inside, Curtis Gupta had moved Michael's laptop, still connected by cable, to the summit of the pile of paper beside his desktop machine, and was entering something through the office computer's keyboard. Geraldine Trayhorn was sitting with a crinoline of fanfold sheets draped round her. She was marking the printouts with a red pen. The cap of the pen was trapped between her lips like a synthetic rosebud.

Rosebud. Gupta had already tried that.

Geraldine looked up as he closed the door. "News?" she asked, whistling sibilants round the cap of the pen.

"Those shares," Munro said. "The ones I transferred to you. Call the broker and sell them while they're still worth the effort."

"Can't." She took the cap out of her mouth. "Can't afford to. I know they're only a handful, but I've lost five hundred on them already. That's half what I owe you for them."

"You don't owe me a penny. Sell the things."

Geraldine just looked at him. Why wouldn't her face move away from its neutral gaze? A shade of an attitude. Surprise, distrust, contempt, infatuation – anything at all.

"Hey!" Gupta suddenly clapped his hands over his head. "Yahoo! Look at this! It's *coming*!"

On the screen, amber in infinite grey, print was tracing itself out in scrolling lines too fast to read.

"Curtis!" It put life in her voice, at least. "You did it!"

"Yes, yes, yes! See?" He turned to Munro. "I got fed up

407

with arithmetic. Tried a hunch. This MICTRA-double-X password. Some of the secret stuff responds to *without trace*, and this other stuff has to be connected. So I took the *trace* out of MICTRA-double-X. The version that works is MIC-triple-zero-X. Bingo!"

"It's stopped." Geraldine was leaning so far forward that she was crushing fanfolds in her lap. "It's *stopped*."

"Shit." Gupta looked at the screen. He shook his head. "It's decrypted again. Double decrypted. But it's still *locked*."

Munro shrugged.

"Sod it." Gupta waved his hands over the keyboard. "Sod it!" Then he typed *Rosebud* and pressed *enter*.

```
Error
These directories are still keylocked
Please enter the correct password
```

They'd left the sticky drizzle of London far behind, but now it was going to rain here, as well. The whiteness of the sky was turning dull, there was a heavy sweetness in the garden.

Pattie Lee locked the Volvo and walked in her flat-heeled, dainty blue shoes across the gravel towards the garage. Such a shame to roll the huge Volvo over the flower bed, but there had to be room to pass. A pity there was no time to leave an apologetic note for Mrs Kenton to find when she turned up tomorrow. She'd probably find the police, in fact, but that wouldn't mend dead flowers. It had been a pretty garden. Pity to say goodbye.

Pattie opened the garage doors. No up-and-over clamorous maws in designer executive country – a pair of hinged, white, wooden doors. She went inside. She left a silence so pure you could hear the air thickening. Nothing but the smell of warm Volvo mixed with crushed flowers, mown grass and imminent rain.

The Renault 19 started inside the garage. Switching cars again was a double security against pursuit. They were going to drive to Wragby while everyone else was still waiting for them to turn up and collect their tickets at Gatwick. Pattie would help him fly the Solomaster to Schiphol, then the next stage was their early morning plane to Oslo. But while Pattie tried to find where he was hiding at Schiphol, and the destination of any alternative flight he might have booked, Michael would be making the hundred-mile taxi drive to Brussels, where his Bangkok departure was due out at dawn.

With money, you can afford any number of tricks.

The red Renault crept out of the garage and crunched past the Volvo. The gravel under its tyres made more noise than the engine. It passed him and halted with its nose pointing at the open gate. He started to walk round the back of the car to reach the passenger door. But the engine stopped. Pattie opened the driver's door and got out. She left the door open. A drop of rain, the first drop, hit the inside sill – a tiny thud on dense plastic.

"Shall I put the Volvo in the garage?"

Michael shook his head. "No need. By the time they think of coming here, it won't matter."

"Right." She walked past him and headed for the garage. A raindrop tapped the roof of the Volvo. More, like invisible pebbles, rattled into the trees screening the road.

Pattie closed one door. Its corner thudded against the stop. "Are you sure they won't find the last password?" She walked three steps to the second door and pulled it round. "It would be a shame if they got to the money first." The door slammed softly home.

"They won't find it. All my passwords are connected, aren't they? They're logically derived, or they're childhood references and so on. There's a method behind them. A constant psychology."

"So they can permutate and speculate." She was coming towards him, passing the Volvo. It had splayed amoeba beads on its roof. "They can find it."

"Not this one. It doesn't connect to any of the others. Not logically, not associatively." He shrugged. He was learning to shrug with his right shoulder alone, while leaving the other one in peace. "It won't fit any system."

Pattie nodded and adjusted the strap of her handbag over her shoulder. "Something to do with Angel, isn't it?"

Smart thinker. He grinned. "My poor fallen Angel."

Pattie nodded again, and passed by.

Too smart. *Far* too smart. Sidetrack her. "Though that isn't the actual password, of course."

"Of course." Pattie reached the door of the Renault. She unslung her handbag, ready to get in. "But it's near enough, isn't it?" She stared at the roof of her car, then at the garden, then the cottage. In the faint rattle from the vanguard of the rain, he knew the basics of what she was going to say next. She looked at him. She said it. "Well, I can't say it hasn't been interesting. It's been very interesting indeed."

He opened his mouth. But he didn't say anything.

"Goodbye, Michael." She turned.

She was his driver. His hand for the throttle and the flaps. He couldn't get out without her! And the bitch was going to *leave*!

He ran in a beach of gravel. He grabbed her by the arm. He hauled her away from the door. He dragged her back past the side of her own car. He was a one-armed man, neither heavy nor strong, but she was too small to resist.

He stopped, holding her arm, clamping flesh against bone. It seemed to be hurting her.

"Michael!"

He shook her. "Don't try to dump me!" How was he going to get in the car, without letting her race away and leave him standing? Get the keys from the ignition. First the keys, then get in the car – the only escape – then wait for her to get in, too.

"Michael! You're an intellectual criminal, not a mugger. This isn't the way you behave!"

"*Isn't it?*" He shook her again. Her head rolled, her hair swung. "Surprise! What are you? A kung fu expert as well?"

"Of course not." Her free hand was swinging round.

Her free hand held the handbag. Its strap floated in trail.
The handbag hit his left elbow.

He didn't know –

– that it could hurt so much.

He was down on his knees, looking at a beautiful world.
Raindrops, one by one, turned quarters and halves of white
gravel dark. The rain was making its pattering sound. A cold
drop hit the back of his neck. Chunks of gravel dug into his
knees. But it didn't matter. Because from left shoulder to left
fingertips was a right-angled furnace of flame.

As if the blow had spun the bits of bone about their bolts.

"Now I know for certain. Thankyou, Michael."

He lifted his head. He looked at her neat blue shoes with
blue laces, her blue tights, her blue skirt and her white blouse.
He looked at her face, impassively Chinese and framed with
straight, bobbed hair. He looked at her dark, dark eyes.

"I suppose you might try driving your Volvo, since it's an
automatic. So I'll keep the key. If I were you, I'd phone
for a taxi and try making a run for it by train. Where did
you plan to dump me? Schiphol? Or the next stop? You're
very transparent, Michael, because you're greedy. And I've
studied you."

Studied him, had she? He tried to rock himself up off his
knees. He got as far as a half-squat. Pattie took a step back, out
of reach. But he had no intention of going for her. He couldn't.
The movement had jolted his left arm and set light to it again.
"You think," he said through his teeth, "you can work out the
password. But you can't. And you need the decrypt programs.
I'm the only one who knows the programs."

"I know that, Michael." She shook her head. "I don't need
you at all." She patted the back of the Renault. "The data's
in here, on your disks in your bag. But I made my own copies
of the data and the programs. Everything but the password to
unlock it all. Now I can do that, too. Goodbye."

She turned away. She walked to the open driver's door.
Her backside swung slightly, sweetly. It was hard-as-nails
fun while it lasted. All the time, he thought he was winning

the manipulation war. By comparison with Pattie, computers were easy.

She got in and closed the door. She started the engine. Exhaust fumes blasted into his face. Tyres ground gravel. When he squinted again through his eyelids, the Renault was turning out of the gate into the lane. It disappeared.

The rain was louder. His shoulders were wet. The stink of exhaust drifted away. In its place came the rising perfume of freshly wetted earth, heavy as sleep.

Pierce called on his private line at four thirty. "I'm afraid things are blank at the moment. The police tell me the Gatwick bookings were real, but neither Tranter nor Lee has turned up for the flight. For the moment they've vanished without trace."

Without trace seemed to be Michael's speciality. "What about the foreign angle, the other end of the fraud routes?"

"Hong Kong, Buenos Aires and all that? We're pressing ahead. But I rather have to tell you that quick results are very unlikely, now. We're going to have to wait for the police investigation to grind into gear. The thing is, the Serious Fraud Office will want to look into it in a big way, so we have to be much more careful. Some of our methods have been a bit illegal. You see what I mean?"

"I see what you mean, Mr Pierce. We don't want to get hung for tracing what Tranter's been doing."

"Precisely. Involving the police does rather restrict our freedom of movement. I'll ring the minute there's anything new."

"Thankyou."

He put the receiver down. The message for Michael at the Orbis building had been a plant. It had seemed so believable, such an innocent gaffe. He'd made it perfect by paying for real tickets on a real flight, convincing the police that Gatwick was where he'd turn up. Michael had made fools of everyone all over again.

What kind of message might Michael have left on the

computer? Munro looked at his desktop. It had been disconnected from the network as soon as trouble hit yesterday, and he hadn't used it since. But earlier it had been on line as usual. What surprise might Michael have slipped inside?

The intercom buzzed. "Miss Symes wants to speak to you. She says it's extremely urgent."

"I'll take it." He reached for the internal phone – and then stopped. Only one thing could be urgent now. At least one of her clients had insisted on selling. The bottom was finally falling out, and MT-Orbis was bound for the abyss. He didn't want to hear it. And he didn't want to make the next decision – sell his own shares while they still had a quotable price, or stay on board as an investor until the bitter, empty end?

He lifted the receiver.

"Robert? It's Sylvia. Have you heard what's going on?"

"What's going on?" He could feel a space in his throat, isolating him from his own voice. He was finally frightened.

"Someone's started to buy."

"Buy what?"

"Shares. Your shares. Well, lower-tier subsidiaries. Not MT and not Siltech or Orbis Air. But your shares are up a fraction – the ones where the buying's going on, that is."

"Buying?" his voice said for him. "Since when?"

"Since about four, apparently, but people have only just started to notice. It's very well-timed – not too long before close of the day, and not early enough to lift the New York prices before they can start buying there, too."

Someone was buying MT-Orbis shares? It had to be someone with a reason to believe there was still a future in the company. It had to be someone with nerve enough to wait until the price had dropped by more than half – and clever enough to do so, in order to pick up twice as much for the money. A significant buy required a very large amount of mobile money, and would take days to prepare. The MT-Orbis collapse hadn't been running for twenty-four hours. So someone must have been ready and waiting. "Who's buying, Sylvia?"

413

A long silence.

"Who is it, Sylvia? The Bryce McFadden Group?"

"Robert – it isn't what you think. It isn't anything to do with me. I know they've only just made us agents for their existing holdings, but they aren't doing the buying through Rowe Spitta Pitts. If they were, I'd have known about it from the start. I think – I think they were hoping some of my other clients with MT-Orbis shares would start to sell, dropping the price even further. If they'd started to buy through us, I'd have had a cast-iron argument to keep the others from selling. Anyway – well, Bryce McFadden have decided not to wait any longer. I suppose they didn't want to risk you going into liquidation by tomorrow."

"If they aren't buying through Rowe Spitta Pitts, Sylvia, how do you know it's the Group?"

"They're buying through another house. Someone there tipped me off not to dump my own shares. So I called Bryce McFadden for an explanation, since we're supposed to be agenting for them with respect to MT-Orbis."

"And what was the explanation?"

"They didn't give me one. They – offered me management of their full portfolio in MT-Orbis, plus control of their buy-in. We disagreed about the Orbis Air move, but they think I know MT-Orbis better than any other consultant."

She was going to play the predator's game. "I see."

"Robert? *Please?* I said no. I turned it down. My boss is *furious*. Think of the commission I've thrown away. A *fortune*. I'm going to be out on the street if I'm not careful. But I said no."

He waited a while. A little bit of honesty and decency, and possibly the dead-end of a good career. "Thankyou, Sylvia. If it turns out you do need help – and if I'm in any position to help – I will. What does the Group's move look like? Am I fighting a takeover now, on top of everything?"

"I don't know. They're doing a dawn raid at the end of the day, as it were. I assume they'll go to fifteen percent in most of your subsidiaries, then accept the statutory pause.

They might not be out for a full takeover. But they want a big chunk of you."

"I see. Which house is it they're buying through?"

"Longman Short. Geoffrey Simmington's joined the move. I'm really sorry, Robert."

SIXTY

"There he goes again. What's left of him. Have you any idea what it's like, Terri? I see a hallucination – in broad daylight – over and over again. I know what it's about. I'm in Angel. Lucifer was an angel. Lucifer got big ideas. I've got big ideas. One helping of fame isn't enough. I know perfectly well what it's about. But that doesn't stop it."

"Does that matter, Ruth?"

"It matters! I see it. I know what it is. But it's just as real. I see it just the same. I talk to you rationally, but it goes on happening. Out of the sky, into the sea, splash. That's frightening. That's really – *really* – frightening."

"But you know it can't hurt you. And you aren't going crazy. You're just very, very tired."

"I think – it's an omen. It looks like an omen."

"To hell with omens. A hundred pounds a mile, with a tail wind to help. You must have made a hundred and fifty thousand by now."

"I've stopped counting. It was a bad idea. I shouldn't have done this."

"Then turn round. Go back. You're only a third of the way across."

"That's a worse idea."

"Well then, stop worrying about Lucifer. You'll be in

darkness in a couple of hours. You won't be able to see him."

"That's supposed to make me feel better, is it? There's another thing about the dark. I'll be on instruments. I mean, Angel's starting to behave funny."

"What do you mean, behave funny?"

"Angel sort of rolls a little bit. And the heading drifts. I think Angel yaws. That didn't happen before. Straight and level and steady, that's how we used to fly. Now Angel sort of slops about a bit. In the dark I won't have the real horizon to help me. I mean, I'm getting tired. Really tired. It's so easy to lose interest in instruments. Little glows in front of you in the dark. It's ever so easy."

"I'll have a word with John about it when he comes back. He's taking a break at the moment. I'll have a word when he gets back."

Ten o'clock. Ripley went home a long time ago. She'd spent the day keeping people off his back, until the evening finally calmed the City, the company, and the panicked upper echelons of MT Holdings. Then she escaped to home and family. She left him a pot of fresh coffee. Now it was almost empty and entirely cold.

New York was getting ready to close, with MT-Orbis shares stuck at half-value, and someone finishing off a buying raid there. The Bryce McFadden Group again. The Group had already been planning to take a bite out of MT-Orbis, and then the unbelievable happened. No buyers, no defensive strength, and shares to scoop up at half-price. Careless companies shoot themselves in the foot. But it rarely happens that a company shoots itself in the head – which was what MT-Orbis did, courtesy of Michael Tranter, its founder.

He might as well see what peripheral fireworks Michael had buried in his personal computer.

Munro switched on. He poured another cold coffee while the machine muttered to itself. Then he typed *SLSS* and pressed *enter*.

```
Silsys Systemizer ST DOS 4.0
Copyright Siltech Systems 1989
Customized: Munro
Do you want to network? (Y/N)
```

He tapped *N* and then *enter*. The prompt for selecting a directory was supposed to appear. It didn't.

Hello, Bob. How did you like my little surprise? Clever, wasn't it? Think you can keep the ship afloat while you try to get rid of the problem? Not without an awful lot of damage. By now you'll have worked out that I was planning to leave. Great big mess in the economy, you insisting on a deep look at our finances, and so on. I had Pattie plant the rumour with Geo-Petro, so that you'd bring the project forward to scotch the scare. Sneaky, eh? I was going to leave the company safe in your hands, but then you hit on this nasty idea of trying to take it from me all by yourself. Oh well, do as you would be done by. You shouldn't have tried staging a palace revolution. Après moi and all that. This message will erase in twenty seconds. It will not copy, print or store. Without trace, you might say. I haven't done anything else in here. Bye!

The message started to dissolve, like deletions in a tray of bacteria dosed with penicillin. The letters went in order, alphabetical bubbles bursting. The last to go were twenty or so *y*s, popping silently one after the other.

The world's foremost hacker had finesse.

John Coates had some new printout spread over all the rest of the stuff on the computer table. Graphics sheets were propped at the back against a teetering row of cheap and empty champagne bottles. Mission Control was starting to look like a tip.

Terri pulled on her shoes and then stretched in her chair. "How does it look?"

John shook his head. "I can't find any problem in these figures. According to the design calculations and the flight test results, Angel should be stable."

"So, what's the conclusion?"

"I think it's just that Ruth is far too tired to be flying anything at all. But we know that."

"We do." Terri decided to stand up. It was half-past ten on her third – no, her fourth – night at this nonsense, and she had no intention of worrying about something no one could put right. "Oh well, it's my turn to sleep. When Mandy gets back from ITN, tell her *not* to wake me. I am *tired*. Ruth decides to go on, and that means we all have to go on. Why did Ruth Clifford have to happen to me?"

"I thought you were getting to like her?"

"Admire. Respect. Understand. I never *like* people, John. It's dangerous." She turned away and headed for the door.

Out in the dark corridor, she was making for the stairs when someone came up the flight from the floor below. He came up slowly, almost hauling himself by the rail. In the dim light he seemed in disguise. His clothes looked as though they'd been thrown on. His hair appeared neat, but that was because it was cropped close to his head in tight and crinkly curls. His jaw had at least two days of stubble, and his eyes were red.

He'd come back, like failure's ghost, to haunt the mission at the end of its run. The take-off was a near fiasco, the design of the canoe assembly had been fundamentally flawed. All of it Chester's work. Since he fled, the mission had at least been mechanically sound. But now Chester Alby was back.

"What do you want?"

He shuffled towards her. "There's a problem."

Terri took two steps backwards. Chester's breath was a stale cocktail of whisky and wine and quite a lot else. There seemed to be a garnish of coffee involved as well. "You've been – bloody hell, you've been on a *binge*."

"Drink problem. Comes and goes. Been a bit bad this week." He shuffled closer.

"It's been a bad week." She stepped back another pace. "Is that the reason Michael passed you over as backup pilot? Did he know you're a – you've got a problem?"

"Course he knows. I've just got the problem now and

then. He never made a thing of it. Knows I do good work."

"You do lousy work, Chester. If Michael knew, what was he keeping you on for? His token black?"

"You should talk." Chester took a look at the door to Mission Control, and began to aim himself at it. "Michael's the best. Only person I've got. He wouldn't give me the push. He knows I can design aircraft for him. I'm good. He's the best."

Terri shook her head. Chester had to be the only senior employee of MT-Orbis who still didn't know Michael was a crook. Michael had made a good job of destroying the company, and Michael was currently being sought with some urgency by the police. "Look, Chester – are you going to turn round nicely and go home again? Or am I going to have to call someone from security?"

Chester looked at her, more or less. The unsteady gaze of his bloodshot eyes was enough to bring tears of sympathy. "Angel. There's a problem."

"Look, will you just go away?" She didn't want another worry, a drunken, broken, washed-up and no doubt eventually weeping wreck of a man. She wanted *sleep*.

"I said – there's a problem – with Angel."

"What kind of problem?"

"Stability. Angel's unstable at very light loadings."

Count to ten, she told herself. Slowly, for your sanity's sake. I come out of the light, where a keyed-up competent engineer says there's no such problem – and out here in the dark I meet this ghost, who says there is.

"I heard on the radio. Ruth Clifford is flying the bonus stage. The loadings get lighter on the bonus stage. The last of the fuel is used. Angel isn't safe now."

Chester's ghost wasn't going to fade away. It stood there, lumpen as dishevelled clay. She blinked, but it refused to go. If she gave it a push, it would just fall over and lie there. It wouldn't disappear. "Look, John's just been over the figures and stuff. Angel isn't unstable."

"I – fixed the figures."

Terri closed her eyes. Overloaded, and hiding in her personal darkness, she asked, "Why?"

"Michael wanted Angel to fly round the world. He wanted Angel in a hurry. So I built Angel for him. I couldn't let him down. He looks after me, he's given me all my chances. He's seen what I can do. But I couldn't get Angel right – not in the time. There just wasn't enough time. So I left the faults in. Not the canoe assembly – fucked that up good and proper, didn't I? But I knew about the stability. I fixed the figures so no one could see – not even Michael. Angel isn't right. Angel's only nearly right."

Terri opened her eyes again. Chester was staring past her towards the night-time window at the far end of the corridor. "If you knew there was something wrong – if you're infatuated with Michael, for God's sake – how could you let him fly in the aircraft? How could you ever think of letting him do it?"

"He'd be safe. He'd fly round the world, and just before the end I'd tell him I'd found out I was wrong. He mustn't fly the bonus stage because then he'd be in danger. He'd land in Florida. I'd feel terrible. He'd forgive me because he'd know he put me under too much time pressure. He'd have his world record and his charity stunt and everything. He'd be all right."

Oh no, she thought. He isn't rambling. This is real. "Why didn't you tell us before Ruth took over the flight?"

"I don't like her. She's no good. She was the only one with him when he fell, wasn't she? I know she was angry. And I know *she* wanted to fly. And I think – I think – he didn't fall. She *pushed* him. I don't like her at all."

Jealousy, Terri thought. Ruth – mainly – had been the one getting into bed with Michael, instead of unrequited Chester. "So you thought you'd just let her fly off and kill herself?"

"No. I didn't say anything because that would get to Michael, and he'd know I'd let him down. I thought she'd give up part of the way. Australia. Africa. I was sure she couldn't do it. Then I heard she was going to finish the

420

mission and land in Florida. All right, doesn't matter, she's better than I thought. Land in Florida and she's safe. And no one would have to know about the problem. No one would know I got it wrong. Not even Michael."

"I suppose no one was going to remember that Angel almost didn't take-off? Or that the canoe assembly nearly killed her?"

Chester waved his hand, dispelling irrelevant vapours. "Then I heard she's flying the bonus stage." He made a second attempt at aiming himself towards the door. "Is John there? Please?"

SIXTY-ONE

At eleven o'clock Munro decided to leave. There was no point in haunting the office any longer. He might as well go to his club, get a stiff drink, and half a night's sleep.

The phone started to ring in Ripley's office. Then the switch sent it through to his own desk. It was the private line.

"Mr Munro? This is Darren Pierce. I'm sorry to be disturbing you so late, but there's been a couple of developments."

Developments. He sat down in his chair again. It didn't sink into its suspension the way it should – as if he'd been thinning out, wasting away, in keeping with his company. "Well?"

"It's rather confusing, I'm afraid. The first point is that the police have been to Tranter's house. His Volvo is there, and as far as can be seen, so are most of his things. What they're most excited about is the computer. But I have to say that with an operator of Tranter's calibre, there's little chance of anything useful being still in the machine."

He didn't need decorations round the facts, not this late in the evening near the end of the second worst week in his life. Only divorce had beaten this. "They drove to the house, dumped the Volvo, and disappeared. Does anyone know where they went?"

"That's the thing, you see. Lee's car was left behind at the house when they set out for London, but it wasn't there when the police arrived. However, they found it about an hour ago – at Manchester Airport."

"I see. And the occupants have flown?"

"Literally, yes. Lee seems to have boarded a flight for Paris, and there she changed to a connection for Cairo. She won't have landed in Cairo yet, but I can tell you now – there's no chance at all that our police will have sorted out an arrest warrant before she's moved on. She's got clean away, I'm afraid."

"And what about Michael Tranter?"

"Well, now – that's the funny thing. He doesn't seem to have taken any flight from Manchester. He's completely disappeared."

Michael had turned himself into a master of disappearances. He and Pattie Lee had separated, and he'd taken an alternative escape route. "He hasn't left from a different airport, I suppose?"

"Well, no – he hasn't. Nor any seaport. To be perfectly honest, I'm flummoxed as to how he'd want to continue. Even if he's prepared a false identity with a passport and what have you, with his injury he'll be extremely conspicuous wherever he goes. Do you see what I'm getting at, Mr Munro?"

"What are you getting at, Mr Pierce?"

"I haven't any evidence at this stage – but it rather looks to me as though Lee might have dumped him."

Michael Tranter's come unstuck, Munro thought. His plans have gone awry! His oh-so-clever frauds were threatened by the approach of the accountant, so he prepared the most spectacular vanishing act of the century. Then he fell down some stairs. So he planned a new escape, led us all by the nose, and got clean away. Michael's been infallible.

Except that somewhere along the line he missed something – and Pattie Lee's kicked him out through the gap! Poor old Michael.

He'd even got so bored with the ease of his success, that he'd started leaving clues behind to taunt his dim-witted victims.

Geraldine Trayhorn wasn't there, but Curtis Gupta was, sitting in one chair with his feet on the other, and staring glumly at the screen. The computer seemed to be checking random passwords – and getting nowhere. Gupta began to wake up. His eyes were open, but the mind behind them hadn't been.

"*Après moi.*" Munro pointed at the keyboard. "Try *après moi.*"

"What?" Gupta got his feet off the chair. They dropped and hit the floor harder than he'd intended, leather-heeled brogues slapping short-pile carpet. "What language is that?"

"French," said Geraldine's voice.

Munro turned. She was standing in the doorway, a cup of vending machine coffee in each hand. She was starting to yawn. The yawn got so wide that it almost closed her eyes. With her mouth stuck wide open she looked less frighteningly self-controlled. By degrees she got her mouth closed again. She shook her head slightly. "*Après moi le déluge.*"

"Oh." Gupta was doing something to the keyboard. The automatic password testing stopped dead on the screen. "What does it mean?"

"Something in French." She came past Munro with the two coffees. "Hello."

"It means," Munro said, "after me, the flood. In other words, after me there's nothing left. The world might as well end. One of the French kings said it."

Gupta looked unconvinced.

"I'm the greatest," Geraldine offered. She put the coffees on the corner of the paper-covered desk.

Gupta shrugged. He swung his chair back to the keyboard. "How do I spell it?"

There's no education these days, Munro thought. "Can you do accents? I mean, can you use the IBM numbers in a password?"

"Um – no, not in ST DOS matched to an English keyboard. It would count as three keystrokes."

"Right. A-P-R-E-S-space-"

"No space in the password."

"All right. M-O-I."

Gupta typed the last letter, and then pressed *enter*.

Error
These directories are still keylocked
Please enter the correct password

"Shit," Geraldine said, and sipped her coffee. "Try the second part."

"Right." Gupta's hands hovered. "How do I spell it?"

"L-E," Munro began. Forget the space, forget the acute accent. "D-E-L-U-G-E."

"Just like English." Gupta pressed *enter*.

Error

"Sod it." Gupta shook his head. Then he stood up and considered his coffee. Even the thread of steam coming off it looked synthetic. "I think – " He looked at Munro. "If it's all right with you, I'll take a little break. Walk up and down the corridors for a while. Good hunch, by the way."

"Thanks," Munro said. Now he was getting consoling pats on the head from a junior deep down in a sub-department. We're all tired, he thought. We're losing our awareness of hierarchy.

"Well – " Curtis Gupta grabbed his jacket and headed for the door. "Back soon."

Geraldine was stifling another yawn. "It feels like that. A flood. Sweeping MT-Orbis away."

424

Munro shook his head. "Not clean away. The Bryce McFadden Group has started buying up our shares."

"Oh." She sipped her coffee, then made a face. "Takeover?"

"Possibly. More probably a carve-up on dictated terms. Buy into choice subsidiaries and prise them loose."

"Sounds bad." She peered into the coffee cup. "Look, this stuff is just awful. And I'm done for. So are you. It's after eleven, so why not call it a day?"

"I'm intending to."

She nodded. "Don't go to the club."

He swallowed. Another crunch, good God, was coming.

"My place isn't splendid." She was looking at him with slightly speculative eyes. "Just the upper half of a house in East Finchley – one of the grotty parts, off the end of Fortis Green. But it's a self-contained flat. It's got more to offer than a room at your club." She put the coffee back on the corner of the desk. "And it's friendlier."

It would be the start of something whose outcome he couldn't predict. It might make a fool of him, it might hurt. It was another human being trying to get a look inside his life. It meant a surrendering of some of the control. It was letting in a little weakness again. That had never been easy.

"Look." She picked a pen off the desk and started to write on one of the memo pads sticking out from the printout discards. "I'll leave Curtis my number, just in case there's any news." She was leaning over the desk, blouse loose, back curved, skirt taut. He didn't stand a chance. "And don't worry," she said while writing. "I promise I won't call you Daddy."

SIXTY-TWO

Mission Time 112.00, UK time 02.00 on Friday. Lucifer was keeping her waiting. He was delaying his night-time dive.

Perhaps he was planning to take her down, too.

The delay might be Angel's fault. It wouldn't be easy swooping on a wobbling target, even one armed with flashing lights.

Ruth kept losing the heading and having to bring it back on line. It would drift a degree or two. Slowly, she would notice. As she watched, another degree would go. As she checked through in her mind, which wanted to sleep, which wanted its dreams, which besieged her last refuge of alertness with a dense darkness – as she checked through what she ought to do, the heading swung another two or three degrees. Each time it took longer to decide which way to push the rudder, longer to do it, and longer to centre it again on the line. She was so nearly asleep that she'd started to overshoot, obliging herself to correct back. She was keeping the course like a snake trying to straighten its tail.

Angel was too eager to turn. Chester told John, and John told her. The long nose and the short tail were out of balance. When an aircraft starts to yaw, slewing sideways to its line of flight, air hits against the side of the nose and the tail. The sideways pressure on the nose tries to push it further round, worsening the yaw. The sideways pressure on the tail tries to straighten it up again, cancelling the yaw. In a conventional design the tail is longer, the tail force greater, and the tail wins. The yaw is cancelled. The aircraft is stable.

Angel had a long nose and a short tail. The advantage was reversed. In a yaw, the force on the nose won and the yaw worsened. Left to itself, Angel would swing into a flat turn, and eventually stall as the airflow over the wings broke down.

The only way to beat the yaw was to put a huge fin on top of the short tail, a great blade pulling through the air and catching so much side force that it beat the lever of the nose. But Chester had designed the tail fin too small, because by reducing the size he reduced the drag, which cut fuel consumption – which was the crucial measure for flying round the world. So Angel was unstable, had no yaw resistance, was far too eager to turn.

It hadn't mattered when there were thousands of litres of fuel on board. The fuel mass had provided inertia to dampen any random swing of the fuselage. The only turns Angel had made were under rudder control at the pilot's command. Now Angel was an empty shell and the sullen inertia had gone. The instability showed.

It was more or less the same with roll. The huge initial weight of fuel had overloaded the flexible wings. It had produced an exaggerated dihedral and a refusal to roll. Now the mass of fuel had been used up, Angel was light as a feather and the wings were unstressed. The upward curve of the dihedral had gone. If a gust tipped Angel to one side, the aircraft would just sit there, leaning over. Without correction the roll would steepen until the wings lost lift – and Angel fell.

Chester had done it to her again.

The bitterest thing was that she'd seen it herself, months ago on Angel's first fullscale test flight. With light ballast, Angel had wobbled in the air. Chester had deliberately ignored it, covering up the fault. Michael had chosen not to notice – after all, he never intended to fly any further than the Indian Ocean, so he didn't need to delay the project for a major redesign to correct an error which would never come into effect. Michael and Chester had joined in a conspiracy of simultaneous silence. After that first flight, they'd both preferred to fly Angel on medium ballast – so that the instability stayed hidden.

Chester fixed the figures to hide the fault. He didn't confess until it was too late. He waited until Ruth was past the halfway point on the bonus stage, with a following wind to the UK but an opposing wind if she turned back to Florida. So turning back was no option. Chester confessed at last, and destroyed himself in the process. But who the hell cared?

It wasn't Chester who was stuck in a lethal machine.

The night in front was much darker over dim and disappearing sea. A vast mountain world of cloud waited for her. Angel rolled and yawed. Ruth thought her way round the walls of a sleepy dungeon, and wavered Angel back on line. It was turning into a deadlocked negotiation. And Ruth needed sleep.

Angel didn't.

In the cloud, which stretched all the way to England, there would be turbulence. A bumpy ride. Angel would have an ally, Ruth an enemy. All the men wanted to take you down. Fathers, lovers, Michael, Chester – and Angel, their Pygmalion machine. They wanted to take you down with them as they coalesced with a burned-out monster during its plunge into darkness, fallen from grace.

Lucifer was waiting in the clouds.

Strange flat, strange bed, strange situation. Strange noises, now and then, from a narrow street and the never-deserted main road round the corner. What was the local crime statistic? How safe was his Mercedes outside?

He felt oversized, cumbersome, condemned in middle age. She was neat, slender, naked and not a hand's width away. Face down in the pillow, she was asleep.

He couldn't sleep. His brain was choked with fearful things. Career destruction, personal ruin, corporate death, hostile takeover or aggressive buy-in, jammed computers, locked-up data, fraud, deceit, disappearing Michael, absconded Pattie Lee. Ruth Clifford, manoeuvred into trying the flight in Angel in order to distract attention for a few critical days – and then enticed into making the bonus stage just to rake in a few extra shekels and save someone else's skin. Guilt, guilt, it was a life full of guilt. And face down in the pillow, sleeping, was the takeover attempt or buy-in manoeuvre for his life –

Some lunatics put their telephone by the bed. He bounced clean off the mattress, then lay there gasping while the infernal thing drilled holes in the dark.

Geraldine lifted her head. She went fishing with a bare arm across the bedside table. The drilling stopped. She propped herself on her elbows, head and shoulders silhouetted against street-lit curtains. She tucked the telephone against her ear. "Hello?"

He rolled over and looked for his watch on the floor. He found it, but couldn't read it, not as an astigmatic smear in the night.

"Right. Hang on." She wrapped her hand over the mouthpiece. "Are you here? It's Curtis Gupta. I can tell him you're not here. Up to you."

Up to me, he thought. Since Michael turned out to be bad, everything's been up to me. So far, all of it's gone wrong.

"He's very excited. Says he's got some good news."

He held out his hand for the receiver. Lying on his back, he had to push the earpiece into the pillow to line it up. With her fingertip she held the corkscrew cable away from her chin.

"Gupta? This is Munro. What's the news?"

No news at all. Curtis Gupta was struck dumb.

"This isn't what you think, Gupta. We're doing an all-night reading of *Bonfire of the Vanities* to raise cash for the company. So kindly tell me what you want."

On the other end of the line, Gupta took a breath before launch. "It's the password you suggested – the French thing. *Après moi.* I tried anagrams, nonsense anagrams, you name it. Nothing. Then I thought, what the French king or whatever was supposed to be saying – kick me out and it's the end of the world. Right?"

"Right."

"And I thought, what he's done to the computer net is pretty much like the end of the world. So – I went down to the computer floor with it for them to try. Bingo! Out come the worms!"

"The worms? The programs he's hidden all over the network?"

"Exactly! They don't have to be physically erased any more. We don't have to comb every line of memory looking for them. They read out on command! We can see how they're built. We can write a program to chew up each one where we find it. It's going to make the search for all the copies *much* faster. We're talking about having the whole system up and running before the weekend's over. Isn't that great!"

It isn't great. It's amazing. A point to our side at last. It's a reason to dance and sing. Don't dance and sing. You're supposed to be the ice-cold executive. "You're clearly involved with your work, Gupta. I'm pleased with the result, and grateful that you told me straight away. I'm very pleased indeed." He handed the receiver back.

"Nice work, Curtis," Geraldine said. "See you tomorrow." When she'd finished stretching to put down the receiver, she turned back, still a silhouette against the curtains. "Congratulations. Right hunch after all. Would you like to celebrate? Can a man of your age do it twice in one night?"

"Go to sleep," he said. "Tomorrow's going to be hectic."

SIXTY-THREE

The turbulence was bad. The weather fronts weren't weak. Thousands of square miles of linked lows bringing heavy summer rain. The darkness was total. But the running lights and the strobes made a stuttering shell inside the cloud where Lucifer could find her.

There were lateral gusts, there was sheer. Ruth had tightened the lap-belt and snapped the shoulder straps into the buckle. If anything happened, she didn't want to fly about loose in the cockpit. She should have climbed above it, as high as Angel could go. But climbing used fuel, and there was no margin left.

She sat in front of the illuminated lines on the VSI, and tried to believe that the tipping and dipping horizon, the oscillating heading scale, the yo-yoing altitude and climb rate figures meant anything at all. In the smooth, then juddering, then abruptly bouncing dark it was very hard indeed. The feedback on rudder and stick made no sense any more, the symbols on the VSI were isolated in a world of their own. Instrument flying isn't easy at the best of times, because of the monotony, the disconnection and the encroaching disbelief. In the stammering flashes of light reflected from cloud, it was worse. After a hundred and fourteen hours, fifty of them without any sleep at all . . .

The sheer pushed the left wing down and the artificial horizon left end up. The roll hadn't advanced more than twenty degrees when she pushed the stick right to correct. The artificial horizon began to come level again. Rolling back to the right, it said. After so much time, her own sense of balance said nothing at all.

The next sheer flung the left wing high and flipped the artificial horizon left end down. She had the stick hard right, and the turbulence was rolling Angel that way, too. Thirty degrees. More. Time to bring the stick back.

Side gust. Another nudge to the right. It didn't help. Altitude creeping off. Rate of descent starting to show. Forty degrees of right roll. Stick hard left!

Forty-five degrees of right roll. Holding. Not coming back.

The heading scale was sliding right. The nose was yawing left. Altitude coming off. Airspeed dropping.

You can wake up so fast!

There was too little lift from the tipped-over wing. Angel was driving forwards but also sliding sideways down the sky. That put side pressure on the nose. It was forcing a yaw. Kick the rudder right and correct against the yaw. Try to turn into the roll. Try to dive –

You can wake up too late.

Angel was slewing round, tumbling over, sliding down. The wings ceased to work at such a flight angle. The control surfaces did nothing at all. Altitude was peeling off and the descent rate rising. The stall warning was already on –

Angel flipped round like a loose leaf falling. The stalk, not the tip, always leads.

431

In the dark there was nothing to see and no help for her eyes. Red flash. Green flash. Blinding white reflection of the strobes. Just the heading scale spinning, the nose-up notch at the top of its ladder, the horizon bar crooked at the bottom of the field, altitude running off, rate of descent accelerating. Tail spin! It's a tail spin! Riding backwards against the useless work of the propeller. Revolving round and round. And falling –

Red flash. Green flash. Blinding white.

Down and round and down. Backwards like a corkscrew through the air. It's a fall. It's the fall. It's the ultimate fall. I got out of every dream! I can –

This isn't a dream!

This is real. This is death at the end of the fall. No Michael to help. No father to jeer. Red flash. Green flash. White.

How long? 3000 feet. 2900. 2800. I flew Angel right round the world. I flew Angel most of the way across the Atlantic. I flew Angel into this aftermath of the sun. And then I fell –

Red flash. Snap out of it. Green flash. Nobody wants to die. Blinding white. I'm supposed to know what to do. 2400. 2300.

You can recover. You have to get the nose round in the same sense as the spin. Get the nose down and turn it into a dive. Then you can worry about ending the fall. The same sense as the spin.

Which way is the spin?

The heading scale is racing round to the right. Red flash. So the nose is turning to the left as it follows the tail round and down. Green flash. So I want to turn the nose further to the left. And roll to the left. White flash. Get my feet back on the rudder bar. Get my hand firm on the stick –

Wait! Don't do it wrong!

2000. 1900. Spinning, dropping, Angel's going backwards down the sky. The airflow over the control surfaces is the wrong way round. Their effect is reversed.

Red flash. I want nose left, roll left, nose down. Green flash. All reversed. Throw rudder right, stick right, stick back.

White flash. 1500.

Do it now! Right rudder, right roll, stick back to the stop. Nothing. Nothing. 1300. 1200.

No more flashes of light. I've fallen out of the cloud. *God please come and help me!*

1000.

The heading scale slowed. The horizon bar lifted off the floor of the screen. It started to level.

It continued to rise –

900.

It went up to the central cross. Angel pancaked in a slow spin.

Reverse the controls again! Left rudder, full left stick, nose hard down. And throttle. Push it right through. Her hand fumbled the throttle. *Try again*. Push it through!

800.

The horizon bar wavered up from the cross. It tipped a little high on the left. The heading scale continued to slide to the right.

700. The scale moved faster. The horizon bar took off. Nose coming down and round into what used to be the spin.

600. Try to roll out. Stick right. Fight to roll out.

500. Rudder centre. Ease off from the dive. Bring the nose up. Bring it up!

400. Stick back. Hard back. Throttle back. Why won't the nose rise?

300. It's coming up. The horizon bar is sliding down to the cross –

200.

Too late. *Why is it too late?*

100.

Almost on the cross. Right on the cross –

Light. In flashes I'm in light.

Left and right. Red and green. White. Hard, faceted light. It isn't like the cloud. Angel's bumping. Red and green again. White. I must be hitting the water. I'll tear to splinters –

Great rolling dragon backs of translucent sliding scales. Spines of foam and coloured fire. Beasts, glistening, out of hell's coldest depths. Strobe-lit in stammering light. Blood red, death green, unnatural white. Great rolling dragon backs rising above me. I've fallen down from grace and entered the pit. They'll crush me, swallow me and grind me up inside –

It's rain slashing the cockpit windscreen.

Waves! Waves!

I'm flying down a valley between giant waves. The buffeting is the turmoil of the surface wind as it swoops into the trough and out again. If my wingtip touches –

And these water mountains move –

Get out of here!

Full throttle. Stick slowly back. Slowly. The mountains tipped. Their rolling flanks subsided. The crest of one slid under her.

For a moment she saw a cauldron by flickering light. A cold cauldron of interwoven water ridges heaving and blundering in staccato steps. A stop-frame film of hell's surface skin, with the beasts beneath. Around it was a circle of absolute night.

Then there was nothing but the rain smears streaked along the cockpit windows as the lights flashed their epileptic colours.

Not extinguished. Not cast down. Not quite.

Part 9

Fallen Angels

SIXTY-FOUR

Outside was a dawn-grey, dark grey alley with rain sluicing grime down the brickwork. It wasn't going to be a nice day. For some it was going to be even worse.

Beside the fire exit, propped against a drainpipe on the wet brick wall, was Chester Alby. His chin was on his chest. Rain ran out of his hair, down his cheeks and into his soaking shirt. The shoulders and sleeves of his jacket were saturated. So were his outstretched trouser legs. His hands rested upturned on the asphalt beside him. Little pools in his palms spilled over on the glistening ground. The base of his drainpipe wasn't cemented in properly, and the grate underneath was full. A wreath of water gurgled out and ran towards the middle of the alley. Chester was sitting in a rippling river.

Wedged between his legs like a grotesque phallic totem, cork pushed part way home, was a bottle of Courvoisier. Well-salaried alcoholics wipe the world out with the good stuff.

John Coates, squatting on his heels, his shirt plastered to his shoulders, shook his head in the rain. Shouting hadn't worked, shaking wouldn't, and worrying was a waste of time. He looked up. "Out cold. The only thing that's going to shift him is an ambulance crew."

Terri nodded. She was leaning through the open doorway, keeping her balance with one hand resting on the push bar of the emergency door. Rain was wetting the sleeve of her blouse, drips from the lintel trickled on her head. "Hospital's official. That will finish him once and for all."

John stood up, still looking at the comatose man. "Not

437

before time. Did you look in the garage? His *car* is here. He *drove* here. I'm glad I wasn't on the road at the time. I'm *really* glad I wasn't in the car he was driving."

Imagine, Terri thought, being in the aeroplane he designed.

"Terri! Hey, Terri!"

Mandy's voice from somewhere inside. Terri leaned back through the doorway, and the heavy return spring started to push the door into her shoulder. "What?"

Footsteps on the stairs, at least two flights above. "Terri! It's Ruth! She's in trouble!"

John was already hauling the door wide open. Terri started running, with John coming right behind her.

The exit door slammed.

The handset slipped when she took it, and fell on the desk. Her hand was still wet from the rain. Mandy scooped the handset and gave it to her again. John was lifting the last one for himself.

"Ruth?"

"I fell, Terri. I *fell*. I fell all the way down. But I stopped myself. I did. I did. I really did. Angel fell. I went down like Lucifer. But I didn't go to hell. I stopped the fall!"

"Ruth! Ruth, calm down. A step at a time. What's happened?"

"I *fell*. The turbulence threw Angel and I lost control. I went into a tail spin. Down and down."

"Christ." John was wiping at water running through his eyebrows into his eyes. "Angel could stick in a tail spin."

"I pulled out. I pulled out. At the last minute. Right down on the sea. I was in between the waves. I've never seen – "

"Christ!" John said. "Get some altitude. Get out of the surface wind. Okay? Climb, for God's sake. But stay under the cloud. You must be getting into daylight soon. You'll be able to see bad turbulence coming from the behaviour of the cloud base. Whatever you do, don't go back into the cloud where you can't see turbulence before it hits you."

"I'm at a thousand feet. I'm just under the cloud. I can't see much, but there's a little bit of daylight."

"You're already at a thousand? When was the tail spin?"

"Half an hour ago. About. Or a bit more."

"Half an hour?" John shook his head. Droplets parted from his hair and his beard. "Why didn't you tell us?"

"I've been – getting over it. I thought I was going to die!"

"You didn't die!" *Slowly*, Terri said to herself. And steady. Make it slow and steady. "Ruth, you didn't die. You got yourself out of it. Try to calm yourself down. You've an hour and a half, perhaps two hours to go to get home. You'll be all right if you calm down."

"*I am calm.* I – am – calm. Why do you think it's taken half an hour to tell you about it? Why, why, why? *I wasn't calm!* I am calm now!"

John put a wet hand over his mouthpiece. "She's cracking up. It's been too much. She's going."

"Surprise," Mandy muttered.

It's up to me, Terri thought. It's entirely up to me. Judge her state of mind, try to contain it, try to coach her home. If we hadn't gone looking for Chester, I'd have been here to worry about her silence. I'd have asked her, this would have happened sooner, and she'd have had less time to wind herself into hysteria. Too late now. "Ruth, two hours, probably less, and – "

"I don't want two hours!"

"Ruth, you got through the previous night, didn't you? We got through – talking – you and me. So we'll talk through the next two hours, and then you're going to be safe. On the ground and home."

"I don't want your psychology! I want *land*!"

"Two hours, Ruth, at the most. We're bringing you down at Plymouth. Forget London. We've got landing permission at – "

"I want the nearest land! Get me the *nearest* land! *I want the nearest land!*"

Terri looked at John. He made eyes back at her – watery, sleep-starved eyes. No good ideas there.

"The Scilly Isles," Mandy said. "That's the first land she could hit."

Terri shook her head. That was crazy. Little inhabited pebbles in the sea. No airport. No facilities. No room at all for the press.

"If you don't promise her something," Mandy said, "she's going to go to pieces straight away."

"There's an airfield on the Scilly Isles." John was rubbing water out of his beard. "I think."

"An airfield." Terri stared at the long wall map. "You think." All the way round the world, back across the wide Atlantic, and our pilot refuses to go the last few miles. Up to me. No Michael and no Munro. It's bloody well up to me. "Will it be open in bad weather? Will it be open at all this early? Will anyone even be there?"

SIXTY-FIVE

I'm all right. I'm much better now. I've got myself under control. Even though the fuel gauge reads zero and I'm waiting for the engine to stop. I used too much fuel climbing away from my fall. But I'm all right now.

The light was poor and the visibility wasn't really there. Just rain descending into windy waves. She'd come on John's approach from the south, and was hoping the INS was still accurate enough to hit the islands in the middle of the rained-in sea. Angel was wobbling all over the place, irregular roll and insistent yaw. The radar wasn't showing her any islands – just a useless mush of clutter from waves and anything else that might be there. It was a midair anti-collision radar. It hadn't got a chance.

440

There was no radar watcher guiding her in, either. Telephoning from London, they hadn't been able to set up anything at all. But once the fuel was reading zero, they stopped suggesting she might want to change her mind.

Come in due north on a course which should take her slap through the middle of the group. Line up on the big island, St Mary's. The peninsula on the left has the old fortress on its top. The tiny neck of land, built solid with houses, is Hugh Town. Go clean over the top of Hugh Town, over the harbour on the other side, circle to the right into the middle of the island and come round to spot the airfield. It's meant for helicopters but it's got five hundred flat yards. Good luck, full flaps and a stall approach, and hit the wheel brake as soon as you touch. With empty tanks there's no fear of a fire if you wreck Angel on the ground . . .

The fortress is at forty-one metres, the airfield is at thirty-six. Altitude is two hundred feet, and that's fine. Airspeed one hundred knots, quarter flaps and a bit of nose up.

There was something coming out of the rain to the left. Surf, rocks, some greenish stuff behind. "Island on my left, John."

"That should be St Agnes. Hugh Town dead ahead."

The island was going out past her wing. Angel was wobbling like a drunk. She'd been fighting that for so long it took care of itself – just about.

There was something behind the rain up ahead. It was higher on the left, it dipped, it rose on the right. Dead on the nose. The INS was a miracle that worked. It didn't come from Chester, it didn't come from Michael. It came off a manufacturer's shelf.

"I've got it. Hugh Town dead ahead."

Rocky shore and tiny cliffs to the right, a buttress of little cliffs to the left. A receding horseshoe of surf straight in front of her. A bit of beach at the head. Short crosswise ranks of roofs soaked with rain. Straight down the middle, straight over Hugh Town. No time for sightseeing now –

The engine cut out.

It didn't even splutter. It just stopped.

The rev needle dropped off the scale. The fuel feed warning was red. The sudden silence *hurt*.

When she lifted her eyes again, wet roofs and a couple of rain-run streets were rushing below. It was the rain hitting Angel she started to hear. It drowned out the slipstream . . .

A bit more beach. Water. A jetty to the left. Rocks round the bay to the right. Moored boats dotting the water dead ahead.

No engine any more. Angel's gliding. If I curve right and try to circle over the island, without throttle I'll lose height on the turn. I'll cartwheel into the ground.

"My engine's out. I've got no power. I'm too low to turn."

"Circle round. Pull up tight. Go for the airfield."

"I'm too low. I know it. I'll have to ditch." Belly land and break open on the sea. If I don't get out I'll drown with Angel. If I do get out, the water's cold, the currents go who knows where, and the life-jacket won't protect me from the surf on the rocks.

Rocks and surf were passing under the right wing. Waves and rain-lash under the left. A hundred and fifty feet. If I'm going to ditch next to the island I need full flaps – speed off quickly but with lift until the last minute. Ready with the flaps –

"Ruth, try a beach."

"I can't see a beach." The rocky shoreline was receding on the right. "What's ahead of me?"

"Wait. Tresco Island. It's less than a mile after St Mary's."

"I'll ditch in front of it." There's nothing in front but waves. The waves will be like the roofs of concrete bunkers. Until Angel tumbles into one and starts to come apart.

"No! Don't go into the sea. There's an inland lake. About half a mile long. When you come over the island, turn sixty degrees left. That should bring you along the line of the lake."

"All right." One hundred feet. It's all choppy, crossing wave crests in a shallow channel. Bound to be full of currents to kill me. An inland lake is better any day. Just one hundred feet, and airspeed ninety knots. "What height will I have to clear?"

"We're looking at the map. We're looking."

Rocks, surrounded by sea, going under the left wing. Angel waves its wingtips at the waiting water. A surf line ahead through the rain. Rocky beach, low land, ending in a rock shelf to the right. Looks like a little point of land.

"Five to ten metres. You'll have to clear five to ten metres. Say fifty feet to be safe."

"Right."

More wave-soaked rocks on the left, the rocky point stretching round to the right. Dim, rainy island. There's a circular pool ahead, off to the left. Trees or something behind it. There's rough grass straight ahead, with a bumpy track, up and down – worse by far than the waves would be. Can't land on that.

Fifty feet. Airspeed eighty. The stall warning starting to flash. I'll stall without full flaps. A sixty degree turn is impossible. The rock and surf go under my feet. There on the left is the long lake. The turn towards it can't be done. I'll lose height, hit the ground –

A beach. On the other side of the point. A long white strip. Dunes on the left, breakers on the right. A long sliver of beach!

Ease right to line up. Flaps full. Line up some more. Let the nose down and –

Landing gear! For God's sake! I'll kill myself yet!

The landing gear lever stuck at the first try. A thump snapped it over. The gear drives growled.

No altitude. Nose up. Flaps full. Seventy-five knots. Stall warning on. Angel's wallowing. Don't put a wheel in the soft sand. Don't put a wheel in the surf. The drag will swerve Angel round.

Seventy. Should have stalled. No time for an elegant flare. I'll run out of beach. Nose up. More nose up. That's the widest part of the beach gone by. Can't see ahead any more because of the nose. *Why won't the wheels touch?*

Bounce. A swish, not a tyre squeal at spin-up.

Left wing going high, Angel going down. Stick left to try and set down level –

A bounce and a lurch and a wrench at the straps. Main wheels on. Dunes passing the left wingtip, water under the right. Can't see where to steer. Get the nose down. Hit the wheel brake and to hell with a smooth landing –

The nose dropped and hit the front suspension like a weight-lifter crushing a pogo stick. Plumes came up each side of the cockpit. Wet sand spattered the windscreen.

Right in front, the beach narrowed to nothing where grassy dunes turned to rock and met sea. Surf, a spout of spray, and nothing beyond it but rain –

Angel stopped.

It was no elegant rolling arrest. It was a slide and a skid and then nothing. Tumbling, eager, bubbling water rushed in underneath the right foreplane.

I'm down. I haven't seen a soul and they haven't seen me. And no one's filmed my glorious arrival – *but I'm down*!

She flipped the catch locking the left window. She tried to do the same on the right. But her right hand came off the stick like a claw, and wouldn't open. Her left arm couldn't reach across to the rightside catch. Her shoulder seized halfway. Her back refused to twist.

She sat for a moment listening to rain rattling on the roof. It trickled down the windshield and the windows. The rest of the world was a sound of breakers and sucking surf, and a busy wind which rocked Angel's wheels into the sand.

She tried to slide the left window open. Her hand could hold the catch, her arm could bend, but her shoulder couldn't cope with the pull. If she'd ditched in the sea, or in the lake, she would never have got out in time. She'd have drowned.

"Hello. John? Terri? It's me. I'm down. I'm on the beach. Would you ring round and send someone to help me? I'm a bit stiff and I can't get out of my seat. And I don't know if the tide's coming in."

SIXTY-SIX

Geraldine was driving his Mercedes again, this time wearing flat-heeled shoes. The morning rush hour on the Holborn Viaduct was awful. The rain didn't help. At least today the weather wasn't interfering with the car phone. It tended to. The technological dream wasn't always sweet. Look what could happen with computers.

"I thought we might start talking straight away," Munro said into the phone. "Would you be happy with that, Geoffrey?"

"I think so, Robert. Under the circumstances."

"Good." Simmington's circumstances, he thought, are as two-faced as the man himself. He means the fact that the Bryce McFadden Group have hired him to run their raid, now that Sylvia Symes has declined. I mean the fact that he's tried making money from my funeral. But be civilized. It pays.

"Business as usual, old chap?"

"As usual, Geoffrey. I see from the overnight trading that the Group has taken fifteen percent of each of our second and third tier subsidiaries. Are they going to declare themselves?"

"The second trading opens, Robert. Everything above board."

Except, of course, for their merchant banker. He watched while Geraldine picked her lane for the one-way round Angel Street. "The Group hasn't got a takeover stake on those figures, and our share price is already back up to three-quarters. We're becoming expensive to buy. Did you know that the income from the round-the-world stunt will meet the SIB cash target, by the way? Ruth Clifford has landed somewhere in the Isles of Scilly, so the bonus pledges are being called in."

"I heard it on the news on my way to the bank, Robert."

"And we've solved our computer problem. We aren't crippled any more."

"I'm jolly glad to hear it, old chap. That was an unfair blow, and no mistake."

"Yes, it was." The Mercedes was standing still. The rush hour traffic wasn't working. The world got worse every week. One day it would all end in some vast internal combustion engine burn-out. "It means we're not flat on our back while the Group does what it likes to us. So, what deal are we going to do?"

"Well now, Bryce McFadden could make life very hard for MT Holdings – divert the income from subsidiaries and run off with the business. Just as you were planning to do to Tranter, really. Of course, your guillotine was elegant, whereas they'd have to resort to some pretty costly hatchet work. So, in fact, my advice to them is not to entertain the idea."

"What do they want, Geoffrey?"

"A single slice, Robert – but a big one, of course. They'd like to trade holdings, give you back their distributed stakes in return for concentrating their ownership in one subsidiary."

That was the obvious deal, if the Group didn't want to pay the price of a wholesale takeover. "They'd want to uncouple their slice from MT-Orbis, I assume?"

"Exactly. The slice they happen to want is Orbis Air. I've taken the liberty of suggesting to them that you might not be too unhappy with such an arrangement."

The car started moving again. Geoffrey Simmington was after a slick, quick deal. He'd be making life easy for the Group and thereby putting himself in line for future commissions. He was making life acceptable for MT Holdings, too: the income from the half-trade, half-sale of Orbis Air would be lower than the expectation from the planned consortium sale, but MT-Orbis would still be rid of its biggest loss-maker. Simmington was playing the gentlemanly traitor. "At a rough estimate, swapping all the Group's acquisitions in our second and third tiers, plus their existing holding at Orbis Air, still won't give them outright control. They'll have to buy on our terms to complete their fifty percent."

"I rather thought you'd say that. What would your terms be, old chap? Not too stringent, I hope?"

"Let's see, Geoffrey. I'd stick with the conditions we were discussing a little while ago. Restricted asset stripping, minimum job losses, retention of structural integrity. As if your consortium had been buying, in fact."

"Well, now – this is strictly unofficial until I've had another chat with them, you understand – but I'm confident Bryce McFadden would be happy to acquire a functioning airline they could turn a penny on, once this infernal recession's loosened its grip. I tell you what, Robert – suppose I buy you lunch at the club? I'll have a confirmation by then, and we can sketch in some of the details. What do you say?"

"That sounds fine, Geoffrey."

"Splendid! I'll give you a ring later to fix the time. Bye, old chap. Good to see you back on your feet, by the way."

"Goodbye, Geoffrey." He put the receiver back on its rest. A surge in the traffic had moved them well on their way towards Cornhill. Geraldine was driving again, not crawl parking.

"Did I hear that correctly?" she asked. "Did you just settle the unloading of our biggest loss-making subsidiary, plus getting the cash inflow needed for the restructuring of MT-Orbis?"

"Yes." He folded his arms, settling satisfied in his seat. "Tell me," he said. "What is it you see in me?"

"Maturity. Power." She joined the queue of cars coming up to the Mansion House. "Slow sex – which is the best kind. Don't ask me to put those in order, though. What do you see in me?"

A young body, he thought. Freshness. Sex in a middle-aged dream. Flattery from the fact that you see something in me. Sum it all up. "More life, I suppose."

There were two police cars in front of the MT building, run up on the pavement with their noses towards the steps. There were two uniformed policewomen beside the reception desk in the lobby. They said it was all happening on the executive floor.

Munro rode up with Geraldine in the lift in silence. With them went half a dozen early-day employees. Michael would have greeted them by name. Well, that was a week ago. Munro didn't learn lists of names so that he could play at being everyone's friend. He didn't steal them blind, either.

On the executive floor, a uniformed police officer was standing outside the door to the boardroom. Inside were the rest of them, grouped round the near end of the table. Curtis Gupta, sleepless in his red braces and rolled-up sleeves, represented company security. Darren Pierce was there in a double-breasted suit which certainly hadn't been up all night. There was a man in a brilliant red and white shell-suit top and blue flannel trousers, and beside him was a uniformed constable. The man in the chair at the focus of their attention, hair badly combed, crumpled jacket over his shoulders, his arm in a dirty sling, was Michael.

Michael smiled.

"Mr Munro," Pierce said briskly. "This is DS Musgrave." He pointed at the man in red, white and blue. "Serious Fraud Office."

Sergeant Musgrave nodded. Munro nodded, then looked back at the smile.

"Well – it's a long story, Bob." Michael's smile turned rueful. "Let's just say Pattie decided to do without me. The number two decides the boss isn't needed any more. Not all that dissimilar to your own decision, really."

"No." Geraldine was watching him. Everyone else had their eyes on the villain, as if he might make a sudden leap for

448

freedom – or just vanish from the chair, insubstantial as all the data he'd deformed, mocking them like a Cheshire cat.

"Fortunately, I wasn't embarrassed for ready cash – always be prepared, and all that. But when I found the police waiting in the dead of night at Dover, I began to wonder if it wasn't time to rethink my options. So – back to the capital city. I left a message on my solicitor's answering machine, then I popped over here and waited for retribution to arrive." Michael nodded at Pierce and the detective sergeant, then he glanced at Curtis Gupta and back to Munro. "I'm told you've more or less solved your little problem with the computer system. I *am* glad."

Michael pitched them into a silence illuminated by his smile.

"Have you done the arrest?" Munro said to the sergeant.

The sergeant nodded.

Munro turned back to Michael. "I suppose there's no point in asking you why? Or how, come to think of it."

"Oh, you can imagine how it is, Bob. These things just turn out to be easy – and very rewarding. Specially when you're rather good at it. You just keep going. Until over-confidence gets you in the end, I suppose. However, I'll be answering questions in the presence of my solicitor – and her QC, by the way." Michael stood up, quite slowly, though everyone else seemed to hover for a moment on their toes. "I dropped in to show you something, Bob. You must have got my laptop round here somewhere. I assume you haven't quite cracked it yet?"

The people in the open-plan area of the finance department were still up to their necks in solving the cash flow crisis. Some of them had been there all night, the others had arrived hours before the start of the normal day. They didn't have time for diversions. But the little parade stopped them in their tracks.

The uniformed officers waited outside. The rest of the troupe squeezed into Geraldine's office, where rain ran on the window and paper spilled everywhere else. The room was choked with the debris of Michael's misdemeanours.

Michael was surveying the jumble of printouts, the glowing computer screen, his laptop connected to it by a cable. "You're lucky this wasn't on line to the network when the worms went in, aren't you?" He fished a memo pad out of a sea of discarded sheets. It was the pad with Gupta's *après moi* anagrams. "I see you found my little clue. I'll deny *any* connection, of course. But you see, Bob, just between you and me – I'm quite a friendly villain after all." He dropped the pad back on top of the sheets. "I thought it best to turn myself in. I'm planning on a minimum sentence, maximum parole, and all of it spent in one of those nice open prisons. I'll be co-operating, as they say in the papers. Besides which, I think my arm could do with some attention. Pattie was quite definite about proceeding on her own."

The detective sergeant was looking impatient, Gupta was looking angry, Pierce was on the verge of being impolite, and Geraldine was looking at him to do something. So he reached behind Pierce and pushed the door closed. "You've already wasted a lot of our time, Michael."

"Quite." Michael tipped his head to look at the screen. "I see you've done everything but open the lock. Nice work as far as it goes." He pushed printouts aside to tidy a space next to the keyboard. Further along the concertina, fanfolds started to slop from the computer table to the desk and nudge cold coffee cups.

Gupta grabbed the cups and moved them to the window sill.

Michael put the memo pad in the cleared space and tore off the top sheet. He excavated a pen and put it on the pad. "That's for you, Curtis. Or for you. Geraldine Trayhorn, isn't it? You'll need to note down each filename the *first* time you look at the list. After you've selected any single file, the rest will never read out again, even with the password, unless you specify the filename. Wildcards won't work. It's another layer of security. If anyone got this far and missed the re-lock trick, they'd only get a fraction of the goodies and the rest would still be safe. Have you found out how much money it is, incidentally?"

"Fourteen million plus," Geraldine said.

"Not bad. Actually, it's twenty-two million. I'm pleased it was so well hidden. Now, let's see." He held his hand over the keyboard. The bottom line on the screen still said *please enter the correct password*, and the prompt was waiting where it had waited half the night. Michael turned his head and eyed Munro. "You realise my motive isn't just co-operation, coming clean, making amends, being a good loser and so on? I'd like you to get as much as possible as fast as possible, before Pattie's had the chance to lift more than two or three million. She wants two million for her parents, you know. Another million for spending money is more than enough, don't you think?"

"Michael," he said. "Just get on with the show."

"Of course." Michael turned to the keyboard, let his fingers hover in the right-hand half of a touch-typer's neutral, then started to tap the keys. A little string of amber letters rippled out from the prompt.

Lucifer.

He pressed *enter*, and the file list appeared.

SIXTY-SEVEN

The rain had stopped, the wind hadn't. Dirty clouds slid overhead in a solid sheet. It was a disgraceful midday for July. With her back to the wind and the rattling grass, with a thin cotton jacket over her checked blouse and black leggings, with her feet unhappy in city shoes on the sand, Terri was obviously cold. There hadn't been time to rush home and change. She'd come out here in a hurry.

Ruth was all right. Ruth was warm. They'd lent her a parka, and a clean T-shirt, and an old pair of cords. The trainers were her own. She sat down, slowly, and landed on all her aches amongst marram grass dried by the wind. She looked out from the dune.

The sea sucked the sand, a seething complaint from each defeated surge. White horses broke further out from shore, and in between was a rolling field of advancing waves. Wallowing in the shifting, sand-grey pasture was Angel. The landing gear, the foreplanes and half the fuselage were submerged. Waves kept swallowing the propeller boss at the tail, and the highest rollers spilled through the windows of the flooded cockpit. Spray, whipped from the crests, sparked along the undersides of the high wings. Angel had flown clean round the world, had parked on a beach, and was drowning.

Down on the tide line, the constable was organising his volunteers. If they left it until the peak of the tide, aviation history's newest exhibit would simply be washed away. The people of Tresco could do better than that. Watching them as they prepared the lines was a two-man Orbis film crew. Nobody else was there. Tresco didn't like strangers from the press.

In front of the shore, the waves were rocking and lifting Angel. An aircraft built on sand.

"How do you feel?" Terri asked her across the wind.

"Oh – " Ruth hunched up, hands in the pockets of the parka. "I've had a long, hot bath. I've had three hours' sleep on a farmer's sofa. I've had bacon and eggs and lots of tea. I'm almost conscious. I even bend a little, if I'm careful." If, she thought, I'm very careful. "The doctor said I'm alive."

"Up to meeting the press? By the time I get you to St Mary's, they'll be there. And in Penzance they'll look like an army."

"I'll cope. If you hold my hand."

"I'll hold yours, Ruth, if you'll hold mine. It's helicopter hops from here to Penzance. I've never been in a helicopter before. I *hated* it. I slept all the way from London. But not in that helicopter." Terri turned back to watch the men coiling their lines on the sand above the surf. "How do you feel about Michael?"

Pass, she thought. That's a bit of a big one. "I'm not awake enough for that. How do you feel?"

"Michael's just sex," Terri said to the sea. "And money."

He meant more to her, Ruth used to think. She turned her cheek against the collar of the parka. Its lining smelled of cigar smoke, bitter and stern from a home far away. Her father's cigars had gone out with the business profit, even before the fall.

"Why did you do it?" Terri hugged her jacket tight and watched Angel in the waves. "I don't mean the fame and glory. I don't mean the celebrity income. I don't even mean the money for your parents. I mean *your* motive. Why did you go all the way?"

"To prove I could." Ruth shrugged. "And to beat Michael."

"Well, you did it." Terri turned away from the sea. She came closer, stepping carefully through the marram grass. Still hugging her jacket, she sat on her heels beside Ruth, facing her, leaning close. "Listen to me. Lots of people are going to like you for this, and it's going to last for some time. Make the most of it, get the money in, and above all *use* it to build a base for yourself so you've got something to carry on with once the fuss dies down. As soon as you can, hire a manager. You can try hiring me, if you think you can afford me."

Ruth nodded. "Business. Never far away, is it?"

"Without business," Terri said, "there's no money, no aeroplane, no publicity circus, no star status, no history books. Don't knock it. Just never let it knock you."

"I'll try."

"I'm serious, Ruth. A lot of people are going to like you for this, but don't make the mistake of thinking they all do. If you go chasing the sun, some people are going to hope you get burned. They'll hate you for being famous. Chester Alby, for example. He's so hung up about Michael, he even claimed you pushed Michael down those stairs. See what I mean?"

Ruth, when she turned her head, saw the first lines snaking

out in a pair of orange arcs, tied together at their weighted ends. The connected weights went into the waves, the lines dropped like loose cheese-wires behind them. One fell into the water in a long hedge of splashes in front of the aircraft. The other fell across Angel's nose. Right first time.

Michael stumbled and tottered and went dancing backwards down the stair. Ruth came sliding and jumping after him. Michael caught himself, precariously, with a grip which was coming undone, which was holding just long enough for Ruth's help to arrive. That had been her instinct, her intention, when she started down the stair . . .

"I did push him. I could, so I did." She looked at Terri, who was staring back at her. "He was in the way."